The Walking Tanteek

JANE WOODS

a novel

THE WALKING

TANTEEK

GOOSE LANE

Edited by Bethany Gibson.
Cover and page design by Chris Tompkins.
Cover illustration by Chris Tompkins.
Printed in Canada.
10 9 8 7 6 5 4 3 2 1

Library and Archives Canada Cataloguing in Publication

Woods, Jane, 1950-, author
The walking Tanteek / Jane Woods.

Issued in print and electronic formats.
ISBN 978-0-86492-910-5 (pbk.). —ISBN 978-0-86492-795-8 (epub)

I. Title.

PS8645.O6388W34 2014   C813'.6   C2013-907296-9
                                        C2013-907297-7

Goose Lane Editions acknowledges the generous support of the Canada Council for the Arts, the Government of Canada through the Canada Book Fund (CBF), and the Government of New Brunswick through the Department of Tourism, Heritage and Culture.

Goose Lane Editions
500 Beaverbrook Court, Suite 330
Fredericton, New Brunswick
CANADA E3B 5X4
www.gooselane.com

For Arthur

If not for you...

You say I am repeating
Something I have said before. I shall say it again.
Shall I say it again? In order to arrive there,
To arrive where you are, to get from where you are not,
    You must go by a way wherein there is no ecstasy.
In order to arrive at what you do not know,
    You must go by a way which is the way of ignorance.
In order to possess what you do not possess
    You must go by the way of dispossession.
In order to arrive at what you are not,
    You must go through the way in which you are not
And what you do not know is the only thing you know.
And what you own is what you do not own
And where you are is where you are not.

    —T.S. Eliot, "East Coker," *Four Quartets*

The cards are no good that you're holding, unless they're
from another world.

    —Bob Dylan, "Series of Dreams"

ONE

The Untouchables sit in a snaggled circle and sing. They sit on moulded plastic chairs and wooden folding chairs with missing slats and old, exploded hassocks that were left out in the rain on garbage day in nearby Orangeville and Schomberg. The hymn they sing sounds as musty and old-fangled as apple pies cooling on windowsills, as cowcatchers on trains, as scarecrows in the corn.

> *I'm kind of homesick for a country*
> *To which I've never been before.*
> *No sad goodbyes will be there spoken,*
> *For time won't matter any more.*

The hymn they sing is as humble as callused hands clutching worn Bibles, as broken-hearted as bowed bodies clustered around icy graves for the very small.

I'm looking now across the river,
Where my faith shall end in sight.
There's just a few more days to labour,
Then I'll take my heavenly flight.

They sit in a circle in their hoodies and stained sweatpants and acid-wash jean jackets from Goodwill. In the hard shafts of winter sunlight angling in through my brother's filthy living room window, they mumble-sing in their tuneless way about what the heart clutches to itself but the mind cannot grasp.

With the exception of the littlest one, they look for all the world like a band of poxy killers for hire.

There's Fred and Frosted Flake and Big Fanny. There's Barb. There's tall Sunil High-Up and short Sunil Low-Down. There's Catou. There's my very own twin brother, Gerard.

And there's Desi, Kevvie's little brother, dressed for this awful occasion in the tan suit and crooked red bow tie Fred got for him at a Pape Street Greek children's wear shop.

The chair that's usually mine, the teetering three-legged stool set between Frosted Flake and Sunil High-Up, is, of course, empty. I'm late. And so I've missed whatever fire and brimstone Gerard saw fit to rain down upon everyone's hanging heads before the singing began.

Beulah land, I'm longing for you
And some day on thee I'll stand.
Where my home shall be eternal
Beulah land, sweet Beulah land.

Still in my coat, shell-shocked and breathless, I'm trying to sidle in surreptitiously behind Frosted Flake to claim my place, all the while watching my brother's eyes. Are they open in cold, hard surveillance or safely shut in private sanctity?

Only a week ago, I was as close to ditching this place and these people and bolting for my life as I'd ever been. It was now or never, my bravest face on tight, breath high in my chest, heart slamming my insides like a crazed squirrel in a cage. This time, I swore, I was really going to do it.

But all bets are off now. I'm paralyzed. I can't move, can't go anywhere. Because instead of me, it's Kevvie who's gone, Kevvie who's taken his heavenly flight.

Only a week ago, he and I were scrambling around on our knees, racing Matchbox cars down the splintery speedway of Gerard's hallway, smothering our laughter in our hands. Five days ago he was hanging off his younger brother's chair in the kitchen as Desi sat at the table absorbed in the *Toronto Sun*, inching down the columns of print with one finger while Kevvie kneed him in the butt, shouting through his cupped little hands, "Des*iiiii*! Can you be *done*? Customers are coming into the store! We have to get busy! Can you *pleeease* be done?"

But it was Kevvie who had to be done. In just a few hours' time, we'll be laying him and his sweet, goofy grin forever under the winter ground.

And my brother's eyes, I see now, are wide open.

Kevvie. All of seven years old, a kid so scrappy and unscrubbed, his mushroom-cloud hair so hilarious, his school attendance so erratic, he should have been a pariah among his peers. But he was adored. It was easy to imagine the mothers of more conventional children picking him out of class photos, asking, Who's this little guy? Kevvie Redpath, the conventional kids would answer, busting out in wide grins at the sheer joy of getting to say his name. He always has the best jokes! Everybody has a crush on him!

Kevvie. He's waiting for us now in town, shushed to eternal silence. Is there still anything left of him, somewhere, that remembers the feverish anticipation of his last day on earth? Seven years old and packed into a van with five other excited grade-two boys on their way to a blowout birthday party, an IMAX movie in the city followed by a wild tear through a McDonald's party room. It was going to be the first party he'd ever been to that didn't feature adults hunkered on his bed, wheezing on crack pipes, or out cold under the breakfast table the next morning.

I need only close my eyes to see what happened next, the van pulling onto the highway, snow blowing horizontally over a pavement that still looks clear, black, smooth. The birthday boy's easygoing mother is driving, one eye on the rear-view mirror as she monitors the cheerful punching and pinching and stuffing of gummy bears into ears behind her. None of the boys is wearing a seatbelt, as there aren't enough to go around, and the ones who did have them at first scrambled out of them the moment her back was turned.

Now the colour leaches from the picture, turning it hard black and slurred white: black pavement, sudden whiteout, black ice. The van skids, plows into an oncoming truck, and flips over several times at high speed before rolling to a stop at the bottom of an embankment. The birthday boy and his friends shoot through the van's windows like birds escaping a tipped cage. All of them are on TV that night, lying where they'd landed in scattered heaps, in their bright little coats. Five dead where they lay, one carried off in a screaming ambulance to live two days more. The mother gets away with two cracked ribs, minor contusions, a heart forever packed in ice.

We're burying Kevvie today, and we have everything under control. Fred, the Untouchables' second-in-command, has made all the arrangements: scouted out the modest funeral home, chosen the casket, even sprung for several buckets of pink-and-white convenience store carnations on his own dime. With Catou, Kevvie's meth-addled excuse for a mother, crouched at his side, he trolled the Internet at the Orangeville Library and found the Lavender Cemetery, an hour-and-a-half's icy drive away.

Kevvie Redpath, from Orangeville, laid to rest in the Lavender Cemetery. It'll be like being buried inside a sunset! This is what Fred tells Catou. Yeah, it's a long drive. Sure, the cost of the hearse rental will go through the roof. But that's why we have Maggie, right?

Yes, that's why they have me. For the hearse, the casket, the burial plot, and its subsequent maintenance. For the winter interment charge. For the headstone. All deducted from my robust bank account, to which my brother, Gerard, sovereign ruler of us all, has granted Fred full access.

We were invited to the joint funeral service organized by the other bereaved families, held this morning at the United Church in Orangeville. Invited to add our coffin to the sad little train in the church aisle.

No, said Gerard, as we knew he would. No, we're going to bury Kevvie ourselves, Untouchables-style. The five other boys who died with him are no concern of ours.

But I went to the funeral. Defying my brother, my heart in my throat, and this is why I'm late to our own pre-funeral service. I spent the morning in the back row of the overflowing church, where each coffin bore a flower-wreathed school photo of the grinning, gap-toothed boy within. Where TV cameras outside jostled the pallbearers loading the hearses one by one. Where grown men stood sobbing, their legs buckling on the church steps.

"Beulah Land" hauls its bedraggled ass to the finish line. From across the circle, my brother's eyes stab into mine. He wags his head furiously in the direction of the kitchen, his face all blue murder. In the instant before I slink after him in practised obedience, my own eyes meet Desi's huge brown ones from where he's sitting next to his mother, graciously holding the ashtray for the smoke she's already lit. I think I see fellow feeling in his eyes, a sweet-natured six-year-old's instinctive sympathy with anyone who looks like they're in for a creaming from the worst bully in the schoolyard.

Gerard kicks the kitchen door shut behind him, his rabid face two inches from mine, giving off waves of wrathful heat.

"Who gave you permission to go out from among us?" he snarls on a gust of smoke-blackened breath. "Let the dead bury their own dead! We are soldiers in the Lord's army, not emotional tourists!" His voice rides piggyback on a terrifying throat whistle, like a frigid wind whipping around corners.

I'm too drained and broken to do anything but hang my sorry head in time-honoured Untouchables-style. Though I'm damned if I'll let him see me cry.

I'd give twenty years of my life for a drink.

Naturally, everybody wants to ride to the funeral home with me in the Trans Am, most notably Frosted Flake, who lusts after the cherry-red car emblazoned with orange-and-yellow flame decals that Gerard confiscated from a former, long-disappeared Untouchable. He lusts after the car almost as much as he lusts after me.

Now he sits mashed up against me, straddling the gearshift, his arms pinned on both sides, which makes smoking tricky but not impossible. Ferret-faced Barb is wedged in shotgun, while the two Sunils are stuffed like giant fold-over sandwiches behind our heads. Everybody chain-smokes no matter the degree of difficulty.

Catou and Desi and Fred and Big Fanny are stuck riding with Gerard in his '79 Chevy Impala, a vehicle so lacy with rust that a strong headwind might easily reduce it to a heap of ochre dust. They're right behind us the whole way; in my rear-view mirror, I can just make out Desi's great puff of hair in the back seat between Big Fanny and Catou. I don't trust Gerard at the wheel for a second. I'm terrified their car will careen off the road and explode in a ball of fire. And I know what I'll do if it does. The others can go out in a screaming blaze, but I will risk life and limb to pull Desi from the flames with my bare hands. I'll burn alive before I see any harm come to him.

Next to me, Flake seems as jittery as I am. He overcompensates by treating us to a string of original jokes all the way to Orangeville.

"Why should you give Viagra to your dog?" He sneaks a sideways look at me, no doubt hoping the saucy reference will turn me on. If I weren't driving, I'd slap him purple.

"This is going to be stupid," Barb irritably informs the window, fogging it with her grey Du Maurier breath.

"'Cause it'll give your dog a boner." Flake snorts in and out of his coke-ravaged nose seven or eight times. A thimble's worth of mucus oozes down his chin. He tries again.

"Okay, how about this? How do you know your laxative sucks?"

I'm trying to concentrate, my eyes jumping between the snow-swept road and Desi's shadowy head behind us. Everyone else is lighting fresh smokes.

"Eh? How do you know your laxative sucks?"

No one has a clue.

"'Cause it don't work for shit!" Snort, snort, snort.

This is the last burst of mirth we'll be hearing in a while.

In the funeral home chapel, we all huddle around Catou in the front row. Her eyes dart like bats from one corner of the ceiling to the other. Does she see angels up there? Catou, Big Fanny, and Barb, the Untouchables women, are big on angels; they're as wild-eyed and spirit-sensitive as Guatemalan peasants. They see demons too, not to mention a Jesus so real you can send him out to the kitchen to make coffee.

Desi, who never cries, cried when they told him, no, he couldn't go to the party with Kev, he had to be seven, he had to be in Kevvie's grade. He doesn't cry here in the chapel. He swings his legs decorously, a polite little man in a cheap suit. Only his hair seethes around his thoughtful little head.

If I keep my eyes steady on him, I can just manage to bear being gutted by this, my second funeral of the day.

Fred conducts the service right here in the chapel, reading the Twenty-Third Psalm over the plain white casket, while Gerard stalks the back of the room in his long black overcoat, the Reaper on a tight schedule. He paces, sits, paces some more. He stands stony-faced while we file up to the coffin one by one to try to say something smart and true about Kevvie.

The assumption, of course, is that Kevvie's safe now in Beulah Land, hanging with Jesus and all the good folks, happy as a little clam. His death is not a major tragedy. There's no call whatsoever for annihilating despair.

But all I can think is, *Prove it, goddamnit!* Because all I see is a silent white box and a howling void where once there was life abundant.

Big Fanny goes up first.

"He was his mama's precious angel," she begins in her gorgeous brocade baritone. Tragedy or not, Barb and Sunil Low-Down are sobbing uncontrollably. Big Fanny gives up and sits, her shoulders heaving. No one else moves. Sunlight muscles in through the windows, a bright beam hitting Gerard smack in the face, throwing every pock and crater into high relief as he strides to the front for his opening remarks.

"In the Father's eyes, the human race, all men, all women, are nothing but grasshoppers," he begins. Then, bless his granite heart, his voice fails him too.

No one says a word on the long drive to the cemetery. The air in the car is blue with smoke. I get us lost twice; it's well over two hours before we pull up in front of the gates. There's no lavender in sight, just a wrought-iron sign tersely announcing, "SINCE 1880." This is where we're going to leave our Kevvie, all by his lonesome with no one for company but a bunch of doddering, griping strangers over a century in the ground.

Jockey-sized Fred in his dress coat, a plaid number three sizes too big, meets us at the gate and walks ahead of us, buffeted by an ice-pick wind. Round and round we drive, to the edge of the back of nowhere at all.

The coffin can't weigh more than a pound of feathers, but Fred, Frosted Flake, and Gerard, both Sunils, and Big Fanny, all standing tall and bleak with the hopeless dignity of laughable humankind, hoist it to their shoulders and carry it to where the grave stands gaping. Tears sheet down all our faces as Gerard slashes a dark cross in the air. Desi holds his mother's frozen hand. Big Fanny moans, "Jesus, Jesus, Jesus," but he doesn't answer. The most we can hope for is that he'll have coffee waiting back at the house.

...

In the five years since I cast my lot in with these people, not a single thing that Gerard promised me would come true has.

You'd think this alone would have given me pause. You'd think wrong.

So many times I've been within millimetres of leaving. But every time, at the very last second, I've pulled up short, telling myself, No, I have to stay for the boys. I have to stay for Kev and Des.

Truly, if it hadn't been for them, I would have — the truth? Stayed anyway.

Because if I were to leave, where would I go? What would be left? My life was hell *before* I became an Untouchable; if I left, I could look forward not only to dust-dry days of searing loneliness with death sidling ever nearer but, as a capper, eternal incineration in the *real* hell I could already hear spitting and crackling just a short hop down the road. This, my brother has assured me, is the non-negotiable fate awaiting spiritual quitters.

I'm terrified of death. I'm terrified of hell. And I'm terrified of my brother.

I'm terrified he might be right about everything.

So I've stayed put, asking myself daily, Isn't at least *trying* to live a life of faith, no matter how much suffering that life entails, of greater value than a soft, lazy life that capitulates to easy doubt? Gerard says so! And who ever said faith would be easy? Who ever said it would amount to much more than a leaky boat on the Niagara River?

These tepid self-pats on the back are what have propelled me for five years from one grinding day to the next. Days without end of selfless service, making myself useful, putting myself last, and focusing on the drab needs of those around me. As den mother to this cockamamie gang, I've become skilled at blustering down all the emotional chaos and general orneriness they can throw at me. In five years, at least a hundred lost, addicted souls have passed through here, jumping and flailing like their eyeballs are on fire or sinking into the furniture, lethargic as alligators in the mud. Dozing off during Gerard's daily Bible studies, drooping around the house waiting for a bed to come up in detox, and, more often than not, taking off before it does to run one more time like excited children after the scrappy, broken-winged, dive-bombing bluebird of substance-abuse happiness.

But the ones who stick around have to be chauffeured back and forth from Gerard's farmhouse in the boonies to the city: to doctors' appointments, to court, to Value Village for new pants without blood and vomit stains. Meds for schizophrenia and fetal alcohol syndrome need to be monitored. The capital-letter cases, the HIVs, the Hep Cs, the ODs, all have to be skilfully juggled. Fines need to be paid, bail put up, groceries bought, floors, dishes, and sheets washed. On and on it goes, the whole sorry junkie sideshow, the result of the Untouchables' various and passionate love affairs with every form of blasting powder or emotional coolant known to man.

That's why I'm here, that's what I do. And according to my brother, I'm saving my own moth-eaten soul in the bargain.

...

Back at the house, I desperately want to slip away while the other grasshoppers are bumping into one another in the doorway, kicking off boots, throwing ratty coats into a heap by the kitchen door. Gerard's post-funeral program bodes nothing but ill; he and Catou are already locked in the pantry he uses as his study, having private words.

The one thing you can be sure he's *not* telling her is that she should be a better mother to the son she has left. Gerard's thinking doesn't follow such prosaic, earth-bound lines. His head floats in the nether-clouds of Beulah Land, and any advice she's getting now will be about how she should step up her self-denying submission to the Father and the Son and grind herself deeper into the dirt in repentance.

Unfortunately for Gerard, Catou doesn't have a submissive bone in her body. I once saw her flip the bird at him behind his back, something not even Flake would have dared. And while I realize this is a wretched day for Catou, I'll go on record right here and say that, bereaved or not, she's the rottenest mother any poor kid was ever saddled with. And I'm one who should know.

No one on this earth could have asked for two more delightful little sons than Kevvie and Desi. But their status in her eyes has always been subject to revision roughly every seven to eight minutes. She'd yank Desi in on one side and Kevvie on the other, mashing their heads against her bony chest, cooing, "You know I love you, don't you, you know I love you best of anybody in the whole wide world, don't you? Tell me you know I love you!" Then in a blink, it'd be, "Can you just wait one fucking *minute*? God, you're so *selfish*! You know what selfish little boys who only think about themselves are asking for? A wallop in the face, is what. Is that what you want? Louder! Is that what you *WANT*?" Then she'd smack them both, hard, or pull their hair till they screamed.

Though if I'm honest—and searing honesty is certainly one of the virtues encouraged around here—I have to admit with shame that part of me understands Catou. Before I met her boys, I hadn't been anywhere near a child since I'd stopped being one myself. If one veered into my path on the sidewalk or in the grocery store, I'd look daggers at it, sending telepathic "Die, whippersnapper!" messages through gun-slit eyes. I was terrified of kids, terrified of their eyes on me, as if in their newness and innocence they could see right through my baggy skin, sour face, and lumpy heft into the boundless sadness beneath.

But on the days scowling Catou deigned to turn up at Gerard's morning Bible study, the boys tumbling after her into the kitchen, my heart had begun to kick its tired heels in the air. Kevvie would be opening and slamming cupboards and cadging quarters from random Untouchables, while Desi would stand sedately by the door, mild as milk, holding his folded copy of the *Sun*. And I'd be digging into my purse for the licorice or the little cars I'd bought to slip surreptitiously into their coat pockets, overwhelmed with a sensation I barely recognized: joy! It was as if I'd stumbled at the last possible minute into a place of promise held empty and waiting for me for decades, my life a debris-littered showroom with *Bankruptcy Sale!* and *Final Weeks!* plastered over its dirty windows, until those boys turned up in the nick of time to save the day.

...

I'm not a live-in Untouchable. I have my own place, where I once, astoundingly, nurtured my own broken bluebird dreams of *la dolce vita*. You can tell by the number of throw pillows in my living room alone. No one decorates like this unless they're expecting a whiz-bang social life to materialize somewhere down the line.

A social life? Really? *Me*? Whatever was I thinking?

But, yes, my home is a million social miles from my brother's wacky mini-Waco compound. I live on the posh thirty-second floor of a vertical green-glass ice-cube tray on Toronto's glamorous lakeshore. I could be looking out all day at dazzling Lake Ontario shimmering all the way to intoxicating Rochester if only I'd had the foresight to take an apartment on the other side of the building.

Twenty-seven years I've lived here, and I'm still the only one parking my drink on the glass coffee table that was so cutting-edge back when Boy George was king. Still the only one sprawled on my exquisite Roche Bobois sofa, gaping slack-jawed at must-see TV. Still the lone snorer in my swanky brass bed.

Let's just pull a curtain of kindness over the whole scene and gently say: I don't make friends easily.

I spent the first twenty of those years virtually guestless, save for the odd sleepover sound engineer or C-list actor who'd call, drink in hand, from my couch to tell his wife he was working late. I'd hear babies crying down the line and would always imagine the patient, capable, betrayed women on the other end as the ones to be envied, rather than me, the barren one briefly and drunkenly holding their men.

I spent the next seven years absolutely alone, except for what can only be described as the worst invisible friend a lonely girl ever had, a furtive *presence* whose locus is my big, beautiful white Montauk chair, and to whom I address all of my scintillating conversation as I kick back of an evening—all right, of every evening—with a drink or three. Or nine.

If this makes me loonier than the looniest Untouchable going, so be it. At least I'm only crazy on the inside. Out in the big, bright world, I'm a highly functioning and upstanding citizen of some small renown: I am, or was until very lately, Toronto's Voice-Over Queen. My three-and-a-half-decade career of skilfully reading ad copy into a microphone has made me richer than Scrooge McDuck, particularly as I've never had anyone but myself to spend my easy-earned cash on.

And yet I've spent precious little of it. Eons ago, I took myself out to restaurants and bars with the faint hope of meeting, I don't know, someone, anyone. I always came home alone. I thought of taking many a trip over the years but kept putting it off till later, and now later has come and gone. I hailed the 1990s by buying a fancy computer, with the idea of hooking up with faceless pals for chatting. I chat with no one.

But spend it or save it, all the cash in the world can't turn a cold and empty glass box at the top of a tower into a home.

For nearly as long as I can remember, I've come back in the evenings to be greeted only by the elevator winking its sleepless red eye at me, pinging a tired hello. It knows my stop like a horse knows the way home in the dark. Once inside, I can deadbolt my door and immediately pour myself an immoderately tall Jack on the rocks, safely hidden from my unknown neighbours, who tiptoe past my silent door on the hall's soft blue carpeting, dinging the elevator and disappearing like smoke. The traffic on the Gardiner Expressway far below swishes by, soundless as fish in a tank.

I tell myself—and my vaporous friend—that some people are simply meant to be solitaries. "*Hell,*" I say out loud for his benefit, "*I've lasted this long. What's another lonesome decade or two?*"

Other times, I think I might revert to feral up here, like a cat left alone too long while its owners drowse on the beach in Acapulco. Men in bee suits will have to come and snare me with nets, slam me howling and clawing, porcupined with tranquilizer darts, into a cage. And cart me away somewhere to be put humanely to sleep.

Yes, okay. So I drink. And have for quite a while now, from long before I ever saw the inside of Gerard's tumble-down, haunted house of holiness. Drinking feels like lighting a crackling fire inside my cold glass box. It feels, at the beginning anyway, like someone's moving all the heavy furniture out of the way, clearing the dance floor for big fun and frolic that *almost* materializes every single time. It's never seemed like a particularly serious problem, since it's never involved anyone but me. Until my induction into the Untouchables five years ago, there certainly wasn't anyone around, friend or foe, to nag me about it. If my mother hadn't called and caught me slurring a couple of times, Gerard never would have found out and no one would have had to go off the deep end over fucking nothing.

Besides. I never miss recording gigs, never fail to deliver the wow factor in the sound studio. Up until recently, I had all kinds

25

of national spots running and wouldn't get out of bed for less than triple scale. Clients are so routinely blown away by my work it's a wonder they don't hoist me onto their shoulders for a ticker-tape parade down Bay Street, stunned by my gilded "Now with fifty percent more nougat!" or my elegantly understated "Eighty percent more of the home-style goodness you've come to trust!" Not only that, but I can skim through medical information voice-overs meant only for doctors, jammed with eight-syllable words ending in "-zoate" and "-xedrine" and "-tryptichloride" in one bright, shining take. I can do cartoon voices for days: adorable rodents, buzzy robots, fairy godmothers, six-year-old boys. Up till not long ago, I was hearing myself everywhere I went: in stores, restaurants, the dentist's office, wherever a TV or radio might be playing, there was I, floating over the city like a spread-eagled cloud-spirit of bustling commerce and rip-roaring fun, fifty miles square.

But then, five years ago, Mum called. She was in way better shape back then, allowing me the relative bliss of limiting all contact with her strictly to the telephone rather than having to personally look in on her alarmingly accelerated disintegration at least once every two weeks like I do now.

On the night in question, she called because she wanted me to lug yet another orange Hefty bag full of musty old-man pants and giant third-hand running shoes from the Our Lady of Sorrows rummage sale up to Gerard's place. She caught me sloshed and hiccupping, kicking back with a mini-crying jag as I conversed in broken shards with my shadowy friend, who lay sprawled in his giant easy chair, grinning ever more broadly the more maudlin and wretched I became.

Six sheets to the wind, rambling like a lunatic about my forthcoming feral future, I sounded pretty much like this: "*Yeah, like a fucking, I dunno, a fucking cat, stuck inside thish, and fucking forgotten, with those whaddyacall'em, darts sticking all over, and jumpy as a cat too, here in my, Christ! This litter box is my home! And I'm going under, ya hear me, going down for the third time and you tell me, who gives a flying fuckeroony, huh? Who? You? Don't make me laugh!*"

I'd just come from the annual agency Christmas party, the most prestigious talent agency in the city, thank you very much. The room all done up in red tinsel like hell's hospitality suite and the entire talent roster of darling buds of May lolling on sofas or standing in hilarious clots, sipping white wine, taking calls and texting, toking up or doing a few lines in the swank marble bathroom, I heard them in there, I wasn't born that very morning. All of them skinny, sleek-haired, bare-armed, their lovely flesh winter-white and goosebumpy as they hung off the arms and braided themselves around the legs of producers and casting directors. And none of them was talking to big, lumbering Maggie, who, as I informed my unfleshed associate, "*hasn't made one fucking, one* real *friend since I was what, ten? Except for, okay, him, wherever the hell he's gotten to, married to that skinny French bitch, and yeah, oh yeah, real nice, you're laughing at me, you fucker, but it's your fault, your goddamn fault I could never ship, chip into, chip away all that, that frozhen, fro-zen fucking, yickety-yack on the surface and be like every other, other people, all warm-blooded and pink in the*

27

face instead of cold as a low-down snake, oh, and did I mention it's all your fault?"

Because there I'd been at party central, stashed in a corner by the drapes, a protuberance in a giant turtleneck sweater, afraid to get up and go to the bathroom for a smoke because people might think I'd noticed I was all alone and was leaving early. Me, the Golden Voice, whose fortune had been made in complete invisibility, who did no on-camera work ever because, for one, I was too damned fat, and two, the minute anyone aimed a lens at me I'd morph into one of the demoiselles d'Avignon, my whole face dividing into separately ruled factions, muscles in spasm, eyes running for their lives, lips and cheeks as pliable as petrified wood.

"Thass your fault too, and her fault, 'cause when you don't have a mother who cares about you, nobody fucking cares when you have a breakdown and lose your way and — stop laughing! Iss not fucking funny!"

Yeah, and so what? I didn't need to be seen. Nobody had to know about my big-boned, middle-aged self muffining over the waistband of my XL jeans because I happened to be sole owner and operator of The Voice of Pure Gold, the huskiest, sultriest, sweetest thing in advertising, the aural equivalent of, as I told my friend just the other night, *"walking barefoot on a bed of cultured pearls buried under autumn leaves. So suck on it!"*

I knew it was generally conceded that I was a pain to talk to, almost pathologically awkward, especially around people I assumed were normal and conventionally successful and happy. I never went to any other parties, never had any film-set anecdotes or wild tales to tell of hobnobbing with Jennifer Lopez or Ryan

Gosling. But the freeze-out on this particular night had felt unnervingly different from the cool yet respectful neglect I'd grown used to.

I wasn't being ignored. I actually *was* invisible. The writing was all over the wall: Golden Voice had till sundown to get out of town.

Over that last year, there'd been fewer and fewer calls. My agent kept assuring me, "It's not you, Maggie. The whole industry's hurting." But I was hearing plenty of commercials voiced by nobodies, saw sassy squirrels and mother mice on Saturday-morning cartoons that should have been mine.

Nor was I surprised. I'd known for a while that something was beginning to sound a little, let's say, off.. Jesus, I was over fifty, and besides, whiskey-curing only went so far in creating a sensational voice; there was a drop-off point after which the returns began to diminish rapidly. What did I expect? The famous gold was going brassy, the sultriness shrivelling into a croak. Words had begun to snag on hooks mid-throat or were forced to crawl upward through mucous sloughs of despond, especially following nights featuring five-plus drinks. I'd begun to sound like a rank amateur, trying way too hard.

Apparently it was now my turn to be meeting the little people again on the way down, etc., all those timid newcomers who'd looked so stricken to see me barge like the *Queen Mary* through the studio doors, all those talent-show winners who'd had to get up on stage with Leontyne Price.

You'd drink too.

My glass walls were closing in on me, the Jack empties and wine bottles in the recycling bin multiplying geometrically by the month. One minute I'd been thirty and then, in an eyeblink, older than time itself. So there I'd sat on that sad night, slumped on my sofa, mournfully sozzled, scarfing a meat lovers' pizza and weeping over a life wasted shilling for triple-protection conditioners and all the goodness of whole grain. And then the phone rang, and my sharp little mother — still her acerbic old self back then — pricked up her ears and barked down the line, "For goodness' sake, Mag Mary! Don't you dare try to tell me you're not drunk *this* time!"

She ratted me out to Gerard. Told him I lived in a tower, hoarded money, worked four hours a week, had time to burn, and a life devoid of any purpose whatsoever.

Unlike him, of course. Because the year the two of us had turned thirty, as I was splurging on furniture for my new home in the clouds, he was fulfilling our mother's dearest heart's dream: kissing the bishop's ring and getting himself ordained a real, live priest.

Back then, it had certainly looked like *he* was the one with the unpromising future. His first priestly posting, in Brampton, had been a disaster. I'd drive Mum out there on Sundays in her crumbling Oldsmobile for the pleasure of watching him say a brusque, testy Mass followed by a dour meal at his new rectory. He'd sit tense as barbed wire, rewarding Mum's bright, chirping questions about parish affairs with monosyllabic, black-browed replies as he balanced lit cigarettes on the edge of his plate or butted them out in his uneaten salad. When I asked to bum a few, he'd shake his head, no, as morose and stubborn as a bloodstain.

Mum didn't know what to think. Gerard was such a far cry from the golfing, schmoozing kind of priest that, for example, her brother, our uncle Jimmy, had been. He never greeted parishioners on the steps of the church after Mass, never cracked a sermon with even the fissure of a joke, never bantered with Phil the janitor after hours as he shoved his push broom around the sanctuary or asphyxiated candles with the long-handled snuffer as if putting out the lights of souls. I shuddered to imagine my brother's death shadow blackening the other side of the confessional screen.

After four stingy years in harness, he was called to the chancery office, relieved of his posting, and urged to seek therapy. Instead, he disappeared.

"He's on priest probation!" I cackled over the phone to Mum at the time. "Maybe no one's allowed to talk to him. Maybe it's a shunning, like the Amish do. Where does he even live now? In his car?"

And Mum: "Don't you dare say such a thing! If he has no money, he knows he's welcome to stay with me!" And then, just as quickly, hardening. "Living in his car. That's just one of your nasty stories."

"You tell me where he is then."

"You've got more money than you know what to do with. Why don't you go find him and help him out? Your own brother!"

Ho ho! As if!

Nor did novenas without end, back-to-back rosaries, or an ocean of mother's tears suffice to bring him back. We didn't see his shining face again till the heady days of Y2K.

He offered no apologies, no explanations. He'd gotten himself a house a good hour's drive north of Toronto. He was still a priest but also, astoundingly, born-again, thoroughly Protestant-ized, and unconnected to any church or parish. Instead, he was running some kind of Bible study-slash-half-assed halfway house for a motley gang of street people whom he'd ferry north from the city in his rust-bucket car, opening cans for them in his kitchen and letting them sleep on his floor.

He called them his Untouchables because in the eyes of the world he had come to know as cursed, they were the lowest of the low.

Our Catholic-to-the-bone Mum was shocked to the marrow.

"A Bible study! Next thing you know he'll be palling around with that Ernest Angley, or that one in the white suit who blows people over. Thank God my mother didn't live to see this."

So, thanks to her meddling, there I was, passed out on the couch, when my phone rang at two-thirty in the morning of my fifty-second Valentine's Day, already a doom-laden twenty-four hours I'd have to drink myself sideways to get through. Though it wouldn't have mattered if I spent my evenings saying the rosary and embroidering Bible verses onto hand-knit long johns for widows and orphans; Gerard would have found something amiss. He could lay a guilt trip on Jesus.

He came through as clear as a bell in frosty air. Though I did try to fight back at first, clawing my way through the murk in my head with a boozy stab at levity.

"Wowee. What a shurprise. If it ishn't old Neliott Ness. And how are you in this wee shmall hour of the morning, eh? Whassup? Whassup with you and your Unfuckingtouchablsh, hee hee hee."

"You need to be up here with us. You can't hide any more."

"Whoosh hid —?"

"You belong here with my people. They are here because they can fall no farther. Every last one of them has come to the end of the line."

"I'm not at the end of any fucking li —"

"My people have all come to the extreme bitter end of hope. My job is to make sure they stay there. Because if a man dies before he's lost all hope in himself, he will be lost forever."

"Well now, gosh. As appealing as that soundsh, I think I'll —"

"Drive up this weekend," he said. It was an order.

He called again the next night, and the next. His preachments were radioactive.

"Your life is a joke. Everything you have, you stole, by lying and whoring yourself in the stinking sewer of greed and gain. I'm telling you that anyone who dies with so much as a dollar in his pocket is deserving of the fires of hell."

And, "There's nothing in your future but failure. You're getting older and uglier. Everything's going to get worse, not better. Your health will give out. All your money buys you nothing worth having. Everything is rushing to a close. Your life is worthless until you kneel in repentance and submission to the Father!"

And *furthermore*, "You have no more control over anything in your life than you will have at the moment of your death. Try to hold on then! Try to stop yourself being pulled into the darkness when your time comes! You must give your life completely over to the Father! It is the death you have come here to die!"

And at long last, the upbeat closer: "Salvation isn't that polite thing they sell on television, the Father giving you a friendly tap on the shoulder. Salvation is what happens when you pull a flopping, fighting fish out of the water and smash its head with a rock on the bottom of the boat! It's like a screaming ambulance carrying a burn victim to the hospital, when all he wants to do is die!

"Without this crisis of the self, there is no life, no salvation! The Father hates the unrepentant human race! We are nothing but grasshoppers in his eyes!"

I knew nothing then about Gerard's little band of disciples except that narrow was the way of salvation and they were a handful of the very few who ever found it. Blearily, I tried to imagine myself existing on the virtual strip of sanctified land no wider than a hallway that he and they occupied, like the last people on earth after the Bomb has wiped out everything, an image from my childhood so steeped in breathless panic I could barely stand to recall it even now.

That book. When I was ten. That was when all the trouble started, the beginning of the end for me.

My dark companion in the chair remembered it too. It brought out the fangs in his smile, which grew ever wider as Gerard rolled out his merry message about faithless, unsaved grasshoppers doomed to die the ignoble deaths of bugs. Because what did the Father care for our deaths, or our lives for that matter, if, for any one of a thousand reasons, we had missed out on his stingily bestowed gift of salvation? All the ripped and ragged hearts in the world were surely nothing but a carnival flea circus to him, all us bugs in spangly leotards performing our little hearts out on the high wire while he sat there yawning in his gaudy box seat.

With four and a half decades of packed-down fear as a seedbed, no wonder it took a mere four days of Gerard's over-the-phone preaching to break me.

The weekend rolled around to find me renting a car and appearing right where he wanted me, in his filthy farmhouse living room, reading the writing on the wall. Literally. Someone had scrawled in black Magic Marker, up behind the cold, dead 1970s-era Motorola TV, what I took to be the House Motto. The words spiralled around the central "LET" like a roaring storm centre on the Weather Channel.

LET NOTHING DISTURB THE!!!
LET NOTHING DISMAY THE!!!!! ALL THINGS PASS! GOD NEVER CHANGES! PATIENCE ATAINES ALL THAT IT STRIVES FOR! HE WHO HAS GOD FINDS HE LAKES NOTHING! GOD ALONE SUFFISES!!!

It felt like a head-butt in the stomach. What was I thinking, opening myself up to all this stuff again? I'd *tried* God, for God's sake! I'd beaten myself senseless trying, and this when I was still young and fresh and relatively resilient. Nothing had come of it. What made me think I could make a go of it again, especially as crusty and used up as I was now?

I stood in the middle of a circle of Untouchables in varied and colourful stages of recovery and/or imminent collapse, feeling like Dorothy swarmed by Munchkins. One by one, they *welcomed* me, grinning and reaching out to touch my long-untouched shoulder. The one I would soon come to know as Frosted Flake gallantly pumped my hand, telling me fervently, "It's great to have you, lovely lady."

I was being inducted into that legendary club nobody wants to join, the one positively chomping at the bit to have me for a member.

Gerard never said a word about my little "problem." He simply told them I was there to assist. Actually, "to serve" is how he phrased it. I'd keep my own place and my still-lucrative work in the city, but I would be making myself available to shuttle them back and forth from town, to supervise the kitchen, and to serve as general all-round gofer. And my whore's earnings from the sewer of greed and gain would be funnelled into keeping the Untouchables clothed and fed and permanently without hope.

This was the first I'd heard of the chapter and verse of my exciting life to come.

I drove straight home afterwards, poured myself a stiff one, and sat staring into the outer darkness, thinking woozily that there might be magic afoot here. Maybe servitude was the way to go, and being up close and personal with my sanctified twin would make a difference. Maybe I could put the alcohol away. Maybe I could relearn how to fall into natural sleep at night.

Maybe the phantom in the big chair would evaporate right out of existence as I made *live* friends—could the Untouchables ever be that to me? Who knew?

Because as frightening as Gerard was, I knew, had known almost forever, that his fierce heart had been seared by the blindingly lit, white-hot core of truth I'd been desperately scrabbling after my whole life. And that the anguish and desolation that had plagued both of us ever since we'd come of age, making it impossible to sink into carefree, normal lives of friends and fun, was something I must address no matter what the cost. Or die trying.

Or die drinking.

But maybe—dare I even hope?—the sodden, shame-faced, cotton-headed prayers I'd been shooting like toy arrows into the night sky for as long as I could remember would at last begin to hit their mysterious Mark instead of arcing and plummeting to the Gardiner Expressway to be swallowed up in the roar of all-season radials.

And so it began. Days when I had no voice gigs—and there were more of these all the time—I'd drive up to Orangeville in the ridiculous muscle car Gerard had given me to do the Untouchables' grocery shopping, dropping everything off at the next flophouse farmhouse down the road from his, where the homeless Untouchables ate and slept when they weren't running amok in the city. Gerard's place was where they met to be chastened, corrected, and biblically bludgeoned, but only Gerard actually lived there, his crumbling shack hemmed in by fell trees looped with tent caterpillar webs, his only company the scritching of the raccoons nesting in the attic and the gurgle of root-beer-coloured water dripping from the taps.

The auxiliary house was run by Fred, the longest consistently sober Untouchable. Gerard had found him living in a cardboard box under my very own Gardiner, and now he served as my brother's loyal vice-regent, ruling over the Untouchables whenever Gerard was busy with his ferocious regime of prayer and Bible-reading or blind and adrift, as he increasingly was, in some mystical ninth dimension.

Fred's place, the Untouchables' dorm, was a warren of doorless rooms with milk-crate furniture and butts stamped out all over the floor. Ash was always dropping from someone onto something; hell could not have had more little fires burning at any one time. Filthy laundry was kicked and wodged into every corner, waiting for me to see to it. Ripped sheets and frowsy blankets hung slack over the cobwebbed windows. The general reek was of feet and vomit and poorly aimed urine. Random Untouchables just in from the streets could usually be found slumped at the kitchen table or eating from the cauldrons of soup and chili that Fred or I kept going on the stove.

The days were long, the years were short. Five of them whizzed by like comets, each day ending with me face deep in the hooch, as wretched as I'd ever been but assuring myself that tomorrow would most certainly be the day the sanctified benefits would start kicking in.

I'm still waiting.

Nor was Gerard ever any damned help. Like everyone else, I was expected to turn up at his Bible study every morning on the dot of eight, but I usually claimed I had work, which was true at least a quarter of the time. Still, while it seemed that everyone in the shining post-post-modern world was wanting *out* of belief, I was shouldering against the jostling surge, barging the wrong way, wanting in. So I made the effort when I felt up to it, though when I did turn up, I was more often than not the only one who had.

Gerard would be sitting at his cracked Formica kitchen table, hunched over coffee that tasted as if it had been boiling for hours on a campfire. He'd tell me I could ask him anything, anything at all. In front of him was his fat yellow tablet full of scribbled notes about the Bride and the Harlot, with "REVELATION!!!!!" written at the top and underlined with such ferocity he'd gashed the paper through.

I'd try not to look at it, attempting rather to open the morning's conversation with domestic topics I thought might soften his grim truculence. Once, early on, I whipped out an ancient, creased, black-and-white Brownie Starflash snapshot with serrated edges that had been in my wallet since time immemorial. It featured the two of us as fat-cheeked, towheaded four-year-olds, standing on either side of our Grandmother Fionnuala, Mum's mum, who was barely taller than we were, save for her snowy Alpine peaks of Marie Antoinette hair. I wore a stiff skirt like a lampshade. Gerard appeared to be in lederhosen. There was still a strong resemblance between us back then, something jarringly medieval in our faces: a cuckoo clock Hansel and Gretel with spinny eyes and kick-out, wooden legs, changelings from the *Village of the Damned*.

Gerard gave the photo a cold glance but said nothing.

"Did you know that one of Grandma Fionnuala's obituaries referred to her as the recently decreased?"

Silence. The flare of a match, the hungry in-suck of smoke.

"Remember how she and Dad used to butt heads? Those godawful Sunday dinners we had to sit through?"

Still squat from the Holy Man.

So there we'd sit, two glum mugs slumped in mirroring positions, his right hand propping his head, my left hand propping mine, his right leg looped over his knee, my left over mine. I had all the time in the world to throw the whole crazy quilt of Christianity up to him, square by wacky square: Adam and Eve bringing death into the world through sin, Noah chasing down the gnats and the polar bears. And so on.

"What's your problem?" he'd snap. "A hellacious worldwide flood. The wicked wiped out. The faithful preserved. What part of that don't you understand?"

All righty then. How about that touchy little item, predestination?

"God is supposed to be synonymous with Love, right? So what kind of loving God chooses a tiny handful of people to care about and pitches the rest into hell?"

A deep sigh from the teacher as he stubbed out his smoke in the Gehenna of his ashtray.

"The love of the Father for his own is incomprehensible to the non-elect. That love is manifested in his plan, which was predestined before the foundation of the world, Romans 8:29. Before the lighting of the sun and the moon, he knew that the Son would become a man in order to take our sin and corruption upon himself and swallow up death in victory. This perfect plan has been completed in history. And so we, living within the bounds of time, unlike the Father who lives outside of it, watch what appear to be people coming to him of their own volition, and other people turning away. But no one has chosen him. He chose *them*, from before the inception of time. The Potter does what he wills with the pots he has made. Faithful is he that calleth you, who also will do it, 1 Thessalonians 5:24."

At which point I'd be willing my frustrated tears to turn the hell around and get back in the house.

"Thanks. You lost me at 'The.'"

I'd look up then to see that his eyes had all but flickered out, the ash from his cigarette a limp grey rainbow.

He'd left time again.

It was his best, most uncanny holy-man trick.

"It just . . . happens. I disappear," was how he'd explained it after I'd witnessed it for the first time over two decades ago in the middle of one of his dismal rectory lunches. It was the only time I'd ever seen his agate eyes soften. "I stop existing in this body. It's called" — and he'd taken a deep, shuddering breath before continuing — "*Interminabilis vitae simul et perfecta possessio.*"

"What's that?" I'd asked sourly. "Do not drive or operate machinery until you know how the cessation of existence affects you?"

All he knew, he'd said, before shutting the conversation down, was that when he came back from his dry run of his own death, he absolutely knew that he knew that he knew.

41

. . .

Five years, my friend. Five years. Every day of which featured noon rolling into Gerard's bare-bones kitchen on the dot of twelve, a carbon copy of yesterday, a dead ringer of tomorrow. If anyone had turned up for Bible study, it would be wrapped at last. Catou might be making herself a baloney sandwich before heading back out into the wilderness of her life. Kevvie might be in the front yard, swinging from one of the repugnant trees. Over by the sunny window, Sunil Low-Down might be tickling Desi, who'd giggle and shriek, twisting every which way and darting quick hands under Sunil's shirt, making him squeal like a dolphin.

It happened every time. The minute Gerard turned his back on his straggling flock, these blessed seven who had made it back, more or less, from their lost street lives, these seven who were the only remaining from the hordes who had come and gone, started busting out all over, blossoming like a field of wildflowers, acting as if it were actually *true* that they were the ones who were supposed to be first in the Kingdom, as Gerard assured them they would be so long as they toed his line. Not Catou so much; she was always brittle and grim, but the others, in their various ways, would wig out, go all slap-happy, as if something true and sweet had miraculously found its way around the daggers and spikes of Gerard's words and into their hearts. Flake would razz Big Fanny, who would start punching him in the head, both of them trying hard not to laugh. Barb and Sunil High-Up would dance around the kitchen, shrieking made-up words to "Born to Be Wild." There was a light in all of their broken faces, a softened quality around the eyes that I

42

couldn't look away from. I had no idea what it was they had, but I wanted it; compared with them, the actors and copywriters and clients I met regularly on the job seemed dried-up, insubstantial, their existences vapid and pointless. The wing-nut Untouchables were connected to *something*, a something that rendered them four-dimensional, or five, or a thousand, their nuttiness fully fleshed and fed from deep, inner springs, their reach long enough to cup Pluto in their bare hands.

Not that this made them any less annoying.

I also knew, without anyone saying a word, that "assistant" though I may have been, I'd never for a second fooled even the most obtuse of them. I may as well have been throwing wild parties for the gang in my apartment after hours. All they needed was one look at my baggy eyes and hard, morning mouth, and "Alky" may as well have been written on my forehead in indelible ink.

But I have to confess that, once in a very great while, and never *in* a Bible study, but only afterwards, while I sat at the kitchen table having a smoke before tackling the cleaning of the reeking bathroom, I imagined that the same light that shone on this lost little band also warmed the back of my stiff neck. It was so fleeting, this feeling, a minute here, five minutes there, but for those moments, I was nineteen again and falling, *reeling* backward into heavenly arms that I somehow knew wouldn't let me fall all the way down. My face would flush with a smile that actually felt genuine, as I was poked in the ribs and tickled by something I couldn't name but knew wasn't fear.

It would come and it would go. And it would *always* be gone by the time I sank onto my couch alone at night.

But far more than the fleeting sweetness of these moments, it was the boys who kept me going from day to bleak, slogging day.

It was eight months after my induction into the fold that Catou had joined us. Like me, she wasn't a live-in; she had her own Orangeville apartment. I'd known nothing at all about her kids until, trudging dutifully up to the house for Bible study on a dark morning in late December, I first spotted her severely compromised, fourth-hand Tercel parked in Gerard's iced-over driveway. And did a double take when I saw Kevvie's tearful little face mashed up against the car window, his nose smooshed like a button, as Catou stomped toward the house in her purple cowboy boots, gearing up for a sound dunking in the Book of Revelation.

Kevvie was hiccupping with muffled sobs no louder than the barking of a restless dog five miles up the road. I peered into the car to find he wasn't alone; there was Desi lying on the back seat behind his brother, looking like a dingy plush toy salvaged from a dumpster, a little brown face in a dirty blue snowsuit with two pointy fox ears on the hood. His stiff arms were flung out sideways, a soother jouncing rhythmically in the middle of his face. Catou had just slammed the front door behind her. It was ten below outside.

Apparently this was where she saw fit to stash her boys for the four or five hours it would take for Gerard to scrub down her nasty soul.

Had she been doing this every *day*?

I pounded in after her, cut Gerard off in mid-opening spiel, and yelled that she'd better hand over the car keys unless she cared to have her head removed from her body like a screw-cap from a bottle. She looked up at me from the floor, unfazed, as she dragged a filthy brown blanket over her shoulders, her obvious concern for her own warmth making the blood rise in my eyes. At the same time, I realized that whatever damage I might care to inflict would only be icing on her personal cake of doom. One of *her* eyes had already been lodged by someone's vigorous fist a half-inch deeper into her skull. She looked as if she'd been eating out of garbage cans and sleeping under bridges her entire life and was hanging on to sobriety, never mind reality, by a fingernail.

She lit a leisurely smoke and raised those iron-cold eyes to mine.

"What's it to you, bitch?"

"I'll tell you what it is to me." And ignoring looming Gerard and the lively interest of the rest of the crowd, I yanked her to her feet by her hoodie and hauled my own fist back in the classic Bluto versus Popeye pre-strike position.

"All right, you fucking fat cow, take the fucking keys, like I fucking give a flying fuck," she acquiesced graciously, digging them out of her pocket and pitching them into my face.

From then on, whenever they came, Kevvie was allowed to bumble gleefully around the house in drooping, pungent diapers, scuttling in and out of the lower kitchen cupboards, banging with knives on the pot and the pan. As soon as Desi could walk, he joined in, though more sedately; he tapped rather than banged. In no time the two of them had sprouted into miniature wild men of Borneo, with huge, lint-flecked shrubs of hair billowing around their droll little faces like storm clouds shot with lightning bolts. The hair and coffee-coloured skin came via their dad, whom we knew only from Catou's description as "the black dude, T.J., or something like that."

She kept her distance from me after that, sitting as far away from me as she could get during Bible study, never meeting my eyes. But, tough as she was, Gerard's preaching had her, like everyone else who dared to turn up, cowering like a puppy at a raised newspaper. Enthroned in the largest butt-scorched armchair in his living room, he ranted like a warlord, thundering, "There shall come in the last days scoffers, walking after their own lusts! And saying, where is the promise of his coming? For since the fathers fell asleep, all things continue as they were from the beginning of the creation! My job is to make it as hard for you as I possibly can! Your faith must be tested every day to the very brink of death! Repentance without ceasing must be your daily bread! Thus does the Father reveal his truth to cursed mankind. Many are called but few are chosen! The human race is nothing but God's sperm cells, a trillion dying for every one that comes to life everlasting! It's like the minnows in the sea in their billions: when the great Net of Salvation is lowered into the water, how many without number will swim easily in and out, untouched, untroubled, jeering, worthless, doomed to damnation!"

Frosted Flake, over in the corner, as far from Gerard as *he* could get, would be wearing the yellow sweatshirt he claimed he'd stolen, the one emblazoned with the words JESUS DROPPED THE CHARGES! When Gerard swung his eyes in the other direction, he'd lean in close to Catou to cadge a smoke. From under the roar of Gerard would come her tight, sanctified reply, "Bite me, dickwad."

...

The boys were in the house now, but I still avoided them for the most part; like I said, little kids made me nervous. I watched them grow from my peripheral vision. And one day, when they were four and three respectively, I walked out of the middle of a horrific Bible drubbing, ducking into the bathroom to hide and breathe some release into my knotted digestive tract, only to find Desi sitting wedged inside the sink with a lapful of kitchen knives, empty Coke cans, and four or five crusty old prescription bottles filched from Gerard's doorless medicine cabinet. Kevvie, shirtless, was indulging in a great arcing pee from a distance of four feet from the toilet, where several baby floaters swirled lethargically. Seeing me come in, he abandoned all control over his aim as he shouted with berserk enthusiasm, "Madam! Welcome to our store! Did you bring lots of money?"

I could hear Gerard's fulminations drifting down the hall.

"The wicked will not inherit the kingdom of God! Tell me, 1 Corinthians 6:9; what the lot of you used to be! Fornicators! Liars! Drunks! Now in your born-again state, what is your minute-to-minute task? You are to chastise! Rebuke! Exhort one another and everyone the Father places in your path! Finish your race! Keep the faith! Be ever watchful! Endure every trial! Evangelize aggressively!"

"Madam!" Kevvie repeated, his fly still open, his megawatt smile so dazzling I had to blink. "Would you like to buy a colouring book for your child, or maybe if you're planning to have a child, he would need this for sure!" He thrust a tattered, fully coloured book at me from a ragged pile at his feet. "Only five dollars! Very cheap!"

"Why is Desi in the sink?"

"He's the storekeeper! We have real good stuff to sell! If you need medicine, this will help you for all sicknesses!" He grabbed a pill bottle from Desi and began battling manfully with the childproof cap.

"It doesn't look like you get a lot of customers."

"Yes we do. Mister Potato Head comes every day to our store," he informed me, indicating a shrivelled, one-eyed tuber in a crooked plastic hat perched on top of his balled-up shirt on the windowsill. "Madam. You can pee if you want to."

"Get outta here, kid, ya bother me," I said, daring to reach out and ruffle his hair. Over in the sink, Desi had lodged Gerard's grimy plastic comb and his grey, splay-bristled toothbrush in his hair, and was running Gerard's gobby razor over his downy arm.

"Give me that before you cut yourself to ribbons! And give me those pills too." I scooped them out of Desi's lap and sank down onto the edge of the low, greasy windowsill where hundreds of dead flies lay with their legs in the air, little x's over their eyes.

"Bring into captivity every thought to the obedience of Christ! Occupy until he comes!" reverberated from the living room. Without my glasses I couldn't make out what all these prescriptions could possibly be for; perhaps some doctor had taken issue with Gerard's much-vaunted leaving of time. But they couldn't be too interesting or the druggies would have made off with them by now. I stuffed them into my pockets.

Kevvie broad-jumped into the filthy, claw-footed bathtub and spun himself into invisibility inside the shower curtain as "Repeat after me!" rumbled down the hall and leaked under the door like black smoke. "Everyone is NOT going to be saved! The vast majority of mankind WILL! NOT! BE! CONVERTED! They WILL! NOT! BELIEVE! And what is the fate of men who turn their backs on the Son of God? Eternal fire! He who rejects Jesus Christ will not see life, for the wrath of God continues to abide upon him!"

"The rat of God cotivues to bite upon him!" Kevvie hollered in insane delight. Gerard fell silent. I was struck dumb with terror; he'd heard! Any minute now, he'd... but no, on he railed. "The word of God is quick and powerful! Sharper than any two-edged sword, piercing even to the dividing asunder of soul and spirit and of the joints and marrow, and is a discerner of the thoughts and intents of the heart!"

"Quick and parful! Tents of the harf!" Kevvie shouted, his face a Halloween-mask glower. His imitation of Gerard was so dead-on that a shrill yelp of laughter escaped me. I immediately covered my mouth.

"If you love me, keep my commandments!"

"If you lub me, key bycomandiss!" Kevvie shrieked, raising both arms over his head, clawing his fingers and lurching like Frankenstein.

"Shush!" I cried, clapping my hand over *his* mouth. "Do you want to get us all killed?"

For a long moment, Gerard was silent again; then the half-hearted, off-key opening bars of "When Peace like a River" began wobbling down the hall, the hymn-sing heralding the end of the morning's tirade.

"*Oh solo miooooo!*" Kevvie yelled over the musically challenged Untouchables. "*With mushroom saaaauuuce! And canned tomaaaaaatoes! Makes you the bosssssss!*" He sprang like a monkey onto the toilet tank and then to the shower curtain rod, from which he swung wildly, aiming his sneakered feet at my head. I tried to pull him off, prying his hands off the rod one at a time, but he effortlessly replaced the one I'd just removed the instant I started working on the other.

Desi piped up from his placid perch, struggling without success to leverage his little self out of the sink.

"I'm finished playing store. I want to play cars. I want to get down."

"Is this really the best place you guys could find to play?"

"It's our clubhouse," Kevvie explained, dropping from the curtain rod to land with a thwump in the tub.

"Please. This is your *clubhouse*? I've never seen such a sorry-ass clubhouse in my life. You didn't even put a KEEP OUT sign on the door. You let *girls* in, for God's sake, and you don't even have any snacks!"

"Yes we do," Kevvie shouted triumphantly, whipping away a pile of towels to display a half-eaten bag of stale cheesies.

"Sorry. My mistake. *Now* it's a clubhouse." I lifted Desi out of the sink and squatted on the floor with them, feeling for all the world like I was fraternizing with Satan as we took turns digging into the pilfered hoard of cheesies, our fingers as orange as the nicotine-stained smoking hands of the Untouchables.

But boys or no boys, every night I still rode my elevator up to an apartment as bleak as an Andrew Wyeth house on a hill at dusk and picked up my drinking where I'd left off the night before. I drank, and I blustered in the direction of the Montauk chair in my new Untouchables jargon, impaling melting ice cubes on my tongue as I informed my friend, *"Hey, I'm just a-trekkin' through the Valley of the Shadow of Death, thass all. No big whoop."*

Ice jittering in my trembling glass, the TV jumping and jiggling with good cheer, I'd trot out my weary defence of my terrorized enslavement for the benefit of the faithful Shade, who lay, as always, stretched out and comfy, feet up, all ears. If a TV comedian distracted me, making me laugh in spite of myself, I was immediately drenched with guilt like slush from a passing car; Gerard's standing orders were for us to resolutely turn our backs on the hell-stench popular culture of the day. But I needed the TV noise in the background; if I'd been in solitary confinement in an actual prison, I'd likely go mad without the distant racket of the other inmates drifting into my cell.

"I know the world deplores and despises believers like us," I'd tell my pal, this while I was still coherent. *"Sure, we're the risible throwbacks to dark times when no one knew anything about anything. Even within the wide Evangelical world, we're North Korea, Stalinist Albania, the purest of the pure, direst of the dire. But why the hell shouldn't we be? Faith is life-and-death business, and since it's supposed to be about the All and the Everything, then why wouldn't it seem, I don't know, a little . . . immoderate? Why wouldn't the path to salvation be as narrow as a gangplank? Why shouldn't the possibility of damnation terrify a person to the point of mental illness? And why wouldn't people only come in Brand A saved and Brand X damned? Yeah, I'm talkin' to you, Mistuh T, dear comrade of my youth, and would it really kill you to pry*

open your jaws and honour one, that's all I ask, just a single, lonely one of my questions with an open, honest answer? Nope. S'what I thought. Geez, back in the day, I couldn't get you to shut up. Didn't know how lucky I was."

Except, really? Really? Only two kinds of people, saved and damned? Talk about wooden characterization! I mean, Jesus, outside of our fart-choked little Untouchables hideaway, there were whole sprawling epochs! Cultures! Histories! A billion variations on ways to live and be! Prussians and Hessians! Tatars and Khirghiz, Mayans and Bantus! How could it all break down to Gerard's insane Josef Mengele of a God, sorting people the minute they stepped off the death train: sheep right! Goats left!

"Why? Did you hear me? WHY? Because the Father said so! Is that it? Huh? Is that the essence of the moral universe? Tell me one way it differs from a blind, amoral one that doesn't give two frothing fucks what happens to anyone at all?"

And so, on to my second drink, as I watched the coloured lights swoosh up and down the CN Tower, the Jack bottle propped against the couch pillows like a tiny boyfriend. Chewing over whatever Gerard had pulverized us with that day, and imagining a parade of similar, terrifying holy men down through the ages: Augustine, Calvin, Bishop Sheen, all scribbling lightning-fast on blackboards big as the sky, chalk breaking, billowing clerical sleeves white with dust. Their crazed thoughts leapfrogging as they worked out abstruse methodologies as intricate as jungle eco-systems, words stacked high as dinner plates in the sink after the Supper of the Lamb, all the systems contradicting one another, with guilt, fear, and broken submission the only constants.

Did every last holy-fool one of them begin life as a knock-kneed, taunted, friendless child, all their philosophies nothing but cut-and-paste jobs to hide broken hearts?

Because Gerard certainly did. But though I constantly reminded myself to keep that in mind when trembling before him, I never could; his grip on some broken thing deep inside of me was too great. And so round and round I'd go, all reason and sense stomped to mash as I found myself entrapped in an ever-tightening spiral of desperation, fuelled by equal parts terror and hope. Terror that my brother, a stranger to all doubt, whose icy road ran straight and true, was right about everything, and that to abandon him and his world would plunge me down the chute to hell faster than a bawling cow into an abattoir. And hope, hope that he who was privileged to see visions denied to the rest of us blindly hopping little bugs had been, whether I liked it or not, vouchsafed profound secrets hidden since the foundation of the world, and that trudging plod for plod in his blood-stained footprints was indeed the only path to salvation that existed in this blasted ruination of a world.

Once I'd gotten a jeroboam's worth of drink into me, I could sit for hours, juggling darkness and light, truth and error, and sorrow and panic over my head like Ping-Pong balls until I passed out, sometimes still in my coat.

And wake up the next morning in an ungainly sprawl, arm dragging the floor like an orangutan's, mouth gaping and packed with dryer fluff, chin sopping with drool, only to heave up with a shudder and a croaked "Fuck it" because the way I felt seemed to be exactly what Gerard demanded I feel; weren't we supposed to mortify ourselves every day, to die to our selfish selves, die that our life might be hid in Christ, die, die, die, etc., etc., etc.? We were to lie down by the side of the narrow road and die till we could die no more. Well, all I could say was: can do, beloved brother. Can do!

And now only Desi is left.

Standing here in Gerard's living room, waiting in dull terror for whatever fresh, post-funeral hell he has up his sleeve, I'm asking myself for the millionth time, my God, my *God*, what the hell am I *doing* here?

And I see Desi, standing with his back to me, still wearing his crackly brown parka. He's studying the elaborate dollhouse Flake made out of Popsicle sticks during a stretch in the joint. Except for the wall motto, it's the living room's lone decoration. It sits on a shelf Flake pounded crookedly into the wall, a split-level dwelling featuring six unfurnished rooms slicked over with clear varnish, like some affluent grasshopper's rustic cottage retreat, all oak beams and handsome blond wood flooring. When it was properly rigged up in his cell, Flake boasted, it had even had running water.

Desi is singing softly, his pitch as true and pure as a running stream.

"*Then my hobe shabbee eternaw. Beulah Lamb, swede Beulah Lamb.*"

It's more than my heart can bear. I look at his straight, earnest little back, and all at once my best self, someone I'd forgotten I ever knew, leaps clean out of the fog. Desi, I think, my eyes welling. Desi, my poor, brave motherless boy. His small self bobs in my blurred vision like a lifebuoy, the last one you see before you go down for the third time.

And suddenly, I know exactly what I'm doing here.

Five years in this desert, and at last, at *last*, there's an answer.

Five years of supposedly learning the nature of Divine love. Five years of clawing myself bloody in search of faith, of cringing before Gerard's lacerating harangues, and suddenly love, actual *love* is standing right smack in front of me. Love with a scrubbed face, walking up to say hi in the inscrutable language of heaven. There are no signs, no wonders. No repentance is required. There is just *love*, scrabbling a message like Anne Bancroft in my Patty Duke palm while my heart bursts like a supernova and all the crooked ways are instantly made straight.

Never mind living for God, love says to me. Live for Desi. Be his mother.

But he has one already.

Sure, says love to me. But not one like you. Not a good one.

Yes. This is what I can do here. And this is what I can be. Not a chauffeur and swabber of floors, not a voice bleating behind a microphone, not a lonely, jabbering drunk. I can be a mother. A mother. It's not too late!

A mother!

And who better? Who understands what it means to be motherless better than I do?

But.

I drink. This I tell myself sternly, in Gerard's voice, ever mindful of his harsh verdicts, his insistence upon stamping out like a spent smoke even the tiniest flarings of favourable self-esteem. The knowledge makes me hot in the face and shy, makes me hang back.

But.

Desi runs through another chorus of "Beulah Lamb," serenading two plastic dinosaurs that lie napping on the shiny Popsicle stick living room floor in front of the beautiful Popsicle stick fireplace that Flake had lovingly stained mahogany with gravy. I can't take my eyes off him. When he finally turns and wanders into the kitchen, a dinosaur in each hand, I follow. His coat drops from his shoulders to the floor, then his little suit jacket. He sits down composedly at the kitchen table in his shirt and tie and begins loping a dinosaur across the kitchen table with his right hand while he eats chips left over from Big Fanny's breakfast, formally, one at a time, with his left. Remembering his manners, he asks the brontosaurus if it would care for one, and if so, what flavour?

"No," responds the dinosaur in a cranky growl.

"Are you sure? Last chance!" Desi slides a large barbecue chip between the dinosaur's pointy plastic teeth.

"Go away!" says the brontosaurus, bouncing to the edge of the table and diving into Desi's lap.

Big Fanny is sitting at the other end of the table, smoking. Parallel streams of tears roll soundlessly from her tiny eyes like waterfalls trickling from caves high in an inaccessible rockface. She sucks back three smokes in a row before addressing Desi with choked cheeriness.

"You know that back in the olden times, Adam and Eve had dinosaurs for pets, don't you, honey?" Her voice is like a rockslide; Desi ducks his head instinctively before answering politely, "I know that." He begins butting the dinosaurs' heads together, making lizard screeches under his breath. Big Fanny sniffs bravely.

"Wouldn't that have been fun?"

"Maybe very dangerous," Desi allows solemnly.

Fred sticks his head in the doorway.

"We're gathering in the living room." It's an order.

Desi slides off his chair to trudge slowly after Fred, his dinosaurs fighting a death match against his chest. Big Fanny follows, nudging him forward with her vast, low-slung stomach.

Fred is already in his regular spot on the floor, cross-legged and bright as an elf in a striped shirt and permanent press slacks from the Bay's boys' department. His fat Bible, dramatically highlighted in six different colours, lies open on the floor in front of him. He always sits directly opposite Gerard's big chair, a servant at the feet of his king.

He grins up at Desi towering over him and announces joyfully to the room, "No one's gonna ram evolution down *this* kid's throat!"

Desi's T. rex lunges at Fred to take a bite out of his shoulder.

"Ow!" Fred rubs the imaginary wound in theatrical agony. "Those are some sharp teeth you have there, Mister Dino!"

"Her name is Gloria," says Desi.

"Stay away! I bite!" squeaks Gloria.

"Come sit on my lap," commands Big Fanny, pounding her giant knees. Desi shakes his head.

"Don't you be sad," urges Barb softly. She sits next to Big Fanny on a canvas lawn chair, as thin, haggard, and perpetually shivering as Fanny is round and overheated. Her sharp face pokes out from the billows of her puffy pink parka like a wasp from a peony. "When the Rapture comes, Kevvie will be waiting at the front of the line to greet you!"

"When?" squawks Gloria.

"Just as soon as the full number of the Gentiles have come in, honey," Big Fanny assures him.

"I witnessed at the funeral parlour," Barb announces to the now gathered group as they light their opening smokes and manoeuvre their saucer and sardine tin ashtrays within easy reach. "I told a lady in one of the other rooms that once you know Jesus, you don't have to worry about death no more."

Ordinarily, I would have ducked my head and said nothing. But something has been yanked tight in me since first setting foot inside the church this morning, and now it snaps with a sting that takes my breath. I spin on her.

"Did you remind her that she was a grasshopper in the Father's eye?" I ask through a clenched throat.

"I forgot. There wasn't time."

"Because that's always such a refreshing funeral pick-me-up."

Every Untouchable in the room eyes me with dangerous interest. Flake, standing just inside the front door, titters, "Dumb ho's always trying to get picked up." But nobody laughs till their eyes have flitted toward the hallway from where Gerard and Catou are bound to emerge at any moment.

"There's no better place to get people's attention," puts in Fred coolly when the giggling has sputtered out. "God commands us to tell people the truth. If you are ashamed of him and his words, the Son of Man will be ashamed of you when he comes in his Father's glory with the holy angels."

"Hoooooooley angels!" screeches Gloria, loping across the rough brown carpet in Desi's soft, brown hand. Both dinosaurs sproing off the top of the TV and begin scaling the far wall where LET NOTHING DISTURB THE!!! spins dizzily around itself.

"Don't walk on the words!" the brontosaurus warns raspily; doing this voice is taking its toll on Desi's throat, especially in this smoke-pit of a room. "There's quicksand in there!"

Gerard's study door creaks open. All breathing ceases. My nerve, so recently roused, fails me utterly.

Desi peers into the hall, but his mother doesn't follow Gerard into the living room. He stands quietly, rhythmically knocking his dinosaurs' heads together.

Gerard drops into his royal armchair, a red brocade affair that looks as if it's gone through a car wash, the arms pocked with burns where he parks his smokes while thumbing through his Bible. Wide, shiny bookmarks like county fair prize ribbons mark every tenth page.

All of us are on tenterhooks, praying, Please, *please* don't let him go for the back where the hair-raising Revelations are stored, where all those bowls of annihilating plagues so dear to my brother's heart are poured out upon the vile earth. We wait on pins and needles for the first words to issue from his hard lips, steeling ourselves for the incantatory rise and fall of his voice, as spellbinding and occultic as the dark whisper of a gypsy in a curtained, airless room.

He lifts his head from his Bible. His eyes remain closed, the better to receive inner teletype data from the Holy Spirit, the better to see the universe he carries inside him, every pebble, blossom, and galaxy explained personally in visions bequeathed only to the few, the proud, the serene.

A smile oozes over his face like an oil spill. Then he leans back, hands clasped behind his head, making a long, steamrolled plank of himself. He says nothing at all.

"Are you all right?" Barb asks timidly after ten minutes have elapsed.

No answer.

Outside, dusk is blackening into full night. Kevvie's all alone out there under the frigid stars, the squirrels and rabbits that have been running over his grave and stopping, alert, having long fled across the hard-packed cemetery snow to the safety of their nests and burrows.

I have to get out. Every fibre, pore, organ, and neuron is screaming for alcohol. But I can't leave Desi till I see what tone the evening's proceedings are going to take.

At long last, Gerard pulls his arms down, steepling his fingers across his chest. A wave of guilty coughing circumnavigates the room.

"Catou has decided she wants to play the victim," he announces evenly. "She believes she has the right to question the Father's wisdom. She's chosen to disbelieve in his love and to rebel against the perfection of his plan." His slow, measured monotone is as hypnotic as ocean tides in the dark. No one meets his inclement gaze. He taps the side of his knee steadily as he speaks, his no-hands cigarette waggling on his lip. Only the stiff set of his neck betrays the hyper-vigilance we all know and dread.

Fred shakes his head, marvelling. Everyone else bores holes into the floor with their eyes. Desi drops to his knees, his dinosaurs whispering hotly to each other in an arcane reptile tongue.

Gerard explodes.

"How long have I been teaching you people that only the Father defines the true meaning of love?" he shouts, his voice sawing the stump of a violent coughing jag. "We don't! How many times have I said that he refuses to be shackled by the ways of corrupt, fallen creatures?"

Silence.

"How many times? Barb! How many times?"

"Lots."

"What?"

"LOTS!"

"How many times, Frances?"

"Way lots," mumbles Big Fanny.

"Sometimes he takes things away from us," Gerard roars, in full throttle now. "And we rear up in indignation and call him cruel. But nothing here is ours! Nothing! Everything, the cattle on a thousand hills, everything is his! Why? Because he SAID SO! He is NOT vicious, he is NOT vindictive, he is NOT mean! He is JUST! A child dies, and we dare to ask—"

"Six children," I remind him smartly. "Six."

"The number is meaningless!" he shoots at me without turning his head. "And we dare to ask, Why, Father? Where do we get the *nerve*? Who are we? Surely it is the Father's right to show mercy or not, as he pleases! It's none of our damned business! His great and all-consuming love is manifested in his *Son*, not in us!" He's sitting straight now, ash dropping onto his lap, his voice blistering the paint on the walls.

"Am I right?"

A timorous chorus of yeses.

"AM! I! RIGHT?"

"YES!" the Untouchables shout as one.

"Fred. Am I right?"

"Oh yes!"

"Frances. Am I right?"

"You are right."

"Are you talking about my brother?" snarls Gloria from across the room "I mean, his brother," Desi amends sheepishly, nodding Gloria's plastic head in the direction of his own.

"You people at the funeral home, you made me ashamed! Instead of standing up like soldiers of Christ, you sat there wallowing in self-pity like a bunch of unbelieving weaklings who have never been taught the truth!"

Sunil Low-Down and Sunil High-Up are sitting shoulder to shoulder on a ratty loveseat, the entire bottom of which collapsed long ago to within an inch of the floor. Only their dark heads and four denim legs hooked over the front frame are visible, as if they're squeezed into a wide barrel. They stare stupidly back at Gerard.

"You two clowns! Tweedledum and Tweedledee! What the hell are those faces about?"

"It is only face I have," murmurs Sunil High-Up, the clear-headed one.

A taut sneer tugs at the corners of Gerard's mouth. He appears about to speak but instead sits up straighter, opens his Bible, and makes a radar sweep of the room. "Luke, chapter fifteen, verse eleven." He turns in Flake's direction. "Will you read, please?" He hands his Book of Doom down the line to where Flake stands, hand on the front doorknob, his jacket zipped, apprehended in mid-bolt.

Flake trudges back into the room and irritably takes the Bible, immediately losing the page. He begins slapping the onionskin back and forth in an angry sweat. Big Fanny looms beside him, urging him not to get all rankle-dankled, patiently turning the pages and indicating the passage. Flake clears his throat nervously several times; literacy is a sore point for nearly everyone in the room. His nose scrapes the paper as he struggles to read the miniscule print, following each line with his stubby orange forefinger.

"And He said... a certain man had two sons," he mumbles, leaving wide gaps between each word. "And the younger of them said, uhm, to his father, uhm, Father, oh, said to his father, oh, that's what he said, uh, Father, to his father" — Flake sighs profoundly — "Father, give me the, the potion of, uhm, goods that, uh, fall, what the hell, falleseth, I can't read this fuc, this damned print, fallesthest to me —"

"Portion. The *portion* of goods," corrects Fred. Barb snickers.

"Portion of goods. And he dividd, divi —"

"Divided."

"He divided them, uhm, into his lyving. Oh. Living." Flake draws in a long breath and barks, "Give me one of your smokes, L.D.," at Sunil Low-Down.

"Never mind." Gerard slams his Bible shut. "I've changed my mind. Forget the Prodigal Son."

"Whoa. Buzz-kill," Flake mutters. And then louder, with a needling smile: "You didn't like my reading?" An uneasy hush drops like a curtain.

"I wouldn't puff out my chest if I were you," Gerard advises him, his tone deceptively benign.

"Why? What did I do?"

"Nothing. Nothing at all. You just keep on playing the fool till the time for the hearing of the Gospel on earth comes to an end. Keep it up till you find yourself in the black place of eternal silence. You'll be begging for one more chance then, won't you? You who have no time for the Way, the Truth, and the Life. It'll be amusing to see how you like no way, no hope, and living death without end."

"Hey, fucking bring it, Jesse James," Flake spits. He kicks the wall behind him a few times in a steady rhythm before kicking himself away to stomp into the kitchen, cupping a smoke and a match close to his face. After a moment, the side door shuts with a bang.

"You know, I try to be kind. I try to be patient. I try to be loving," says Gerard with a long, mock-sad sigh. A wave of irony-appreciating snickers crosses the room. "I try my damndest to teach you people the difference between truth and error. Why am I getting the impression swine are running hog-wild over my pearls?" The nervous laughter ramps up, the relief that Gerard has gone for Flake and not them palpable in every face.

I pick up my boots and tiptoe out onto the front porch, avoiding the ragged hole someone has stamped into the middle.

Then I run, coat and boots still in my hand. I rev the Trans Am, my eyes on the curtainless front window, expecting someone to come flying through the glass at any minute. My heart breaks for little Desi trapped inside, but I can't stay another second.

Moments later, I pass Flake hitching by the side of the highway, see him in the rear-view mirror turning in slack astonishment as the car he so loves hurtles mercilessly past in the freezing dusk.

I roll into Fred's kitchen the following afternoon, hoping against hope that Desi will be there, but only Barb sits at the table, rolling her day's stash of smokes. When I ask where everyone is, she just shrugs.

"How did it go last night?" I ask, sliding into the chair opposite her.

"It went like shit. Father Gerry tore Catou's ass up so bad, calling her names and stuff, that she just took off, yelling and cursing him out. She said we're never gonna see her ever again."

"Calling her what names? What did she do?"

"She was sad, what do you think?" Barb refuses to meet my eyes, aware she's telling tales out of school and not knowing whether I can be trusted. "He said she didn't have a right to be sad because Kevvie wasn't hers, he only belonged to the Father."

"What about Desi? Where's he?"

"She took him. She like, dragged him out, without even his coat on. They took off in her car. Fred told me he saw she didn't even turn on her headlights, she was in such a rush. After that, Gerard got royally pissed and kicked us all out."

I leave her there, turn right around, and head for home. All I can think of is Desi trapped seatbelt-less in her terrifying car, doors held on with duct tape flying off as they career blindly down icy roads in the pitch-dark. Did they make it home? Are they bleeding in a ditch or lying on slabs at the morgue? And if they're alive, will she change her mind and come back? Will I ever see him again? And what right do I have to care? Look at the kind of mother I turned out to be. No better than Catou, turning tail and leaving my boy in the lurch because I couldn't wait to get home to my bottle.

Oh, Desi! Desi, I'm so sorry! Please, please be all right! Please come back! I swear I'll make it up to you. I'll make everything up to you!

But Catou wasn't kidding. Days turn into weeks with no sign of them. I'm beyond desolate, eviscerated, my throbbing anxiety and howling sense of loss mitigated only by the fact that Fred claims to know that they're still in Orangeville, that Desi is still in school, and Catou is staying more or less clean.

I know what school he goes to; it wouldn't be hard to find out where they live and drop by. But Catou scares the shit out of me, not least because she's the only person I know who has ever openly defied my brother. I toy briefly with the idea of skulking by the school playground just for a glimpse of my boy, but this seems too creepy even for me.

If Desi never comes back, I don't see how I can endure this Untouchables life any longer. Even if I disintegrate entirely and drink from the moment my eyes creak open in the morning till I fall unconscious at night, even if I never address another word to a living soul, it can't be worse than being in Gerard's house without Desi in it.

And still—*still*—I'm afraid to jump ship.

Why? I mean, for God's sake, woman, *why?*

I'll tell you why. It's because no matter how much time and effort I've put in, I still can't believe that these five years of grudging self-sacrifice have done a single thing to recommend me to the surly Father and his unfathomable Son. I've done nothing to attract their gimlet-eyed attention or earn their curt approval. And Gerard says, "If the thought of hearing Jesus say at the Throne of Judgment that he *never knew you* doesn't scare you, then you're lost beyond all possible hope."

Oh, it scares me all right. Not only does Jesus not know me, I couldn't pick *him* out of a lineup if my life depended on it. Five years in, I still don't have a clue who or what he is. When, in my pre-passing-out stupor, I make feeble attempts to pray, it's to an imaginary Jewish Johnny Cash, same initials anyway, black-robed and gravel-voiced, with a banged-up face, a friend to the addled and mangled, whom I can just barely imagine drawling, "Sit down here beside me, hon. I'll pull you out of that burning ring of fire."

But who also shot a man in Reno just to watch him die.

But gradually it occurs to me that maybe leaving the Untouchables can be accomplished cautiously, a few quiet steps at a time. Maybe I can *ease* my way out, strike a happy medium by joining the congregation of a welcoming church somewhere, thus appeasing Gerard—as long as it's the fundy kind of church he approves of—and not entirely abandoning my cock-eyed quest for faith. I can't imagine the church that would be harsher and less forgiving than this place. I can pick one out of the phone book and just roll myself down the aisle atop the wreckage of my life like a castaway hunkered over a barrel. Surely they'll be delighted to have me, and then it'll just be a simple matter of gradually transferring my allegiance until I can close the door of Gerard's place behind me for the last time.

I haven't darkened the door of a church since Gerard's Brampton days, and have never set foot in one that wasn't Catholic, having been brought up believing that Protestants were the Enemy, every last misguided one of them doomed to the eternal flames. So the first church I step into looks and feels all wrong. It's as golden as Satan's front tooth with slanting sunlight, its walls painted a spartan white. There are several ominous, vaguely African flags up front. There are no statues, no candles, no Sacristy Lamp All-Seeing Eye. There's a minister in a business suit, a lectern instead of an altar. The place fairly hums with brisk, quotidian efficiency, and I think with a sinking heart that no one is going to hear my prayers in here. In the church of my childhood, prayers knew how to proceed, how to pass through the labyrinths of ancient, pneumatic tubing leading upward into the clouds. But these people just lift their eyes skyward, state their bald requests, and sit down again.

Still, Protestantism has an appealing, fun side Catholicism doesn't. I can't help nursing a fond vision of huge, glistening women in sumptuous hats slamming tambourines and shouting, "Can I get a witness, bruthah? Can I get a witness, sistah?"

Swaying choirs, heaving like the sea, hands whip-slapping, shouting praises to a glad-tiding Jesus: a healing for every heart-ache! A promise for every problem! Come all ye who are weary and heavy-laden, and lay your burdens *down*, Halle*lujah*!

With this bright picture in mind, I devote my Sunday mornings to sampling one venue after another, a battered worldling limping over sanctified thresholds, drawn like a moth to the porch light. Greeters with shiny smiles thrust glad hands at me in vestibule after vestibule and then turn gladder faces to the next person, always a likelier prospect. There are no thundering choirs; this is Canada. "Worship leaders" drag the congregations through endless Praise Songs, the lyrics projected on giant screens overhead, and everyone sings so sweetly, so whitely, all hands waving like Saskatchewan wheat, everyone but me tingling from the brush of angel wings.

There are usually coffee and squares afterwards in the basement, where smiling folks loom into my line of vision to ask for my testimony. I smile woodenly, croaking some balderdash about how I'm sure the Lord sent me to this very place this very morning, any declaration of faith feeling to me as if I'm hawking magic weight-loss pills or X-Ray Specs. Then I clam up to take my rigid stance on the edge of the nearest group of florally dressed ladies of a certain age. On only my second Sunday, I hear one lady earnestly tell another, "It's okay to go into a bar if you're there to lead someone to the Lord." The first seven words clang in my head like Chinese gongs; I can't wait to beat it the hell out of there. Noon is no longer too early for me to begin imbibing.

For two months I work my dogged way through the Baptists and the Brethren, the Nazarenes, Presbyterians, and Lutherans.

Though the atmosphere is positively frolicksome compared with Sundays at Gerard's six-hour home-church fright-fest, they all preach the same hard-line message as he does: get saved or burn. Though it's hard to take seriously when the message is coupled with what strikes me as a shocking lack of decorum. A youth group puts on a puppet show where huge, goofy heads with yarn hair bob up and down the aisles shouting, "Hey! You know that dude they crucified for our sins? He's alive! Pass it on!" A pastor dressed like Peter the Fisherman in hip waders and a red hook-on beard roars, "Do we know how blessed we are that God let us be born into an awesome country like Canada where we had a chance to hear the Gospel and be saved? Will you open your Bibles now?" And there follows a windy rustling of pages as I think, Please, I beg of you. Kill me now.

I try in church. I swear I try. But every week I stumble out into the light after listening to the same insane death-and-resurrection story that I'm obligated to swallow in its entirety or the Father will bloody well know the reason why. It's no different than being at Gerard's. I can try, I can wish, I can strain, I can fake it, but with helpless tears, my arms hanging limp, I simply can't get it down.

Why does everyone else find it so easy? What's *wrong* with me? Why can't I take comfort the way they can, why do my fears still rise up and choke me every hour on the hour? It's not that I don't want to believe. I do, I *do*! But it just doesn't work the same magic on me as it does on everybody else.

And yet, I won't, I can't give up. Somehow, there's just enough belief, just enough hope in me to keep me from throwing in the towel. Or it's just raw, shrieking terror; I honestly can't tell the difference any more.

I'm in Gerard's kitchen washing a week's worth of dishes when in marches Catou, unannounced, trailed by April sunbeams and little Desi in a Spider-Man tee-shirt, his thin brown arms as garish as a sailor's with wrist-to-shoulder press-on tattoos.

And immediately out she marches again, alone, gunning her car through the last patches of April snow up the long dirt drive to the highway. A rainstorm comes up fast and swallows her whole.

Desi sits on a kitchen chair all afternoon, kicking the table leg, watching Untouchables come and go. Finally I make him a grilled-cheese sandwich, and as he eats, he tells me calmly that his mother said to tell us she isn't coming back for a while. I ask him how long a while.

He shrugs. "Maybe when it's winter again."

I knock at Gerard's closed study door to give him the news.

"Call Fred. They have room over there," he says brusquely through the door.

"He's not staying in that insane asylum! I'm taking him home with me!"

"The hell you are."

"What do you care? I've got room. I can look after him. I'll get him to school, I'll—"

"I forbid it!"

"Why?"

"You know why." Yes, I know why, and I finish his tirade for him: you're a drunk, that's why. You're not fooling anybody, probably not even Desi.

I stand stupidly, without defence, as Gerard violently yanks his door open and stamps into the kitchen. I follow, praying he won't be rough with Des, but he simply throws open the door to a tiny room off the kitchen, where a bare mattress lies on the floor, and goes straight back to working out Bible cryptograms, instantly forgetting all about him.

The next morning I drive up with an armload of my own sheets, a pillow, and a down comforter. I find Desi alone in the kitchen toasting hot dog buns on a fork over the roaring-hot stove burner. The following day I load Gerard's cupboards with strawberry jam and chocolate cereal, and pack his squalid refrigerator with pizza pops and juice boxes.

Desi never goes back to school. The week after he arrives, I'm stuck doing a long film narration and can't come up at all; in my absence, one Untouchable or another has taken the messages when the school, to whom Catou has apparently given this number, calls to ask about him, garbling them beyond hope or forgetting them entirely. It's close enough to summer that the school just lets it go.

It isn't hard not to notice him in the house. He plays the Game Boy Flake stole for him a year ago, his hands jumping for hours like fleas. He sits at the kitchen table reading the newspapers Fred brings him. He plays checkers with himself on a beat-up board he found stuffed into a cupboard. He lies outside under the gruesome trees and whispers to his dinosaurs.

I resent every interminable voice gig, every stupid Untouchables errand that keeps me out of the house. He's been there a week when, coming by with groceries in the middle of a Bible study, I find him pensively setting newspaper funnels on fire at the stove and blowing them out, the flying sparks grazing his thunderclap hair. Terrified, I root through drawers till I find a pair of rusty, loose-hinged scissors and order him into a chair.

"No more playing with the stove, you hear me? Sit. I'm going to give you a trim, mister."

He sits without protest. The *Sun* lies on the table, and he appears to be reading it upside down. I begin chopping off chunks of hair; it's like cutting through a mattress, springs and all. Huge Brillo tumbleweeds roll down his back and bounce on the floor.

"What's Frosted Flake's real name?" Desi asks suddenly as I hack and slash.

"It's Trey, I think."

"Oh yeah, I forgot." He pauses to reflect. "Then how come he's called Frosted Flake?"

"Beats me. It suits him though."

"If it was my choice, I'd call him Frosted Flakes in a dish on a tray."

"Good one! You should suggest it to him."

"He told me he was a testarestrial from Mars," says Desi solemnly. "He said he had Martian horns on his head under his hair."

"Sounds about right to me."

He turns a page of the paper, reads for a while. In the living room, the Bible inferno is raging, Gerard raining down plagues of wrath and destruction onto the slim crowd of Barb and Big Fanny.

"The Moabites *deserved* to be slaughtered, and so do you! He says: If you love me, keep my commandments! Do you think God is averse to judgment? He wiped out the heathen peoples of Palestine in their thousands with the back of his hand! Do you think he's going to go all soft on you if you disobey?"

"So is it true?" Desi asks, after finishing the editorial page.

"Is what true?" I'm panicking; how can I discuss slaughter and deserved death with this boy who's had this life?

"About being from Mars." He turns his enormous eyes up to me. It's the first anxiety I've ever seen in his face.

"Not a chance, Lance."

"I'm Desi."

"I know, Joe."

He ponders this.

"Are you teasing me, Bruce Lee?"

"Yes, Jess. Are you teasing *me*, McGee?"

"Yes I am. Ma'am."

When I sweep the hair up off the floor, I stuff a fat gob into my pocket and take it home, where I keep it on my night table in a jade green porcelain bowl.

I can't stand the idea of him alone in that house. I begin leaving at 6 a.m. so I can be up there in time to kidnap him before he can absorb a word of Gerard's vociferant screed. And in order to look sharp at that hour, I have to dispense with a good three-quarters of my evening libations.

It turns out to be easier than falling off a log.

And the emptier my glass, the emptier yawns the great Montauk chair. For the first time in as long as I can remember, my nights are spent well and truly and wholesomely *alone*.

In no time at all, we've worked out a routine. By seven I'll be parked in Gerard's driveway waiting for Des, a born early riser, to whack open the screen door and gallop toward me, my grin boiling over at the sight of the bobbing thornbush on his head, his inside-out tee-shirt, the raspberry jam on his muddy-coloured chin.

"Whoa! It's my main man!" I shout, backing in a hurry down the driveway before Gerard, lurking unshaven on his sagging front porch in pyjama bottoms and an old blue suit jacket as he kicks piles of butts onto his dirt lawn, can stop me.

Desi, belted into his seat beside me, is no bigger than a twig.

"No Bible study for you today, Ray," I tell him cheerfully.

"You mean no Bible study for *us*," he corrects, my heart swelling to the music of the plural pronoun. After a moment, he remembers to add, "Russ."

The first stop on every outing is the ritual car wash. He can't get enough of the soapy torrents running down the Trans Am's windows, the enchanted forest of multicoloured brushes, the thrilling suction-dry. We pull out into the morning sunshine with beads of water chasing down the windshield and glinting on the flames roaring toward us across the hood, purified and ready to roar hell-bent for leather into the wicked city.

If I have a voice gig, I take him along with me. At first I turned down any job that might've lasted longer than an hour because I was afraid he would be bored. But it turns out he has patience to burn, and lives especially for the grand days when I have cartoon voices to record. Before long, all the sound engineers are giving him high-fives, and clients in the control room let him follow along on the animation storyboards.

The rest of my Untouchables errands I pawn off on Fred so the remainder of the day will belong to Desi and me alone. I take him to the zoo and to Riverdale Farm. I take him to the Science Centre, where he walks sedately from one exhibit to the next, reading all the information aloud, sounding it out syllable by syllable.

"The Per...mee...an...ex...tin..."

"The Permian extinction."

"...extinction...took out nin...nine...ninety-nine...of all animals on earth, the Cret...cretass..."

"Cretaceous. And that's ninety-nine *percent*, not ninety-nine."

"...two-thirds of all speck..."

"Two-thirds of all species, including dinosaurs, which allowed mammals to thrive and become the dominant land vertebrates." I finish for him. "How did you learn to read so well? These are hard words."

"I'm the best reader in my class."

"You just learnt it and ran with it, huh?"

"You can't run in school, fool." He thinks for a moment. "Except at recess. Jeesess."

He stops to study an elaborate artistic rendering of pre-historic vegetation. "Do they have a picture of Adam and Eve someplace?"

"I doubt it."

"Yes, because probably cameras weren't invented yet."

I stand behind him, reading over his head as the Science Centre pummels us right and left with ciphers and formulae, jumbles of letters and numbers more dense than Desi's hair. All around us, life is broken down into its inexplicable parts, scribbled on a 360-degree blackboard by goggle-eyed scientists. A single human cell more complex than the Apollo 13 spacecraft! Thousandths of millionths of millionths of centimetres, speeds of one divided by ten thousand million million million seconds! Hundreds of millions of nebulae containing ten thousand galaxies each! A cosmos thirteen billion years old, featuring, at this moment, Desi and me, on stage, now playing, one nanosecond only!

I rest tentative hands on his shoulders and lower my chin into his hair. It feels springy and smells of dust bunnies. Just the feel of it tickling my chin turns everything around us into a joke, a wild guess. Or outright lies.

"If I had a powerful Cyclops eye, I could see where Kevvie is. Heavy fizz." He takes a deep breath, the way he does when he's thinking something deeply through, and I wonder how much he truly understands, considering the garble of doctrine that surrounds him. Only a week ago he told me with a wry smile conveying gentle benevolence toward his silly, youthful self, that he'd thought Kevvie would be back the morning after his burial, rubbing his eyes in the hall in his blue underpants, hogging the bathroom, and fighting with him for the last of the Cocoa Puffs.

"You miss him, eh?"

"Well." He sighs a deep, adult sigh. "Every day I just get used to it." He waits a beat. "Do you think we might see my mother walking around one day?"

"Probably not at the Science Centre. But you never know."

"You never know, McSchlo."

I buy him a new set of Mr. Potato Head parts, and on rainy days, we go to my apartment and make Mr. Zucchini and Mr. Banana Heads and laugh till our stomachs hurt. Or we order pizza and watch cartoons on a TV that works. I sit beside him on the sofa while he operates the remote, this delicate little bud, his big burr head held up by such a tiny stalk of neck I'm afraid it might snap at any sudden movement. He watches, mesmerized, his mouth open, his breath audible. His laughter brings astonished tears to my eyes. I want to touch the back of his neck, to fluff the soft column of down and tickle him behind the ears, but I'm too bashful to touch him with my veiny old wino paws.

We watch a cartoon boy with a bald head chat earnestly with a little bird on a stump. I had voiced the bird myself in the studio, and I chirp along with the TV in a high-pitched tweet, to Desi's giggling approval. The bald boy's eyes, like Desi's, are bright with anticipation because my bird has promised him a surprise. A *nice* surprise. I sit on the couch and watch the boy and the bird, *my* boy and *my* bird, and I want to know what that surprise will be with all of my dashed and disappointed heart.

...

We have the whole summer together, straight through to the end of August. Then, one morning, Catou, fresh out of detox, resurfaces at a Bible study. I'm stuck in the city, an unusually full workday for me, peddling tampons, homeowner's insurance, and dishwasher rinse agents. I have no time to drive up to get my boy. There's a terse call from Gerard that night, and Desi doesn't get on the line for a chat. I imagine him perched on a kitchen chair, showing his mother his new tattoos and studying hers. Smiling shyly at the floor a lot. Tactfully not asking where she's been for the last four months.

Deep inside my spreading maternal bulk, my bones go ice-cold.

Next day, no one's waiting for me as I pull into the driveway. But as I come through the side kitchen door there's Desi, his shining face pulling my focus like a full moon in a perfect summer sky. He stands at his mother's side with a new board game tucked under one arm, his other little hand on the back of her chair like a polite waiter who's just seated her.

I hail him in high, good cheer: "Mister Redpath is in the house!" He doesn't even look at me, dropping instead to his knees to lay out the game Catou has given him, which involves plastic men racing through a maze while a timer ticks off the seconds. He begins setting it up as neatly and precisely as if he's laying a banquet table, cards perfectly stacked, timer ready, four men at attention and ready to roll. I can hardly blame him for being excited when checkers with half the pieces missing and Left Behind: The Board Game, a thoughtful gift from Fred, are the only other ones he's ever played.

"All set to play your game?" I ask, leaning down and daring to stroke the back of his pipe-cleaner neck. It seems to warm him; he grows tawnier, a timid smile sweetening his face.

"If someone wants to play it with me."

"How does it work, Dirk?"

"You need four players, and what you do is, you have to catch the robbers before they excape from the bank, but first you have to pick a card which tells you how many minutes you can get. Then you set the timer for like if you get two minutes you set it for that, and then if you lose, like if the robbers get away, the timer goes beeeep and you're out. I hope you'll play, Mummy," he says, turning to Catou and away from my hand. "It's not hard. It's a game that all can play, and—"

Catou cuts him off. "I hope I'm not gonna hear you've been a bad boy while Mummy was away."

Desi shakes his head earnestly as Flake, who has just ambled in with Big Fanny, scrapes a chair back and sprawls opposite them, watching through narrowed eyes.

"So what have you been up to all summer?" Catou asks, lighting a cigarette and baring her teeth in the overacted, wise-ass grin of a chimp.

Desi thinks it over carefully before replying

"Child's activities," he answers finally. Flake and I laugh, and Desi's smile widens. He takes a tentative seat on the edge of his mother's lap.

"Ow. Get off, you're crushing my organs," grouses Catou. She rises with grunting effort to slide him off, inadvertently stepping into the middle of the game, toppling the cards, and nearly crunching the timer underneath her boot heel. Desi bends quickly to shove everything out of harm's way, taking a quick in-breath that doesn't come out again. Then he stands, blue and green men in one hand, red and yellow men in the other, gauging the shifting mood in the room, waiting his turn.

"Do *you* guys think I'm going to make it this time?" Catou inquires belligerently of her small audience.

"No," says Flake at the same time that Desi says softly, "Yes, you are."

"You'll make it if you just keep putting one good foot in front of the other one. Good foot, I said. Not the other one," advises Big Fanny, polishing off a pre-Bible study breakfast can of chocolate cake icing. "Just 'cause you can't see Jesus don't mean he can't see you fine."

"I see him all the time," reports Catou smugly.

"In my dream I had once," Desi offers, a happy light in his eyes, "there was green water, and I was standing on the bottom and I saw Jesus walking toward me. I felt all spooky." The room falls silent at this, granting him centre stage. He seems to grow a few inches, fill out around the shoulders.

"How did you know it was him?" asks Flake.

"He was wearing his outfit."

Flake snickers. "Which one?"

"The white one. He only has one. Then a big wave came and he drownded in it!"

The room explodes into hooting laughter, Desi's happy shouts cresting all the rest, as I think wretchedly, Desi, oh Desi, when you pass through the waters, I will be with you, and when you pass through the rivers, they will not sweep over you, no, not on my watch, Desi Redpath. Not on my watch, my dearly beloved boy.

"My game takes four players," he reminds us brightly when the laughter has died away.

"I'll play," I tell him. "It sounds really fun."

"I need two more!" he says, crossing his fingers for luck.

"Hey, you mopes," I throw over my shoulder, beginning to scour coffee cups at the sink so no one will see my filling eyes and wobbling lips. "We need two more players for Desi's game."

"I'll play," says Flake. He yawns expansively and lurches to his feet, strolling over to where Desi stands sentry by the game. "What's this thingy here?" he asks, crouching with some difficulty to pick up the timer.

"It beeps and the red light flashes. It tells you when your time's up. See, the rules are written inside the box," Desi explains, eagerly thrusting the lid at Flake, who holds it up first a centimetre and then an arm's length from his eyes.

"Dude! I can't read that tiny shit."

"I'll read it to you," offers Desi, but Flake has already creaked to his feet, slapping his pockets for smokes.

One by one I slam the cups upside down onto the rubber tray, thinking furiously, Why the hell can't Jesus make these pathetic loons be nicer to Desi? What the hell good is he? Why doesn't he whip Catou's ass? Yeah, I know he's busy emptying the ashtrays when no one's looking, busy making sure nobody starts a fire in the trash or knocks the coffee pot off the stove, but if he's even *close* to the person I imagine him to be, old J.C.

in his black rockabilly clothes, his hair water-combed straight back, that old scourge wound like a pothole in his chin...if he were that person, his heart would *break* for little Desi! And *he* can do something about it!

Desi sinks to the floor under the sunny window and begins warming up the little men, walking them for practice around the perimeter of the game board. Dropping down behind him, I whisper in his ear, "Hey. I'll play with you, Stu."

He looks up at me sadly. "It has to have four people."

"Then I'll play all the other guys. I'll take all their turns. Just pretend I'm three people." I wink at him. "I'm big enough."

"It won't work."

"Sure it will. Come on, let's try." My smile feels clownish, maniacal.

He looks up at me with no expression and begins listlessly restacking the cards, obsessively lining them up so that they touch the edge of the board on all four sides. He sets the timer down in the middle.

"Who do you want to be?" I ask. "Because I think I'd like to be yellow man, Fellow Dan."

"I'll be...I'll be..." He rubs his chin thoughtfully. "I'll be blue man!"

"Excellent choice, Boyce."

"Okay. Who goes first?" he asks, enlivened and scrambling to his knees.

"Youngest player always starts. It's the law, McGraw." Already my own knees ache from being folded under me on the bare linoleum.

Catou has run smack into Gerard on her way to the bathroom. Now, from the living room, drifts the not-unpleasant sound of him laying into her.

"What gives you the idea you can run from the hand of God by going out from among us? You belong *here*! There's nothing for you out there! You've learned nothing! You still refuse to accept that the Gospel is going to cost you everything, all your illusions, all your ridiculous hopes! And the stupidest illusion of all is that everything is somehow going to be magically different somewhere else! There *is* nowhere else!" Something, probably an ashtray, crashes to the floor. "Never mind! Leave it! I said, *leave* it!"

"Is Father Gerry mad at my mother?" Desi asks timidly, putting down his man and sitting back on his heels.

"I don't know. It sounds like she wants to leave again."

"We is, I mean, we are. She told me we're going to...um...I can't remember the place. Where Mummy comes from." He takes a stab. "I think its Monkeytown."

"Moncton?" I ask on no breath at all.

"I guess so." He's looking hard at his game, won't look at me.

"When?"

"Tomorrow."

We sit in silence for five minutes while my flash-frozen heart splinters into shards. Finally I whisper through my sealed throat, "Aren't you talking to me any more?"

"I don't have anything to say."

"Okay. So...shall we play?"

"The game's all ruined now."

Catou slinks back into the kitchen, tense and defiant, and stands over us, the Colossus of Rhodes, one scuffed cowboy boot on either side of the game.

"You weren't afraid Jesus would beat your ass for breaking my watch?" she asks Desi, reaching down to slap him with light malice on the cheek. "He told me he was really mad at you because of that."

"No," says Desi faintly, as vulnerable as a violet in a patch of poison ivy. He raises his eyes then to both of us, pleading, "Don't tell Father Gerry about the watch, okay?"

"Not a chance, Vance," I assure him. "Your secret's safe with me, Smee."

Catou slides into a chair, her hard eyes veering in my direction. Hunched at the table, tricked out in all her adornments: eyebrow ring, nose stud, vermilion hair, and tattoos the length of both arms, she looks like a venomous jungle salamander, her forked tongue flicking in and out.

"What did you call him?" she asks me. I busy myself studying the notes to Desi's game, pretending not to have heard.

"What've you been doing with my kid all summer? He's gone all weird."

"She was taking care of him, being a mother to him." Flake is staunch in my defence, but I know that if I look at him with gratitude, he'll run with it, so I don't.

"Grandmother, more like," sneers Catou. "Great-grandmother, more like."

"She looks better than you. You look like shit on a stick," Flake swipes back.

"Yeah? Well, you look like barf on a scarf." This makes Desi giggle.

"What's so funny?" Catou demands, her voice a knife slash. "Aren't you even sorry your brother's dead? Aren't you sorry I won't see him any more, ever, *ever*?" Desi's smile drains away; he hangs his head, and although everything I know about mothers and sons doesn't amount to more than a teaspoonful of acid, in that instant I see all his years marching ahead of him, years of hanging heads and bafflement that will in time corrode into anger, rage, revenge, and ruin.

I should know.

"You *will* see Kevvie again," murmurs Big Fanny, draping her pillowy arms around Catou's shoulders and pressing up against her like the Hoover Dam of faith, the concrete-hard, death-defying bulwark of "I *know*!" and "I *will*!"

And all I can think is, Sure. Life after death is a crapshoot; anything can happen. But life after Desi is not going to be worth the shallow breaths it will take to sustain it.

I turn up at Fred's with groceries a week later to find Marty, a long-departed and supposedly cured Untouchable, and Flake cutting lines of coke on the kitchen table, both of them too high and too slow to hide the evidence when I burst in without warning.

I ignore them, shoving the groceries into the cupboards and the fridge. A linoleum tile sticks to my shoe and accompanies me about the kitchen, thwap-thwapping amusingly. I can hear smothered chortling behind my back.

"Nice going," I snap. "Keep it up, bozos. If Gerard finds out what you're up to, your asses are toast."

"You're not going to tell him," says Flake with a sly grin.

"How do you know?"

"Because you're good people."

"Is that right?"

Not remotely intimidated, Marty cuts several more lines onto the begrimed tabletop. They snorf up two apiece.

Flake sits back in his chair and turns his frank, happy face my way. I shoot him the fisheye.

He grins right back. "Why don't you share some of this very excellent blow with us, sweet thang?" he asks, waggling his hand in a beckoning gesture.

"Get serious. Where's Fred?"

"Out serving the Lord," says Marty with a lip curl of contempt, obsessively winding the end of his long, scrappy ponytail around his left index finger. "He took Gerard's car and went into TO."

"How can you tell people not to get loaded when you don't know what you're missing?" wheedles Flake, twirling his sniffing straw like a tiny baton. Yesterday, Barb peroxided his hair and gave him a pixie cut; he looks like Bert Lahr in a Debbie Reynolds wig.

"Where'd you get that stuff?" I ask, as if I don't know by now that someone is always hitching an unauthorized ride into the city to stake out the old panhandling corners or cash a welfare cheque they've held back from Gerard's compulsory communal pot. More often than not, there's contraband in someone's pocket.

They both snigger, greatly pleased with themselves, two bad boys caught stealing pie from Granny's pantry. Flake lowers his head for another prolonged snort.

"You can't help us if you don't know what we're up against," he repeats reasonably. As he extricates a fresh smoke from his pack, a jumble of little baggies tumble out of it onto the table, reminding me that, of course, he got his disability cheque a couple of days ago.

I've spent the last six evenings drinking myself comatose. I'm a lead weight on two crumbling legs. Death is a matter of supreme indifference, chastisement by Gerard only marginally more intimidating. I take a deep, shuddering breath, and Flake's eyes, spinny as they are, bore straight through me. And I know that he knows that he knows.

"This isn't going to get back to Gerard?"

"No fuckin' way!" Marty assures me gallantly, patting the empty chair beside him.

Flake holds out the four-inch straw as reverently as if it were a magic wand. I reach out, take it, bend my head to the table, and give it a whirl.

Heaven blows in like a hurricane through the open windows.

Who *is* this person, suddenly, miraculously anguish-free and grinning fit to bust at Flake and Marty, while Flake and Marty beam and chuckle right back at her? I feel as if I've been impersonating myself every single day I've spent on earth until now.

"You're one sassy bitch," Flake congratulates me, patting my arm and giving me the glad eye. "I mean that in a good way."

"Of course you do." I laugh merrily.

"No, I mean it, man. I didn't know you were like this. I mean, I know you're nice, but I thought you were kind of like some schoolteacher, or..." He trails off, unable to control his sheepish smile, his hot blush.

"More like Gerard, you mean?"

"Well, yeah. You're his sister, and, I mean, you kind of have the same look, so I kinda thought—"

"Of course we have the same look. We're twins."

"No fuckin' way!" Flake's and Marty's jaws hang unhinged.

"Fuckin' yes way."

"But he's so scrawny! And you're—"

"So fat?"

"No, no, not fat. Exactly. You're, uh"—Flake combs his mind for an elegant, irresistible compliment—"fat in a good way." His eyes do a broad, fond sweep of my chest.

"Aren't you the sweet-talker."

"Dude! You're red as a beet!" cackles Marty.

"I'm just teasing you," I say, patting Flake's arm, letting him know that if he wants to touch me back, he can, for today anyway. I vacuum up another small line, feeling like Oprah with two dazzling guests, a woman of the people, smoking and laughing, relaxed and excited all at the same time.

It's such an astonishing novelty to be sitting in the company of grown-ups and not be bored, furious, or terrified. Flake and Marty begin falling all over themselves showing off, topping each other's stories, playing to the boss's sister. I hear about old drug busts, botched robberies, life in stir, detox horrors. I queen it up shamelessly too, purring and flirting in my brown sugar voice, egging them on. I find out about the day Gerard showed up at Fred's in the middle of a drug party similar to the one we're having now, how people had to be stuffed squealing into closets until he left. That, and a hundred other behind-the-scenes indiscretions I've never dreamed went on.

"I'm tellin' ya, eh," says Marty with deep satisfaction. "Life around here is like, you think that movie was crazy, eh, that *Plan B from Outer Space*? Well..."

This has me oozing to the floor like an eel, to Flake's exquisite delight. And then we all do another line! As a solitary drinker with only a drear shadow in a chair to talk to, I've been suddenly and profoundly enlightened as to the concept of the communal binge. I want to go on like this for weeks, for years, forever!

Eventually the talk turns back to Father Gerry. Marty and Flake know things. Like where Gerard had been during his disappeared years.

Out West, Marty informs me. Edmonton.

"Get out!"

"Oh yeah. And then someone died and left him this huge fuckin' stash, eh, sacks and sacks of cash, dude. Like, ten million."

"Naw," counters Flake. "More like a half a million."

"Half a million, my ass, dude!"

"Who? *Who?*" I ask one, then the other. They don't know. The story going around was that he'd saved some Edmonton cowboy junkie's life, the eternal one most likely, since the guy had definitely cast off his mortal coil but not before leaving Gerard a great honking earthly reward.

Father Gerry refuses to talk about it.

"That's how he got the cash to set up this place," says Marty. "And to bail people out of jail, and buy clothes and shit for people. Dude, used to be he'd do anything for anybody, eh, give you anything you needed, no questions asked."

"Naw, he invested that money," Flake cuts in. "Don't ask me how I know. He keeps this place running out of the interest."

"The hell he does. You're all living off me," I point out, not without pride. I get up to turn on the bulb hanging over our heads. In the glare of white light, both of their faces collapse like old vinyl couches. I can only imagine what mine looks like.

"Okay, so that's where he got started, out West. That's where he got saved; he told us that part. He'd thought 'cause he was a priest he was made in the shade, but he didn't know Jesus from a hole in the ground," Flake says. I'm dying to ask him, in all earnestness, *do you*? But he's busy opening a beer from a case pushed into the cobwebbed back of a low cupboard. "You guys want some? It's warm."

"I'd love one," I say promptly, but then, overcome with a rush of druggy paranoia, ask, "What time does Fred get home?"

"Late. Don't sweat it," drawls Marty.

Flake first knew Gerard as a spectre haunting the back walls of AA and NA meetings and clinics, and stalking the streets in the same ancient, stained overcoat he wears now, carrying a backpack full of convenience store sandwiches and clean syringes. He befriended the worst dopers and drunks, took them to the hospital when their bodies broke down, sat with them all night so they wouldn't yank the intravenous drips out of their arms and hightail it back to the street. He snuck smokes with them right by the oxygen tanks. He'd talk to anyone, the crazed, the corner preachers, the bellicose and blasphemous. He slept outside with them in winter where they camped around Nathan Phillips Square or under the Gardiner. People who trusted no one trusted him. He took them straight up, no questions asked, just the way they were.

I'm shocked speechless: Gerard, speaking the language of love? I feel as if I've taken a blow to the head.

"He said if Jesus came back today, it was us he'd want to talk to, not some bigass shits," Marty puts in. Flake laughs in concurrence, his roughly jostled teeth in the bright light the colour of sweet corn. "Too bad he changed, man, went all whack. He stopped going to TO and stayed holed up here 24/7 with his Bible, and pretty soon ya couldn't even talk normal to him."

Flake cracks open a second tepid beer. "But when I first met him, he was okay. Weird-okay but okay. He came up and started talking about God to me one night when I was hard up, puking and freezing in thirty below in no fucking coat at all, and I listened to him. Didn't have no choice, dude, he'd stick to you like glue till you broke down and said okay, you needed Jesus. He'd buy you coffees and Big Macs and he'd wait for you when you were sleeping it off at the shelter or in the park. You couldn't get on his bad side, and you couldn't shake him. He'd give you his last smoke, I swear. Fuck me, man, we need another line." He begins chopping three more fat ones with a kitchen knife, raising my spirits considerably.

"So, anyway, he drives me up here one night, and I'm thinkin', This is fucked up, any minute this freak's gonna jump me, and I had a knife on me, fuckin' nine-inch-blade, so I was thinkin', You're living your last breaths, man, if you fuck with me. But he didn't do shit. He made me soup and fixed up the mattress in his little room there and then he says, Y'know, I got a whole bunch of people like you who come up here out of rehab and shit and they're staying clean" — here they look at each other and burst into wheezy guffaws — "and then he says, I have my own church that meets here every morning and you're welcome to join us anytime."

"And you're thinking like, *church*?" Marty smirks. "No way, ho-zay! But it wasn't like regular church, eh. It was just him talking to us and we could talk too, but he wouldn't take no crap from nobody and after a while you start thinkin', fuckin' A, dude, I can get my head into this. When he said drugs and stuff was the same as those old dudes in the Bible worshipping gold cows, man, I tell ya, that just blew my mind."

"I was clean for a whole year," says Flake smugly. "Still am. I just take a vacation once in a while."

"Yeah, but," I venture when I can get a word in, "he rides you guys so hard."

Flake snorts his line and lights his seventy-fifth smoke, blowing three perfect rings over his head.

"That ain't nothin'. I got my own head to think with. He's always telling like this thing or that thing is true 'cause it's in the Bible, but what he don't know is the Bible wasn't even published until like two hundred years after Jesus croaked. I had a friend told me that, is how I found out. Father Gerry don't know everything. You have to take it all with a grain of salt, man."

"Wow. You've got everything figured out," I say in my husky, glamorous way, looking straight at him, aching to be drawn out, questioned, probed about *my* life.

Flake looks straight back at me. Our locked gazes hang frozen as he lassoes me with three more perfect smoke rings.

"I like listening to you talk. Your voice puts me in a good mood."

"Does it, now?"

"Yeah. You sound just like the lady who, when you call up Social Services and leave your message, the one who says, if you're calling about clinic hours, press one, all that shit."

"That *is* me."

"Get the fuck outta here!"

"I did their voice mail system. I've done lots of them. I'm answering phones all over town as we speak."

They stare at me, speechless.

"You're awesome," whispers Marty when he can find his voice. Flake's eyes are sodden with love.

And so we sit, snorting back rail after rail with steadily diminishing returns, until my knees are jiggling uncontrollably under the table. I keep telling myself, just one more, just one more, and then I'll get up and leave. But I know I won't budge from my chair because if I do, the huge, sweet blossom of hope and friendship and belonging that's hovering just out of reach, holding off until the perfect moment to enfold me in its sun-warm petals, will go limp and brown and fall in dry husks to the filthy floor.

Time roars by. At eight-thirty Fred phones to say he's ministering to the homeless at a Coffee Time. He doesn't know when he'll be back, maybe not till tomorrow. He's trusting Flake and Marty to hold the fort. Flake, who answers the phone, returns to our table of dissolution and idolatry, yelping, "The party never stops!"

My teeth are grinding themselves to nubs, but when he empties another baggie onto the table, I won't, can't leave until it, like all hope, is gone.

Around midnight, Marty produces a couple of Quaaludes from his shirt pocket and announces he's ready to crash. Flake wants to go into the city, promising me that he'll score some more to keep us going all night. By now I'm hideously bored, have heard every tired junkie boast ever invented, and yet, with every line, the sweet feeling tiptoes back for a minute or so, just enough to keep hope weakly thrumming. My turn to talk might be just around the corner!

"Let me drive," wheedles Flake, but I nudge him irritably into the Trans Am's passenger seat, perhaps a mistake, since he doesn't seem a tenth as wired as I am. He adjusts his seat till it's almost horizontal and scooches back, arms behind his head, closing his tired, red eyes. How can he relax? I don't know if I can get us downtown without blasting out of my seat and whipping ten times around the earth like Superman. I feel metallic, pingy all over, my heart bouncing off the windshield and dancing on the roof like Fred Astaire.

Even with his eyes closed, Flake still has a great deal to say.

"Do you believe in aliens? I do. I seen 'em, man." His voice scrapes away at my brain like curettage with a rusty knife. "They're everywhere. Besides, how do we even know we're not living in a hologram, man? Did'ja ever think of that? Like, how do we know we're not just blips in some alien dude's computer game? I saw one of them motherfuckers once."

He waits for my stunned reaction. I remain flintily impassive.

"You believe me?"

"Uh-huh."

"Huge motherfucker, looking right at me, behind the Bay, middle of the night. I swear he knew every thought in my brain. He could've killed me just by blinking his eyes. I've never been so fuckin' scared in my life. I swear on my mother's head, I never—"

"What does Gerard have to say about all this?" I cut in crossly, focusing on the highway lines swooshing by, each one like a fat, stress-relieving line of coke I can't have.

Flake harrumphs. "He thinks he knows all the truth there is. I ain't tellin' him shit."

I drop him off near Queen and Sherbourne; he tells me he'll be back in a flash. As he disappears around the corner, I urge myself to move, you idiot! Squeal those tires! Go home, now! But nothing will obey me. Every part of me, against all reason, wants more drugs, will settle for nothing less. And true to his word, Flake is back within five minutes, sliding in, grinning, slamming the door.

"We're goin' to your place, right?" he sniggers. Till that moment, it hasn't dawned on me that we're going anywhere. But I so badly want what he's suggestively patting in his jacket pocket that I simply nod, gunning the engine with unnecessary force.

In no time at all we're in my elevator and rising. I pray no one will see us in the hall, though I make an awful racket trying to fit my key into the lock every which way, dropping the whole set several times. Once inside, Flake announces he needs a drink to chill, and do I have any downers by any chance? I tell him I have some Valerian capsules for sleeping.

"We'll do this, and then we'll take 'em," he says, holding up a cloudy little balloon with a dusting of white powder on the bottom.

"Is that all you got?"

"Uh-huh." He ducks his head evasively. "I didn't want to wait around for my guy, so I got this and took off. Whoa! Is that your waterbed?"

"No. Sit down."

He eases himself onto my swell couch. The leather is a close match to his face. I go to get whiskies for us both, and before I know it, he's snuggling up behind me in the kitchen, nuzzling my neck with his dripping nose, whispering, "You rock, Maggie May."

"Go sit down!"

"Okey-dokey-doo. This place is fuckin' ace, man. How much you pay to live here?" He slumps back onto the couch and begins playing with the remote; I *hate* seeing him paw something that once brought so much pleasure to Desi. I set his drink on the table in front of him, downing mine in three gulps.

"Just checking if there's any porn on," he says, grinning up at me. The clock on the kitchen wall reads three thirty-seven.

"You have to go now."

"Aw, c'mon. You can let me crash out here for the night at least. Why don't we—"

"No!"

"Come *on*," he croaks hoarsely, pulling the edge of my sleeve, trying to get me down beside him. "Please. You're so pretty. I won't tell Father Gerry, I promise. Be a friend, Maggie." His arms begin snaking around my legs.

"I said no! You have to go, now!"

"Aw, come on. Let's do a line, okay?"

"If you don't go now, I'm going to tell Father Gerry everything that happened. I won't get in trouble. But you will."

He lurches to his feet and stumbles against me, grabbing both my arms and holding them in a wrestler's lock against my sides. Who knew he was that strong? We waltz awkwardly around the room as he tries to steer me into the bedroom and I try to wrench myself free.

"NO, NO, NO, NO, NO, NO, NO!" But even as I say it, I'm thinking, Just give in! What'll it cost? Give in, get it over with, and then maybe he'll leave.

He bumps me clumsily against the wall next to the bedroom door, mashing his mouth into my face. He smells like a house gutted by fire.

"Get the fuck *away* from me!" I push him as hard as I can and he staggers backward. His face crumples, then hardens, and I realize I'm in for the beating of my life.

But Flake is an old man, a fifty-year-old living in the war-torn body of a man of eighty-five. He's down for the count.

He takes the Valerian bottle from the coffee table, tosses back a handful, and falls onto the couch, immediately teetering sideways. Surely herbal pills can't be working that fast! If he falls asleep I'll never be rid of him. I'll have to marry him. I begin tugging him to his feet by his shirtfront, and once he's up, I aim him toward the door and start shoving from behind. Now that he's given up, he's easier to manoeuvre. I get him out, and down the hall and into the elevator, which is still stopped at my floor. If he passes out in there, I'll pretend I don't know him. I ping the button for the ground floor and send him on his way.

I feel jangled and hard-core mean, like I've just kicked Jesus out of my house.

I go back in and crawl into bed. My heart goes on slam-dancing for hours. I throw the blankets on and off until well after nine. I have a voice-over gig at ten-thirty and my nose is blocked solid, the Golden Voice as nasal and rattly as one of Flake's aliens. I shoot half a bottle of Dristan up my nostrils and cross my fingers. When the elevator door opens for me, Flake, praise the Lord, is gone.

I never ask him where he went. I never have the chance. I never set foot in Gerard's place again.

TWO

I'm a big girl, but this is ridiculous.

Come evening, I'm so heavy, so torpid, it's all I can do to hoist myself from the couch, both arms straining at maximum capacity. For every actual pound of body weight, I seem to be lugging an extra five, so leaden am I, so listless and stagnant, so inert.

You'd think with all the crying I've been doing, I'd drop a pound or ten. But it doesn't seem to work that way.

Meanwhile, Mistuh T hovers nearby, lighter than air, silent as the tomb. Though he's gone all sluggish too in his old age; he didn't always spend his days and nights flat out in a chair. But then, neither did I.

I'm not certifiable. I *know* I'm alone up here in my cheerless aerie. I'll always be alone here. Life holds nothing more for me now. It's over. Little Desi was my last feeble hold on love, my last connection to humanity. My last reason to get up in the morning.

But I have to talk to *someone*. And who's been with me longer, knows me better than the grinning miasma over there? He's brother, father, and mother, closer to me than they ever were, a shadow crowding my back and, against all reason, a source of bleak strength during the worst times of my life, when no one else had so much as a limp hand to offer.

He never shrinks from the difficult stuff, never pretends that life is anything more than a bowl of rotting cherries swarming with flies. And he's such a good listener! What better companion for a black-hearted bitch like me?

So I ask him, "*How about a little chinwag, my friend? While we sit here tapping our feet, waiting for the big End-Time fireball to consume the cursed earth and the legions of the wicked?*"

But first things first. Glass. Ice. Bottle. Pour. Tilt. Swallow.

"*Ah! All the lip-smacking, home-style goodness I've come to trust! Cheers, old buddy!*"

I'm not even crying over Desi any more. It's been three weeks after all, and I'm big and I'm tough. I can take it. And on the bright side, I never have to lay eyes on another Untouchable until we meet up again in Beulah Land, hah!

No, the weeping I'm doing now is for the future, not the past. Except the future grows out of the past, a blighted, tortured, tree-like thing of bumps, knots, and claws sprung from a bad seed embedded deep in some gaping fissure in the heart. I'd like to blame Mum for everything, and I pretty much can. But it was Dad who really got the ball rolling, when I was only ten, giving me that damned book no child should *ever* see. Handing it to me with that smug face, saying, "Here, I think you might get a kick out of this." He wasn't even a reader, so what the hell was he thinking? Did he just pluck it off the best-seller list, thinking, like I did, that it was a *Beach Blanket Bingo*-style teen frolic?

Maybe it was my fault. I trusted him completely so I never even glanced at the back cover, with its sensational warnings about doomed survivors desperate for a miracle, a shocker for the Atomic Age, etc., etc. And maybe no one else would have freaked out the way I did over a novel about the end of the world. But it was certainly the beginning of the end of me.

Fred used to get on his high horse with the gang, lecturing them sternly about how people could open themselves up to demon possession by fooling with Ouija boards or watching porn. Maybe that's what that book was to me, the gates to my soul suddenly left unguarded, swinging wide open, fear flapping in on a thousand webbed black wings.

The Fear. That's what I called my friend back then, before I knew his name. And just the thought of it…

"Lord, help me, I need another drink, and pronto."

Yes, except before I become too debilitatingly inebriated, I'm stuck with the niggling, obnoxious task of arranging about seven thousand pills into their individual plastic compartments and labelling them with billboard-size print because otherwise Mum will whine, "I can't *seeeeee*, Mag Mary. I'm *old*, Mag Mary." Please! Join the club, woman! Besides, she can *seeeee* perfectly well to knit all those heinous outfits for her unspeakable dog. She can *seeeee* my cab pulling up outside her building so that she can get all cagey, pretending she doesn't know it's me banging on her door at least twice a week now — and it's only going to get worse — making me cool my heels while she chats with the dog, taking a good ten minutes to wade through the litter on her floor to let me in, shooting me the evil eye when I ask her why she hasn't put away the laundry I did for her last week or wiped up the soup spilled on the kitchen table four days ago.

Of course, the one thing she *can't* see is her way clear to asking me how *I'm* doing. As in, "What's life like for *you* these days, Mag Mary?" thus giving me the chance to open my heart, spill my daughterly guts. "Ah, it's grand, Mother. I'm living pretty much like you do these days, sitting home night after night just like you there in your couch corner. And boy, do I drool with excitement, looking forward to coming here so I can watch you deteriorate in real time, that innocent face plastered on you while you cool your heels and sit pretty, waiting for me to come and *fix* everything, manage what's left of your money, for example, so you don't end up living on cat food and getting evicted from this hovel you moved into, all because Gerard told you poverty would be good for your eternal soul. And as a bonus, I get to mop your filthy floors, *and* clean up all the dog shit, *and* change your sheets, *and* get your groceries, *and* Gerard never lifts a sanctified finger. But, golly, Mum, thanks for asking."

She's positively avalanched downhill these last five years. Six, seven years back, she never needed checking up on. The only times we'd meet face to face was when she'd call me at six in the morning, snappy and businesslike, and order me to be at her apartment at eight sharp, where she'd meet me at the door with yet another bag of rummage-sale crap: scorched teakettles, mismatched cups and saucers, used tube socks, stuff I was to drive up to Gerard's *immediately*. My begging off only inflamed her ire.

"Are you so busy, Mag Mary? Is your life so full and important? Can you really not find a spare hour for your brother?" No, frankly, I couldn't. I invariably dropped the bags into the dumpster outside my building for some lucky lost soul to find.

Now it's like I never left the Untouchables. Which, of course, is just the way Gerard wants it. The last thing he said to me after I ditched him and his merry pranksters was that if I wasn't going to stay up there slaving for them, then I should start taking proper care of Mum in her malodorous old age. All right, the malodorous part's mine. But what a perfect, parting knife-twist in the ribs that was. He *knows* the way I feel about her, knows I hold her entirely responsible for the ruin of my life.

My big break for freedom has gotten me precisely nowhere. Gerard still has his hooks in me, is still yanking the same old marionette strings, making me dance my clodhopper jig to his uneuphonious tune. Telling me I'm supposed to be forgiving her seventy times seven thousand times because if I don't keep my hand in even this much, if I don't at least *pretend* to want to do right by someone, I can count myself a total goner, a waste of good flesh and bone, a first-class ticket holder on the greased-lightning express to hell.

Yep. The boy's still got it.

So now, instead of keeping track of the two Sunils' meds, I get to monitor hers, and she's on so many I can't believe they aren't tearing into one another inside her, kicking and karate-chopping her bloodstream into a pink froth. Any day now I'll turn up to find her spontaneously combusted on the couch, nothing left but a heap of chicken-sized bones and smoking ash. There are sleeping pills, tranquilizers, anti-hypertensives, anti-coagulants, thyroid meds, diuretics, anti-depressants, and the latest entry, Aricept, for her creeping dementia. There are laxatives, fibre pills, antacids. What is her doctor thinking? The labels alone would confuse a neuroscientist, never mind her murky head: take once daily, take as needed, take morning and evening, take three times daily, before meals, between meals, on an empty stomach. This must explain why I kept discovering unopened pill bottles under sofa cushions or in the bathtub drain and finally had to take *this* situation in hand along with everything else.

"I raise my glass to you, Mother, and to you too, my fine feathery friend! Only meds yours truly needs are in this sturdy bottle, Old No. 7, Tennessee sour mash whiskey. Dead simple instructions for use on the back: Please drink responsibly. Ha! Am I not the very soul of responsibility? Do I ever miss a single night?"

I suppose I have a nerve, ragging on Mum for living in squalor. I haven't emptied an ashtray, washed a dish, a sheet or a towel, or picked my clothes up off the floor since the day Desi left. There are more pizza boxes strewn around than at the Alpha Omega house after pledge night. I do sweet fuck-all and *still* I'm bone-weary. Is my blood even circulating?

The last time I remember feeling like this was back at university, the first time my life came crashing down around my ears.

I had just enough energy this morning to drag myself out to a voice job. And then proceeded to botch it shamefully, pitching and reeling through a sand-dry narration for the Department of Fisheries and Wildlife, eighty takes for every paragraph, countless clumsy, amateurish stumbles while I tried to work around the pound of pebbles lodged in my throat. Meanwhile, the clients, in plain view, were exchanging many a significant look, so it's doubtful I'll be bothered by Fisheries and Wildlife again any time soon.

"*But, hey! You know what? Fuhgeddaboutit! Because I'm home again, home again, jiggedy-jig, with a big, fat cheesecake on my lap, a whole bag of Chips Ahoy!, and several large, revivifying drams of moonshiny tipple in my immediate future! What is there not to love, pray tell, about this merry life of mine? Bottoms up!*"

I am so going to regret this in the morning. The older I get, the worse my hangovers are; last Sunday morning was one of the worst in recorded history. I felt so ill, so beaten-down, hopeless, and ashamed that it seemed there was nothing for this prodigal daughter to do but pick up my old church search where I left off in April. If the Father won't accept me in *this* pitiful condition, I reasoned cloudily, then he really has nothing but soot and storm clouds where his heart should be.

It seemed like a good idea at the time.

I flipped open the phone book, shut my eyes, and stabbed my finger onto the church page, the better to allow for supernatural guidance. Then I called a cab. In no time flat, I found myself marching into a Pentecostal church and sitting down to an interminable service featuring boisterous guitars, thumping drums, and fervent shouting in tongues, just the balm for my poor, beleaguered head.

A good hour and a half in, I was about to beat a glum retreat when the preacher suddenly grabbed the screeing microphone and requested the hall to hush, all heads to bow, and every eye to close. Then he asked who wanted to ask the Lord Jesus into their hearts.

I guessed I wanted to. So I did the solemn, hungover, imbecilic thing and raised my palsied hand.

Why? Don't ask me. Far greater minds than mine would be stumped by this one. How can someone doubt everything like a madman the way I do and still believe? No wonder Gerard still has me on emotional speed dial. I took nothing away from the Untouchables but this flabby faith of mine that just barely manages to keep all the loose, crooked pins holding me together from shooting out in all directions.

The congregation was so nice to me afterwards, though the fact that they all knew I was that day's savee proved they'd been peeking through their hands the whole time. They crowded around me the way the Untouchables had on my first day, assuring me that my name was now inscribed in the Lamb's Book of Life, though it didn't dawn on a single one of them to ask me what that name happened to be.

There I was, washed clean in the Blood, slouching in the pew all squinty-eyed as they informed me I was now an adopted child of the King, that jealous tyrant who murders wantonly, sweeps billions into hell, and breaks hearts with happy impunity.

And I thought *my* dad was a card.

Being washed in the Blood may look good from heaven's perspective, but it confers zero in the way of magical powers; Mistuh T, Jack, and I were right back on the job Sunday night as if nothing had happened. Nor do I think I'll be heading Pentecostalward again any time soon. I know churches, and I know the drill. I won't last another week in those rowdy pews. No, sorry, I've stood up and done my bit. Jesus, the next move is yours.

I've got enough on my plate as it is. I'm already feeling

nauseous, anticipating having to explain this pill business to Mum for the thousandth time tomorrow while she sits there and talks right over me to her one-hundred-and-forty-year-old wonder-pooch, telling him at *length* about a birthday party she went to in 1937. Or throwing out the question, "Is green or yellow a better colour for a little boy doggie's booties?" for debate. I yearn now for the days of old when she could barely bring herself to speak six words in succession to me. The older she gets, the gabbier by the second, every last word of it aimed at the seedy fleabag huddled at her feet. Even on the phone with me, she'll be talking to him while I sit glumly eavesdropping. Gerard almost never takes calls from her any more, as they put such a serious crimp in his repenting and exhorting schedule.

And yet, every time I go over there, knowing exactly what I'll find, I can't help it: I keep expecting to walk in on her old 1968 self, sitting up pert and alert, knitting away on an Irish fisherman's three-quarter-length car coat, her sharp little cable twister between her teeth, the pattern unique to the Moriartys so we'll be able to identify her body in case she's ever shipwrecked and washed to shore three months after the fact. The shrivelled, juiceless husk that peers up at me from behind her smeary glasses never stops being a shock. As wretched as she looks, though, she's still loosened up enormously over the decades, enough to pretend, at least sometimes, that she can actually stand having me in the same room.

Fine and dandy. I'm pretending my ass off too.

She'll be knitting all right when I turn up tomorrow but with nothing pert about her. No, she'll be sunk six inches deep into the form-fitting bucket seat her sofa's moulded around her butt after all these years, her needles slowly churning out a fluffy onesie for Winky, sad-eyed poodle of the lowlands. A game try, but her chain-knitting days of yore have pretty much gone the way of all flesh.

She used to clack those needles like a fiend, no sooner sliding off the last piece for a sweater than she was looping on wool for a fresh project. Those icepick spikes seemed to grow right out of her hands; I was always terrified that she might suddenly go for my jugular with one, except that murder by knitting needle is a pretty roundabout way to off someone. It would have taken hundreds, thousands of teeny punctures; her matchstick arms would be falling off and I'd still be hale and unbloodied as I calmly and politely inquired as to what she was so mad about.

Ah, Mother. Such fond memories! If she wasn't sitting prim as a post in church or saying her beads or helping Gerard memorize the facts and stats on the backs of his holy cards, she'd be hunkered down with a pattern book on her lap, needles chittering away like sharp little teeth. All the wool that passed through those clenched fingers could've circled the equator forty times, her hands like industrious little plows laying down furrow after furrow of oat and mulberry and aubergine. The damn woman could knit and cook at the same time, standing at the stove purling the salmon mohair while she flipped the Friday fishsticks or working the ruby mitts while the beets boiled. If the scarf or mitts or sweater weren't for Gerard, they were for her, all those creations stacked and colour-coded in her closet, whites and beiges, tangerine-coral-pumpkin-peach, aqua-lavender-chartreuse-lime. Except she never wore a single blessed thing she'd made, was always in those hideous grey skirts or a brown dirndl and a shapeless beige blouse. Maybe she intended to wear them in some distant, shining future—maybe she was exactly like me in that respect, putting off trips, postponing happiness for later, always later—but meanwhile they piled up like exotic provisions, luscious preserves put up in preparation for the coldest woman on the planet's infinite winter to come.

And there was always something new to make, more frost to ward off, because Gerard wasn't getting any heftier, skeletal blue and shivering even in summer. Her arms were forever pumping over heavy-duty, arctic-wear ski sweaters with fearsome caribou antlers locked in alpha-male conflict across the chest, intended, I supposed, to protect his barely fleshed ribs from the wrath he inspired in so many of our easily offended school cohort, not to mention in me.

Kids instinctively hated Gerard, but this was nothing to the animus that raged between the two of us. It must have started back in the minus-hours of our lives, a beef born in the womb that we dragged into the world with us like a triplet. We probably spent our first nine fetal lunar cycles orbiting each other amid the entrails and sewer pipes, slow-mo slugging with our little pidgin limbs in the darkness to the tom-tom beat of our mother's heart.

We spent our formative years leaping out at each other in murderous ambush. Neither of us ever had fewer than eight swollen bite marks at any given time. We pulled out enough of each other's hair to stuff a mattress. He threw boric acid into my face, hoping for the pleasure of watching my features melt from my naked skull before his eyes. I locked his arm in a vise in the basement, where he wasn't discovered for four screaming hours. He released giant garden spiders in my bed. I tampered with the brakes on his bike, wrestled him to the ground to set his hair on fire with Dad's lighter, baked his pet turtle, and smashed a mirror over his head. Fifty years later, he phoned me in the wee hours to kindly suggest that I admit I'd come to the bitter end of my hopeless self.

This is one holy man who truly knows from grudges.

But the mayhem I *dreamed* of doing put all my real-life exploits in the shade. I fantasized night and day of doing him the kind of grievous harm that would require many major surgeries to correct: pressing a hot iron onto his back, or sewing his eyelids shut while he slept. But where would it have gotten me, once the thrill of conquest was over? He'd just run off wailing to Mum, who would hug him to her birdy bosom and tenderly wipe away the gore. Then she'd wedge a chair against the kitchen door so they'd be barricaded in there like the good saints in heaven while she made him foot-high stacks of French toast, my favourite food. I'd sit in the outer darkness, my back against the door, howling with rage, desperately praying for her to "slip" with the big bread-cutting knife and accidentally slice his poultry neck from ear to ear, oops, darn it! I'd hear him in there, gurgling like an old radiator before he expired at last with a sideways flop of the head. There'd follow a hasty funeral, a few days of mopey faces, and then we could — at last! — proceed to the glad business of getting on with our lives.

By the time we were six, strangers refused to believe we were twins at all. I was such a little pudge, popping the buttons off my blouses while he slunk around with his whippet belly and sinewy old-man arms, the easiest kid in the world to beat the stuffing out of. And *still* Mum loved him to delirious distraction, and so did Jesus and *his* Mother, and all the beat-downs in the world couldn't transfer a single jot of that love to my bankrupt account.

Although there was that one day. One day, when the eye of the hurricane passed over. One day, out of all those years of sucker punches and head-butts, of raging jealousy and rabid revenge. One day of purest light out of thousands.

Does Gerard even remember?

Sunday, February 12, 1961. We were eleven, our childhoods on the slow wane, our mutual loathing unabated. We came home from Mass that day same as always, but instead of flopping in front of the TV in sullen fury or poking each other with stray knitting needles, we—who can believe it?—set up shop on the kitchen table to make valentines!

It was all his idea.

I can still see those valentines too, lumpy with glue bubbles, smeary with ink globs from our ballpoint pens, decorated with friendly, happy faces cut from musty old *Life* magazines we'd found in the garage. There was the cheerful Culligan Man, the grinning Texaco gas jockey, all manner of apple-cheeked Norman Rockwell children. And we didn't just make valentines for kids at school, we made them for all the ancient, crabby people on our street, and it never even crossed our minds to write anything jokey or nasty on the back. To Mr. Greco three doors down, we wrote: *You have nice flowers. We hope your garden is always good (In sumer that is.)* And to mean old Mrs. Kirkland, who never answered her door on Halloween: *We know you are a widdow, and we are sad about it. Have a happy valentine's day!*

It was jumping-up-and-down cold outside, but our little twin hearts were mushy-warm as we raced up and down the street stuffing the cards into mailboxes with our woolly mittened hands, running like the wind before we were spotted. Gerard had on his dorky plaid earflap hat and I completely forgot to point out what a chucklehead he looked like in it. And then, when all the valentines had been delivered, he suddenly pressed, of all things, an item he'd clipped from the newspaper into my hand, concerning a nine-hundred-pound man named Happy Humphrey who had "slimmed down" to seven hundred pounds.

Oh! Slimmed down! We were beside ourselves, tears freezing on our faces. Every time our laughter was on the verge of dying away, one of us would shout, "He SLIMMED DOWN to seven hundred pounds!" and we'd lose it all over again, bent double and screaming. There was a picture with the article of what appeared to be a sofa dressed in overalls with an apple-sized head on top, sitting at a picnic table holding a knife and fork, beaming to beat the band, and not once did Gerard remember to remark on the expanding girth of *my* stomach.

But then, two days later during the class valentine exchange, full of happy trust just like the ding-dong he was, he gave the only one he had left, the special one he'd saved, the prettiest, least gluey one with the paper lace and the border of gold stars and the picture of the Norman Rockwell Mother serving a fat turkey, to Andy Rearick, a stammering kid with no eyebrows who wore a bow tie and stood at such insanely fierce attention during the singing of "God Save the Queen" that the whole class would be snorfling back mucus and could barely croak our way through "God save our gracious."

I made sure the word got out about that valentine. I also threw in some choice, mostly false tidbits about a certain someone still wetting the bed.

We were pretty used to Gerard coming home with black eyes and split lips and bloody noses, so the stern correction he caught for going all sweet on Andy was nothing out of the ordinary. But, Jesus, the way Mum carried on, fussing and fluttering, applying compresses, stroking his hair, and then making him a batch of chocolate-sprinkled cupcakes no one else was allowed to touch.

Really, who could blame Dad for saying she'd turned him into a prancing fairy?

I knew he'd find a way to repay me. So I put up my dukes, dancing from one foot to the other, spoiling for our next heavy-versus-bantam-weight bout.

But Gerard never looked back from Happy Humphrey day. He never said a word, never tried to get even. He just squared his spindly shoulders, strapped on his halo, rounded up his private honour-guard of angels, and walked away from me into his own exclusive future.

Is that the memory that lurks at the bottom of my fear of him, that clanging evidence of his superiority and inherent greatness? Because all I really need to do when he starts rubbing my nose in the steaming pile of my own loser-hood is to think back a few years from that day to the memory of his scrawny ass backed up against the house in Uncle Dermott's backyard, those Moriarty picnics we had every year, all Mum's people, babies thick as dandelions underfoot, Grandma Fionnuala swanning around on Dermott's arm under a pansy-covered hat big as a sombrero. Twenty thousand cousins packed in shoulder to shoulder, hollering, spitting watermelon seeds. And Gerard and me, always dressed wrong. I'd be parked in a lawn chair in my hot blue suit and white gloves, which Mum forbade me to take off even to saw with a plastic knife and fork at the squirting sausage on the caved-in paper plate in my lap. And there'd be Gerard in his plaid sport jacket and mad-scientist glasses, heaps of scapulars and holy medals bulging inside his shirt like a tumour, trying to fade into the bricks and thanking his lucky stars that wearing his good clothes spared him the ignominy of being roped into games of tag or Red Rover and having to hear Dad cup his hands like a megaphone to holler, "You run like a sissy!"

Cousins would be shooting by him one by one, knocking his glasses crooked, yanking his hair, the rest of them in a clump by the side of the house, hooting and snorting. Gerard would stand there frozen in martyrly rictus, pretending not to notice, turning the other cheek, and then the other and the other till his face was nothing but a spinning blur.

Mum would be propped in her lawn chair like Miss Priss, looking straight ahead, never cracking a smile or loosening up for a second, not even seeing Gerard in his awful plight. She was socially inept to a frightening degree — the chip doesn't fall far, does it? — and totally wrapped up in her own misery. Of course she was *supposed* to be miserable, yoked to a heathen like Dad, though you'd never know from the look of her how she managed to get herself into the family way outside of the bounds of holy matrimony. Of course I didn't know about that then. But even I could have beat her up by the time I was ten, and should have, all five-foot-four of her, those mosquito arms, that pinched-in waist, that flat, uninspiring chest. And yet she scared the life out of me.

Why Dad took her stingy bait, I'll never know. Or she his, as he had all the lady-killing skills of Popeye. I imagine him on one of their courtship dinner dates, his elbows on the table, shoving aside the silver ice cream dishes and saying in his flat-bottomed way, "Pretty good grub, yup, but when are they gonna clear away this crud?" Talk about a match made in the lowest circle of hell, never mind his heathen ways and sneering contempt for all her religiosity and for the Church. When she'd get the rosaries out after supper, he'd pitch his *TV Guide* clear across the room and stomp downstairs to his den, turning on the TV down there super loud, leaving us pious three to recite the Glorious Mysteries while *77 Sunset Strip*'s pistol shots and car chases percolated upward through the floorboards under our tortured, shifting knees.

Then there was the time Gerard won a statuette of Mary for a perfect recitation of the multiplication tables and tried to offer her a quiet home on his dresser. Dad no sooner saw her holding court among the jungle of wildflowers Gerard had picked in tribute than he hurled her out the window into the rhododendrons, hollering, "This is a house, not a goddamn church!"

I was beyond thrilled to see plaster Mary land kersplat in the bushes. What good was she if she couldn't even see through Gerard, the most transparent of all the world's good-doing children? And if she really *had* appeared to him like he claimed that morning, zombie-walking down to breakfast with his eyes spinning in his head and hives all over his face ... if she had, then why didn't she grab him by the ear and shake him like a mop the way Sister Miriam did to Billy Barr when he asked her if she'd happened to catch *Naked City* last night?

Really. As if Mary the Mother of God had nothing better to do than to sneak into our house at three in the a.m. of a fine summer morn, tiptoe into his bedroom, swish around in her starry robes examining all his dumb airplane drawings and A-plus test papers, and finally peer down at him sleeping, curled up with his girlie rosary looped around his fingers. His eyes must have popped open to find her face an inch from his, her lapis lazuli eyes dripping with stern beneficence and blood-chilling understanding. I imagined her making a beeline back to heaven to report on him, God the Father hunched like Sitting Bull at the table in the Holy Kitchen, taking it all in, making a mental note: here was someone to watch!

If it had been my chunky, slovenly self waking up to find the Queen of Heaven looming, she'd have given me a smart cuff on the ear and quipped, "That's for nothing. Wait till you've done something."

I was a rollicking kid back then, before the Fear had begun its campaign of assault on my soul. I certainly wasn't Mum's child, delicately cut from crepey black funeral bunting like Gerard. No, I was every inch Dad's daughter, hacked with a Bowie knife out of raw cowhide, a laugh-a-minute gal with energy to burn and dukes always up. I had school pals all over the place, played every sport there was, could beat any boy at anything.

As for Dad, let's just say he was no Atticus Finch. He loved to tell me he was "a born nose-thumber," and yes, he was poorly behaved to a quite spectacular degree. He'd stop at nothing to stick it to the holy side of the family, starting with those breakfasts he used to have waiting for us all post-Mass on Sunday mornings. We'd come trooping in dressed in our Sunday clothes to find him flipping eggs in the kitchen, and no sooner had we sat down to the table than he'd announce he'd fried them up in his own snot. This would make Gerard frown and Mum slam the bedroom door, but it made me laugh like a hyena. And then he'd pile a stack of old jazz 78s from his teenaged days onto the turntable and crank them up so loud you could hear them five houses down the street.

I knew beyond the shadow of a doubt that he really, really liked me. I was right up his alley. I also knew that every breath Gerard drew rankled him to the bone. Nor could he abide the upstanding Catholic Moriartys, always taking a powder the second we'd get to one of Uncle Dermott's picnics, only to turn up again hours later, listing around a corner of the house, privately lubricated to the eyeballs. He'd attempt to insinuate himself into the backslapping nuclear cloud of red-faced Moriarty uncles, trying to talk sports but totally lost when they started in on Irish football or the ponies. Even Uncle Father Jimmy the priest fared better than he did, hoisting a convivial Molson with the boys in his long black dress, all the men talking right over Dad, edging him out the same way we girls did at school to someone who was totally beyond the pale. He'd lurk a while on the fringes of all that Celtic bonhomie, lips grim, arms hanging, absolutely cast out. At long last he'd call me over to ask me six times in a row, what did I think of my old man?

"He's fine."

"No, what do you think of your old man?" Then, madder: "Damn it, I asked you what you thought of your old man!"

Not much later I'd find him beet red and passed out, snoring in the back seat of the car.

Who else did we have but each other? Mum had turned her resolute Catholic back on him years ago when I guess everything that had ever needed to be said had been. She had an endless stream of sweet nothings to dribble into Gerard's delicate seashell ear, but Dad and I got her hard, zipped mouth from dawn to dusk, no matter what he pulled out of his sleeve to aggravate an outburst out of her. As for me, she always made me feel like an extra package delivered by mistake along with the good twin, as in, "We didn't order this. Stick it in the back of the closet; otherwise I'll have to dust it."

Of course after a brewski or six, Dad stopped being playful and got nasty, talking mostly to himself while I eavesdropped. Even when I was too young to know what "lousy in the sack" and "thinks she's going to hell for getting knocked up without the priest" meant, the words "strait-laced, poker-up-the-ass malarky she's shoving down that little fairy's throat" had a very encouraging ring to them.

We had us a time, we two pals, tossing the football, hitting flyballs out of the backyard, or just parked on the sofa with popcorn in front of *Hockey Night in Canada*. I was the son he never had, and perhaps, looked at charitably, he was merely overestimating my native resilience when he did me the honour, on my tenth birthday, of giving me *On the Beach* to read, putting it into my hands with a steely-eyed nod, which I manfully returned. I ran right off, sprawled on my bed, and began reading about the end of the world, which, up to that moment I'd been positive was permanent, a handful of people with only weeks to live clinging to the southern edge of Australia as they waited for the radioactive air to arrive and kill everyone and everything forever and ever and ever.

I couldn't even touch the book after I'd finished it. For weeks afterwards, every time I thought of the horror of that story, I'd concentrate hard on the chug of a lawnmower outside or the smell of the cut grass through the open window. Or cars whooshing by, dads heading for the hardware store, mothers driving kids to softball practice. Or a song playing on the kitchen radio, Rosemary Clooney urging me to come onna her house. Those sounds, those smells, gradually worked on me like a hypnotist's watch: back to normal, back to normal, back to normal. *This* is what's real, not the other thing.

And so I slipped back into my former "Hey, boys and girls!" childhood daze—but not all the way. No, never again all the way: from that summer on, there was always one open window on the world that I couldn't shut, no matter how icy the winds that blasted in, whipping the curtains to the ceiling, leaving etchings of frost on my puny kid's heart.

That was the damage *he* wrought, or at least the opening salvos of it. Grandma Fionnuala also had her own unique contribution to make, particularly on the nights she deigned to dine at our humble Prentice table. She never hid her preference for her raft of successful sons, seven in all, and their lovely wives and attractive, well-behaved, devout children. Coming to our place was a profound sacrifice for her, surely noted in heaven and inscribed in gold on her Permanent Record.

We'd no sooner have tucked in our napkins when she'd introduce the one topic of discussion Dad couldn't handle to save his life: catechism drills. She'd rap her knife on her plate to shut us all up, breathe in the edgy silence, and then inquire briskly, "Who made us? Gerard."

"God made us."

"Mag Mary. Who is God?"

"God is the Supreme Being, infinitely perfect, who made all things and keeps them in existence."

"Very nice, with your gash stuffed full of potatoes. Gerard. Who is God?"

"God is the Supreme Being, infinitely perf—"

"Fine. Very good. Let us enjoy the bounty before us, sadly without the benefit of anyone's having taken the time to say a proper grace."

She'd stare for a long time at her heathenish, unblessed food before laying down her knife and fork and folding her hands in her dark lap. She'd shut her eyes then and sigh in a strangulated way, as if the devil himself had his claws around her throat.

"Do we all know that if we were to shed every last drop of blood for Jesus's sake, it still would not be enough to get us into heaven without the intercession of the Blessed Virgin?"

Sometimes Dad would just snort, "Aw, hell!" before scraping his chair back and carrying his plate, knife, fork, napkin, and beer down to the basement. But on other nights, the best ones, he wouldn't leave. Instead, he'd start right in shovelling humungous loads of food into his face and chewing extra loud, his mouth open so we could see the mangled mess sloshing around like clothes in a washing machine. Then he'd burp loud as a gunshot and tilt back in his chair, arms behind his head. He'd grin right in her face, and it was all I could do not to pee my pants on the spot.

Better still, he'd get up and put on one of his Sinatra records at top volume and start strolling around the table lip-synching into the fireplace poker like a Vegas crooner, snappy tunes like "That Old Black Magic," "I've Got You Under My Skin," and "In the Wee Small Hours of the Morning." He'd lean over her shoulder, his mouth smack against her ear, the songs leaking out off-key from under his breath while the jazzy Nelson Riddle orchestra honked and swayed behind him. But I had to hand it to her: she was tough. Because no matter how long he'd keep it up, he couldn't get her to look at him. Meanwhile, Mum and Gerard would sit stiff as tombstones offering it all up for the souls in Purgatory.

Not me. I'd just grin and grin, kicking back for the excellent floorshow with another heaping helping of potatoes and gravy.

Only when he'd gotten tired, or gone to the bathroom, would Grandma finally crack, muttering, "Merciful hour!" on a stream of spittle before crossing herself three times in a row. Then she'd look over at Mum to inform her smartly, "He should have been jailed the day he was born."

But the fun stopped there. After the meal was over and she'd kick-started her digestion by watching Bishop Sheen on TV work out some theological posers on his dusty blackboard, she'd settle back in her special chair and begin unspooling the priest-lore that was all for Gerard's goggle-eyed benefit. She'd spin out tales of our Uncle Jimmy's glorious life, the respect and honours showered on him as well as the sore trials he had to endure, the slatternly old wagon in curlers he was saddled with as a housekeeper, the strain of having to whip those bad articles in the Altar and Rosary Society into shape.

This preamble completed, she'd launch into a series of wild yarns about long-ago Irish saints: crazed monks clinging to rocks in the sea, swooning in solitary ecstasies, holding on to crags with one arm, ready to drop like a rock if Our Lord or Lady wished it so. Or living in tiny stone beehives they couldn't straighten up in. Standing naked in freezing lakes for hours just for the zip of it. Taking flying leaps into stinging nettle bushes, hoping to get a grim laugh out of God.

All of which would suddenly lead her to cry out as if in profound pain, "I don't expect the lot of you to care, but the Holy Name Society raised six *t'ousand* dollars this year, thanks to the generous giving of Our Lady's blessed servants, none of whom I saw sitting around the table tonight!"

Gerard would hang his saintly head and she'd reach over to pat it tenderly.

"Poor mite. It's a rocky path in thin shoes, is it not?"

Mum would come in then from doing the washing-up, wiping her hands on an apron besprigged with happy, dancing pots of geraniums, clearly meant for some other breed of mother in some far distant house. She and Gerard would snuggle on the sofa, holding hands, while I had the smaller, scratchier armchair all to myself.

"Perhaps you'll be one of the blessed Saints yourself one fine day," Grandma would say, her circumflex eyebrows right on message. Gerard would duck his head to hide the proud smile spreading like measles over his face, while from the basement would arise a strangled "God*damn*it!"

"Are you ready to give up everything, even life blood, for the love of Jesus and his Mother and the Church?" Gerard's smile would wobble a little, sagging at the corners. "Does it seem hard to you, lad?"

"No." Which shameless lie would then propel her into the crowning jewel of the evening, the blessed Croagh Patrick speech.

"Let our own beloved Saint Patrick be your lodestar in life! You can hardly do better, my bright-eyed boy. Patrick fasted and prayed for *farty* days and *farty* nights on his holy Reek, the one we call Croagh Patrick in his honour. He vanquished the she-demon Corra by hurling his silver bell at her and he drove every last *voiper* in *Oireland* into the sea, and I don't wonder if he wasn't often thanked for his troubles! And some people, knowing all this, are still too *moighty* to spare a few thin dollars for the St. Patrick's Day Altar Society. I'm not mentioning any names!"

She'd pull her hanky from her sleeve to snuffle and dab at her dry eyes while the guy on TV downstairs shilled enthusiastically for Ipana and Gerard bent over and pretended to tie his shoelace, smirking his face off, his brush-cut hair seething like a hurricane around the still centrepoint at the crown. And from up on the mantle, his First Communion picture would leer down at me, the evil twin, who was going to feel pret-ty bad when he finally stepped up to take his place at the top of the guest A-list for the big, blowout Supper of the Lamb.

Speeches done, she'd leave us at last. I'd march upstairs with my face parked in neutral, whistling a happy tune. And then climb into bed with the sickest heart in the world, gagging into my sopping pillow long after the light was out. Because I wasn't just a non-starter in the saintliness sweepstakes and a stranger to the bosom of the woman who bore me, but I was being eaten alive from the inside out by a terror that was all jaws, filed teeth, and foul breath, slavering and ripping and tearing without mercy at the cowering prey of my unprotected heart.

It wasn't the same as the *On the Beach* fear, though it was related. This Fear was its big bully of a brother, or perhaps even its unholy sire, since I'd first caught it, like a deadly virus, at school, not a week into my primary education.

I was no match for it. For all my stalwart fists and roly-poly rawhide, I knew I was way worse than weirdo Gerard had ever been. I was a gigantic fake, one of those total pain-in-the-ass kids who ruins everything for everybody by having a heart attack on the scary ride at the amusement park, or the dumb-ass doofus who chokes to death sipping her milk backward through a straw.

Because, slouched at my grade-one desk with a pretzelled stomach, I'd heard Sister up at the blackboard tapping with her pointer as she laid down the First Great Law of Horror.

"All Catholics dying in a state of grace, after time served in Purgatory, go straight to heaven. Everyone else is damned to the eternal flames. Forever. Everyone. Hindus, Moslems, Jews, Pagans, Protestants. Unbelievers. There are no exceptions."

I wasn't scared for me. I was in with the in-crowd, perfectly safe unless I screwed up the "state-of-grace" requirement, which I fervently vowed I would never allow to happen. No, I was scared for the person I loved best in the world, the one who'd taken to *me* from the jump, because that person wouldn't set foot inside a church if they were serving free beer while the organist thumped out "Take the A Train."

I could just see poor Dad snatched up by a sky-hook, dangling over the flaming pit from which he'd never, ever escape.

He looked so startled, so completely unprepared, kicking and flailing in his lawn-mowing khakis and white tee-shirt with the Luckies rolled up in the sleeve, and I couldn't do a damned thing for him, his fate sealed, his bones as good as ash already.

It was horrible and it was absolutely going to come true. There was nothing I could do but pull a carapace tough as tent canvas over myself and refuse to think about it. And thumb my nose at old Mother Church, who didn't want me anyway. And pull simian faces at the nuns behind my desk lid. And stand on my bike pedals, no hands, and laugh and defy death on every screaming downhill slope I could find. Because Dad's scoffing was the source of my night terror, but it was also the never-ending, steady fuel for my daytime strength.

After all, in the bright sun of noon, he was getting away with it just fine!

And look at me now, all these decades later. The state-of-grace thing completely shot to hell and the bottom of the last downhill slope coming up *fast*. I'm older than Grandma was back then, and this flat-lining life as a resentful drudge in the service of a mother who has never lifted a finger on my behalf is all I'm ever going to have, ever! My God, if I *didn't* drink? My nerves would be sparking and popping, sizzling like cold water splashing into hot oil. Every eve of every visit to her I'm a wreck, all that carnage awaiting in her apartment, the fly-strewn dishes, the endless *reasoning* with her I'll have to do, trying to talk sense into a block of cement. I'd take Untouchables drudgery over this any day; at least they were good for a laugh once in a while.

It's true, her nun pals from St. Bernadette's help out, dropping in on her when they can, quietly straightening up a few things. And Mrs. Penniman, her neighbour in the next apart-ment, keeps an eye on her in between my visits. She has a brisk, no-nonsense way about her and can command Mum's respect in a way I never could. Mrs. Penniman's good at little things, like running out to pick up Mum's prescriptions, and getting her to wear her glasses on a chain around her neck so she won't be constantly bonking her head on end tables as she crawls on the floor groping for them. Mrs. P. also checks in to make sure Mum's eating the frozen dinners I get her, often heating them in her own microwave when she finds Mum angrily stabbing at the ice-hard contents with a fork. She makes sure she's at least taking the pills she *has* to take, the ones on whose pill compart-ment labels I've pasted little gold stars. She also comes in once a week, unasked and unthanked, to clean out the bathtub and coax Mum into it—I could *never* get her to do it—as well as keeping her supplied with adult diapers. She's the only person Mum will allow to accompany her to the doctor, though lately she's been refusing even that.

Mrs. Penniman also keeps me apprised of Mum's more colourful adventures, like setting out for the supermarket on a steaming day in June, wearing her winter coat and boots, and coming home with one green bean in a plastic bag. Mum swears it never happened.

I know Mrs. Penniman doesn't like me, that she considers me neglectful and cold, though she's too polite to say so. I don't know how long she'll be willing to keep her hand in; if I had my way, she'd do everything there is to do for all time. But she's over seventy herself, and besides, this is starting to look like a round-the-clock job for paid professionals.

But. Except. However. Even the *thought* of having to uproot Mum and put her someplace else, and then *pay* for it, leaves me seething with resentment, beaten about the head with anvils, pulverized into inertia.

She doesn't deserve my help. Where the hell was she when I was twelve, that wretched age when you need a mother like you need air, when Dad's consulting firm started sending him on overseas assignments for months, jobs no one else wanted but he jumped at, anything to get shut of his bitter wife and creampuff son. He probably lived the Rat Pack life of Riley when he was away: parties, booze, blackjack, broads. And the more he was away, the more he shrank into a stick figure with zero domestic input, leaving Mum and Gerard to rule like despots. And when he *was* home, he began avoiding me, and I only needed to cast my eyes downward to know why.

It was the breasts. The damned things inflating into watermelons overnight, and he completely stopped looking at me, only addressing the air next to my ear if there was something he *had* to say, his eyes never dropping below my chin level. But I looked at *his* eyes, and they were critical and cold, they were *disappointed*. He'd invested so much in our father-son bond, and I'd gone and let him down just like every dumb broad on earth could be expected to do.

It didn't feel overtly sexual, like he didn't dare look because he'd be swept away with lust. No, it was just the busting-out femaleness of these massive torpedoes that forced him to turn away in, there's no other word for it, disgust. All the work and time he'd put into our mutual alliance against Mum and Grandma Fionnuala, against pansy Gerard and stuck-up Mother

Church, against females in general, had gone belly up. The helpless shame of it all, never mind the weight, slumped me over like a comma until Mum threatened in sharp, three-word bursts to put me in a posture brace.

My rollicking days were ended. The boiling embarrassment at my new, repulsive body drained like a poison drip into my adolescent soul, which in turn bought advertising space on my face. Pimples began ganging up, making sport of me, arranging themselves in plainly discernible constellations and configurations that mirrored each other on either side of my nose: two Big Dippers, two Cassiopeias, two ornately coiling Draco the dragons. Mum silently left a few experimental bars of black acne-busting soap on my bed, but when I continued to look as if I'd been dragged by the heels face down over a gravel road, she gave it up in quiet revulsion. I'd probably've been better off raised by wolves.

"Let us call a halt to the proceedings at this sad juncture and raise glass number I've lost count in a heartfelt toast to wolves!"

The longest sentence she addressed to me in the years between thirteen and seventeen was "There's hand-washing in the basement," the words bitten off and spat as her nimble fingers raced through a freakish-looking grape and vanilla harlequin-patterned vest with patch pockets that would never see the light of day, unless it was for Gerard. But it meant I'd leaked blood onto something, which called forth her second favourite sentence, the one with which she eased me into my reproductive years: "Cold water gets out blood." In the basement, next to the laundry tub, there'd be a stained sheet or underwear that wanted scrubbing by the filthy perpetrator. And once in an extremely great while a fresh box of Kotex would make an unheralded appearance on my bed, once in a while not even close to being often enough, so that I usually had to go without it and didn't know where she hid hers. I was mortified to death to bring the subject up, let alone stand at a checkout counter to buy my own out of my lunch money, which I needed anyway to keep myself in Clearasil. So I had to make my own inefficient pads out of fat wads of toilet paper, which after an hour would begin to shred into rank brown strips that moulted from under my skirt unless I walked down the school halls pigeon-toed and knock-kneed.

But how could she be concerned with such mundane matters when she had far, *far* bigger fish to fry?

Aunt Baby was the first one to fill me in on that score. Sweet, hefty, blushy-faced, tapioca-thighed Aunt Baby spilled the whole steaming, gassy pot of beans about Gerard's exalted future into my lap one afternoon at a Moriarty picnic as we sat together polishing off an entire cherry pie between the two of us. She was already in her novice robes by then, and looking good too, as they covered up her astonishingly thin hair and big round tummy, the two reasons we'd always called her Baby instead of Fiona. She was the youngest Moriarty, Mum's only sister, but she couldn't have been less like Mum or Grandma had she been a Japanese man. Grandma was always telling me, "You favour my Fiona," which she did not intend as a compliment. Of course she was pleased that Baby was a nun, but did she have to be such a big, homely one? Or, for that matter, so easygoing and friendly? Nuns were supposed to be fearsome creatures, stern defenders of the Faith, not smiling, gentle, or joyfully self-indulgent when it came to third helpings of dessert.

Baby just always had that good word to say about everyone. She was sweet as dumplings to me, but then she'd turn around and be just as sweet to Gerard. I realized nunship required this of her, but in my book, it was an egregious dereliction of simple human duty.

"You must be very patient with your brother, Mag Mary," she said to me between heaping forkfuls of gelatinous pie and ice cream. "He has a special mark on him. He may have the vocation. We are all praying and offering up Masses for him, asking Our Lord to guide him as he finds his way."

And I thought to myself, how could this *be*? God had to be an idiot! Gerard had *everybody* fooled, kneeling for a hundred years after Communion, his hands splayed over his face like giant spiders. Or taking his turn as star altar boy, Father Moretti's pet, which made him privy to all the backstage secrets, though he wouldn't cough up a single one no matter how long and hard I punched him. Mum and I would be in our front-row seats at seven o'clock Mass, and sometimes at the nine as well if some other boy couldn't make it and they called Gerard to work a double shift. She would be melting and sighing, patting away tears while he pranced around in his lace outfit, offering the paten, tinkling the little bell, holding up the chalice, speaking *Latin*, for God's sake, and kneeling in an adoration that didn't look remotely faked. He was sure-footed and graceful up there behind the red velvet ropes, his paper-white face raised heavenward, eyes shut, praying hands arranged just so. Next to him, all the other altar boys looked like stooges and stumblebums.

And sure enough, two years later, he quietly confirmed his glorious vocation at a Sunday dinner table surrounded by his fainting-with-pride grandmother, his sobbing-for-joy mother, and his big, fat, blighted, and abandoned twin sister.

He was home safe. Free. A made guy.

As for Dad, he greeted the news with a simple, eloquent "Aw, hell." Under the circumstances, it fell a little flat.

And as for his big, fat, blighted twin, left in the lurch as he prepared to take his heavenly flight? Nothing good, unless you count all those thoughtful, silent gifts I never asked for that Mum left on my bed: rubbery, midriff-bulge underwear in boxes featuring matronly ladies in pensive moods, stiff, medieval garments that got humid and mossy-smelling and left raw red welts all over me. And because she was offended by the yellow stains under my arms, dress shields, gigantic half-moons plasticized like hospital sheeting and mortifyingly visible under my regulation white school blouse and only under mine because all the other girls managed to stay sweet and powder-dry, crisp and permanent-pressed all day long. Maybe she would've loved me if I'd been one of those girls, but I was the farthest of cries away, my horrible, greasy skin forcing me to duck into the bathroom stall at school three times a day for a complete stripping and refinishing. The sight of my naked face was so unsettling I had to work in private, crouched in front of the metal toilet paper dispenser, a murky, forgiving mirror, while I hurriedly swabbed my face with brown toilet paper squares soaked in rubbing alcohol, the bottle wobbling dangerously between my knees, and reapplied a fresh top coat of Clearasil. The bathroom would be smokier than a tavern, feet bunching up under my door, someone always pounding and yelling abuse. I never left until the bell had rung and the last straggler had stamped out her butt and departed.

Gerard's puberty schedule lagged light years behind mine, his pituitary gland still asleep at the switch as he marched into high school, his skin baby-soft, still lugging his elementary school briefcase full of wildflower drawings and Mother's egg sandwiches, her grotesque hand-crafted snowmen frolicking under his school blazer.

At home, I kept strictly to my room unless food were being served, up to my eyeballs in puppy love, mooning over the muscle-bound lunk who had smiled once in my general direction in English class. I'd failed to notice he wasn't wearing his glasses; I was probably just a smear on the air to him, so, mercifully, he never saw the answering grin that ate my face like leprosy. Of course I know now that this is what happens to girls who embarrass their fathers: they continue to embarrass themselves in matters of love for decades to come. But back then, I was convinced that heaven had meant the two of us to be, and all year long, I shamelessly hoisted the flaming torch of my adoration in public, my face red as a baboon's rump whenever he passed by, and blubbering, wailing, and clutching the lockers for support when he took no notice of me at all. When he wasn't around, I wormed his name into every conversation, all the girls stamping their feet and shouting at me to "Quit it!"

I had never lacked for friends in elementary school, but by high school, I had lost the knack of talking to girls my own age, never mind boys. My childhood friends drifted away into cliques, none of which had any room for a hulking, besplotched thing like me. But all that exasperated female stamping made an

134

impression on me: being noticed and discussed even negatively was at least a foot wedged in the social door. All I needed was a gimmick to squeeze the bulky rest of me right on through.

I'd always been able to make Dad laugh by imitating people on TV. And I don't mean just laugh, but sputter and clutch his belly, this even after he'd stopped looking below my chin. I could do Tweety Bird and Olive Oyl, Lucy and Ethel *in conversation*, and Daffy Duck, Donald Duck, and Foghorn Leghorn engaged in a full-on, three-way, feather-pulling dust-up. I could do a flawless Elvis, and all four Beatles. My Grandma Fionnuala impression was so dead-on I scared the pants off *myself*.

But the voice I selected for the relaunch of my rambunctious reputation was that of Mrs. Wasserman, the lady from Long Island who lived two doors down. Not a day went by in summer that we didn't hear her hollering up and down the street at her husband or her kids in her explosive New Yawk honk: "*Hahrry! Haow many toimes do I hafta cole yeou? Get in heah, naow!*"

I tried out a few practice sentences on the two or three girls who were still talking to me. I'd say, "What's thyat on yeh pyants? Wawtah?" and "Oh moy Gawd, didja get yeh haeh done?" I killed! Kids would suddenly smile and lean way in to listen, their mouths agape, asking, "How do you *do* that?" So I just kept turning up the volume and the New Yawkiness, standing up straight, jutting my big butterballs, and hollering all up and down the halls of academe like I was, to use the popular expression of the day, Her Majesty, Queen Shit.

I was back! I was loud and I was rollicking! And I found that I could get away with saying just about anything as long as I didn't use my natural voice. Gangs of C-list girls followed me like paparazzi, heatedly whispering to one another, "What *will* she say next?" Or so I thought. But more importantly, boys followed too, and unlike the girls, they stuck around after the novelty had begun to wear off. Sure, it was the runty, nearsighted ones with the braces and dandruff, but they were no less horny for all that. Pretty soon I was climbing out of parked cars and ditches, tramping home from school at dusk, a big-titted blimp of a girl, who talked like Fanny Brice, my skirt twisted sideways, blouse hanging out, humungous bra hiked up around my neck, the weenie loser I'd been with already scampering off to tell his slavering friends what base he'd gotten to with me.

I'd arrive home to find Gerard all cozy in the kitchen, sipping hot chocolate and doing his math homework while Mum hovered over him speaking whole sentences, *paragraphs* even. So nobody noticed me slinking into the bathroom to repair my destroyed face and pick the sad twigs of love out of my hair.

"Oh. Ohhh. Morning. Ohhhhh God. Oh, and look at you, lookin' so chipper over there in your chair. Guess I passed out. Ya miss me, Mistuh T?"

I roll off the couch, thinking, if I'm not careful, it'll soon be Mistuh *D.T.* There'll be *Lost Weekend* bats flapping around in here, blood seeping down the wall while I scream and claw my face. Which is what I want to do anyway, as the day's agenda ripples into grimy focus.

I splash cold water on my puffy face. Knock back a brimming shot glass of Jack for my stomach's sake. Finish off the cheesecake with two hands. Flounder around the apartment searching for the car keys, my head bricked in solid, my eyes a couple of running sores, until it dawns on me, I don't have the old flame car any more.

I change my shirt. Gobble seven or eight cookies. Almost throw up. Brush my teeth.

Twenty minutes later, I'm lurching out of a cab in front of Mum's building, sunlight searing my eyeballs white, wondering if she's lurking behind the blinds up there, getting ready to trot out her standard lecture about how shamelessly profligate I am, taking cabs everywhere when I should be thriftily saving for the many rainy days my pathetic future surely has in store.

Thank God she still seems to know who I am; so far I've been spared the sight of her tugging open six or seven mental file cabinets, flinging useless yellowed documents right and left, stumped as to who this Mag Mary in her vestibule might be.

The door's unlocked. Good thinking, Mother! Just the thing in a building full of low-lifes like this one. I poke my head in and, voilà, heeeeere she is, slumped over the tangled wool in her lap, her glasses hanging off her face, the TV tuned to an extremely loud daily Mass, but not loud enough, *never* loud enough to drown out the frenzied yipping from Winky that heralds my every intrusion into this black hole of dereliction she calls home.

There's the usual jumble of dirty cups on the coffee table, as well as the breakfast plate with the remains of the toast I made her last weekend. No more the dainty, close-mouthed chewer of yore, her be-crumbed teeth are resting on the plate among the petrified crusts, leaving the bottom half of her face sucked grimly inward. The rest of the apartment is in an equally

137

sordid state, the bathtub littered with dog feces, and crusty beige mounds of doggie puke in front of the TV and behind the door to the kitchen. There are piles of newspapers everywhere, and grocery flyers, telephone bills, up-ended cups, and laundry that needs doing by you-know-who. She'd have been right at home up at Fred's place.

The TV organ groans away as the tele-communicants shuffle forward to receive the Body and Blood. Sunk into her happy place, Mum bows her head and mumbles while I sit at the window watching furtive shadows flit behind the windows of the apartment building across the street, remembering the handful of times I brought Desi here. I can still see him perched on the edge of the big armchair that once cradled Grandma Fionnuala's righteous behind, tracing circles on his knees, patiently waiting for it to be time to leave.

I know I'm lucky to find her sleepy; the more-than-usual fogginess will curtail the chitchat with Winky. Still, she perks up from her sanctified reverie to announce, not unlucidly, "I don't like thish television Father. He'sh too old to shay a proper Mash." Her diction, without her teeth in, is as slushy and imprecise as mine after several tall, cool tumblers of liquid comfort.

"He's a chicken compared to you, darlin'."

"Don't you shtart. I'll shlap you."

"Do you mind if we turn it off now?"

"Shister Angie's coming by thish afternoon with Communion for me. You should shtay and take Communion, Mag Mary. When was your lasht Confession?"

"Mum, I'm a Protestant now. Try to keep up. We shoot our sins straight up to God." It's far too difficult to attempt to keep her abreast of my current non-Untouchable, or would that be Touchable, status.

"Catholicsh got there firsht. Firsht is besht."

"Can I make you something to eat now?"

"I'm not hungry, dear." She flicks the remote, stopping to watch a fellow in a tinfoil spacesuit reprimand some bickering puppets, a show Desi would have loved.

The conversation unspools as it does every time. "Mum, you need to eat something. Do you want a soft-boiled egg? Did you have supper last night?"

A long pause. The puppets chatter.

"I don't remember."

"All the more reason."

"Ish that my phone ringing?"

"There's no phone ringing. That's Mrs. Penniman's vacuum."

"Gerard promised to call me."

"Well, sit tight. That wasn't him."

I turn on the frizzling fluorescent light in her tornado-struck kitchen, remembering how Desi would have followed me in, pointing to an empty can of soup on the counter to announce in an excited stage whisper, "You believe in this! You did a spot for it last week!"

"A spot! Listen to you!"

But he's not here, his absence a fistful of cotton in my throat.

"Is this green bread all you have?" I call to my mother.

"There'sh no shuch thing, Mag Ma—"

"Mum, I *told* you to make a list of the things you needed and I'd pick them up for you. You can't, oh! Well, that's nice. And your dustpan is in the freezer because...?"

It's a very long moment before she works up an answer.

"Gerard told me not to plan ahead. He shaid the Father would provide, but only if I gave no thought for myshelf."

"I see. So, does the Father deliver groceries now?"

"I am never alone here, you know," she croons, her mind having made one of its spectacular grand jetés to parts unknown. "They're all here with me." Her weak voice lilts, taking on a Pat O'Brien brogue; she sounds just like Grandma Fionnuala, only more so. "Fairiesh," she adds by way of clarification. "Yesh. Oh yesh."

Behind the bedroom door, Winky pukes melodramatically.

"Well, isn't this charming. That damned dog—"

"You let him be! Don't go in there! He's jusht clearing his tummy-tum. Mag Mary, don't go in there!"

The familiar high water of jealousy sloshes over its banks, the wave cresting and smacking me hard. My mother's twittering little heart, given freely in her liberated old age to dogs and nuns and fairies and a son who barely has time to give her the occasional uplifting lecture, but never, *never* to the waste of space she raised as her daughter. But Gerard has ordered me to let all that go, to forgive everything, over and over; otherwise, the Father will turn his regal back on me and I'll be without hope. Again. Sigh.

"Mum! Someone has to clean it up! No wonder it stinks to high heaven in here."

I shove open the door to her dark, fusty bedroom. Winky is quivering on his haunches next to her unmade bed, dry-heaving over a pungent stew of vomit.

"Is Dizzy with you?" she calls from the couch, having inserted her teeth at last.

"Yes, he is, Mother. He's invisible, but I'm sure you can see him fine!" I prod Winky hard with my foot, snarling, "Your ass is out of here, Bub," as I slide open the screeching balcony doors and land a solid kick on his hind end. He skids all the way to the outer railing like a puck into the net. After a stunned moment he rises with starchy dignity on his arthritic legs, looking martyred and infinitely woeful as I slam the door shut on him.

Back in the living room, I sink onto the couch. Mum sits tight-lipped, wrestling a stubborn smile for control of her mouth.

"So it's fairies now, is it?" I ask in the same stage Oirish brogue she's adopted. I don't know what's turned her so ostentatiously Irish in her old age, unless it's the hours she spends listening to jigs and reels on Radio Erin, the tweeting of the pennywhistle causing her all manner of mournful upheaval.

"Yes. Oh, yes. It's as true as true can be, or my name isn't..." She stops, stumped.

"Sheleighleigh McClunahan," I offer sourly. "I don't suppose you've run this fairy theory by Gerard."

"Gerard doesn't have to know everything," she mumbles peevishly.

"You look like her," Desi once remarked out of the blue as we piled into the getaway car after an hour in her airless apartment. "You have the same face, and Father Gerry has a kind of mean one, but the same too."

"We all have big chins and weensy mouths," I conceded as he sat quietly studying me. "Is my face mean too, like Father Gerry's?"

"Sometimes. But not when you're talking. Only when you're just thinking."

I busy myself in the kitchen slapping strawberry jam on toast, thinking, The hell with cleaning this place up, I'm in no goddamn shape for heavy housework. Meanwhile she sits perfectly still and blessedly silent, her breath rasping in and out like a slow tide. I imagine the spirit inside her twisting hotly, excitedly this way and that, like an animal that's nearly gnawed its way out of a trap, that feels the holds loosening, the cool forest beckoning. Her dentures are out again, hooked over the side of a dirty cup; it's her way of telling me I can stuff whatever it is I'm going to try to get her to eat.

Her amazing extractable teeth were her most mesmerizing feature in Desi's eyes.

"How old is she?" he asked me once as I took his little hand in mine to cross the street in front of her building.

"She is five hundred years old, my lad."

His jaw dropped.

"She's eighty. Eighty years old."

He took this in, adjusted.

"How can she eat without teeth in?"

"I'd rather not think about it."

"How old are you?"

"Guess."

He pondered.

"Eighteen?"

"Good guess, Jess!"

"Thanks, Shmemanx."

Too bad he missed the golden years of her old age, back when she was making casseroles and crocheting slippers for the nuns at St. Bern's, helping out at the convent and in the church, always a net over her hair, a mop her constant companion. Being around the sisters, she'd seemed genuinely happy for the first time in her life. Sometimes she'd call me at seven in the morning, so upbeat and full of beans she'd even remembered to include *me* in her life, unless she'd dialled the number by accident.

"I'm working with the sisters this afternoon. I've got all the pews to polish with lemon oil, and the vestibule walls need a good, thorough scrubbing."

"Those gals sure latched on to a good thing when they found you."

"Yes, and isn't that typical of you to come out with a mean remark. Sister Claire is always telling me how much they appreciate my help. I like doing for them. It gets me out of the house, and the sisters are wonderful company."

"Can't they give you something easier to do? Next thing you know, they'll have you rotating the tires on the church van."

"I'm plenty fleet enough. You mind your own business. Sister Anne is two years older than I am and she scrubs floors! If you're so worried about us, why don't you step over and lend a hand? You've got enough free time to clean forty churches."

But round and round the days had gone, dwindling her by increments. As I pounded the hamster wheel of my career and eased into my grim Untouchables years, I never gave a thought to what she did with all those identical days running one into the other, days of porridge and tea and toast, days of gazing out her window at the silent trees behind the building across the street as they announced the seasonal coming attractions.

Now she can sit for hours once she's run out of things to tell Winky, her once manic hands folded in her lap, doing nothing but shrinking. Even Desi's legendary patience used to fray after too much time spent in death's fetid waiting room, the poor kid pressing up against my side to smoosh "Cummee gooooo, *pleeeeeeze*?" wetly into my upper arm. Except now I'm thinking that the second we left was when the action began in earnest, the fierce tug-of-war as the fairies grabbed her hands and feet, resuming their ongoing attempts to haul her bathrobed and diapered self through the shimmering veil.

Maybe *that's* the setup, Gerard and his stern afterlife logistics be damned. Maybe this whole world is nothing but a baroquely overdecorated doorway through which we're squeezed out into the Land of the Fairies, kicking and screaming just as hard as we did when we were squeezed in, like my twin and me, rabid as Curly and Moe, squashed together in the birth door, scrabbling like wildcats to be the first one through.

I have no idea who this little old woman circling the drain in front of me is. She's never told me anything about herself. The paltry gleanings of her and Dad's courtship that I possess came from Dad's beery mutterings and snide tidbits Fionnuala sometimes let drop, a story basted raggedly together from veiled references to a long-ago August night when her errant daughter Moira had come home from the Ex shockingly past her curfew, followed by a series of hushed, besotted telephone conversations in the hall with a boy she'd assured her family was Catholic. Said boy had only had to go to Mass once with the family, nervously jumping up when they stood, dropping to the hard kneeler a second after they did, making the sign of the cross backward. He'd even taken Communion, grimacing, I imagined, as he loped back to his seat, surreptitiously trying to scrape the sticky wafer from the roof of his mouth with his little finger.

Not many Sundays after that, young Moira had keeled over in a dead faint at the Communion rail, as comely as Loretta Young in some old black-and-white tearjerker.

They'd tied the knot behind everybody's backs, running off starry-eyed to Niagara Falls. They'd come home in an entirely different, high-noon frame of mind, Moira weeping non-stop, overcome, I can only presume, with the marital equivalent of buyer's remorse.

The magic lantern had plumb sputtered out. Mister and Missus Everlasting Regret took up grudging residence in a tiny, upstairs flat on Euclid Avenue. Dad never showed his face at Mass again, and Fionnuala, horror-struck at her daughter's lapse from grace and the Faith, began campaigning vigorously for an annulment on the grounds that Moira had been hypnotized and kidnapped against her will. The campaign died on the vine when it became obvious from the growing gap between button and buttonhole of Moira's skirts that the marriage had been hasty for the very best of reasons.

So Moira, glutted with guilt over her free fall into sin, turned into Mum. She began setting out for Mass every single morning, determined to worm her way back into God's good books. She refused to share even a sip of her husband's beer. She steered clear of all movies not featuring priests or nuns. She buttoned her blouses up to her chin and cut her long Katharine Hepburn hair into a severe Joan of Arc bob, the two kiss curls against each cheek her only concession to softness and style.

But she was stuck with us soon enough, if it was penance she wanted so badly, stuck with chasing us around their drab *Honeymooners* flat as we scuttled like greased weasels into the shadows. I saw a picture of her once, standing on the sidewalk in front of their house, wearing a cocked and feathered Robin Hood hat, gamely displaying her little twins for the camera. Baby Gerard slept bundled up against her neck. I was squeezed under her other arm like an unwieldy clutch purse, or a football, threatening at any moment to splurt out and away.

And now here I am, patting her birdy claw on my way to the door and blessed escape, my hand resting as briefly as possible atop hers, a lightning sketch of the heart of the universe, love transmitted from generation to generation, the young seeing the old out as we square our shoulders and step to the head of the line. Or something like that; I'm probably the last person you want to ask about mush-headed sentiment and warm family feeling.

"Put the Mash back on," she orders, her voice sluggish, eyelids drooping. "You go along. I'm jusht having a little nap, dear."

"I'll call to remind you to take your pills. If you get confused, just go over and ask Mrs. Penniman to..." Her eyes fly open. She clutches hunks of her yellow robe in frantic white fists.

"Winky! You've left him outshide all this time! Let my baby back in, Mag Mary! He'll roasht in that shun!"

On the way home, the cabbie has the radio on, and as usual, my ear is cocked to hear if one of my now infrequent commercials will play. On long drives in the Trans Am, Desi used to catch every one, listening closely to the entire message, putting fine bottled waters and the friendly service at Ed Dodd's Chev-Olds on his approved product list before telling me solemnly, "Everybody

146

in the whole world can hear you if they turn this channel on. But they don't know what you look like. Only I do." This would be followed shortly by, "Do we *have* to listen to this kind of music?"

"Don't you like jazz, Chazz?"

He'd frown in perplexed concentration before intoning flatly, "Big Spider Back."

"What?"

"He just said the guy playing music before was called Big Spider Back."

"Don't tell me you don't like Big Spider Back!"

"I guess they call him that because he's black and also has very long legs and arms."

"You've hit the nail on the head, Ted."

"You've bit the snail on the bed, Dead."

I'm back home by one o'clock and crawl into bed for the nap I've been aching for all morning. But I can only clamp my eyes shut. Sleep won't take. I get up and pour a drink, a triple, the words "big spider back" circling my head on an endless loop. I feel mean as a black widow, the hourglass on my belly very nearly emptied.

My constant companion shimmers airily to life in his chair.

"*I know what you think. You think it doesn't matter a good goddamn if she dies alone in that wretched apartment because, according to you, that's all that's in store for anybody anywhere anyhow. Lights out, then obliteration. So why not hate her with everything I've got? There's no reckoning, no comeuppance heading my way. Least not according to you.*"

But just in case there *is* comeuppance, I think I pulled it off okay over there. I didn't lose it for once, didn't yell at her. Will I get any points for that? Will it suffice as the first of the seventy times seventy million forgivenesses required of me?

Sometimes I wonder if Gerard doesn't hate her as much as I do. Not for abandoning him, but for *never* abandoning him. For dogging him every step of the way into the future she'd so desperately mapped out for him. What in the world would he have become without her constantly on his back? A kind and simple man, a lanky Happy Humphrey? Loving husband to, let's go hog-wild and say, Rick? Rainbow bunting around their front door? The mind boggles.

I remember him at eighteen, stumping up the stairs from the basement, graceful as Frankenstein, his face properly splotched now with its own volcanic islands and archipelagos of acne. All spruced up in a navy blue collegiate sweater (store-bought, reindeer-free) and maroon tie, his brown corduroys swishing and sighing. He'd spent his entire senior year, apart from school and daily Mass, underground, in a curtained-off corner of the basement, a monkish cell where the succubi surely came for him at night, hovering over his narrow bed like gulls at a ship's rail. He'd spent all summer down there too, putting in hard, rheumy-eyed time on his back, squinting at the flea-speck print in twenty-pound volumes slotted into the deep concavity beneath his ribs, his reading lamp arching its swan neck from his milk crate bedside table, solicitous and gently encouraging, while the washing machine chugged away in the background.

Meanwhile, up above where summer birds twittered and breezes blew, I sat at the kitchen table eating Apple Jacks and swaying to the sunny sound of the Lovin' Spoonful dinning from my transistor. And while I was buttoning up my white Dominion Stores cashier uniform, sweetie boy was down in the dark, spit-shining his Latin and getting the jump on first-year Metaphysics, Philosophical Anthropology, and Scholasticism. *Fides quaerens intellectum*, don't you know.

Standing at the top of the stairs, all spiffed up, he must have been feeling damned smug, considering how the entire student body of our high school had vented its considerable spleen upon him for four long years. Every day he'd trudged to school and home again, head down, hands fumbling at the beads in his pants pocket, exciting unfathomable umbrage in his peers: Hey, Pizza Face! Hey, Jizz-breath! Hey, Faggot! Legs suddenly thrust into aisles had regularly sent him, books, and glasses flying. Salacious slurs to his character had been scratched for all time into the wood of our desks, his name taken enthusiastically in vain every day, every hour, every minute by someone, somewhere.

But with Mum's unflagging help and inspiration, he'd offered it all up, devising stringent, penitential fasting programs to bleaken his life even further: Tuesdays, Thursdays, and Sundays, refusing everything but water and the stale heels of bread she'd saved for him in a special Tupperware container. And every Saturday morning she'd been on the job, spiriting him upstairs by distracting Dad, who was home with us for a two-month stretch and sitting unshaven and fogged-in at the kitchen table behind a smoke and *The Star* sports section. She'd pour him extra cups of coffee, butter unasked-for slices of toast, sometimes even *speak*, thus allowing Gerard to slip out the door unnoticed and unmolested, to lope like a giraffe for the bus to his weekly top-secret confab with the Diocesan vocational director.

And picture this: Prom night, me at the screaming peak of my New Yawk loud year, revered and feared, the lauded captain of the girl's field hockey team, now that my skin had bowed to my mighty will and cleared up enough to allow me to engage in sweaty activities in public. I had an actual prom *date*, and left the house on his arm, shoehorned into a giant pink Liberty Bell of a dress afroth in ruffles and bows, which upon my return featured discreet streaks of dried vomit trailing down the front following a copious beer-puke into the wet sand at Cherry Beach as the dawn of my childhood's end came up like thunder. My date long ditched, I pitched sideways out of bad boy Billy Barr's car onto our front lawn, from where I bludgeoned my way into the house, reeling from one wall of the hall to the other on the way to my bedroom. And whom should I meet coming in the opposite direction, a ghost ship passing in the night, but Holy Boy, smelling of fungal mattress and oily rags, on his upstanding way to seven o'clock Mass.

But back to him at the top of the stairs, a suitcase in each hand, tough as a tuber and ready to roll. Nametags sewn into all his clothes. Scholarship papers all in order. Mum, nearly as-phyxiated with emotion, whispering, "Tu es Petrus" into his greasy neck. The poor child had a crippling forty-minute journey ahead of him to his residence at St. Michael's College, where he'd be living in poverty and chastity with all the other boy- wonder ecclesiastical students given the nudge by God that year. And after all the years ahead of marching in lockstep with other tense, mirthless, cold-water-washed boys, swishing their skirts down long, bleak corridors, keeping strict custody of the eyes, agonizing over creeping concupiscence, scrupulously avoiding "special" friendships, the kind everyone knew could get you expelled... after all that, he'd emerge a Master of Divinity, and after seminary and Holy Orders an actual *priest*, privy to arcane knowledge and the jealously guarded secrets of Heaven. Imagine! My scrawny, pomegranate-faced brother a pillar of sanctity as he elevated the precious bread and wine, the incomprehensible Magic jolting into the elements like an electric charge from his gizzard hands.

And picture me watching both brother and mother surreptitiously from the living room couch, sour as piss, pretending to study the back cover of *Another Side of Bob Dylan*, holding up Bob's scowly face to stand in for my own. I was wondering what else might there be in those suitcases of his. A framed, autographed photo of St. Thomas Aquinas? A Saints and Holy Martyrs All-Star Team calendar? A spare pure heart, polished to a fare-thee-well, in case the original got smashed?

I noticed him looking quite coolly over Mum's head at the door, thinking, I'm sure, Mother, what have I to do with thee?

In half an hour I'd have to leave for work myself because *some* of us, ignored by our Heavenly Father, were still required to work for a living. Gerard hadn't had to get a summer job, of course. Pray without ceasing, oh adored and blessed son, Mum had urged him day and night. And rest without ceasing while you're at it, for your labours in the vineyard will soon require all of your strength, my precious one.

Vineyard, shminyard, was what I was thinking. And what a shame Dad wasn't there to see him off. *He'd* have had a few choice words for the occasion.

Mum stood with him waiting for his cab, which was taking for-fucking-ever. Of course he was too manly and self-sufficient to let her drive him; otherwise they could be playing this tender scene on the steps of his residence, a million miles from my prying eyes. Though, perhaps with luck, there'd be an unforeseen accident on the way: the cab blindsided at a busy intersection, Latin dictionaries and ironed underpants flying, carnage for days, God just as surprised as anybody!

Dad had only recently left again for four months in Oslo to do consulting for some branch of the fishing industry, instructing ice-block-headed Norwegians on fish efficiency. With just Mum and me occupying the main floor of the house, it'd been a rowdy summer of slammed doors and white-hot invective hissed into sodden pillows, till both of us learned to keep to our respective lairs, like rooming house tenants hiding out from the law. I'd kept my morale up with some blistering diary writing, all of it to be eventually turned into a major motion picture, when certain people were going to be fixed for *good*. Other than that, I'd done sweet fuck all but slouch on my hip behind the cash register at Dominion, punching in prices in a fever heat of irritation, while prissy housewives dared to push their overloaded carts into my aisle, burbling, "Are you open for business?" Their gap-toothed, piggy children, mashed into the child seats, kicked their pudgy legs and grabbed at the gum and chocolate bars next to the cash. My outraged soul never once stopped screaming, "*Don't you know who I am???*" as I tossed egg cartons willy-nilly over my shoulder, too fast for my brain-dead bag boy to catch.

Being loud had served me well. I had a dim sense that I may

have, once in a great while, veered across the border between entertaining and obnoxious, but being a loud person meant you didn't have to worry about that stuff. In my last year of high school, I'd even managed to attract a few friends, though from this distance they look more like parasitic groupies in search of a host. Nevertheless, I strode the halls like an Amazon in my plus-sized blazer, my gorgeous river of mahogany hair long enough to sit on, my heaving, celebrated prow of a bosom straining behind my gap-fronted blouse, announcing my arrival whole seconds before the rest of me got there.

I had left all my old fears in the dust, the future a wide-open grin. My big plan was to be a journalist, though I was unclear what that was exactly. My grades, while not sensational, were university-worthy enough, though increasingly I'd been having a hard time reading, my eyes seeming to stall whenever I tried to move them sideways. By the end of grade thirteen, I couldn't get past page six of anything without nodding off. But I'd done well enough to scrape my way into McGill, whose principal attraction wasn't academic excellence, but its location in Montreal, far, far away from Mum and her jiggedy knitting hands and withering, bone-hard silence.

So a week to the day after Gerard left, there was I, booked on the overnight train, a glowing picture in my head of arriving in Mo-ray-all fresh with the morning sun. I'd stride purposefully from the station, chin up, bust foremost, hair streaming, while cabbies honked friendly salutes and good-looking French boys spun on their boot heels for a second look. Strangers would hand me daffodils. I'd try on shoes, struggle with packages, get caught in revolving doors, and laugh till I puked.

Mum came to the door in her nightgown, her hair spooled around plastic rollers, which told me without the wastage of a single word that she'd never had any intention of accompanying me to the station. There was a half-finished sweater sleeve in her hand, a ball of fuchsia wool trailing all the way back to the chair she'd just left. She leaned in for a quick, awkward clinch, her first attempted hug in eighteen years. Her face suddenly so close, her head bumping mine, the sour gardenia smell of her face cream rubbing off on my shoulder, all threw me badly. I was holding a ratty, overflowing duffle bag in each hand and had a purse as big as a mailbag strapped crosswise over my front like an ammunition belt. I had to put the bags down to reciprocate, but before they hit the floor, the hug had been rescinded.

"Stay out of trouble," she said.

"Haven't I always? I'm not a complete moron."

"Call once you're settled at the Y."

"Yeah, yeah," I said, already waddling down the front steps lugging everything I owned, my cab honking. The door closed behind me. Hallefuckin'lujah!

I didn't sleep for a second on the train. Instead, I and the me reflected in the black window leaned our heads together like conspirators, watching the penlights of nocturnal Ontario flit by. When the sun finally came up to say bonjour in Montreal, I was all a'jitter, my palms sweaty, my hands aching, my stomach swarming with bees.

I had a map, courtesy of the student union. On paper, the Y was an easy stroll from Central Station, but I had to stop every twenty paces, put down my bags, and rest my arms. I had oozing blisters on both palms. No cabbies honked. No one smiled. Home was thousands of miles away, smudgy, all but erased. I was deliriously happy.

The student union had also provided me with a typed list of apartment and rooming houses, mostly in the McGill ghetto. I knew as soon as I entered its precincts that this was the place for me: it was Funky Town, swarming with gabbing, long-striding young people who all knew exactly where they were going and what they were about. Music, *our* music, poured from the open windows: The Doors, Paul Butterfield, the Stones, Dylan. Far-out boys bearded like Romantic poets and girls in headbands and buckskin sat on stairways and windowsills, rolling smokes from packages of Drum and shouting unbelievably hip epithets at one another. It was outtasight! There were so *many* of us, the young, the hip, the future most excellent rulers of the world!

I tramped two whole days before managing to snag a broom closet with a Murphy bed and rusted-out hot plate, to which I had to slog up four flights of dark stairs straight out of *Crime and Punishment*. The windows were painted shut. The landlady was tiny and round, with a name like Mrs. Babushka. There was a common room on the ground floor, where I could see bell-bottomed legs flung over the sides of raggedy, mismatched chairs. The TV was on, the pedestal ashtrays overflowing. The bathroom, half a mile down the hall from my room, had a hole in the ceiling big enough to crawl through. When I turned on the buzzing light, forty thousand cockroaches bumped heads and bolted.

I set my bags down in my room and stood in front of the

cankered mirror over the dresser with the warped drawers. I combed my exquisite hair over my face so that it fell two inches on either side of my nose. I hung my new Navy Surplus pea jacket and hip, homemade bells on the old coat rack in the corner. I couldn't wait for the chill weather so I could step out in my attractive new fall ensembles.

My last few free days I spent sleeping and cooking Kraft Dinner and entire boxes of Minute tapioca in the one dented pan provided by the landlady. There wasn't a soul on earth to tell me what to do. I blew off orientation; all those notices stuck up everywhere for Frosh Week and beer blasts and dances all seemed so Mr. Novak-cornball to me. I was here to be serious, not to lark around like Shelley Fabares on a tear. My new course books lay stacked on the floor beside the coat rack. On the shelf over the hot plate was the book I'd brought as a wry memento of my childhood: my sad little copy of *On the Beach*.

I got around to calling home a whole week after I was supposed to. Mum didn't seem to have noticed the delay.

"Everything's fine," I told her. "I've found a great place to live. Classes start day after tomorrow. Yes, yes, there are churches on every block. Masses every hour on the hour."

"I haven't heard word one from Gerard," she cut in, unaccountably loquacious, her breath catching. I could hear the clickety-click of needles like a tiny train down the wire, but still, I was taken aback. I'd assumed the two of them would have had a hotline buzzing night and day, with God listening in on the extension. How dare Gerard try to out-rebel me!

"Maybe they don't allow them to use phones. No phones, no pools, no pets. Maybe they have to grow their own food, and do the plowing with mules." I allowed a space for laughter and applause, then rolled on: "This morning I caught two cockroaches strolling across my pillow holding hands. When I turn on the light in the bathroom at night, there's an army of them all lined up in formation on the floor, doing parade drill."

She barely let this sink in before blurting, "I wonder if I should call St. Michael's and ask if everything's all right."

Bowled over by this long-winded speech, I told her, chortling, that I was only just now leaving for Mass and would certainly put in a good word.

When classes began, I made it a point to sit way in the back of the steeply raked lecture halls like a hawk in a tree, watching the profs scamper like mice at the bottom of a ravine. No wonder I didn't spot Liam right away; all I could see were the backs of heads descending like shrubs down the slope.

It didn't take me long to cotton to the pleasant truth that they didn't give out detentions for sleeping in class at university. You didn't even have to turn up. Nobody noticed. Nobody cared. I lost the thread sometime in the first three days, my size-sixteen bulk squeezed into a size-zero desk, daydreaming about my psych prof, a draft dodger with a groovy beard. I understood nothing. I thought of going out for field hockey or track, but suddenly I was too tired, drained and fagged out to the point of narcolepsy. From the raging fireball of a year ago, I was atrophying into the two-thousand-year-old liberal arts student who required eighteen hours of sleep out of every twenty-four.

Besides, I hated everybody. All the kids around me were so hopped up all the time. What for? And where did they come up with all those questions in class? I didn't have a single word to say, loud or otherwise, to a living soul. I was supposed to be reading *Walden* but instead was putting myself to sleep at night by rereading *On the Beach*. I knew the story already, it was easier.

And God, what a story! Though this time around, it didn't scare me so much as mystify me: a handful of people left in the entire world, hanging by their fingernails to the frayed hem of southern Australia, weeks left for the earth to live, corpses strewn everywhere, and still they were going to cocktail parties with nice couples from the neighbourhood.

That was what higher learning in a wicked world was beginning to feel like to me.

But then,

then

then

(Oh, mama!)

Liam loomed.

Right in the seat next to me in Literature of the American Romantic Movement. Liam Cushnahan, mop-headed and funkalicious, with a knockout Irish grin that split his face like a big, juicy melon. This grin was aimed in my direction. But unlike my high school idol, Liam could see.

I opened my mouth, ready to wow him with a New Yawk witticism. Nothing came out. I was struck dumb, but at the same time, astonishingly, I felt *at ease*! He was looking right at me, *at my face*! I could tell he liked me, and not for the usual reasons. He just did!

We were boon companions in no time; the boy was right up my alley. We passed notes, cut up, whispered jokes, criticized everyone harshly, and laughed till our sleeves were drenched with snot.

Except,

he already had a girlfriend.

He told me about Dorothée in a note slipped to me in class.

We met this summer in Simpson's basement

We both were buying socks.

Her hair in braids,

Her granny shades,

She was a super fox!

Dorothée Samson. When he told me everyone called her Sam for short, I thought she must be a barrel of yucks, a real party-hearty gal. Instead, she talked slower than a bug slogging through molasses on crutches. But she had that kootchy-koo accent, and those huge brown eyes the colour of—let's be frank —cockroaches. And honey hair. And jeans that fit like the skin on a plum.

"She Belongs to Me" was their song, he told me. She loved Dylan, and it described her perfectly, he told me. She's got everything she needs, she's an artist, she blah blah blah, he told me. With that Eeeeee-gyptian ring that sparkled before, during, and after she spoke because once she got rolling on Camus or Schopenhauer, illustrating point after point like anybody cared, whole teeming galaxies came into being, lived, and died.

I was of the opinion that he never understood a thing she said. But he was so eager to learn! I could have retched.

At first, when we all went out together, I knew she didn't

think I was any competition. But gradually I noticed her keeping a buzzard-eye on him, and it dawned on me she was jealous of the way we were always laughing together. She never got any of his jokes. At the pub we went to when it was just the three of us, she'd stare morosely into her beer, drawing curlicues in the wet rings on the table while we farted around and made merry far into the night.

All the same, I couldn't stand the way he acted around her. Taking her arm, pulling out her chair like Manners the Butler. He always seemed so smitten with her when she was around, but when she wasn't, he forgot all about her! I wanted her to bugger off, find some wizened, tweedy professor with elbow patches and a pipe to wax philosophique with.

And what in God's name did someone like her see in Liam? What would she have said if she'd seen us getting thrown out of that bar, one of the fun ones we went to when she wasn't around, thrown out at two-thirty in the morning because we were laughing so hard we'd tipped our table over and I'd wet my pants, sitting on the floor howling while Liam tried to haul me up by the shoulders? And that night with Marc and all the rest of them, when, the more lagered up we got, the funnier the word "lumpenproletariat" became. Walking all the way back from the Main to the ghetto with our arms around each other, the six-foot purple scarves I'd spent a month clumsily knitting for us — Mum would have been so proud! — looped around each other's necks, both of us with the bends from hilarity.

When Liam and I were together, I almost felt perfectly all right.

But I never had him to myself for long. Mostly, if I wanted to be with him at night, I had to follow him as he followed

Sam to that wretched pub on the Main, four tables joined together, all of us squashed in around a hell-scape of beer bottles and Armageddon ashtrays and frighteningly articulate chat enthusiasts who had read every book ever written, spoke all languages and knew all things, and who loved nothing more than to sit around shouting political jargon at one another and declaring points moot till you wanted to jab lit smokes into your own eyes.

I sat there trying to look jaded and aloof, pretending I knew what "moot" meant. I despised them all, the bushy-haired girls in ponchos knit from baling wire, the guys in identical proletarian lumberjack shirts and construction boots, masquerading as loggers or miners on a spree in the big city. Everybody yickety-yacking about monopoly capitalism, Browderism, the cybernetic revolution, Frantz Fanon, the FLQ and the SDS, when they weren't hailing the glorious National Liberation Fronts of places I'd never dreamed existed.

But more than all of them put together, I loathed Marc, the captain of this ship of fools, with his brain-numbing blather about taking up the task, promoting the slogan, forging strong links, hoisting high the glorious red banner. Marc, with his Ulysses S. Grant beard and breath that could split the atom. We all knew never to sit downwind of speechifying Marc: blah blah *Little Red Book*, blah blah dialectical materialism, blah blah Great Proletarian Cultural Revolution exclamation mark, exclamation mark, all of us taking great care to breathe in and out exactly when he did.

I wanted to club them all to death with extreme prejudice.

"Super freaks" was what Liam called them. And "cool heads."

The way he sat there nodding all night, chain-smoking Gitanes, his Shirley Temple hair artfully dishevelled, mumbling, "Far out, man" and checking to make sure Sam heard him. I wanted to make a citizen's arrest, have him hauled up on simpering charges. I knew he was faking his face off. He could parade around in that dumb army surplus coat all he wanted, with VIVE LA RÉVOLUTION written in black Magic Marker on the back, the words marching around the circumference of a huge peace sign. My poor, sweet baby; did he really think that was going to impress those grim stalwarts?

As for me, I didn't dare open my mouth, not even for a sycophantic "Right on!" I knew instinctively that my old New Yawky ways would cut no ice with this crowd. I was thousands of miles out of my depth, so far out at sea I was a speck in their spyglasses.

I lived for the nights Sam wanted to go home alone. I thrilled to the sight of her diminishing in an easterly direction, heading back to the Badlands east of the Main where she dwelt with her own kind, leaving Liam and me free to walk home together inside a snowflake paperweight, all purple sky and swirl, and then, that sudden lurch sideways that stopped my heart, a whoosh of snow in my face as Liam swooped me off my feet and leapt with me like Nureyev over the snowbanks. Leaping! With a fat sack of potatoes like me!

When he told me he and Sam the Sham had decided to go to Europe for the coming summer, I felt like I'd been cold-cocked. He was rabid about it, couldn't wait to get to Denmark and Sweden because the people over there weren't into head games and mindfucks like they were here. They were all into their own groovy bags, and the vibe was outtasight. They'd never had a war there on account of they weren't hate-mongers and all hung up over sex. You could make it with anyone you wanted to over there, he said. Nobody cared.

But I knew he'd be making it with Sam Enchanted Evening, all summer long, under Delft-blue skies, in castles and Alpine meadows, under the Eiffel Tower, hanging off the sides of fjords. And I cared plenty.

Then he told me he wanted to marry her! The guy who wasn't into head games! The king of free love was as moony as Bobby Vee, droning on about their ideal wedding: on a beach, naked, Sam already swollen with his sweet love child. The minister (Ginsburg, if available) would be in golden robes. Dylan would play at the reception.

When he asked me if I'd come, we were standing at the corner of Milton and Durocher while he rolled a joint right there in the street over his bended knee, wind shrieking around us, his fingers stiff and clumsy.

I feigned lightheartedness by channelling old Fionnuala.

"Well, put some clothes on ye and your slatternly jade, and try to look dascent at least."

He passed the joint to me, saying, "This is how it should be all the time, beautiful people sharing love, just like the flowers do." Then he planted a smashy kiss smack on my blue lips.

For one precious second I saw myself as the little wifey in the bib overalls with the love child on my hip, toiling on the hippie sensimilla farm in Copenhagen that surely lay in our future.

But then he pulled back, ruffled my hair, and slung his knapsack over his shoulder.

"Gettin' on me nerves, ye are, Paddy," I spat at him. "Ye'd best be scurryin' along."

He gave me a darlin' grin and a salute.

"Beat it," I snarled, but he was already sauntering up Durocher, zingy on his feet, a sunny song in his heart and nary a thought to keep his two ears apart.

But, oh. Clueless and close-mouthed, I was fresh meat to old Marxist Marc. He had that furtive way about him, the sad-sack sidle of the pedophile who always knows exactly which woebegone kid in the schoolyard to go for. I wasn't halfway through my first term before he'd started trying to recruit me, boring in with his Rasputin eyes. But no matter how many times he explained what dialectical materialism was, I couldn't retain it for more than seven seconds.

I didn't understand him, but he scared the pants off me just the same. Because what if he was right?

"All our questions about the origins of life will be answered one day," he claimed grandly. "Once man knows everything there is to know, no one will ever have to fear anything again. We'll all eventually die, like the animals we are, and our petty, individual stories will end then and there, in nothingness." This caused a great, steaming geyser of "No!" to shoot through my brain. "But we can still know that one day, mankind will have all the answers, and all its troubles will come to an end."

Sez you, I thought to myself, hanging tough, refusing to even open the tattered, coffee-ringed copy of Feuerbach's *Thoughts on Death and Immortality* he forced on me, those being the two dead-last things I wanted to talk, much less think, about. I was only there in that pub because Liam was. My stomach was always killing me. I knocked back three or four beers nightly, but they never seemed to take.

Some nights Marc turned up with his knapsack full of copies of *China Reconstructs*, an obligatory purchase at fifty cents a pop, and hilariously unreadable. If I couldn't stay awake for *Walden*, how could I survive "Chairman Mao's concern for our millet crop warms ten thousand households?" But the pictures! All those stagy scenes of eager-beaver militants in laundered and pressed worker or peasant outfits, gathered around some glowing, good-looking comrade who had all the answers and then some, waving the *Little Red Book* in the air, setting hearts aflame. All those fierce folks shaking their revolutionary fists at everything, including, and perhaps especially, God.

All religion was going to be abolished in the future, Marc assured us. Class-conscious workers like the bold, revolutionary Chinese had no time for superstition and backward thinking, all of which would soon be swept into the dustbin of history. Man would build his own paradise on earth. All human instincts would be under perfect control. The working class would create a race of Supermen who would run the world as if it belonged to them and not to some imaginary old bugger in the sky.

When I first heard all this bold talk of no God, half of me felt a tremendous weight being lifted from my heart. But it gave the other half of me the oddest sensation to just, well, *erase* him. I was so used to the lack of religious concern I'd begun feigning as a child, coupled with my raging jealousy of Mum's and Gerard's allegiance to a Church I hated because it was so crazy about them, that I was startled to realize that all this time I'd been living unconsciously in the dead centre of a universe that I still believed was breathed out of God's nostrils, as if he were The Wind in old storybook drawings: no body, just a giant head with long white hair like some crazed drifter. And huge puffy cheeks, eternally blowing out cloudy gusts of Universe.

And when I tried to imagine the universe all on its own without him, when I tried inking him out of the picture for longer than it took to forget what dialectical materialism was, my chest filled with evil fumes. Just Universe. No God. Nobody looking at me. Nobody there at all! Jesus, Mary, and Joseph, all whisked into the dustbin of history!

Well, I told myself, at least now you can do whatever the hell you want.

Sure I could. So why did I feel like a kid lost in a department store, locked in by accident overnight? All that terrific, wildly coveted stuff, free for the grabbing. The toy department! The bike shop! The candy counter! But all alone, in the dark, it wasn't any fun any more. Worse. It was horrifying.

Yes, but at least you won't have to worry about hell, I told myself. Except that hell, cancelled out by Meaningless Void, turned out to be no kind of exchange at all.

Going to that pub night after night after night left me no time for studying. Afternoons, if I wasn't in class, I was curled up on my Murphy bed sawing logs. The idea of sitting alone in my room, especially at night, trying to read, made my stomach roll and pitch. I didn't even want to be in the library unless Liam was there.

And as bored and cranky as I felt propping up my chin on two hands in the pub while the talk roared around me, when the end came and everyone began scraping back their chairs and shouldering into their coats, my knees would buckle in panic.

Walking home beside Liam comforted me, kept the big Fear away, at least until we'd reached the door of my building. Then the night started for real.

I thought I could handle this terrifying thing that had got hold of me, thought I could bounce back from it the way I'd bounced back, more or less, from my *On the Beach* fright when I was ten. But somehow, my bouncing mechanism had gotten jammed. The rehypnotizing watch swung stupidly, uselessly before my eyes. The daze of distraction would not come, and the abyss yawned lazily inches from my feet, flush with all the time and space in the world.

Paralyzing Terror waited for me to wake in the morning, having sat patiently on the edge of my bed since long before dawn, nursing a metaphorical cup of coffee. The second my eyes opened, it pounced. It hung about me all day, a wolf snarling over a kill, gnawing on my neck, its breath reeking of entrails. "*Nothing lasts,*" it wheezed in my ear. "*Nothing. Nothing. The more beautiful things appear, the more pointless they are. Every second you live brings you closer to Nothing at All, and not just nothing at all, but infinite nothing at all, oh yes, because nothing is the one thing that does last and will last forever and ever with you in the middle of it except of course it's not really you and it's not really in the middle of anything, ha ha, and as for infinity, just the concept of it's enough to short out your entire brain, so even if you're alive forever, even if it's in heaven, the idea of nothing ending ever is so petrifying that my suggestion to you, sweetheart"* —the voice wheedled in summation—*"is to cut the whole mess short this afternoon. At least you won't have to think about it any more. Please. You're just a couple of blocks from the Metro. That renowned third rail will fry you so quick, you'll never feel the smash of the train. Do yourself a favour, honey bun. Act now, and spare yourself decades of senseless turmoil and grief."*

"*I can't,*" I whispered back brokenly.

"*Why the hell not? It all comes out the same in the end.*"

"*Because—*"

"*Because what, cretin? Use your head. Finish it now. Things will never be any better than this. They'll just get worse. Life is a bad joke. End it now!*"

"*I can't because—*"

"*Because?*"

"*Because when I look into my eyes in the bathroom mirror, I can't live without me.*"

"*That's your answer?!?*"

"*I and me look at each other in that busted-up bathroom mirror, and the two of us share this fantastic, unbelievable secret. Except, except that me won't tell I what it is.*"

"*Jesus H. Christ. You're even more of a moron than I thought you were.*"

. . .

Meanwhile, the word from home had become increasingly bizarre. Mum kept asking me if I'd heard from Gerard, which was so unlikely, I was beginning to think some real rascality was afoot. How could she possibly have lost track of him so soon?

Meanwhile also, class participation and tests continued to be worth fifteen percent of final grades. I had to get out of bed. I had to get my ass to class.

So out I'd set, stopping at the dep for three or four Mae Wests and a takeout coffee, the Fear riding my shoulder like an excited kid at a parade. I scanned the tops of buildings for jumpers, monitored the sidewalk for fresh chalk outlines or the just-hosed-down stain some recent jumper had made when his head hit and burst like a cantaloupe. I could think of nothing else. The universe was pointless, and even if I was too frightened to check out early, others weren't.

I also craned my neck every few minutes, watching for the huge, soundless bloom of a mushroom cloud below Sherbrooke Street. Someone was going to push that button, sooner rather than later: a photo-flash; millions dead, no time even for God to intervene.

Take that, miracle of life!

The entire creation lay in ruins. I tore everybody I saw, every body, into charred shreds of meat that I hung from trees like bloody rags, like obscene clumps of tinsel, imagining how everybody I passed would look after a plane crash. My mind never stopped churning up fresh questions: What will *I* look like after jumping in front of a subway train? Answer: Ground round smeared on the track. What happened in fires, what happened in explosions? Answer: Arms, legs, heads, all helter-skelter, black skin marshmallow-crisp. How about Hiroshima? Easy: Little kids with schoolbags, running in a screaming wind tunnel, suddenly vaporized into their own negatives.

The grinning gargoyle of a TV in our common room was on all the time. The War was always playing. I couldn't not look at it. When I went upstairs to my room, I took all the images with me, the blackened faces of boys my age, their heads tied with bandanas, flooming into frame from behind elephant grass, from behind galloping streaks of fire. All those choppers rearing up like spooked horses, or hovering over treetops, the earth smoking beneath them. Or falling, spinning like ducks felled by a clean shot to the heart. Boys running bent over, the grass whistled to its knees by the rotor blades. Dead boys hanging backward over barbed wire, faces snipped from the bone and flapping. Boys trudging, filthy, spooked, like addled old men.

Surely they were thinking the exact thing I was: You'll have to kiss it all goodbye eventually, so why not get the jump on it now? It's the only plan with legs, universally applicable.

And yet, astoundingly, nobody else seemed to be bothered!

I knew everyone *said* they were, all the indignant kids sprawled around the common room, smoking and shouting hip abuse at Cronkite and LBJ, but the minute they went outside, everything was all right again. I saw my fellow students striding through the snow, all abustle with clear, prosperous thoughts, nothing but wide, straight roads ahead for them. Everyone seemed so juiced up about ideas, debate, argument, about writing and thinking, about carving swaths of territory for their brilliant future selves. Weren't they students in a world-class, vibrant, exotic city full of Earnest English and

Frolicsome French, jam-packed with theatre, music, poetry readings, rallies, forums for hot debate, and celebrated speakers pounding podiums?

Meanwhile, Gerard remained incommunicado. I could hear Mum down the phone line, her knitting fallen to the floor, wringing her hands to bare cartilage. I told her she should send Grandma Fionnuala and Uncle Dermott over there, seeing as they were paying for a fat chunk of his rarefied education. Have them frog-march him to the telephone, shouting, Call your mother, Holy Boy! Or burn in hell!

"I should have known that's all I could've expected from you," she snapped before hanging up on me.

Well, what did she expect?

By December, the only class I hadn't dropped was Literature of the American Romantic Movement. And I wasn't doing the reading for that one either, except for *Moby-Dick*, which we weren't even supposed to start till next term. But I'd leafed through it one night, trembling before the heft and girth of it, and had stumbled across these words: *There is a wisdom that is woe, and a woe that is madness.*

I knew instantly that Melville knew my ravaged, secret heart.

My woe that was madness was the sickening understanding that, without some kind of God in the sky, everything was absurd. Absurd surd surd, absurd is the word: all the books used it, all the current thinkers tossed it around, sprinkling it on everything like pixie dust. Everyone agreed that everything was absurd, but no one seemed to mind. The word conjured up clowns and circuses, chuckles and silliness. Certainly nothing to get your bowels in a vise over.

And certainly nothing to engender a woe teetering on madness.

In desperation, and feeling stupider than shit, I'd begun running tests by the hypothetical God I'd been brought up with, just in case he was there. Such as: If you exist, make three red cars pass in a row.

Sometimes they did, sometimes they didn't.

If they did, I still didn't believe it, even though I'd sworn that this time I positively would, that this would be the decisive test. Instead I said, all right, if I was right about taking the red cars as a positive sign, please make three yellow cars pass in a row, as a confirmation that I was right about the red cars. That'd cinch it because there weren't many yellow cars around, and *never* three in a row.

Once I saw two school buses right after I'd asked for yellow cars, and I inquired of the sky, Is that your way of telling me two school buses equal three yellow cars?

But you could ask all you wanted. It was impossible to tell a no from a no-reply.

I didn't want to go home for Christmas, but I wanted even less to stay in Montreal alone over the holidays. The idea of "home" had become unreal, a dim candle flickering in a tiny window somewhere in a general westerly direction. I'd scrabbled through my one exam, blowing smoke right and left; I'd never gotten beyond page seventeen of *Walden* and had crammed the

Coles Notes for *Uncle Tom's Cabin* like a death-row last meal the night before.

Liam and I said goodbye at the bus station; he was off to his parents and sister in the West Island, where he hadn't shown his face since the term began. He was still trying to josh me out of a fight we'd had earlier in the day.

I'd been sitting on his bed in a snaggle of tie-dyed sheets unwashed since September, watching him pack. He had Dylan on and that damned song came up, *their* song, "She's got everything she needs," etc. I ordered him to stop singing along.

"You sound like scrap metal rattling down a drainpipe. Stop it! I'm the only one who should sing." But he kept right on, so I shrieked even louder to drown him out till the guy in the next room started banging on the wall.

"*She's a hypnotist collector,*" I sang with gusto. "*You are the walking tan-teek!*"

Liam broke right in half, his gut completely busted.

"It's not the walking tanteek, you dolt! It's 'You are a walking *an*-tique.'"

"The hell it is! What do you know?" I picked up the needle and dropped it a millimetre back. "Listen for yourself, fuckbrain! Hear that? It's plain as day! You. Are. The. Walking. TanTEEK!"

"Maggers! There's no such thing as a tanteek!" He was helpless, weeping, literally slapping his knees.

"No, *you're* the one who's wrong! It makes perfect sense. She's a hypnotist collector, and he's one of the hypnotists she collects. The Walking Tanteek is his stage name."

"*What?!*"

"What do you mean, what? The Walking Tanteek is a

hypnotist who follows her around like a zombie, hypnotizing her and messing her up because she thinks she knows everything, like she's so foxy and cool, all that painting the daytime black shit, and her stupid rings…what the fuck is so funny? Stop laughing at me! I can't hear you, I'm not listening! Shut up!"

Once he'd gone, I'd set about Christmas-izing myself for my own journey home. Thinking about the old fireside rituals, cards from the neighbours and myriad Moriartys lined up on the mantle. Dad's annual stencil work on the front window of two martini glasses leaning tipsily in toward each other over a prickly nest of holly berries, though he might not have gotten back from overseas in time to do it. And the tree; surely there'd be a tree this year, even though Mum would have to see to it all by her lonesome. But she'd do it. She'd put out the Christmas candles. She'd loop a red velvet bow over the stair railing. She'd make shortbread. She'd do it all for sure, if Gerard were coming home.

And he surely would be, re-emerging from whatever dripping cave of prayer and abnegation he'd been crouching in for the past months. Hell, even Bishop Sheen brightened up for Jesus's birthday.

I called home to say I'd be there in two days. Mum sounded harried, telling me she was in the middle of baking; she was probably knitting Holy Boy a sanctified black priest dress as she spoke and couldn't wait to get off the phone so she could twist a damned cable or something.

"Your brother is doing fine, by the way, thank you for asking. He called last night. He's keeping a straight-A average, which is why he's been so hard to reach. Just like I said."

She'd never said anything of the kind, never mind so many words to me in succession, ever. She was clearly back to her tart little old self. I hung up with a sore stomach, thinking I'd be keeping my own academic performance close to my chest for the duration. There'd be plenty of time to buckle down and make good after the holidays.

But with Liam gone, there was nothing to hold the centre in place. Waking the next morning to a deathly quiet house, no shouting in the halls, no doors banging, no coffee smells wafting over the transom, everyone but Mrs. B. gone, I caved in like an abandoned mine.

My bed was drenched, my hair soaked. My nightgown stuck to my skin in transparent patches. My breath was so high in my chest I could only pant, like an overheated dog. I swung my stiff legs over the side of the bed, but my toes, like the man said, were too numb to step.

But they were going to have to because I had to escape the echoing charnel house around me, or die trying. I pulled on an assortment of clothes from the floor in short, arthritic bursts, buttoning them all wrong, leaving zippers where they stuck halfway, my topmost sweater on inside out. Then I barrelled down the stairs and outside into an arctic wind that slammed me back against the door.

Walking always made the Fear lift, like wet sheets in a heavy wind. It was the rhythm of it, the steady right, left, right, left; it was the same thing I suspected all that knitting did for Mum. My thoughts had to break a sweat to keep up with me, unlike that wolf-thing that followed me everywhere, grinning, its tongue lolling, exhaling clouds of foul vapour. I sped up, trying to see if I could force it to trot, or even lope to keep pace, but I never succeeded. I walked fast, and it walked too, easily, smirking at my efforts, its eyes pinwheeling, claws click-clacking on the icy sidewalk, tick-tocking like a crazily swinging watch.

I knew who it was now. It was my own, hideously creepy, personal Walking Tanteek.

I walked east as far as Papineau, then north to Henri Bourassa. It was thirty below and falling, but I had on four sweaters, a coat, and a six-foot scarf mummied around my face. Right, left, right, left. I was hot as blazes, walking fast, head down, and yes, yes, at last I'd gotten the Tanteek panting at my heels, wheedling at me to slow down.

At Henri-Bourassa I turned and walked all the way back. I turned west at Dorchester and soon spotted the sharp green spire of St. Patrick's Basilica, a spring shoot breaking through dead, grey stone. The Tanteek nipped my heels, marching me inside, ready for a rest at last.

I sat at the back, a pea under a towering heap of mattresses. People, mostly women in dark coats and mantillas, were lining up for Confession, slipping humbly into the confessional to emerge mere minutes later, a new bounce in their steps. They eased into the pew to recite a quick, lenient holiday penance, five Our Fathers, five Hail Marys, and a quick run-down of the grocery list for tomorrow night's party.

Religious obscurantism: that's what Marc would have sneered. But Marc wasn't there. Instead, it was the talking Tanteek in my head that had gotten its wind back and was hectoring me hard.

"Better go back to church now before it's too late," it slobbered in my ear, its whine arch and ironic. *"Look at Gerard: he doesn't*

have any trouble believing all this crap. Do you think he worries himself sick about death and annihilation? No, because he puts in the time, does the hard work, and in exchange, God shows him his sunny face, and everything in his garden is roses. So what's your excuse? What are you doing that's so important?"

"*I'm here now, aren't I?*" I answered sulkily, even as I thought, Yes! How sweet it would be to believe with a full heart! How safe I'd feel! Full of grace, beloved, approved in the highest circles. And there was really nothing to it. All I had to do was be different from now on! Same as I'd done the night I'd decided I was going be loud: I'd just lain in bed and ordered myself to change, right — on the count of ten — *now!*

Okay then! Done! From now on, I'd be nice to everybody! I'd pray! I'd do a good deed daily! I'd come to Mass every Sunday and then some! My heart would be light, my conscience clear! And then just watch God's eyes light up! He'd be so grateful, he'd shower me with attention, the good kind! He'd bend over backward to come up with some clear answers for a change! My terror would melt like mist. After all, good people didn't fear death; why should they? It was just a ticket home, one last ride on the night train!

And as a bonus, people would fall all over themselves loving me. I'd be swarmed with new friends! I'd be, why, I'd be normal!

A priest slapped past me down the aisle in the same kind of galumphy brown rubber boots kids wore, the unattached buckles jingling like spurs. He genuflected before the altar. He was young, blond, nice-looking. He surely had the answers to all my questions. I could ask him the best way to get started on my new, godly life.

"*Sure,*" mewled the Tanteek, hidden inside me now, incognito; this was the House of God after all. "*Go ahead, what's stopping you? He's going to get away if you don't hustle.*"

"*What should I say?*"

"*Fuck if I know. Tell him you're haunted by death and eternity. Tell him you've forgotten how to live. I promise, it'll make his day.*"

"*Never mind. He's probably French. He won't have time. He won't know anything. He'll start hammering on me and I'll have to get down on my knees and swear I believe in the talking snake and infallible popes and the punishment of eternal fire for eating meat on Friday. I'll have to say, a dead man coming back to life? Sure! No problem! I'll have to rejoice about all the Protestants and the entire population of China and my own father going to hell, for nothing! Don't you understand? I can't do it! Not for peace of mind, not for a free pass to heaven, not for anything. I just can't!*"

The familiar geyser of hopelessness shot from my gut out my eyes, my nose, my mouth. My legs, my arms, all the hope left in me blew outward in the horrible flash.

There was no, absolutely *no* way out!

Back on the sidewalk, I pulled my coat close, hiking my purple love scarf up over my mouth. The wind was coming straight at me now, so cold it burned. But I was afraid of the Metro, afraid of what the Tanteek might make me do. There was only walking left, walking against an ice-wind that pushed back hard all the way home.

By the time I got on the train the next day, the Tanteek was partying like a madman in my head, staggering around, yelling, puking, throwing chairs. Heaving TV sets out the window. I had to be insane, going home in this condition.

I pictured Mum, flour-dusted and perspiring daintily, looking up sharply from her rolling pin as I lumbered up the walk with my duffle bags full of dirty laundry. I pictured Gerard, oozing success, his skin all cleared up, holding forth over the Christmas turkey, arms spread wide in sublime righteousness, lecturing us all on the Doctrine of the Real Presence.

I'd decided my best hope was to go home in disguise.

I'd costumed myself as one of those fierce little gals from *China Reconstructs*, the kind of apple-cheeked, bob-haired lass who posed at the tops of craggy peaks, gun-metal eyes fixed on the horizon, a long rifle slung over her back. Nothing ever got that gal down, not trekking in cloth shoes through the mountains all day, not having to go to political night school every single blessed night of her life. Not having to maintain unceasing vigilance against hidebound capitalist roaders. Not having to denounce her own stooped and hobbled grandmother for Backward, Negative Thinking and Poor Party Spirit.

I'd folded my hair in fourths, making two fat, stumpy pigtails bound with several rubber bands apiece. I wore the cloth shoes and quilted jacket I'd picked up in Chinatown, even though they were barely warm enough for April. Proletarian craftsmanship at proletarian prices: already the stuffing was leaking out of the quilting, and the jacket didn't come near to closing. Not one of the billion-plus Chinese was as lavishly buxom as I was.

Lastly, I had an olive-drab men's cap, one I'd gotten for Liam that wouldn't fit over his tumultuous hair. I'd glued a blazing red star onto the front of it, cut from the stripe on one of my dishtowels.

The only thing missing was a gun.

Dragging my bags down the escalator at Central Station, I pretended I was marching ramrod straight into a remote mountain village flapping with red banners. In the midst of a gaggle of adoring poor and lower-middle peasants, I stopped to hold up the *Little Red Book*, warmly reminding them that militia women love battle array, not silks and satins! Always bear in mind the Party's basic line! Recognize counter-revolutionary currents, you people! Let us not deviate from the wise course charted by our beloved Chairman!

I'd called home once again the day before, stopping at a payphone a few blocks from the church, my fingers so frozen I could barely press the dime into the slot. Called collect, on the off chance that Dad might be back home, that he might even answer. But it was Mum's voice that piddled down the line as the wind howled and rattled the phone booth.

For a moment I was paralyzed, voiceless. After several icy huffs, I finally managed a pathetic squeak.

"Is Dad there?"

"He gets in late tonight. I'm in the middle of something, Mag Mary. I have to let you go."

"What about Gerard?" I squeezed in, but she'd already hung up.

I had books with me for train reading. One of Sam's philosophy textbooks that she'd left at Liam's place and I'd pilfered. *Moby-Dick*. My Philosophy of Religion textbook for next term, when many new leaves would be turned.

Marc had caught me browsing through that last one just after I'd gotten it. He'd sat down all unbidden next to me in the caf and started jawing away, withering vegetable matter and tender hearts for miles around.

"Philosophers have only interpreted the world. The point is to change it. What are you getting embroiled in all this religious obscurantism for? You should be studying something more useful to the people."

"I wanted to, but Sorghum Farming 101 was full."

He kept leafing through the book, shaking his head in disgust.

"You have to realize, our personal fates are meaningless. The only meaning is to be found in common struggle, holding high the banner of Enlightenment, which has reached its most lofty pinnacle in Marxism–Leninism–Mao Tse-tung Thought."

What he didn't know was that the book had the goods on him too. It said that Marxism-Leninism was a religion just like any other. It said that the very nature of humanity was to seek transcendence, and to keep finding it in new ways. All atheists like him were doing was loading their sacks of meaning onto different, equally rickety wagons.

I would have found out more, but as usual, my eyes glazed over as soon as I turned the page.

Now on the train I'd opened it again, purely as a diversionary tactic. I believed it would utterly confound nosy onlookers to see a revolutionary cadre studying a book on the philosophy of religion. A total mindfuck!

As I waited for the train to get moving, I reviewed the teleological, cosmological, ontological, and moral arguments for the existence of God. I briefed myself on uncaused Causes and unmoved Movers. All the while I could hear Marc as if he were breathing down my neck from the seat next to me, warming to his theme, badgering me to "look at your historical analysis!" Parisian Communards, Moscow workers, Angolan and Cambodian peasants paraded across the page, tracking mud over the words.

"Apply the principles of dialectical and historical materialism!"

Yes, and that meant, uh, that meant, something like, the fusion of theeee . . . sis and antithesis! Okay, I got it. Now I can . . .

Pooff! Gone again.

I opened Sam's book, hoping that'd shut him up. Out marched Hume and Wittgenstein onto the parade grounds pulling a float carrying a mock-up of Ferré's metaphysical models. The voice at my ear ranted on. *Can you draw a positive conclusion as to the existence of God with a valid argument in which God does not appear in any of the premises? Huh? Can you? Huh? Hah! Didn't think so! It can't be done without begging the question. Now try this one on for size: God is the author of everything in the world. Evil is something in the world. Therefore God is the author of evil. Ha hah! And again: Evil exists. An omnipotent God could destroy evil. A benevolent God would destroy evil. Therefore, since evil is not destroyed, God is omnipotent and malevolent in some way, or God is benevolent and impotent in some way, or God is both malevolent and impotent, or there is no God.*

The correct answer was: D! No God! Occam's razor sliced off the dross, the simplest answer plopping into my lap like a fat bunch of grapes of wrath.

The seat next to me was empty, as were the two facing. At least they must have appeared so to everyone else on the train.

But, in fact, not Marc but *way* worse, the stalking Walking Tanteek had metamorphosed into humanoid shape and sat sprawled next to me, feet on the seat across from us, one bony arm flung round my shoulders, expansive with the excitement of a journey.

It peppered me with questions. *"What if the train derails and goes up in a fireball? Won't all you fools' holiday plans look a little silly then? Look at that old lady across the aisle. How much time do you think she has left, huh? An hour? A week? What about yourself? Same deal, right? Do you realize this train is nothing but a bunch of connected tin cans carrying gobs of pointlessly animated clumps of sentient meat to meaningless things they call 'homes,' when in fact they're all moving closer every second to total annihilation?"* The Tanteek was so cheery and upbeat, full of swagger, talking a mile a minute, poking me in the ribs. *"Don't forget, little lady, on top of everything else, that you're on an accidental planet spinning pointlessly through infinite space!"*

The more the train burrowed into Ontario, the less snow there was. Leaden clouds chugged along beside us, keeping pace. The horizon closed over the sun like a swollen eyelid. The darkening streets in the towns we roared through glistened with cold rain.

In Brockville, where we ground to a screeing stop, people dashed awkwardly from the station to the train in a downpour, holding up slick, wobbling umbrellas, their bags bumping against their legs. None of them boarded my car. Two big German shepherds that had been chasing each other around the platform, tripping up the rain-blinded passengers, suddenly came to a dead halt, turned their heads, and stared right at me.

Their stern faces registered mistrust, disapproval. I met their gaze for as long as I could stand, which wasn't long. I didn't dare look back till the train had begun to move, and then I swivelled my eyes fast in their direction. One had bounded away; I could see him sniffing the ground under the eaves of the stationhouse, nosing among the damp potato chip bags and cigarette butts.

The other one was still looking at me.

But it's not me, I thought. He sees the Tanteek. Animals can see all kinds of invisible stuff.

I narrowed my Chinese eyes at him, craning my head around to hold his stare as we picked up speed. The bastard never blinked.

At Kingston, the platform was jammed with Queen's students, jostling, laughing, the girls holding sodden newspapers over their heads. Through the window, there was barely a sound to be heard, till all at once the compartment door slammed open, swinging the volume needle crazily into the red. They thronged the aisle, reeking of wet wool, throwing their bags over the heads of people already sitting in order to get dibs on seats three rows away. Everyone had dripping hair and cheeks rosied by the December wind. They were bruisingly loud, thudding down the aisle, bags pressed into the backs of the ones before them, shouting cheerful profanities at friends farther up the line. The elderly woman across the aisle shrank against the window like a leech jabbed with a stick.

The Tanteek grew rigid, fell silent. A wispy blond girl in a powder-blue ski parka slid into its seat, threw a quick smile my way, and began jamming her bags underneath us, crushing my legs against the wall.

Sorry, she said, offering another, briefer smile. I pulled my glowering red star cap down over my forehead, silently advising her to take troubled note.

A girl and a guy had fallen into the seats facing us. The girl, who was beautiful, was already brushing out her long, wet black hair, pulling gobs of it out of the brush as she worked, tossing them over her shoulder. Her boyfriend pulled the brush out of her hand, pinned her back against the seat, and kissed her hard as she bucked and sputtered. It made me think of love-drunk Liam kissing gorgeous Sam in front of the whole gasping world, and then sitting back to bask in the glory of being loved by such a ravishing thing.

I treated them both to my Chinese pit bull face. The girl took one look at me and laughed out loud.

I ducked my head, in full, fiery body blush, concentrating hard on bold revolutionary thoughts: We of the Bamboo Forests will always follow the Party! Tenacious fighters forge ahead unceasingly! Resolute steelworkers boldly fulfill the quotas of the five-year plan ahead of schedule! I am such a hopeless shithead!

I opened *Moby-Dick* blindly, my head still down so my tears would plop into Melville's ocean and roll away unseen.

When we finally pulled into Union Station, I thought for one wild moment that there might be someone to meet me. But I looked in vain over bobbing heads in the throes of happy reunion, hailing and hugging and scattering for the exits on their way to home, sweet blessed home. Never mind, I told myself sternly. Learn from the people's steadfastness in fighting and forging ahead! Take the subway, fool!

There was no snow in Toronto. The flattened grass was brown, the bare trees hangdog. Coming up my old front walk, it seemed I'd been away forty years. Everything was smaller, dingier, the paint chipping away around the window frames and the front door, the strawlike stalks of plants in the garden still slumped where they'd keeled over in November, staked to sticks with garbage bag ties.

There were no stencils on the windows, no tee martoonies too many. But I could make out the grey silhouette of an unlit tree behind the closed drapes.

"I'm hoo-ome!" I shouted from the entranceway. The house echoed like a mausoleum. I slid open the closet door to hang up my coat and tried again.

"Hell-ooo! Your prodigal daughter has returned! Come all ye faithful and hail her!"

Not a word. Not only that, but it was past suppertime and there was no sign of anything like a meal being gotten ready.

"Guess what! I just got a big fat zero on my Lit exam!"

For a moment I thought I could hear scuffling sounds rising from the basement.

I strode into the empty kitchen. Not a pot on the stove, nothing but some skimpy butter tarts covered with a tea towel on the counter. I inhaled four of them on the spot, then marched to the head of the basement stairs.

"I *said*...I'm *home*, you unrepentant capitalist roaders!"

Uncle Dermott's huge head loomed suddenly out of the gloom as he tiptoed upstairs, a shushing finger pressed to his lips. He was an alarming sight, his hair gone completely white since I'd seen him last. He bore down on me like a Santa Claus parade float, all florid face and swollen stomach crammed into a green-and-red felt Christmas vest a'frolic with appliquéd bells and snowflakes and candy canes.

"Everyone's downstairs, saying the beads for your brother," he whispered on a rush of breath fairly reeking of distilled spirits.

"What for? Who's everyone?"

"Shhhh," he warned before turning and heading back downstairs. I couldn't ever remember him being in our house before.

I followed him. There was low murmuring coming from Gerard's curtained-off sanctuary. It sounded like something from the last movie I'd seen with Liam: Minnie and Roman and all their cronies droning up the devil behind Mia Farrow's bedroom wall.

What the hell? I took hold of the edge of the curtain and peeked around it.

There were Mum and Grandma Fionnuala on their knees, eyes closed, hard at their beads. Dermott stood with his hand on his mother's shoulder, his face puckered into a rosy mask of tragedy. In the bed lay Gerard, grey as a tombstone. His clavicle spiked out of his upper chest like tent poles. His eyes were sunk deep into purple sockets. His long hands, fingernails chewed raw, were clasped on his chest in the traditional pose of the pious corpse.

I tromped upstairs to my room and slammed the door.

What used to be my room, I noted at once. Now it was serving as an all-purpose, walk-in storage closet. As rude welcomes went, this really took the cake. My eyes were scalded with self-pitying tears as I stepped over piles of cardboard boxes, old lamps, and stacks of books to reach my bed, which was heaped with magazines, out-of-date coats, sweaters, old kitchen appliances, and shoes intended for Goodwill. I crawled underneath the blanket with the pile of junk on top of me and pulled the pillow over my head. The sheets smelled like a forest floor in late November.

I was awakened from humid sleep at intervals, dimly conscious of the slamming of the front door, or the doorbell buzzing, of rustling movement and voices from the living room too faint to identify. People seemed to be going and coming all night long; the noise would wake me for as long as it took to register, then I'd fall right back to sleep. It was only much later that I was jolted awake by the throb of music so loud it shook the bed, rattling the debris on top of me like a minor earthquake. Under my window shade the sky was a deep lilac that didn't look like dawn.

Sitting up with a start, I realized I'd slept all night and all day, right up to the very cusp of Christmas Eve.

Outside, a drab freezing rain was falling. The grass had a silver crust, over which a few dun-coloured birds hopped aimlessly to the thump and thunder of *Benny Goodman at Carnegie Hall*, which could surely be heard seventeen blocks away. The smell of roasting meat drifted under my door. Someone had finally seen fit to cook something.

I stumbled into the hall, smelling like the bottom of a hamster cage, my clothes crumpled, pigtails tearing at my scalp where they'd been smushed crooked under my head for so long. Swinging "Loch Lomond" blasted from the living room. No one but Dad would have put that on, but he was nowhere in sight. I threw open the door to the kitchen. Two heads snapped sharply my way, Dermott's and Mum's, both of them thick as thieves, caught in mid-secret confab.

"Oh! So sorry," I mumbled, backing out and shutting the door. In the hall, pressed against the wall like a fugitive, I strained to make out the conversation.

"You'll have to take Father McMillan's word on it, lovey," Dermott was saying. I'd taken quick note of the suspicious silver flask he was holding under the table in his pudgy lap. I knew Dermott well enough to know that his involvement in this crisis would be peripheral at best; most likely he was putting in yeoman service as Fionnuala's driver.

"Yes, he's a pious, devoted boy," he went on, "but you have to understand, there are limits. He's not in training to become a desert monk after all. Look at Jimmy, now. He's managed to live a fine, upstanding life as a priest without turning his back on the human race."

Mum cut in, frantic. "No! I believe my son. If he says he has been swept up to the third heaven like St. Paul, then it has truly happened! I won't listen to anything or anyone else!"

"He needs medical attention, Moira. It's not normal, all this crying and refusing food and floating off into the ether. He should be hard at his books. Something has gone badly wrong, lovey."

Oh! Wafting odour of rat! So he'd been doing well, pulling in all A's, had he?

I strode into the living room and just as suddenly sprang back. I'd missed seeing Grandma Fionnuala from behind because even with her Dairy Queen hair, her head didn't clear the top of the chair back. She sat staring at the dying embers of a fire someone had made, not a muscle twitching in spite of the Carnegie Hall riot hammering and clanging around her. She, too, was in festive dress, a long-sleeved, high-necked silk confection in a crazed red, black, and white geometric print that looked positively psychedelic. Inside it, though, she appeared fresh off the Famine, as if her diet for the last five years had been bowls of grass dunked in the blood drained from skin-and-bone cows.

Even her hair seemed thinner, her exhausted coiffure slumping on itself like an empty hot water bottle. She'd taken off her shoes, her outstretched feet smaller than my hands, the sturdy stockings a glum brown at the heels and toes, like real feet of clay. Her varicose veins lumped out under the fabric like a load of furniture badly tied down with a canvas tarp. Her arms lay like dead weights along the chair arms.

The Christmas tree was urging her to smile, all tarted up with ornaments, the tinsel thrown on in heaping handfuls. But it was plain her holiday had been spoiled. The grand gala with the cream of the Moriartys, Jimmy and Seamus and Michael and the wives and the kiddies and grandkiddies, held in her sprawling Mafia-don home in Woodbridge, had been shot to smithereens. She and Dermott had apparently been stuck for the last little while shuttling back and forth to stew with the Moriarty bottom feeders.

But the music! It was Dad's classic touch, expressly designed to rile her to the marrow of her soul.

I looked down the basement stairs and saw that Mum had gone down, and Dermott had disappeared. She stood alone at the bottom, as immobile as her mother. Her head hung, her shoulders slumped. Her hair, which had been a bouffant, pecan brown when I'd left in September, now looked coarse and dry, of no nameable colour at all.

I noticed too how her sagging pouch of a stomach swelled under the scab-coloured Christmas dress she'd worn for seven years running. The dowdy hem hung unfashionably below her knees, from where the tributaries of her own complicated river system of swollen veins descended.

Look at her, I thought with satisfaction. So withered. So haggy.

That little stomach mound had once been my home. Okay, our home. *Co-locs*; that's what they'd call us in Montreal. Roomies. The two of us jammed into yin-yang formation, gnawing like rats on our umbilical cords. There hadn't been any new tenants since we'd vacated the premises. Almost two decades of disrepair and neglect were taking their toll. The beams were falling in. The place was a flophouse.

Suddenly, footsteps, as Fionnuala loomed from behind and squeezed by me, leaning on the complaining banister, easing herself down to the basement one stair at a time, toddler-style. I flattened myself against the wall as she passed without a word, her bony rump sashaying comically in time with the jungle drums on the record. Mother and daughter disappeared together in the direction of Gerard's hidey-hole, which had taken on the tremulous mystery and terror of a sideshow freak exhibition.

I crept after them, slinking into a crouch behind the hot water tank. I could hear them both creaking audibly onto their knees as they began doxologizing in tandem: "*I love Thee, Jesus, my love, above all things. I repent of my whole heart for having offended Thee. Never permit me to separate myself from Thee again. Grant that I may love Thee always, and then do with me what Thou wilt.*"

Gerard's voice bumped along after theirs, a broken-down wagon hitched to the back of a Mercedes. The whole basement reeked of vomit.

The prayer ended. There was a brief, charged silence, like the pause between movements of a symphony. I held my breath. Some tiny creature scrabbled along the wallboard behind me. I could hear feet walking over my head upstairs, the whole ceiling vibrating to big band mayhem, tootling clarinets, sprawling trumpets, and crazed drumming, capped by torrents of applause.

Fionnuala broke the silence at last.

"Our Lord and Lady have given you your marching orders. You are to leap back into the battle, young man. You are to keep on fighting. Your superiors were put there by God to discipline and guide you, and you must obey them as if the Lord himself were issuing the commands. They have specifically ordered you to fast only at the prescribed times, and not to take extra burdens upon yourself. You are called to a plain, Spartan life, but not to starvation and self-destruction. If you don't eat, how can you keep up the energy you need to study? Kindly tell me that, would you now."

From Gerard, an unintelligible mumble.

"The diocese believes you have a vocation!" Fionnuala cut in smartly. "The Bishop believes so. Is he deluded, then? Father Finnerty and Father McMillan believe so. They're willing to offer you another chance. Who are you to question their insight? Where did you scrape up that blather and nonsense?"

Where indeed, I thought with rising spirits. The plot thickeneth!

The curtain didn't reach as far as the wall; around the edge I could see Gerard's head flat on the pillow, tears crashing like breakers over the crags of his cheekbones onto his sopping pillow. He opened his eyes for a moment only for them to drop instantly shut like windows with a broken sash.

"Our Lord and his servants are not to be trifled with. You deal cavalierly with him, young man, at your immortal peril."

"But that's...what I'm trying to...tell you," croaked Gerard, forced to compete with Liltin' Martha Tilton leaking down through the ceiling. He tried to raise himself on his elbows but fell back with an audible thump.

"You don't, you don't know," he whispered. He lay panting, helpless, a shell-shocked recruit being hastily patched up, packed full of flimsy stuffing and stitched together without anaesthetic, made ready to be sent back to the front.

Back in my room, I shoved everything, books, magazines, shoes, coats, and two broken toasters, off the bed onto the floor. The volume of the music was suddenly lowered, and the tidal wave of stuff as it landed sounded like the back wall of the house was giving way. Then, silence.

And then, all at once, Dad's voice from what sounded like the living room.

"Who's for some hooch? I declare the bar officially open!" This was followed closely by an even more jovial, "Yep, I'm back, and when I'm here, we play by my rules, Dermwood. My house, my rules!"

Where the hell had he been hiding?

I ventured into the hall, passing the dining room where Dermott was making himself useful, trying to jam the extra leaf into the dining room table. He kept hoisting the heavy slab against his stomach and valiantly, blindly aiming it for the open space in the middle. He missed every time.

"Now you do as you're told!" he scolded the leaf right to its face as he lay sprawled over it atop the table, still clutching both sides, the strain causing gin blossoms to pop out on his face like hemorrhoids. "I've got better things to do than fight with you all day!" With a mighty effort, he heaved the leaf up again and staggered backward against the wall, but it escaped his grip and crashed to the floor, narrowly missing his toes in their gala, candy-striped socks.

Suddenly I heard, "Marge!"

No one in the world but Dad had ever called me Marge.

He'd come right up behind me, a rainwater-clear drink in his hand, a jaunty lemon slice straddling the glass. He raised it aloft, clinking the ice. Dermott, enlivened by the friendly sound, scuttled out of the room and was soon rattling bottles in the makeshift bar Dad had set up in the living room, sloshingly refilling his little flask.

"Well, finally, here's *one* of my kids," said Dad with welcoming gusto. "Is the Preacher still down there in the tar pits surrounded by sobbing women?"

"Yep. What the hell is going on?"

"Marge, for chrissake, would you go down there and tell him to get his mackerel-snapping heinie up here and say hello to his old man? He was down there when I got back the other night, and there's been nothing ever since but religious nitwits I

194

never invited crowding me out of my house, and hand-wringing and rosaries flapping in the breeze. I had to check into the goddamned Holiday Inn to get a decent meal and some shut-eye."

"How was Oslo?" I asked, giving him a hearty slap on the back. "Oh, wow, Daddio, it's about the groovy sideburns!"

"Not bad, not bad at all. Some terrific people there." He stroked the sides of his face as if he'd only just noticed the excess hair. "So, you think your old man's groovy, do you?" He snapped his fingers a few times like Dean Martin Live at the Sands. "What do you want to know about the fisheries business? Fask me about the issheries, baby! Anything at all!"

Without waiting for my question, he stepped into the living room and flipped the record over, dropping the needle down with care and giving the volume knob a hefty twist. "Sing, Sing, Sing" began rocking the turntable.

He set his drink down and picked up his slippers from beside the couch, slapping them on his knees in time as he sang along. *Yam boogie, yam boogie! Rahda rahda rahda rahda rahda rahda rahda rahda rah. Yam booo-gie, yam booo-gie!* The slipper that veered off to the side to bash the invisible cymbals was right on the money every time.

"Hey! How do you like Mr. Krupa?" he shouted at me over the din. Behind him, Dermott had dropped recklessly into Fionnuala's chair and picked up a newspaper from the side table, giving it a crisp rattle meant to imply sobriety and incisive thinking.

"All this bleeding heart fuss over the Tet Offensive," he announced over his shoulder, causing Dad to lean over and turn the music up several more notches. The drums sounded like artillery.

"If you ask me, it's all the more reason for making sure the Cong get their faces pushed in!" Dermott shouted over the din.

Dad continued drumming like a maniac, his head jerking up and down, his eyes closed, taking one solo after another in a crouch, then leaping to his feet as the horns blatted like Bronx cheers. There was another burst of applause from the Carnegie Hall audience, at which he paused to nod in gracious acknowledgment before bending again to his task, flailing and hammering the air, the chair arm, his shins. He knew the whole drum part by heart, right down to the cowbells.

Dermott flapped his paper, lit a cigarette. "You wanna get me an ashtray?" he hollered somewhat belligerently to Dad, who was now on his knees, whacking the slippers against the side of his chair. Getting no response, he flicked his cigarette into the fireplace, pulled his flask from one of his Yuletidey pockets, and drank deeply.

Benny's clarinet loop-de-looped the room like an elegant bee. Dad's shoulders and eyebrows arched this way and that along with the rampaging band. I couldn't stop grinning. Instinctively, I knew just what he was up to: this was his version of New Yawk! He was elbowing a space for himself, demanding homage and recognition. Hell, he *invented* New Yawk!

"Sing, Sing, Sing" was a long number. Just when I thought the slipper drumming would carry over till New Year's, he slammed his air cowbells and brought the band home, tossing the slippers over his head and bowing to the roar of applause before whirling around and lifting the needle abruptly from the record.

In the sudden interstellar silence, he picked up his glass and made a beeline for the bar.

"Ask me anything about the fisseries!" he ordered, lifting his full glass to me. "Hey, Marge! It's good to see ya!" For a moment he forgot to keep his gaze aimed above my chin. I blushed like a brazier.

"Can I have some of that?"

"Help yourself." He held out the gin bottle, it's bold Beefeater striding purposefully toward me with his long, sharp stick. "Just don't let your old lady catch you." He leaned over and jammed a loose plug into the wall, lighting the tree up like a Ferris wheel.

"How do you like my work? Did this the night I came home and not a damn person helped me hang so much as a hank of tinsel."

Now that it was lit, I could see it was his work, all the ornaments crammed into the front, the string of lights drooping like downed wires after a hurricane.

"It's very nice." I said. My cool, lemony drink raced down my throat like a spark running along the detonator wire to cartoon dynamite. My insides caught and went kaBLOOM!

God*damn!* This gin had beer beat all hollow!

"Hey! Maisie!" Dad shouted into the kitchen, where Mum, having risen from the depths, was hacking greens for a salad. "Are we going to sit down and eat or do we have to chew the table legs off?"

She emerged primly to set a platter of singed meat loaf down on the table.

"Meat loaf? It's Christmas Eve!" Dad bellowed in indignation.

"The turkey is for tomorrow," she replied, stiff as a fork.

"Will Old Hatchet Face and her big growing boy be joining us for chow tonight?"

"I'm not going to turn out guests on Christmas Eve. They've foregone celebrations of their own to be here. Mother's just having a few last words with Gerard." Yet another ornate utterance out of her; I didn't think the sum of her communications with Dad over the last eighteen years had amounted to more than one or two typewritten pages, double-spaced.

"And will the mental patient be joining us?" He tossed back a long, full-bodied swallow. Mum swallowed hard herself, clearly calling upon the universal communion of saints to maintain her stability.

"He's not feeling up to it."

"The hell with feeling up to it. He gets his sad-sack behind up here in three minutes and counting or I'm going down there and haul him up by the hair!" He took another long swig, then turned to the record player to shuffle through the pile of old 78s he'd set out on the table next to it, stacking several onto the spindle. The first one clattered down.

"'Pennsylvania 6-5000!'" he announced to the room at large.

One by one, we eased ourselves in around the table that someone, presumably Mum, had finished putting together and laid indifferently with napkins and silverware. No one met anyone else's eyes, no one having a clue how to speak to more than one other person in the room, if that. Grandma, up from the depths, her face cheery as a battlefield, speared a slab of meat loaf from the platter and passed it to Dad, who made her hold it aloft while he rolled his entire drink, ice and all, down his throat. I slumped in my chair, daring Mum to take note of the drink in *my* hand. Meanwhile, Dad extricated a pair of sunglasses, of all things, from his shirt pocket, and sat drumming his hands on the table, a real hepcat, cool and oblivious behind his shades.

The next record dropped.

"'Sheik of Araby', with Coleman Hawkins and His All-Star Octet," he shouted around a mouthful of meat. It sounded like old-fashioned cartoon music to me, springy and slaphappy, with big-rumped mammies in turbans and goggle-eyed krazy kats. I wondered how soon I could arrange for another drink.

Dad began drumming again with the cutlery, knife on gin glass, spoon on plate. No one said anything. He drummed, we shovelled in the eats. The Sheik of Araby folded up his tent and stomped away. Down dropped the next record.

"'One O'Clock Jump,' ladies and gentlemen! Featuring that outstanding tickler of the ivories, Mr. Count Basie, and His Orchestra!" Fionnuala grumbled something fervent but inaudible into her napkin.

"After this, we should put on one of my records," I offered sociably. "Maybe start living in the twentieth century." When no one replied, I decided to throw caution to the winds and stepped to the bar to fix my own drink, taking advantage of Mum's brief run to the kitchen for more potatoes. Half gin, half tonic seemed about right. The lemon slices were gone; my first sip went down like chilled rubbing alcohol.

And I thought to myself that the truly great thing about drinking, never mind mingling with your whacked-out family, was that it made you forget all your existential and metaphysical woes. It zazzed up your blood, made every cell in your body stand up with a raised fist and an unshakeable opinion in your personal favour. I was on top of the world, the meanest muthuhfuckuh in the valley!

I reached for Dad's pack of smokes on the table. Fionnuala, irritated beyond endurance by the music, scraped her chair back, a lightning bolt vein on her forehead visibly throbbing. She disappeared down the hallway to the bathroom. Dermott, too, got up, shuffling into the living room, back to his paper. After a minute or two, he could be heard snoring like a cartoon fat man, his lips vibrating, exhalations long and whistly.

I was flush with fiesta spirit, though the unstable room was tipping sideways a little every time I moved. I wanted to reach for the ashtray next to Dad's plate, but I wasn't sure I could complete the complicated manoeuvre without falling out of my chair. I stubbed out my smoke in my uneaten green beans and glugged down the rest of my drink. Where had this stuff been all my life? To think that I'd spent the last four months suffering the persecutions of the damned, raw as a naked babe on the frozen tundra, when this stuff was being bought and sold in stores everywhere!

Grandma reappeared and sat down primly on the edge of her chair. The mechanism wheezed, a fresh record kerplopped. Dad sprang to his feet, waving the gravy ladle in the air and crying, "'Cherokee!' Hey! For an extra helping of this shoe leather meat loaf, who can name three bandleaders featured on weekly radio programs from 1935 till 1949?" Not waiting for an answer, he strode toward the bar.

"Way to liven up the party, Dad! I could use another drink there while you're at it." Out of the corner of my eye I spotted

Mum scuttling down the basement stairs with a generous plate of food.

He dropped ice into his glass, poured in the gin, came back to the table. "For a scoop of mashed potatoes, who's handling sax and trumpet duties in this number?" He was clearly not going to make me a drink, so I wobbled over to the bar to tend to business.

There was no one at the table but Fionnuala to answer the quiz question. She icily declined.

"The names I was looking for were Charlie Barnet and Billy May. Mashed potatoes go to me." I saw Mum, her face all undone, duck back into the kitchen with the same full plate of food she'd gone down with. Grandma followed her in, shutting the door behind them.

"Now, then," said Dermott, suddenly awake and alert and hovering over the bar, filling a glass with some amber-coloured stuff from an as yet unused bottle. He raised his glass to Dad as he prepared to whip up an enthusiastic show of audience participation.

"You had your Bob Crosby on the radio, I remember him." I had no idea anyone else but Dad knew any of this stuff.

"Bob Crosby is one. Who else?"

"Why, there was Matinee at Meadowland on Saturdays, that was with Jimmy, no, Tommy Dorsey," Dermott corrected himself hurriedly as a thundercloud darkened Dad's face. "And wasn't that Cab Calloway on once a week?"

"Well done! A scoop of cold spuds for the stocky fellow in the clown vest!" Dermott flushed red as a side of beef at this highly unusual approval. Another record hurtled down, more jungle

drums and a bass that thumped like a headache. Dad hailed it
with a flourish of the gravy ladle.

"'The Big Noise from Winnetka!'" He pointed his knife
at my chest.

"You! I want three of Bob Crosby's sidemen. Ten seconds
or less. Go!"

"Larry, Curly, and Moe."

"How about Irving Fazola on clarinet? How about Muggsy
Spanier on trumpet? How about Nappy Lamare on guitar?"
he yelled, a splodge of mashed potato oozing down his chin.

I burst out laughing. "You're making that up!"

"The hell I am!" He banged his fist on the table, making
the record skip. "Moira!"

No answer.

"MOIRA!"

Mum appeared in the kitchen doorway wearing dripping
yellow rubber gloves.

"I thought I told you to get my son up here. It's Christmas
Eve, damn it!"

"I'm washing up the pans," she replied with prim asperity.

"I said go get him! That's an order!" He shoved his chair back
and made as if to stamp after her, forcing her to bolt down the
basement stairs followed by Fionnuala. Another record dropped.

"'Harlem Airshaft,'" Dad remarked placidly, sitting down
again. "The Duke." He raised his glass. "To the Duke."

"We certainly enjoyed the Duke in *The Green Berets*," opined
Dermott as he settled into a chair in front of the TV. "I took
the boys to see it. An excellent motion picture, and a real lesson
for our times!" He leaned forward, turning the TV on and

cranking up the sound. The news was on, chopper propellers thwacking behind Cronkite's voice.

Mum rematerialized in the kitchen doorway, wringing her rubber-gloved hands, her chin up and defiant, to announce in an unnaturally high register, "Fiona will be stopping by tomorrow."

"Fiona? You mean that damned nun?" Dad barked, his shades slipping down the bridge of his nose.

"Yes, that damned nun," Fionnuala barked back at him, the first time I'd ever heard the d-word issue from her lips. I don't think she was even aware of it herself.

"What the hell for? Don't they have Christmas in the nun house?" But Mum and Grandma were already back in the kitchen, the door kicked rudely closed behind them.

"I thought I said Gerard had to be up here in three minutes! Am I still running this house or aren't I?" A lob of Dad's spittle landed on my cheek. The sound on the TV mounted another notch, treating us to a choir yelling "Oh Little Town of Bethlehem."

Fionnuala marched back out of the kitchen.

"Dermott!" she snapped, making him jump. She wagged her head vehemently in the direction of the front door and he leapt up to follow, Mum trailing morosely after them. Much heated whispering ensued as Dermott helped Fionnuala into her stiff black Persian lamb coat. She gazed sternly into the mirror on the closet door as she balanced the matching pillbox hat on top of her hair stack, then bent to pull her plastic galoshes over her shoes, clutching Mum's shoulder for balance, making them both stagger. The door banged shut behind them at last, with nobody having bothered to say goodbye.

Dad slammed back his chair and swung round the door to

the basement, taking the stairs two at a clip from the sound of it.

Yes! Another drink!

I'd just spun the cap back onto the gin bottle when I heard many heavy feet mounting the stairs. Dad appeared first in the living room doorway, flinging his arms wide.

"Your chair, sir. What'll you be having?"

Gerard listed sideways, a long reed in a high wind.

"Siddown!" Dad bellowed, all congeniality spent.

Gerard groped blindly for the chair back. Touching base at last, he fell toward and over it, his head drooping. The music had stopped.

"Stand up straight, for chrissake! You're not a goddamned invalid!"

He hauled Gerard backward by the collar of his pyjama jacket. Stretched to his full height, I could see that he was shockingly reduced from his already severely whittled self. His head had been recently and indifferently shaved. His lips were brown and crusty, and he smelled rank as a gas station toilet.

"Get this boy a plate of vittles!" Dad commanded. Mum trotted into the kitchen.

"Sit, sit," Dad insisted, with the largesse of a delighted host. Gerard didn't move. Graciously, Dad pulled out the chair with him still draped over it and, yanking him sideways, manoeuvred him into position in front of it. With one hand on Gerard's chest and the other on his back, he folded his son like a paper Halloween skeleton. Gerard sat, head hanging, hands knotted in his lap. Dad kneed the chair in from behind with extravagant force. Then he dropped to a crouch to rummage through the records on the shelf under the record player, methodically removing a fresh assortment from the sleeves.

Mum slid a plate of cold meat loaf and potatoes under Gerard's nose. The record player jumped to life.

"'Opus One,'" Dad shouted, clumsily jumping up again. "Tommy Dorsey and His Orchestra!" He hoisted me out of my chair from behind, dragging me to my rubber chicken feet.

"Stop it, stop it!" I was crying, but he'd begun dancing me around the room. I cramped double with laughter, trying to pull away, but he wouldn't let go, spinning me one way, then the other. My stomach rose to critical levels and fell again, rose and fell. He was not a good dancer. He unspooled me, reeled me back in, his breath boozy and smoky, smells I associated with Liam, boys my own age. Giddy, shrieking, I grabbed the rest of his drink off the table as he swung me by, knocking it back just before he looped me into a Cyd Charisse dip under his arm. I stumbled in the opposite direction, hopelessly entangled.

The music was all busted out and swollen with happiness and hope, the same bright phrase tearing around and around after itself while violins swayed like palm trees in the background. I pictured the horn section rising to their feet in their white jackets, the girls in saddle shoes, the young soldiers clustered round the bandstand or swinging their girls around the dance floor. They'd had such a jumpin' soundtrack to their war, no hard edges, no heroin-fuelled, screaming guitars.

"*Oh, to dance beneath a diamond sky,*" I shrilled in exhilaration, knocking over two chairs, "*with one hand waving freeeeeee!*"

Gerard lurched to his feet and made for the stairs. Dad's arm shot out in mid-spin, intercepting him by the seat of his pyjama pants, exposing his concave, fungus-white backside.

"Where do you think you're going? Siddown!"

The song sprawled to an end and we both fell against the table, heaving like marathoners. Gerard tried gamely for a second dash. But he was in worse shape than Dad, who stepped neatly to the head of the basement stairs to stand with his arms braced against the doorframe, blocking Gerard's way, still huffing mightily. I collapsed, wheezing, onto the couch. The room was doing figure-eights, my dinner rising all the way to my tonsils before sliding reluctantly back down again.

"Sit down and eat like a man!" Dad barked. "And when you're finished, you can tell us all about why you ran away from that damned divinity school."

I sat up straighter, incredulous.

"You ran away?"

"He ran away," spat Dad in disgust. "Disappeared for two weeks and your mother had to call me in Oslo, bawling, Come home, Gerard is lying in a ditch somewhere. Then where does he turn up but in some damned fleabag rooming house on Dundas, panhandling, living on bread and water, blubbering like a baby all day long, till the landlord finally called the police. For the love of Christ, if you don't want to be a priest, why don't you just open up your goddamn mouth and say so!"

I turned to Dad, dumfounded.

"Mum *called* you?"

"I don't want to be a priest," said Gerard.

From behind the kitchen door, I heard Mum burst into wild sobs. Another sour wave crested in my throat. I willed it back down, but it was like stuffing a live squirrel down a drain.

I forced myself to focus on Gerard, straight eye to straight eye. There was nothing of the known world in his face. He sat like a ragdoll flung into the chair, twisted sideways, slumping on his knobby tailbone. His arms were thrust out straight in front of him, circling the full plate on the table; his hands, on the far side of his plate, kept rolling and unrolling his napkin. He never took his eyes from his work.

This wasn't my brother. This was a returnee from an alien abduction. Or a helium balloon we'd let go of, a speck in the distance, lost for all time.

Gerard cleared his throat, and I held my breath, feeling like a witness to the pre-teen Jesus preaching to the elders in the Temple. Another record dropped.

"Taaaaan ... ger ... eeeen!" crooned the singer from some impossibly remote galaxy of joy.

"The only reason we exist is to die," said my brother. His voice was rusty and grinding; the words crawled up out of his throat, looked around, shivered and shrank. His whole body jiggled as if he were on a runaway train. "Nobody sees the truth. You all worship yourselves as idols." He stopped, spent, and closed his eyes for a whole minute, still jiggling. Then he sputtered to life again, as if a new record had dropped in his head.

"Your eyes are sealed shut and your consciences are seared. But my eyes are open. Life is nothing. As soon as you think you've found it, you've lost it. All you can do is throw it away."

This cut *way* too close to the bone. My heart was careening into walls like a bird that had flown into the house by mistake while the cat sat motionless, watching with glittering eyes.

"Aw geesh," said Dad at last. "Now you've got us feeling all bad. Shucks."

"Tangerine" ended. The ragged fire ticked in the fireplace, the spindle mechanism creaked and whirred. In the kitchen, Mum blew her nose. The next record splattered down.

"'The Big Crash from China!'" Dad proclaimed. "Bob Crosby and His Bobcats, featuring Ray Bauduc on drums and Bob Haggart on bass!"

No one moved. "The Big Crash" sounded like a crazed blind man running around someone's kitchen, knocking into pots and pans, bashing everything in sight with sticks.

Dad bent to fiddle with the knobs on the TV, the sound all but drowned out by the cavorting Bobcats.

"Apollo 8 is going to be broadcasting from the moon's orbit," he announced, sounding awfully cool under the circumstances. "I'd like to catch—"

"The warissanasheet," floated toward us from the dining room table.

"What?" shouted Dad, cool no longer.

"The world is an ash heap. It's all chaos. Everything that lives inside of time is pure evil straight from the pit of hell."

"Is that what they're teaching you in priest school?" Dad inquired with a sinister leer, swaying as if on shipboard, his drink sloshing over the sides of his glass.

A new tune began thumping, its horns muted and arch.

"'Tusks-edo Junction,'" Dad began, but Gerard spoke over him with something very like authority.

"It's what God has taught me."

"In person? Like, in a real voice?" I asked, sitting up, trying to focus my eyes on him.

He took a deep, steadying breath. His answer flew out so fast it seemed to be all one long word.

"He lifted me up and called me his own and in a flash of time so short it can't be measured I knew the meaning of all things."

Mockery died in my throat. It was as if he'd set himself on fire right there in front of us.

My brother knew things! He had *answers*!

Now Mum was standing behind his chair, eyes streaming, knotting and unknotting her fingers, knitting something only angels could see. Dad took this as his cue to sidle up to her, crook his arm around her waist, and begin dragging her about the room to the lazy music, holding his drink in the hand behind her back. It was as if he'd uprooted a tree trunk.

I had to crane my head around the two of them to shout at Gerard. I was too inebriated to care what I said.

"So, if you know the meaning of all things, big shot, tell me why God wipes us out, like he just, just, bumpsh us off the table by accident, and doesn't even notice. Tell me why he doesn't, doeshn't even *care* when little babies and, and children in Vietnam are left lying in the road all burnt, and people are, I mean, you think that's how he *wants* it? Because we're all evil?" I tried to stand, but my knees refused to participate.

Gerard mumbled on like a drunk in a doorway, but he wasn't

answering me. "I'm the evil one!" he whispered, with a wet, backward sob. "I'm evil, I'm evil, I'm evil."

Dad was still manhandling Mum across the floor like a corpse he had to drag to the graveyard. For a moment, I thought she'd swooned. I imagined the two of them in their whirlwind courtship days, sliding drunkenly around the floor of some saloon where the chairs were already stacked on the tables, him in a snappy suit, her in a long, slinky satin dress. Dancing in a clutch, butts protruding. Waiters rolling their eyes.

He gave up at last, dropping her like a bag of bricks onto a dining room chair, and turned to stumble in my direction in some kind of partnerless foxtrot. Halfway over, he tripped on a bunch-up in the rug and sprawled against the couch, spilling the rest of his drink. But he took no notice, his eyes suddenly riveted to the TV screen, where a wedge of grey moon could be seen flickering against a black background.

Mum was the one who had the presence of mind to turn the music down.

"That's Bill Anders!" Dad said in a garbled way, pulling his chair up to within an inch of the screen.

"I hope that all of you back on earth can see what we mean when we say that it's a very foreboding horizon," said Bill. And there was the speckled, shimmery moon over Dad's head, looking like an airplane wing or an oddly cut slice of pie. Bugs seemed to be swarming over it. Bill seemed put off as well, remarking that it was, "a stark and unappetizing-looking place."

"Sounds like our living room," I muttered under my breath.

"...this smooth region called the Sea of Tranquility..."

I looked at Gerard. He was the only one not watching. His face was in his hands and he was weeping helplessly.

"...you can see the long shadows of the lunar sunrise..."

"They're moving!" Dad cried, tapping the screen, making it buzz with static. "They're flying right over the surface! See how the landscape changes!"

The wobbly moon was doing voodoo on the tides inside my belly. My mouth went dry, as my throat tried to swallow itself.

"For all the people on Earth the crew of Apollo 8 has a message we would like to send you. In the beginning God created the heaven and the earth..."

I seesawed down the hall, making the bathroom in the nick of time. Up came potatoes, meat loaf, ketchup, all as recognizable leaving as they'd been going in but soured in a toxic spin cycle of gin.

"...and God saw the light, that it was good: and God divided the light from the darkness..."

Dad had turned the TV up. I could hear every word.

"And God made the firmament, and divided the waters which were under the firmament from the waters which were above the firmament..."

I reclined on the bathroom floor. The room still spun but more politely.

"...and the gathering together of the waters called he Seas: and God saw that it was good..."

Even with the gritty mat under me and the metallic reek of the low-slung plumbing an inch from my nose, I felt much better. I wondered if I could handle another drink, get back the good feeling from before. I promised myself I'd stop sooner this time.

"Good night, good luck, and a Merry Christmas, and God bless all of you—all of you on the good earth."

From the living room, sounds of a tussle. And then Gerard's voice, suddenly clear, strong and even.

"I hate your guts! I've always hated you!"

"Hey! Feeling's mutual." Dad's shrug and grim smirk were audible even from where I lay.

"You're lost! Hell is forever! If you don't fall into the dust face down and repent—"

"Aw, knock it off, ya goddamned pansy!"

My last thought before passing out was of the astronauts in their tin can craft afloat in eternity. I knew we'd never see those guys again. No one could look at the dark side of the moon and continue to live.

That night, after I'd finally crawled down the hall and into bed, I dreamt about the War.

I was alone somewhere, "in country," wearing only a wet brown canvas poncho. In the distance were mountains, perfectly serrated, like giant, horizontal knives. The sky was mud yellow; the swampy ground sucked hungrily at my feet. Burnt tree stumps poked up from a river of foul, green water that I recognized as the Mekong. I knew there were severed heads floating in that water.

In the yellow sky floated a broken hunk of moon, and I knew that we, the soldiers, the warriors, were responsible for breaking it, and that it could never be repaired. This was all the moon people were ever going to have from now till the end of time.

Heaped behind trees, mounded against fences, were the bloated carcasses of people and animals. Snakes laced in and out between the bodies. The few huts in sight were roofless, and spiders the size of hubcaps hung suspended across the broken doorways. It was criminally hot. The leaves dripped some sweet secretion, some tempting, poisoned syrup. Jungle birds swooped overhead, cawing in desolation. Monkeys hidden in the trees hiccupped and grunted.

That's why they call them grunts, I said to myself. This explained a multitude of things.

The burnt huts were hung with fetishes: hairless, limbless dolls that were supposed to protect the people who lived there. I looked at the blackened, smoking wreckage, trying to imagine how the people had felt when they were hit anyway. I could still see some of those people. They were melted on the walls, and their wild eyes, as if painted in, were huge and rolling up.

Far down the road, shimmering in a mustard haze, lay a city. It had towers and turrets like the Emerald City of Oz. I thought to myself, Go there. Walk straight, don't look right or left. It will be different there than it is here. But I didn't believe myself. It'd be no different in the city. No one would be living there. There'd be nothing in the burning streets but filthy, torn plastic bags swirling in funnel winds.

The Enemy, I knew, was still out there, hidden between the lethal peaks of the mountains, behind thick curtains of vines. The hyper-stoned Cong, crazed to kill. I remembered how we'd admired them back in the pub. I wished to hell I were back there now. The Cong had No Regard for Human Life. Their cause was just. Bullets couldn't stop them, nor machine gun fire, nor rockets, nor artillery, nor strafing with liquid fire. They could crawl over razor wire, burrow under cement. I stood paralyzed. All possible roads led to hell.

I became aware of music drifting toward me from the direction of the city. Dance music. Of course, I thought, remembering: the Dorsey band had been engaged by the USO to play for the troops. They must not know I was the only one left. Now I could see them off in the distance, rising from their seats in perfect synchronization, horns lifted, trombone slides wooshing out and back. As I walked closer, I saw that most of them were shirtless in the appalling heat, their big white bellies glistening with sweat.

They played and then they sang, holding their horns aloft in their right hands, pumping their arms to the beat of the drums. A vocalist in a white jacket stepped up to an old-fashioned microphone and began crooning about the moon in all its splendour, which shook me because hadn't he seen, didn't he know? In between phrases, the band threw in their two cents' worth: "*Have a little faith in me!*" and "*Tra la la la la!*"

Then I was awake. The music was still thudding through the walls. I sat up and immediately fell backward, my skull mortared in, my throat Sahara dry.

Mum shoved the warped door across the carpet, poking her head in.

"We're going to the nine o'clock. You'd better hurry."

I hadn't been to Mass since summer. Not even the groovy guitar Masses they put up flyers for at school. Just the thought of the groaning organ, the snap of the kneelers, getting up, sitting down, getting up again, drained me like a vampire working at my neck. Our prayers requested for the souls of the following. The swinging censer, the poisonous High Mass clouds billowing over our heads. The tinkle of the Sanctus bell and the Elevation, and then God's big shadow as he swooped through the room, a quick drop-in, like Santa, on a tight schedule, just passing through. The priest delicately separating the wafers in the chalice, which I now knew to be a swear word in my new Quebec home. The chalice, the lid on the chalice, the host itself, and the little gold house it lived in, all emphatic curses, as light on the tongue as froth on champagne.

"I'm sick. Go without me."

"You're not missing Mass on Christmas Day!" But she wasn't all that scandalized. She'd foreknown my damnation all my life. Still, the door closed with unexpected force.

The music had stopped. Voices rose and fell. I heard a muffled clattering from the kitchen, cupboards opening and shutting, the whistle of the teakettle. After a while all was silent.

I spent the next hour and a half trying to fall back asleep but couldn't. My head hurt with an ache from outer space. When I got up, I realized I had the shakes, which I found wryly amusing; what kind of an alcoholic was I going to make if one night of tepid carousing could fell me like this?

In the bathroom I drank nine glasses of water. A truck had driven over my face in the night. My hair, still bound with rubber bands, was a lumpy mat of hemp. The few clean clothes I'd brought were still in my bags in the hall. In the bedroom, I peeled off my smelly top and pulled on one of the bigger old sweaters lying on the bed, a Moira original from a decade ago, turquoise and fuzzy, the breast pocket embroidered with a little grey poodle. I'd coveted it when I was ten.

Tiptoeing into the basement, I peeked behind Gerard's curtain. Gone. Couldn't eat, couldn't stand up straight, but couldn't miss Mass either. Asshole.

I waited a good twenty minutes before going back upstairs. Dad was alone in the kitchen, in his plaid bathrobe, looking spectral, elbows propped on the table, a cup of coffee pressed against his forehead.

"Merry Christmas," I ventured. "If you don't mind my saying, you look like holy hell."

He put down his cup, stared into its black depths, said nothing.

"I think I have a hangover," I told him, trying to make it sound fun. "My head feels like someone stuffed a bowling ball into my brain and sewed it up."

"There's coffee on the stove," he answered grimly, then looked up at me suddenly.

"You didn't go to church."

"Nope."

"Have you had it with all that stuff?"

"I don't know." Really? Did he want to talk religion with me, to talk *seriously* after all these years of—

"Goddamnit, where does she keep the small spoons?" He was tilted back in his chair, twisted sideways, rummaging violently in the silverware drawer behind him.

"What small—"

"The small spoons! The small spoons! God*damnit!*" He bashed the drawer shut. The silverware inside just laughed at him.

I poured myself some cereal from the same box I'd left unfinished in September. The flakes swarmed in the bowl like a plague of locusts. There was the smell of a bird beginning to sear in the oven. On my way to get milk, I saw boxes of frozen broccoli and asparagus tips thawing in the sink. I put the milk back, poured the cereal back into the box.

I decided I belonged in bed and turned to go, but Dad's voice waylaid me.

"Small combos. Bands within bands. Name me any such combo of three."

"Why would I know anything like that?"

"The Benny Goodman Trio, Teddy Wilson on piano, Krupa on drums. Number two: Tram, Bix and Lang: Frankie Trumbauer on C melody sax, Bix on cornet, Eddie Lang on guitar. And their only number was—"

"'Why Don't We Do It in the Road.'"

"'For No Reason at All in C.'"

"Well, that's just peachy keen."

"How about groups with four?"

I said nothing, thinking darkly, no wonder Mum hadn't spoken to him in eighteen years. This uncharacteristic impulse to take her side unnerved me until I remembered that it was all her fault he'd gotten this way in the first place.

"The Benny Goodman Quartet: Hampton on vibes, either Dave Tough or Krupa on the skins, both acceptable. Martha Tilton on vocals. Also, Woody Herman and His Four Chips. Give me a group with five."

Tears were ganging up on me. Didn't *anybody* in this wretched family know how to talk to anyone else like a human being?

"Tell me about your trip to Oslo. What's it like there? Are the people really free?"

"Artie Shaw's Gramercy Five: they played two numbers only, 'Dancing in the Dark' and 'Smoke Gets in Your Eyes.'"

"Are you listening to me? I said—"

"You also had Red Nichols and His Five Pennies, featuring Benny Goodman and the Teagarden brothers. Krupa on drums. 'Sheik of Araby' was their tune."

"Oh, really? So that's what Oslo's like. Gosh! And the people?"

"Groups with six: Will Bradley's Six Texas Hot Dogs. Ray McKinley on vocals and drums. One number only: 'Basin Street Boogie.'"

"Oh wow. Hot dogs. And here I thought Norwegians lived on herring in salt sauce."

"Also, let's not forget J.C. Higginbotham and His Six Hicks. Or the Benny Goodman sextet, who brought us 'Rose Room.' Now. Groups with seven. Tommy Dorsey's Clambake Seven..."

He got up as he talked and set about searching for a frying pan and spatula. He found bacon in the back of the fridge and started dropping strips into the pan. The smell and the spitting made my stomach and head scream in unison.

He began cracking eggs into the bacon fat. Making too sudden a turn, he caught his bathrobe sleeve on the panhandle and the whole mess toppled over and sloshed to the floor.

"For the love of *Christ*!" He kicked the pan viciously against the refrigerator and hurled the metal spatula all the way into the living room, pounding out of the kitchen just as the front door opened and Mum and Gerard bustled in on a rush of frigid air. I could hear her whispering as she tugged off her boots and then stood aside for her poor, ailing boy to do the same. In a split second, he'd shot past us and down the basement stairs.

She appeared in the kitchen doorway, hands flying to her face in shock.

"Mag Mary! Good Lord! Did you make this mess?"

"Of course! Always accuse me first! Nice Christmas spirit you picked up there at Mass," I offered sociably. "No, I'm not the culprit, sorry to say." I backed out of the kitchen, leaving her standing over the spreading lake of grease and egg yolk.

Christmas morning proceeded ominously apace. The four of us sat as if we were at gunpoint, opening last-minute gifts of cheap, embossed-cover paperbacks and boxes of drugstore chocolates. That ordeal ended at last, Mum sucked in a deep, preparatory breath.

"Fiona will be here around four," she announced in the same foreboding tone she'd use to tell us that an army of zombies was marching on Don Mills.

Dad looked up sharply.

"Does Bubba Wubba need another shoulder to cwy on?"

No answer.

"Is Sister Finnoodlehead staying for Christmas dinner?"

"She's welcome," Mum answered evenly. "And you're to address her as Sister Brigid." Ten words! Apparently she was no longer giving an inch on anything.

"Is Finnoodlehead up on her girl band singers?"

"If you want to play those childish games all evening, I'm sure I can't stop you."

219

"That's right. You can't. Marge! Girl singers! Rosemary Clooney and Frances Wayne. Whose band featured those two particular songbirds?"

"Yeah, Dad. Like I give a shit."

He dropped into a boxer's crouch in front of me, throwing light, playful jabs to my arms and neck.

"Quit punching me!"

"Aw c'mon, Marge! Play the game! C'mon! I'll give you the first one. Woody Herman. Now, who sang 'Sentimental Journey' with Les Brown and His Band of Renown?"

"Quit punching me, I said! Why is that funny? *Stop it!*"

I tore down the hall, slammed the door to my room, flapped down the shades, and flung myself onto the bed, hands at my sides as if I were on a slab in the morgue. I imagined Gerard two floors below me in exactly the same pose, tears dripping into all four of our ears.

The buzz of the doorbell jolted me from dead sleep.

"Test question before entering!" I heard Dad shout. Outside the weather had taken a pathetically fallacious turn for the worse, the sky leaden, sleet pinging like handfuls of rice against the window glass.

"What were the respective signature tunes of Artie Shaw and the Harry James Orchestra?"

Aunt Baby. Sister Brigid. I pushed up on my elbows. I hadn't seen her in so long.

She was standing in the entranceway, hung with many veils, shrugging off a man's brown trench coat. There was a befuddled smile on her face, as she'd been roped into a quiz before even getting out the "hell" of hello.

She pulled the rubbers off her sturdy black brogues and lined them up neatly against the wall before coming shyly into the living room, smiling round at Dad snapping his Rat Pack fingers, at Mum in her apron, and at me.

"Merry Christmas, all," she said softly.

"I'm still waiting for my answer," said Dad.

Baby sank uncertainly onto a corner of the couch, nervously smoothing her black skirt over her knees. The room fell silent. Everyone stared at different spots on the wall, faces wavering between frowns and smiles.

She'd aged a lot about the body. She was considerably heavier, but the sugar cookie face mashed in behind her wimple was unchanged. She wore glasses now, little rimless nun glasses. My heart lurched toward her, and she smiled in my direction but made no move. I wondered if she knew who I was.

"Didn't you forget to cross yourself before sitting down?" Dad asked genially with just the rumour of a smirk.

Baby smiled, blushing.

"My wife crosses herself every time she goes to the bathroom."

Baby tittered nervously, setting off another fraught silence.

"Mag Mary," she piped up finally. "I almost didn't recognize you over there. How grown up you are! How is it going at university? How are you finding Montreal?"

"I just get out of the train and there it is."

She looked confused.

"No, I meant, how do you like—"

"I hate university! I hate everyone alive!" With this dazzling proof of just how grown up I was, I turned tail and stormed back to my room.

When I slunk sheepishly back to the living room an hour later, Mum and Baby had gone AWOL. Spike Jones had just dropped onto the turntable, the first song bursting into rude life, a strident commotion of whistles, honks, razzberries, and bells. Dad was laughing ferociously at the silly record as he ostentatiously removed ornaments from the tree, tossing them carelessly into the box they were kept in the rest of the year.

"What are you doing?" I cried.

"What does it look like I'm doing? Christmas is over. I'm taking down the tree."

"We haven't even had dinner yet."

"The hell with that," he said. I slumped onto the sofa and watched as he continued his frenzied work, savagely ripping an armload of tinsel from the tree and flinging it into the fire where it flared and sizzled like molten mercury. He crunched two ornaments in his bare hands, pitching the shards fireward, still laughing in a frantic, barking way.

Mum appeared out of nowhere and marched over to the record player. With an energetic snap of the wrist, she turned the decibel level down from jet engine to a barely discernible hum. Dad, wildly aflame, whirled on her. Her face crumpled like a raisin, choked little bleats emerging from her throat as tears I'd never known she possessed began to splurt from her eyes. She backed away from him, arms raised to protect her face, until she reached the wall and could back no farther. Dad began turning in frenzied circles, looking for something to grab and heave, to give full vent to his murderous rage.

A fat, red Christmas candle soared across the room, missing Mum's head by a half an inch. Foaming oaths followed. Paternal garments were rent, paternal hair was torn, a paternal shoe was banged repeatedly against the wall until the plaster imploded. The vibrations caused Spike and his manic pals to skip and skid, the needle skating erratically across the record.

"Quitcher damned blubbering! I said *quit it*!" Dad's arm shot out, aiming straight for her face, but she ducked and with a scream ran blindly toward the kitchen, passing too close to the record player and knocking it to the floor with a deafening crash. The Spike Jones platter leapt to safety, rolling across the room, a wild tire spinning away from an overturned car.

I could hear her in the kitchen, wedging a chair under the doorknob. I could just make out her muffled voice. I assumed she was talking to herself, that she'd finally lost her last marble.

Dad threw open the front door with a mighty bang and charged outside, trying to pull on his coat as he ran. He was, however, unable to locate the sleeves, finally just flinging the coat over a cedar bush in the front yard. The car vroomed to life in the garage. He backed out with a roar and tore away, fishtailing down the icy street.

I stood in the middle of the room, afraid to move for the longest time.

The doorbell buzzed fiercely, twice. I opened it, expecting to see Dad, back for another spitting, snarling round.

Instead, there were suddenly two huge cops in our piney-fresh living room. They lumbered around, examining the damage in their stiff, rustly, winter police coats, stepping on crinkly wads of paper, taking up all the space, knocking flimsy angels and ornaments off of tables. The kitchen door had been opened a crack, a line of mud brown filling it in.

"Come on out, Ma!" I called to her. "The coast is clear!" Both cops looked me over suspiciously, but I fixed them with my Brigade Leader fish-eye.

"Why don't you ask *me* what happened?" I suggested to the younger, cuter one. But they didn't seem to think that was necessary.

Night fell and the house settled into jittery calm. Mum was locked in her room. I sat on my bed into the wee hours with the pilfered gin bottle, taking raw sips of the fiery stuff whenever I could stand it, trying to get myself to pass out. Lying down, squeezing my eyes shut, then getting up after ten minutes to drink some more.

Next thing I knew I was slipping and sliding down the icy street in my cotton Chinese shoes. I'd grabbed one of Mum's coats from the closet by mistake; it was impossible to close around my gut. The sleeves of the bulky poodle sweater bunched up annoyingly inside the coat sleeves. I felt like an unmade bed. I started walking fast, the Tanteek hot on my tail.

The clouds had all blown away, and there was the usual urban pepper spray of stars in the moonless sky. Dizzy with gin, I stopped in the dead middle of the street.

"Who's up there with you?" I shouted at the stars. "Is it just you guys, or is there someone else? Can you see me down here? I want an answer, and I want it fucking NOW!!!"

Silence.

"Speak up! I'm dying down here! Don't you even care?"

A car skidded by on the ice, lightly grazing me. My feet

swooped out from under, my ass hitting the ground hard. I threw my head back and bawled like a heifer felled by a train.

When I stopped, the silence dropped again, bundling me like a shroud. There was no one about. The only sound was the faint electric buzz from a thousand strings of Christmas lights.

I sat in the middle of the road, scowling up at the stars. They seemed, what? Friendly? Kind of. Benign, like a bunch of old folks sitting on a bench, watching kids play some rude, noisy game. They radiated not love exactly but weary understanding. Tolerance. Forbearance. Wry amusement.

"What's got you so spooked, girly?" they seemed to be asking. "If it's death you're so afraid of, why, you're already halfway there! Your Tanteek has walked you so far out into the darkness that the worst of it's already over."

"But I want to live," I whimpered. "If possible, forever."

The stars nodded back at me, the way old people do when you take the time to say hi if they're sitting someplace all alone, and they want to let you know they appreciate the greeting but don't want you to come any closer in case you have a knife.

I picked myself up painfully and kept on walking, cobbling a skittish plan for my future. No one was holding a gun to my head to stay here. What was stopping me from moving to China? They'd have me, if I swore to them that I had nothing but the revolution to live for. Then all I'd have to do would be to get up every day and work till I dropped at whatever revolutionary task they assigned me. I could tend water buffalo or drain the marshland with all my heart, winning greater victories with every passing day. Or I'd write for *China Reconstructs*, anything they told me to. Hail the No. 5 iron ore-smelting brigade's bold smashing of the nefarious plans of the capitalist roaders! Anything!

Life would be so clear. Wind and thunder stirring, red sun rising in my heart!

The seat of my pants was soaked through. The cold had sobered me up considerably. Head down, I headed for home and straight to the basement.

Gerard's light was still on behind his raggy curtain. I yanked it aside. His collapsed old-man's face rolled in my direction. His pillow was lying across his stomach, his head flat on the mattress. His haunted face in the glare of the nighttable lamp was slick with oil and swarming with newborn pimples.

Baby sat on a folding chair next to the bed, her head drooping, snoring lightly.

"Are you gonna tell me what's going on with you?"

His eyes closed, slow as a lizard's. His head rolled away to face the wall. His voice, when it came, was colourless, odourless, like carbon monoxide.

"I'm having a nervous breakdown."

When he turned his face back my way, it was unaccountably lit up with droll frivolity.

"Get out! I'm so jealous!" I pulled up the other chair, leaning forward eagerly. "Did the College of Theological Knowledge do it to you?"

The twin knobs of his shoulders jolted upward and dropped back. Tears, only recently dried, recommenced. He wiped away a shiny rope of snot with his cadaverous hand.

"Nobody understands!" he breathed hoarsely. "Mum writes to me four times a week, asking for the moon, telling me I'm her one hope and joy. I'm her only reason for living. She sends me novena cards, asking me to get her stuff from God like I have my own private hotline. What am I supposed to..." He stopped to honk back what sounded like a quart of phlegm. Then his eyes met mine, direct, lucid, and alight with inner fire.

"I saw heaven. I was there. I was really *there*! And it's, you have to believe me, it's *so* much better than here!"

This was more information than I'd dreamed possible. Gerard confiding! My heart swelled. Could Happy Humphrey be far away?

"So how did you—?"

"What was going on upstairs, before?" He pushed himself up onto his crab's leg elbows. "Why did the cops come?"

A spark jumped between us, the wordless communication of twins, or maybe just of youth. His face was tentatively ironic, a millimetre away from a smile.

"How did you know there were cops?"

"Baby told me. She went up just as they were leaving. The racket was unbelievable. The living room's right over our heads."

"The pigs came because Dad went berserk. Three guesses who called them, and the first two don't count. I heard her in the kitchen, whispering so she wouldn't get caught."

"Berserk how?"

"Throwing stuff. Knocking Mum around, like she doesn't deserve it. But when the fuzz got here, everybody clammed up. They asked Mum if she wanted to press charges, but she took a minute out from bawling to politely decline."

"Stupid cocksucker."

"Gerard!" I was genuinely shocked.

"I told him I hated him and I meant it."

"Mum told the police she wants a restraining order. Which is really rich, since the whole fiasco is her fault, just like everything else."

Gerard said nothing.

"Don't think she isn't pleased as punch about all this. Anything that makes Dad look bad suits her to a T. She probably planned everything to happen this way just so she could come out looking like a saintly martyr."

Gerard's face crumpled. "I'm sorry," he whispered brokenly, not to me. He eased himself down flat, closing his eyes. Unwilling to lose him so soon, I clutched at his pyjama sleeve, trying to tug him back to me, to bring that wan smile back to his chapped lips.

"Uncle Dermott thinks you need to see a shrink."

Silence.

"Were you really living in a shit hole on Dundas?" This galvanized him all right; he jacked himself back onto his elbows and whispered savagely, "So what? What's it to you?" before collapsing again. His eyes swerved surreptitiously in Baby's direction, but she snored on, crumpled up in her veils as if she were sleeping in a laundry bag.

"It's fucked up, is what it is to me."

"Shut up."

Long minutes passed. The furnace came to life with a sudden roar, making me jump.

"Are you going back?"

"Yes."

"You know you don't have to."

"Yes I do."

"Why? Why can't you just be a good person? Why do you have to be a priest? Just because it's what Mum wants? Do you have to live your whole life for her? Don't you have a mind of your own?"

No answer.

"What if you're not cut out for it? Geez, you're like one of those stupid, die-hard kids who just *has* to make it to Broadway when everybody's telling you, kid, you got no talent."

No answer.

"Plus, you can't go back if you're having a breakdown."

"I had it. It's over now."

"You're kidding, right?"

He flopped his head my way, hot poker eyes boring into mine.

"You don't have to sit there feeling sorry for me, or superior either." He took a deep, sandpaper breath, his clavicle nearly colliding with his chin. "Sickness is the natural state of the true disciple of Christ. He calls us to be ready for death at a moment's notice. Being sick for his cause is a blessed privilege." He stopped between each wheezing sentence to haul in air. "When we're weak and all the fight's been knocked out of us, then it becomes easy to let go of our wills and submit to him." He coughed hard, knees jerking up to his stomach.

"Is that why you're not eating? Because—"

"Anyone who has ever really heard him speak…" He stopped, sobs beginning to wrack him all over again. "When he speaks, really speaks to you, he, he…throws you down and, and…"

I watched in alarm as he writhed and gasped like a caught fish on the bed. Baby continued to snorfle on; he must have really put her through the wringer.

"Sickness and, and death and loneliness are precious," he croaked at last. "Pascal tells us that all the evil in the world comes from people who aren't content to sit alone in their rooms."

"Yeah, well, for his information, it's never done me a fucking bit of good." I was on the knife-edge of yanking aside my protective curtain of quip and irony and spilling my whole sad story to this favoured, albeit obnoxious, child of God.

"So did you get this sickness and death stuff from your Flagellation 101 lecture notes, or did you think it up all by yourself?"

He ignored me. In her corner, Baby gabbled something and shifted, cracking her head up sharply. Her eyes sprang open. Then her head dropped again.

As if on cue, Gerard burst into lusty, histrionic tears. Something in me twanged and snapped. I slapped him hard across the face. Then I slammed a left hook into his sunken stomach. He lay flat and unresisting but wailing as if the she-demon Corra were gnawing at his balls.

Baby's eyes snapped open, slowly focusing on the two of us.

"Mag Mary! Goodness, what time...Oh dear. Oh dear, No! Stop! What's the matter now?" Gerard was convulsing, heaving, clawing his hands down his face. Baby fairly tackled him where he lay, throwing her big body down on top of him, crooning, "You have to stop. Shhhhhh. Stop. Stop. It's all right. Do as I told you, remember? Just do as I told you."

She stroked his sodden head, his pimply face, whispering calming words I couldn't hear. Gradually his heaves became shudders, his shudders slackened to laboured breathing. At long last he lay quiet, eyes closed, his work here done.

"What did you tell him? Can't you see he just wants attention?" I said sulkily. "You're falling for it like everyone else. He can have a giant, kicking, screaming freakout any time he feels like it because he thinks he's the only person with problems. Mommy's precious darling. Give me a fucking break."

Baby said nothing. She caressed Gerard's arm, still whispering private heavenly counsel into his ear.

"What are you telling him? Why's it such a big secret? Why can't you tell me too?"

Baby pulled back from Gerard and in one burly lunge grabbed me by the shoulders, hauling me with unbelievable strength onto her lap. I sank down into a deep cushion of cloth, feeling like a giant ventriloquist's dummy.

"What's bothering you?" she asked evenly. "Tell me."

I gulped air for a long time. She waited, Gerard hiccupping mildly in the background.

"Something's really wrong with me," I whispered brokenly at last. Nothing else would come out. But she was a nun; she should know what was wrong without my telling her. Talk to me, I begged her silently. Tell me that one magical thing that will take away all the pain, all the fear. Do your job! Tell me what holds *you* together!

"Are you questioning your faith?" Baby asked gently.

"Questioning?" I cried, rearing back. "There's nothing there to question! That stuff isn't real life! It doesn't work for shit! Oh! I'm shocking you, aren't I?"

"Not much. Go on." Her calm, her gentle smile, fed me the strength I needed. I gulped in a great, desperate breath and took the plunge.

"Baby, I'm afraid like, all, all, *all* the time. All my life I've been afraid." I was rolling the edge of her veil into a thick tube, letting it spring free, rolling it up again. "I'm afraid of everything there is. I'm really, really sick, Baby. Sicker than him," I added, narrowing my eyes at Gerard's comatose form. "I can't *stand* thinking about the war, and babies being burnt up, and then it'll be my turn next and, unless, unless maybe the secret is somewhere else?" An idea newly born chinned itself up to my lips and over. "I mean, maybe God hides the way things are made from us so that, when someone gets burnt alive or torn to pieces, it doesn't mean anything, like, right away they wake up somewhere else, someplace good, and it's like they didn't even really get hurt? Because the secret of life is somewhere else? Could that be the answer?"

If Baby knew, she wasn't saying. My bright idea shrivelled like a spider sprayed with Raid. Panic swelled afresh.

"I'm so scared! What happens to us? Where do we go? Oh God, I'm so scared! I'm so scared! I can't stand it!"

"You won't be lost," said Baby soothingly, restraining my jerking arms in a vise grip.

"Lost? What do you mean, *lost*?" My heart plummeted and hit bottom; this possibility had *never* occurred to me! Did she mean people could be literally...lost? Overlooked? Sent spinning off into blackest space, forgotten, alone with myself *in saecula saeculorum*?

Baby, unperturbed, rocked me lumpily back and forth. "I'll tell you what I told your brother. Just let yourself fall into God's arms."

"Why? All God wants to do is scrape people into hell like old chicken bones off a plate!"

"Shhhh. Fall into his arms."

"*What* arms?? He doesn't have any arms! Come *on*! Doesn't it seem suspicious to you that everybody talks about him but nobody *sees* him? It's the Emperor's New Clothes. There's nobody *there*, Baby! Why won't you admit it?"

"There's a lot we don't see. Some things are tuned to a frequency our poor eyes can't penetrate."

This stopped me cold; it sounded vaguely scientific, faintly plausible. A string in my heart pinged.

"Fall into those arms you can't see," she went on, calm as moonlight, "and you will discover that they're there. Just let yourself fall, even though you're afraid, even though you don't understand. You don't have to understand. He'll catch you. You'll recognize him, I promise you. All you need is enough faith to let go and fall. I know you have that much."

"You're wrong."

I closed my eyes and let her rock me. I felt as if we were suspended in infinite space over a cobweb hammock of hope.

"I just want to feel normal again," I whispered at last, putting a heavy, testing foot to one of the shimmering strands.

"Shhhhhh."

My heart gradually slowed, and my spirit, while not soaring, at least tried to jump a few inches into the air, kicking its muffly Chinese heels together. I imagined God standing way below me, chuckling, holding out his arms while I stood, paralyzed, on the window ledge of a burning building forty stories up. What choice did I have? Where the hell else was I going to go?

For a moment, my heart nearly burst with relief and hope. If it was all really true, I could live and be safe! Baby thought it was true, and she was the nicest person on earth. She must know what she was talking about!

She shifted her weight under me, sliding my bulk from one black knee to the other, like a ship's cargo rolling across the deck as the ship rode the swells.

Maybe believing in God was like the sea. Already my hope was fading, my light dimming. But I could sense it getting ready to swell again, to pull back in the other direction. Maybe it would just keep doing this, back and forth, on and off, in and out, for the rest of my life. All I'd have to do was learn how to ride it out.

"Do *you* ever think God is one giant crock?" I asked in a tiny voice.

"I've had my moments."

"Really? When? Tell me!"

"You'll be just fine," she answered with a set to her jaw that made me distrust and respect her at the same time.

"I'm too young for this, Aunt Baby." I gulped against her neck.

"You've no need to be afraid of him. He forgives everything."

A hundredth part of me believed her.

The rest believed Gerard. Because even in his wrecked state, there was no weakness in him. He had no weakness because he wasn't afraid to be wrecked, to run aground, to crack to splinters on the rocks.

For a long time I sat basking in the golden afterglow of

paralyzing fear, the nightmare that really had been one after all, the car wreck swerved out of at the last second, the ice that had cracked ominously but never broken through. I sat on Baby's big lap like a dumb but increasingly cocky kid, shooting prayers up to what I imagined as some soft-hearted and easily outwitted geezer in the sky.

Besides. What geezer couldn't I outrun, if it turned out he was a hateful old crank after all?

Gerard had rolled away from us to face the wall, his knees folded to his chest. Baby reached out to lay her hand on the spiny ridge of his back. Her other arm was still around me. She sat between the two of us like a conduit, and no one said a word, until she finally whispered, "I have to get up, sweetie. My legs have both gone completely to sleep."

All the rest of that winter in Montreal, I was jumping into God's invisible arms every twenty minutes. They kept getting lower. It wasn't like jumping from a building any more. It was like jumping from the moon into a water glass.

Nothing was better, nothing was fixed. My old pal the Tanteek was still panting at my side like a hideous, slavering hound, jumping up and pawing me every chance he got, his black tongue slobbering over my face, his evil-smelling muzzle poking into my ear, woofing and whining for me to leap onto his back and ride away with him. Since no one else could see him, they'd simply see me hunched and floating above the ground, clutching the air in white fists.

I took Blaise Pascal's gloomy advice, holing up in my grim

little room and skim-reading *Moby-Dick*, combing through it for the good parts the way other people troll through books for porn. If I was anyone in that damned book, I was Pip, the cabin boy who jumped out of the boat in a blind panic every time they set out after a whale. Pip, who found himself left alone at last in the middle of the eternal blue sea, abandoned in disgust by the hard-working, no-nonsense whalers. Pip, no more than a pinhead bobbing in the rolling emptiness, rescued at last but too late, his mind shattered, his reason salt-corroded to a rusty shell.

I skipped far more classes than not. When I wasn't in my room, I was out Tanteek-walking, head down, counting my steps, trying to break the ten thousand mark before I turned back, still desolate, for home.

One Sunday I rounded the last bend to find Liam perched on my rooming house steps, bright as an all-points bulletin. For weeks he'd been trying to cajole me out of the darkness; he thought it had to do with my disastrous academic performance.

"Geez, Maggie, don't sweat it. If you flunk out, you flunk out. There's more to life than reading a lot of dead guys' books. Come on, man! You only live once!"

That's the *problem*, numbskull, I wanted to scream at him.

But today he was rolling out the big guns. He opened his palm to display two sea-and-sky-blue tabs of acid resting in a nest of grubby tissue and pocket fluff.

"You need your mind opened, Maggers," he smirked, adding, with a sly wink, that I should ask Alice beause she'd know.

Destabilizing myself even more seemed like the dumbest

move imaginable. But I wanted him to be proud of me. I also wanted to do something Sam wouldn't do.

It was Sunday; we had the whole day free. We went to his room, where he soon had banks of candles going on his dresser, on his cluttered desk, on his wobbly dinette table. No sooner had we lain chastely side by side on his bed, waiting for the drugs to kick in, than he cried, "Let's pretend we're on a magic carpet!" And happy, happy boy, he began bumping up and down on the mattress, eyes closed, arms flapping.

"Oh, wow! I can see the air molecules! I can see Paris! Now we're flying over Sweden! Look at all the beautiful people! Watch this, Maggers! This is what I'm gonna do when I really get there this summer! I'm gonna steal my old man's movie camera, and *paaaan* just like this, *slooooowly* over everything I see!" He was leaning over the edge of the bed, holding the invisible camera to his right eye, the left one squinched shut. "We're going to *EXPLOOOOORE*!" he shouted, bouncing to his feet on the bed, rocking and swaying like Washington crossing the choppy Potomac.

Where's the good acid that makes people jump out of windows, was what I was thinking. Fuck Sweden! Try living for fifteen minutes in the Bergman movie of *my* life, you pop-eyed twit.

Bored and black of heart, I was beginning to think we'd swallowed a couple of blue aspirin when I noticed that the notes of the Hendrix tune he was playing had suddenly been incarnated into thousands upon thousands of thumb-sized leprechauns who streamed out of the stereo speakers and proceeded to bounce on my stomach, carom off Liam's head, and sproing back and forth between the walls. They swarmed the room like the demons from Pandora's box, wearing thimble hats and tiny frock coats, each one's teeny teeth bared in its unique-as-a-snowflake goblin grin.

I closed my eyes; they were still there. I went to sit under the kitchen table, hugging my knees, burying my face in my hands, but Jimi kept churning out more. I could feel their high-heeled boots hammering my shoulders, their wee, leathery hands gripping clumps of my hair as they Tarzan-swung to the far corners of the room. They tried to burrow up my nose. They tried to run up the legs of my jeans, the little perverts, faster than I could slap them away.

Out the window I could see giant icicles, huge mothers, six feet around at the top. I must have crawled into a cave thick with stalactites. The cave was a waiting room, a holding cell, and God, the Separator of the Right from the Left for all eternity, was making his unhurried way toward me, flicking a riding crop like lightning, Josef Mengele meeting the train. His eye behind his monocle was huge; it jumped like a fish. He shattered me with two words: Goat. Left.

And then I was in hell, to where the Tanteek had been walking me all along.

But hell wasn't what I'd thought. It was silent. There was no fire, no screaming. I sensed rather than saw endless cracked concrete and chain-link fences, a cold ochre sky. Nothing terrible was going to happen except this: every day from now on was going to be the exact copy of the one that had gone before.

Nor would I be alone. My no-exit world contained two eternal companions, ancient crones, one little and bony and the other a huge, stoop-shouldered hulk. The two of them were tight; they'd been together forever. They resented the hell out of having to drag me along.

Every day we three would be setting out for the no-frills hell supermarket, where the cans were unlabelled, greasy, and half squashed, where desiccated, dirt-clumped root vegetables lay scattered in filthy bins along with black bananas and hunks of green meat. The whole time, the big one would never stop talking. She'd keep pointing out all the wares to her friend, whining, I bought those peaches last week and they were terrible. Had to throw them all out. Let me show you those cookies I got that were just terrible, she'd say, every single cursed day, her friend trotting at her heels like a terrier, with a rapacious grin and spittle on her chin. And me trudging behind them like a cow on a rope. Back and forth to that supermarket with the sputtering fluorescent lights, carrying our stuff home in grimy plastic bags to a bare attic room with ceilings too low to stand in, our arms nothing but bones, our eyes lolling like marbles in their sockets.

I was going to feel as if I were living inside a dry-cleaning bag. And it was going to last for as long as it took an angel who picked up one grain of sand every ten thousand years to empty all the deserts in the world, and then do it all again once for every grain of sand there was in the universe. And then to do it all over again for every star. And then to start all over again from the beginning, and again and again, world without end, amen.

I hunched under the table, paralyzed, while Liam jounced and pirouetted, chattered and sang. The Jimi-chauns were on me like fire ants. It was a waking coma; I couldn't speak or move, but I could see and hear everything. Every time Liam flung out his arms or tossed his handsome head, he left silver trails and red slashes in the air, like nighttime car lights in a speeded-up film.

The silver and red trails looked like hope; they spun out from him until they hit the walls, where they were abruptly snuffed out and replaced by more. Watch how beautiful the cigarette in his hand is, I told myself. Watch his lips, watch his rippling sleeves. Don't tear him into bloody pieces. Don't see him dead. See him *now*. Ask him to sing louder; it's hard to hear way down here! I tried to mouth the words, my fingers scrabbling at the floor like some trapped, wild thing.

I don't remember coming out of it. It blew over and left me. I saw Liam roll a fat joint, and I wondered aloud when he thought he was going to have enough drugs in his system. That's when I knew I was okay again.

He was scuttling around the room, pulling garbage bags out of cupboards, rooting in his junk drawer for string. He said, "Watch this and trip out, man!" He lined up a bunch of pots full of water on the floor and tied a green garbage bag to the pipe in the ceiling. Then he tied another one to the bottom of that one. Then he lit a match and set it ablaze.

Blobs of liquid blue flame floomed up and dropped into the pots underneath, hissing and sizzling. He was beside himself, his eyes lit up with green fire. I watched him in awe, marvelling at how at home on the earth he was. He strung up three more bags and lit them all, whooping and hopping like Rumpelstiltskin. The beads around his neck might as well have been human eyes and ears. I knew the place would go up in a fireball any second, and there was nothing I could do about it.

But of course it didn't happen. It so often doesn't.

He turned on his clunky, rented TV. Ed Sullivan was on. Liam sat with his nose to the screen watching some corny old dance team in sequins and pomaded hair. "I can do that," he cried, breathless and sparkly with self-knowledge. "My body knows how to do that! I can do those steps, and those leaps, and I don't even have to think about it. I have perfect dance pitch!"

He turned the TV up as loud as it would go, and the stereo, too, shouting, "Mixed media, man!" The Ray Bloch Orchestra was in a fistfight with Big Brother and the Holding Company. I felt strangely at home. I crawled out from under the table and climbed onto the bed, a ship doldrummed on a flat sea with no place to go.

Liam was still punchy. He sat next to me, riffling my hair, his face shiny, cheeks carnation pink.

"Man, dig this old fart singer. That's the kind of music my old man digs. Whoa, bummer. Why am I thinking about him? What a bringdown. Shit, man!"

"What's wrong with your old man?" I asked, my eyes shut, my arms feeling long enough to turn the doorknob fifteen feet away.

"He's plastic, man."

"What's your mother like? Is she cool?" I asked, trying to sound interested.

"I hate his guts. He drove me crazy over the holidays. Man, I hate going home."

I tried again. "Is your mother cool?"

"Yeah," he said. She agreed his old man was a hopeless drag. They'd gotten married way too young. It was the worst mistake she'd ever made. She was into politics now, which he could respect, especially for someone her age. She ran lots of committees and stuff, used to teach elementary school but then she'd started writing this column for the local paper.

I was waiting for him to finish because I wanted to tell him about *my* holidays. I'd never talked about my family with him, nor said a word about my spectacular Christmas. Then again, he hadn't asked.

He said, "Sure, it's the Establishment press and all, but she gets to say her piece and she gets people pissed off at her. She even ran for mayor. Blew my mind, man!"

I thought he meant mayor of Montreal, but, "No, no, mayor of our town on the West Island. Anyhow, she lost. She demanded a recount, but they wouldn't do it."

"My father took off on Christmas Day," I told him. "He never came back. Some phony-baloney woman claiming to be his secretary came and got his clothes." But that was as far as I got; the needle stuck there, and anyway I didn't think he'd heard me. I just sat on his bed, while the Tanteek stood next to me marching in place, stiff-armed, like a broken robot.

Then, in the blink of an eye, it was April, the long, dark school year over, no more pencils, no more books. And crazy warm too, July-warm, that night we went to Debbie's house.

Debbie, a friend of Liam's sister Charlotte, who was in

pre-med at McGill, was having her engagement party at her parents' house, way out on the lakeshore near where Liam lived. That very afternoon, I'd irremediably botched my last exam. Liam laid some wine on me to cheer me up, a whole bottle's worth. I told him, Never mind, who cares, I'll start over next year from scrash, go into languages, something tech, tech-nickle, with rules, vocabulary lisths, easy-to-understand shit. What the fuck. Lang-guages. I'll fucking blow everybody's minds, go work at the UN, and give me that back, who said you could drink that, that's my glass! Gimme that! I'm not drunk. Okay? Thass right. Feeling no pain. Thass right. Fuck off.

All the snow had disappeared overnight, buds coming out, grass plumping up underfoot. "We'll go barefoot!" I said. "Dig it!"

We passed the hash pipe before the bus came. I felt all right. Better than all right. There'd be a punchbowl at the party, right? More likker, right? Any friend of Charlotte's was an enemy of ours, right? That was the only reason we were going, to give the finger to Liam's uptight, overachieving, Establishment-pleasing sister. I'd met her a couple of times; I'd never encountered anyone with such low wattage. "She takes after my dad," Liam had sneered, summing up and dismissing his sister with a sharp finger flick.

"We'll try rapping with the straights," he snickered as we slid into our seats on the bus. "But if we hate it, we can always split."

A giddy little boy in the seat in front of us clambered up onto his fat knees, beaming, to show us the toy truck he'd been vrooming up and down his mother's shoulder. He had both of us grinning, and in my secret heart I was thinking, Maybe one day we'd have a little sweetheart like him of our own. My heart swooped upward on a jet of gas, my brain calculating at the speed of light: children are beautiful, children are pure, children are the essence of hope. Hope is Life. Then Life unspooled before me like a blurry, bright yellow and blue home movie of sunlight and flowers, heedless laughter, and someone's loving arm around me. I thought: There's so much to live for! Everything is going to work out just fine! Then the rocket I was clinging to looped over like a giant question mark and the little boy grew up in front of me. I saw his eyes blown out like windows in a hurricane, saw him carried on a stretcher by men running bent double under the churning propellers of Chinooks. He wore a helmet with a picture of Snoopy on it. His toy truck hung around his neck with his dog tags. I saw him tossed senseless into his grinning, steaming grave where he'd mottle and putrefy and stink and disappear forever. Life looked so stupid now. There was no reason for it to live, and no escape for anyone trussed up in its sticky, murderous web.

I needed more drugs, was all. We sucked back another pipeful, sitting in the squishy mud of Debbie's front lawn before hobbling up the front walk feeble with laughter, our arms around each other, high on our own greatness. Drink awaited inside. And plastic music! Bad vibe alert, we snorted, our legs crumbling beneath us.

The living room was packed with girls dressed like the talent on Lawrence Welk: pastel dresses, empire waists, hair ringletted and stacked high. The boys were all junior executives in tight ties and snappy jackets, clean wheat jeans and desert boots. "Watch out for the freeeaaaks," we cackled at each other, slobbering guffaws on each other's shoulders.

Debbie and her mother in twin madras hostess skirts were working the room like geishas, bending with silver trays of cocktail weenies and olives on toothpicks. We cleaned out the whole tray, twice over. Then we flopped into their big armchairs, me with my dirty feet up on a hassock, Liam, red-eyed and burpy, his big, hot Frye boots trailing mud and wet grass over the thick pale carpet. Charlotte's face was pure evil, although the other guests seemed to forget about us quickly enough. Hordes of giggling girls sat demurely on the floor around Debbie, legs folded sideways just so in their tight skirts, while she opened her gifts: crock pots, hair dryers, his-and-hers barbecue aprons. Mr. Debbie-to-be stood behind her, clucking and smiling, a quiet sherry in his hand. The girls squeaked and squealed. Liam and I sat sneering at the happy fray, having arrived giftless, which was further proof, as if needed, of our grand detachment from everything proper, well bred, and phony.

Debbie was holding up the darlingest pair of one-piece jammies for the crowd to admire when a freight train hurtled through the French doors and mowed me down in my chair.

There were pots, there were pyjamas, and then there was nothing but "*No point! No future! Because you're all going to die!! To die!! TO DIE!!*"

The chair spewed me out of its mouth straight out the French doors and into the back garden. I broke into a run down the sloping yard that ended at the edge of the lake. The grass was slippery under my bare feet. I was running, sliding straight into the fourth dimension, Tanteek claws around my throat, and no way back.

I fell onto the tiny, stony beach, sobbing in white terror.

After a very long time, I felt Liam's hand on my shoulder. "Whoa! You on a bad trip?"

I saw him as if through the wrong end of a telescope, tiny and perfectly contained, his eyes lit up with adventure and loopy good times.

"Come on!" he yelled. There was a rowboat pulled up on the shale of the beach. "C'mon, man, it'll be far out!" He pulled off his boots, held out his hand from the far end of the universe, and pulled me into the dark little boat. Then he ran behind it, pushing it out into the quietly lapping waves, before leaping like a pirate over the side, shouting, "Too far fucking out!" at the sky.

He sat facing me, rolling up the sleeves of his pink Mexican wedding shirt, clattering the oars into place. Behind us, the long dark Debbie yard rose to a heaven of bright windows, where the party petered on in safe, well-lit splendour. No one missed us; no one came running with waving arms to the beach to stop us.

I crouched in the stern while he rowed, thinking, He's got nothing to do with me. He's a grown man. The muscles in his arms undulated like nests of snakes. His head was thrown back, and he was singing, "Row, row, row your boat," trying to get me to smile.

He stopped after a few minutes, holding the oars against his chest, and leaned forward, mystified. "Why are you crying?"

"There's...no...way...out." I was pitching and gulping, rocking the boat dangerously. "Nothing matters. There's no reason for doing anything! I'm so scared, Liam. I'm so scared. I can't get it to stop. There's no way out! We're trapped!"

"We were having such a good time! Don't, don't, Maggie Muffin. It's going to be okay."

"It's *never* going to be okay!" I was frantic; he didn't know, he couldn't see!

We began drifting, turning in circles, his arms dangling over the sides, fingers trailing in the black water. Useless lights of people's pointless, temporary homes winked at us from the shore.

"There's no such *thing* as okay. We're all going to die, and really soon. Where will we go? Why did we have to come here in the first place when it's all for nothing?"

My chin was slimed with mucus. I was freezing in the balmy air. The boat was perched on top of the water for now, but at any moment it could be hit by a meteor, flipped over, sucked under. It was only a matter of time. Below us awaited hungry, yawning creatures of the wet and the dark, unspeakable tentacled plants, aqueous Venus flytraps with multiple eyes. Also awaiting: Pip's water-logged mind, of which I wanted no part, no part at all, not now, not ever.

Liam's face was a sailor's knot of perplexity. Could I be the only person on earth to see the truth? Debbie and Charlotte, and Mrs. Debbie with her twin flipped-up commas of hair, and dopey Mr. Debbie in his plaid pants, sitting on the edge of the sofa among the flibbertigibbet girls; none of them saw it! They'd rudely dismissed their deaths long ago. They were barnacled tight to the stuff of life, hopping the stepping-stones of good times, looking forward to many more, until —*pop!*— they'd burst like soap bubbles, painlessly, into nothing.

Why was I the only one who could see it? Why was I the only one who was *bothered*?

"Liam, am I going insane?"

"Hey! Don't freak out! It's outtasight to be insane! Crazy

247

people are the real seers, man!" He leaned back on his elbows and addressed the stars. "The so-called normal people are the sick ones. The more normal you are, the sicker you are, ipso facto." He started giggling. "Ipso facto. Flipso flacto. Cripso crakto!" He grabbed my knee and wiggled it back and forth. "Zipso zapso! Schmipso schmapso! Hey, c'mon! It's funny, man!"

He looked so pretty, his curls bunched like grapes around his face. I was sure his necklace of multicoloured beads had been hand-strung by Sam, his happy head lying in her lap as she recited from the *Rubaiyat of Omar Khayyam*.

"Maybe it means you're beginning to really think. Thinking can be dangerous to your health!" he advised me cheerfully.

"What do you mean? I'm beginning to *really* think, or I'm *finally* beginning to think?"

But he'd begun singing again, tunelessly, a sea shanty to which the only words he knew were "ear-lye in the morn-ing." The boat dipped gently, the waves slapping the sides. Cassiopeia went swinging across the sky. Down on earth, I was swallowing hard.

"Melville says," I squeaked and stopped. I took a deep breath, began again. "Melville says, 'Mortal man who hath more of joy than sorrow in him cannot be true. The truest of all men was the Man of Sorrows.'" I hoped he'd at least give me credit for memorizing a line with "hath" in it.

He took out his damned pipe and filled it from the baggie in his back pocket, muttering about ripoffs, not enough hash to see us through the night's adventures. He looked up at me. A light switched on in his face. He, too, had literature to share. He began to declaim.

"The sea is calm tonight, my friend, something something, the moon something, the French coast, the cliffs of Dover, anyhow, what the fuck, oh love let us be true, for the world which lies before us like a land of dreams, so something, beautiful, so new, has, has, I really know this, Sam loves it, has, has neither joy nor, nor light nor love, nor certitu...tainity, nor what, nor, um, certainty, nooooor, oh yeah, peace, peace, man peace, nor help for pain, yeah, that's it, and we sit here on a darkening plain, thaaaaaat's it, swept with something, struggle and flight, where ignorant armies clash by night. See? You're not the only one who memorizes stuff!"

He held out the lit pipe to me. "That's all the truth you need to know."

"I don't want any more. No, Liam, I mean it!"

"More for me then."

He stretched his legs out, leaned back, closed his eyes. My knees knocked against the gunwales.

"Does this stuff really not bother you, or it does and you're just not talking about it?"

"Neither." He put the pipe to his lips again, sucking in and exhaling with a phlegmy wheeze. Then he knocked the pipe on the side of the boat, pocketed it, and lit us both cigarettes. We inhaled simultaneously. He leaned back once more, expansive as God, holding all the aces.

"I'm too interested in life. By some fluke, I happen to be here, so while I am, I want to *be* here. Plenty of time to be dead later on." He threw his arms above his head, emitting a wolf howl: Arooooooo! The boat bounced.

"Oh, maaaan! This stuff is too fucking great!"

I unleashed a wail like an air raid siren.

"Hey! Hey! Hey!" He reached for me, took my face between his hands, touched his nose to mine. "You're never going to understand the meaning of life, so don't think about it. Just live! Sure it's hopeless, but just don't look at it. Live for today. Eat, smoke, and be merry!"

He was behind a firewall. He couldn't hear me at all.

"It's too late, Liam. I can't go back. What I know is the only true thing there is! It kills everything else."

"Well, come on, don't cry about it." He took both my hands in his. "Be cool, Maggie Muffin. Oh, man! Now what? What did I say?"

"Listen to me. Please, just listen to me! Don't laugh!" I was trembling so hard my teeth chattered. "Two ships are passing out at sea. The *Pequod* is Ahab's ship, remember? You read it. The other one is the *Bachelor*—"

"Bachelor in Paradise," he interjected, grinning inanely.

"Please! No stupid commentary! Just listen!"

"What's this got to do with..."

Yes, what's this got to do with, I thought. We weren't on Melville's ocean. We were on a stupid, flat lake in Quebec, in a stolen rowboat. We were nowhere and nobody.

Shut up, I answered myself. You are one among billions, no more but no less. Keep going. Try, for God's sake!

"Listen!" Another deep breath, the clanging of my iron will in my ear. "The *Bachelor* is all lit up, remember? Everyone on board is carousing and dancing."

"I don't remember. I didn't get past chapter three."

"Listen to me, Liam! Stop rooting through your pockets! They've come through bad times and trouble, but the *Pequod* is heading to the place they've come from, and it's a dark ship and gloomy and everyone on it is afraid. The two captains catch sight of each other. The captain of the *Bachelor* raises his big thing of ale and shouts, Come aboard! Come aboard! And Ahab shouts back at him, from the darkness of the *Pequod* deck. He shouts, 'Hast seen the White Whale?' as they pass each other, passing, passing the whole time."

The words hurt coming out. There was more of my heart in them than could squeeze through my throat.

"The *Bachelor*'s drunken captain shouts back to Ahab. He shouts: 'Heard of him, but don't believe in him at all! Come aboard, and I'll soon take that black from your brow. A full ship we are, and homeward bound!'" I took a deep, steadying drag of my smoke and pitched it over the side. "And Ahab said to himself... *pay attention*, Liam! Ahab said to himself, 'How wondrous familiar is a fool! Call me an empty ship and outward bound.' And the *Bachelor* sailed away all full of party cheer with the wind behind it, while the *Pequod* kept on going, fighting the wind the whole way."

My breath swelled and retreated like sails blown out full, empty, full. Empty. Waiting.

"I can't believe you memorized *Moby-Dick*! You're amazing! How did you do that and still manage to flunk the Lit exam?"

"It memorized itself," I answered dully.

"Hey! Just try to relax. When you come down, the bad feeling will go away."

"No it won't. You don't know. You're blind." I watched the

shore lights slurring in the rippling water. My speech receded to the hidden place from where it had been summoned, slamming the door behind it.

"C'mon. Don't go wacko on me." His eyes narrowed ever so slightly.

"You said people who didn't think were the sick ones."

"Yeah, but you can make yourself sick, and you're going to if you don't pull yourself out of this. C'mon. You were fine before. You'll be fine again."

Breathing in, breathing out. Breathing through a throat blocked with refuse, scrap metal, black fumes. I breathed to the waves only: The wisdom that is woe, the woe that is madness. I breathed out to my friend, the black night.

We brought the boat back to shore, caught the bus back to the city. Liam was bright and gabby, trying hard. It wasn't his fault. He talked about dropping out of university, about maybe going to ballet school, about how brilliant Sam was. About growing his own dope and hoping to see Dylan at the Isle of Wight in the summer. I felt like his grandmother, stooped, weary, ugly as roots in the rain, walking the Tanteek on a leash. I counted my breaths, in and out, all the way home: one, two, four thousand and six, four thousand and seven.

The Tanteek got into bed with me, as usual. He promised he'd never leave, that he alone understood.

The next day, I called home, collect, from the wall phone in Mrs. Babushka's kitchen. There were gilded icons in the corners with red lights burning in front of them, a bright yellow plastic tablecloth, and a centrepiece of artificial blue carnations. The calendar over the phone had Cyrillic lettering under a picture of a smiling, flaxen-haired peasant girl in an apron, holding a lamb.

Mrs. Babushka was baking plate-sized cookies with raisins in them. She didn't offer me any. I didn't blame her. How could she stand all of us thronging outside her door night and day with our smoke and our stinking feet, our demented music and shrieking and door banging?

I hadn't called home since March when Mum had given me to understand in twenty-five words or less that she was now a woman alone and that Gerard had steadied himself and was doing magnificently. The badly listing ship had been righted and set back on course, its mutinous crew thrown to the sharks. There was no other thing that wanted saying.

She picked up and accepted the charges with an intimidating briskness, barking, "What" as soon as the operator was gone. Her voice was flat, uneasy, a stick held out in front for protection. Then it was my turn to talk.

I humped over the phone without a word to my name. Nothing came out but gulps and sobs. Mrs. Babushka slipped tactfully into her living room and shut the door. I cradled the phone against my shoulder, looking at that happy peasant girl, her happy little lamb. Mum was the one to finally break the shuddering silence.

"That fellow from the Dominion wants to know if you'll be back this year."

"I...don't know."

"You don't know."

"No. Tell him no." I hung up.

...

The arrival of summer calmed me somewhat. I achieved a steady state of melancholy, already several rungs above suicidal. I got dressed. Ate. Walked. Sat on park benches with bags of chips, watching everybody scurry hither and yon.

I tried sitting in the backs of churches, but it made my stomach lurch dangerously. I didn't want to tempt fate, so I quit. I never knew what they were talking about anyway. None of it had me in mind.

I found a summer job as a finisher in a dress factory just north of Jean-Talon, psychological light years from the McGill ghetto. I sat all day at a low table heaped with garments, cutting the hanging threads off after the buttons had been sewn on, the hems zinged under the needle. Italian and Greek ladies sat in long rows, whipping sleeves and yokes through their humming machines with the rhythmic precision of galley slaves.

The ghetto, hot and steamy, was all but deserted for the summer. Except, of course, for Marc. He took to dropping over in the evenings, loaded down with pamphlets, newspapers, tracts. Bruno, his new acolyte, came with him. Bruno was half Mohawk, short and stick-thin, with lanky brown hair styled like Hitler's. He was missing a few foreground teeth and put me in mind of a chimney sweep. But he had a grin I liked. A little like Liam's but not so damned cocksure.

The two of them sat on my Murphy bed talking revolutionary shop till I passed out. I didn't care. Once, I asked Marc to give me a straight answer on what it would take to end the war.

"We must all come under the discipline of the working class, by which I mean working class theory. In the final stage of moribund imperialism, a people's war on a protracted basis is the only way to guarantee world peace and help the Vietnamese, and all oppressed people." My heart sank. How the hell long was *that* going to take? Yet the sound of the two of them yakking away soothed me. Besides, I could hear Liam's voice shrieking all the way from Europe: "That Bruno, he digs you, man!"

At night, when no Marxist-Leninists came to call, I had the common room TV all to myself. I watched variety shows and sitcoms, curled up on the lumpy couch. Sometimes Mrs. Babushka sat with me, watching through her thick bifocals, understanding nothing, her eyes, behind all that glass, like ancient pennies thrown into a fountain, in vain, for good luck.

We watched the war together. The Mothers of Invention, or the Airplane, or Junior Walker drifted from the odd window on the street and into our open one. On my day off, we watched the news at noon before she switched off the set to disappear into her kitchen. The picture tube burped shut after sending off a few arcing flares. In the dark, in the jungle, somewhere inside the TV, I knew the war was still going on. I tried to imagine a lull in the fighting for those boys, tried to imagine them huddled together under banana plants, toking up, passing roaches. I hoped they could snatch a moment of peace that way.

I took a page from Mum's brief, concise book, suddenly comprehending the soothing relief of personal silence. I hardly spoke at all the whole summer, except to repeat slogans after Marc: Take up the historic task! Seek truth from facts! I graduated to two packs of smokes a day. My voice started to sound like rusty, gurgling pipes, and I liked it that way.

Liam came back from Europe the last week in August, golden

brown, his hair bleached and streaked, his grubby Eurail Pass sticking ostentatiously out of his front pocket. He couldn't stop talking about Paris, Rome, Vienna, Amsterdam, all the groovy heads he'd met that summer. His only regret was that Woodstock had come and gone without him.

He took to calling me "sister" in the peace-and-brother/ sisterhood spirit of the times. Thank you, sister. Are you coming, sister? His lofty, sanctimonious detachment seemed like the worst blow of all.

We picked our courses haphazardly, neither one of us intending to see any of them through. We registered for classes in September when it was still sweltering. He wore shorts, and his Europe-knowing legs were the colour of chocolate milk. With my white skin, long sleeves, and un-sunned face, I felt as insubstantial as smoke.

A week later he announced that he was born to dance, not to kowtow to the Man. He dropped everything and started taking dance classes, four, five a day, at a cheesy, fly-by-night dance academy way to hell and gone in Longueuil. I hardly ever saw him.

Meanwhile, Bruno started sleeping over. It was no big whoop, becoming a woman and all.

I stuck it out all the way to Christmas before dropping out for good, trailing after Bruno to rabid little meetings held in classrooms at night, ratty red banners lettered with screaming yellow slogans hung over the blackboards. Sometimes we went to people's houses, grim apartments with no furniture and grey venetian blinds drawn tight. Someone always put a rolled-up blanket over the telephone, in case the RCMP or the CIA were listening in to our urgent meetings, which were chiefly held in order to plan more meetings. I went out with some other humour-free comrade in the wee hours to stand at factory gates, handing out leaflets and tracts as the sun came up. Every day, the same oppressed proletarian took a leaflet from me and asked, "C'est quoi, ça? Du porno?" as rich, working class laughter erupted all around me.

It was easy to pretend that I went along, right down to the profession of atheism. It was the perfect cover. Nobody needed to know about my regular falls into the gossamer net. The Marxist-Leninist world was as narrow a road as anything Christianity might ask of me, and it was just as easy to fake. Mostly I sat at the back, as was my way, passing under the radar. It was nice to feel numb. It was nice to have a vague sense of purpose. I thought if they really were going to change the world, then it'd be good to be on their side. And if they didn't, well, too bad. I didn't much care either way.

Bruno worked as a recording engineer in his day-to-day, bourgeois life. He ran off clandestine copies of the important comrades' speeches in the studio at night after everyone had gone home. One night he hustled me into the studio to read an introduction on one of the tapes. He liked my voice, he said; it had a real militant quality. Some of the comrades had remarked on it. Those tapes flew off the meeting book tables at three dollars a pop, and dour, Fortrel-wearing revolutionaries began coming up and complimenting me. Apparently, I reddened their ears, inflamed their revolutionary ardour; some of them actually trembled as they shook my hand, me, a mere hanger-on, a no-name scrub.

Liam called once, to invite me to his spring wedding, burbling away about commercial auditions and the dancing life, and all his funky new friends with their beautiful bodies and long silk scarves and arch attitudes.

"Yeah? Well, when the revolution comes, you'll be the first to go," I told him smartly, thinking to myself, The people's quick thinking stops an enemy agent!

He hung up on me.

And that was that.

Mere days before Christmas, I informed Bruno that he was getting on my nerves, and I wanted to go back to Toronto. I packed up and left that very night while he was at an urgent meeting.

So there I was, coming up the front walk once again, hoisting my old kit bag. Home was a shadow of its former self. Gerard spent all holidays now on retreat. Mum, supported financially now by her many successful brothers, mostly sat on her bed, watching the TV she'd wheeled into the bedroom and knitting afghans by the wagonload.

Meanwhile, the Tanteek, that old shape-shifter, shucked and jived its way through the pores of my skin, where it lurked like cancer cells laying low until the radiation passed over, hiding behind polyps and valves, snorkelling through my bloodstream, breathing through reeds. Gathering strength.

And now sits, grounded just like me in this sad, suffocating room, reminding me every time I lift my head that I'm still, even now, only walking in place, going nowhere good.

THREE

God is said to work in mysterious ways, but this thing that's just happened, this gift, this largesse, this utterly gratuitous bounty, seems as jaw-droppingly bizarre to me as a spaceship full of good fairies landing on my coffee table to zap me all over with rib-tickling, rainbow-coloured delirium rays.

Because only four weeks and three days after booting Flake out of my fortress of solitude, after kissing off the Untouchables forever and resigning myself to a sour, arid life-in-death as sole caretaker to my sour, arid, death-in-life mother...I pick up the phone and what do I hear?

Liam's voice.

Liam's voice, out of a cold black sky. Liam's voice informing me that, amazingly, there are only six M. Prentices in the phone book, and wow, he hit the jackpot with number four!

He's been living in Toronto for eight years, he says. Sharing a duplex with his mother.

I'm knocked senseless. I can only take in every fifth word.

When I suddenly notice he's stopped talking, that a silence has opened up and it's my turn, I gabble the first thing that pops into my mind.

"I can't get far enough away from *my* mother."

To which he burbles, "Oh, Gail's great fun. You'll have to come over and say hi."

As my heart gradually slows to a canter, I begin to piece his story together: eight years ago, a swell job offer here. Mother Gail, a merry widow these past twenty years, chomping at the bit to get out of anti-Anglo Quebec. His sister, Charlotte, already here for a decade. And no, he's no longer married; no, no longer dancing. Ancient history, babe, he tells me ruefully, my heart bumping its head on the ceiling at this casually tossed-off endearment.

"I work in information systems. I had to quit dancing when I just about severed my Achilles' tendon trying to do leaps I'd never been trained for. So I went back to school and learned computer programming. Sad to say, I'm really good at it."

"Schmuck. Eight *years* you were here without looking me up?"

"I thought you hated me."

"Please! *You* hated *me*!"

Back and forth we banter, nervous as hell: Leafs versus Habs, St. Lawrence versus Jean-Talon, brown Toronto hulking under its low webbing of wires versus big-sky-country greystone Montreal.

A shrieking pause. He asks me to dinner.

"You'll be sorry. You'll keel over dead when you see me. I'm as big as a house."

"I've always favoured ample women," he replies, smooth as butter. Ample! I feel like a sleek jungle cat draped over a tree limb.

"Maggie, I don't care if you've grown a second head," he continues. "I *really* want to see you."

I arrive at the restaurant twenty minutes early, nauseous from nerves, not to mention two Jacks gulped down on an empty stomach and a half-litre of perfume poured down my neck. I take a table by the window, watching for him without a clue as to what I'm looking for. I recognize his swivel-hipped, flamenco walk rounding the corner from a full block away. He's wearing a natty tweed cap and a fat white sweater, as if he's stamping through the peat bog, rounding up the sheep. I have to sprint to the washroom, where I stand for ten minutes dry-heaving over the sink. When I finally emerge on unsteady legs, there he stands, just inside the door, looking lost, squinting through his glasses (*glasses!*), the lenses fogged over from the cold. I freeze, my heart going bumpedy-bump, waiting for his eyes to find me.

Recognition floods his face. Oh! I burst out laughing. It's been thirty-seven years, and he's not a day older, and neither am I!

Although, upon closer inspection, I note that he's not wearing the face I visualized over the phone. While the hazy picture in my mind is slowly being made flesh, I confess: some of the air leaks out of my giddy balloon.

Then he moves in for a hug, and in the clutch, his cap is knocked askew. I pull back to discover, reeling, that he's bald as a doorknob. His head sits like an egg in the cup made by the scarf wrapped several times round his neck. There's a fan of deep wrinkles around his eyes and two deep gullies between them. His head, without the hair, seems freakishly small. He looks like a turtle.

But the scarf is purple!

I go limp at the sight of it, and just in time, for I've been slapped by a wash of, what? Contempt? Yes. As if only turtle-headed Liam has aged, as if I've discovered a shameful flaw in him, exposed for the first time.

And then he turns his head and, to my profound chagrin, poking out from between layers of scarf is a four-inch, pewter-coloured, old-bald-guy ponytail.

"Well, that thing's gonna have to go," I tell him, giving it a smart tug as if it might come off in my hand. I sweep him with a critical, head-to-foot once-over, wanting him to take note of me doing it before I add, more softly, "You still have the scarf, I see."

"Of course I still have the scarf! Do you have yours?"

"It's in my closet, hanging on a sacred hook. It hasn't been out of the house since the winter of '68." And all the while I'm thinking, His voice! My God, I could pick it out of a choir of angels!

But it's his laugh that finally saves him, the laugh of '68, of tie-dyed sheets, the lumpenproletariat, and ballet leaps in the snow. My engine floods all over again, thrilling to the comely grid of his still-handsome face, spoiled only by the wicked curve of his upper lip, the left side snagged as if on a tiny nail. It was always the flaw that made him spectacular.

He voices my thoughts exactly.

"You're more beautiful than ever," he says all in a rush, his cheeks flushing as if he were fourteen.

"Get atta heah witcheh biootiful! I'm a hideous old bag!" But inside, I'm hopping, jumping, screeching: The one that got

262

away! The one that got away! Right here in front of me! The one that got away!

He follows me to the table hard on my heels, whispering wetly into my ear, "I see you still have those big, strong field-hockey legs." I detect genuine lust in that whisper. I feel huge in his eyes, *good* huge: iconic, like one of those colossal Fellini women, legs spread, hands on hips, haystack hair tumbling all over the place.

Everything begins to pick up speed.

Gingerly feeling our way, we let one another know that the right one just never came along.

After he and Sam split, he tells me, there were a few second-string girlfriends but nothing serious. And no one at all for the last seventeen years. He just gave up on love, he says. And God yes, he's well over old Sam.

"We had no business getting married. It was horrible. It was over after the first six months, but we stuck it out for four miserable years."

Ha hah! Take *that*, skinny French hootchy girl!

"It never seemed to me you guys were all that close. Not the way we were."

"I thought I loved her. But what did I know?"

"Any kids?"

"No, thank God." A pause. "You?"

"Nuh-uh, not me."

"How long did it last with Bruno?"

"I can't believe you remember Bruno! We lasted four and a half minutes."

"And after that?"

"After that, squat. I've been making money, my dear, not love." I proceed to tell him how invisibly famous I am, enumerating recent TV commercials he might have seen or, more to the point, heard.

"That was *you*? No wonder I loved that ad! And the one for the panty liners! I always got the funniest feeling listening to that, like I'd forgotten something important but couldn't put my finger on it. That was you! God*damn!*"

"So we both got a shot at showbiz, more or less."

"Less for me, I'm afraid."

"Ah well, it's overrated." I wave a big, grandiose arm, giving fame the kiss-off as I drain my third glass of wine. Already my elbows are on the table, people around us glancing over whenever I open my mouth. "It was all just a fluke anyway. I flunked out of McGill, in case you were wondering. So I was back here in TO waiting tables at this greasy spoon on Parliament, and who should stroll in but this guy Luc from my old commie days. He used to help Bruno make recordings and stuff. So he recognizes me, and it turns out he's a defector too, into Carlos Castaneda and peyote, the usual route out of Marxism–Leninism. Anyway, he was working in a recording studio here. So, long story short, he got me an audition for a shampoo commercial, and I got it, snap, just like that, first try. So I kept going to auditions and getting work hand over fist, and before I knew it, I'd joined the union, quit waitressing, and had myself a red-hot career."

"Croikey! I'm in the presence of a star!"

"Don't get too excited. 'For the lips of a strange woman drop as an honeycomb, my dear, and her mouth is smoother than oil; but her end is bitter as wormwood, sharp as a two-edged sword.'"

He looks at me blankly.

"From the Bible. Proverbs." A beat. "It's a joke, son."

"The Bible. God, don't get me started! I had that crap stuffed, you'll never believe it, but it was Sam who was into it, a complete one-eighty, bright as she was. She got this idea, when the marriage was coming apart, to drag me out to this dingbat commune up near Sainte-Agathe. It was beautiful up there, the whole peace and love, back-to-the-land thing. Anyway, that's how she sold me on it. But I wasn't there two minutes before the thumpers started crawling out of the woodwork. Prayers every morning, holding hands, singing hymns, superstitious voodoo crap from morning to night. I couldn't wait to get the hell out of there and back to the sanity of mass-consumer culture."

I take another long gulp of wine. I'm hot as an oven.

"The consumer culture part was a joke too," he allows gently, looking worried. "I only meant it looked good, relatively speaking."

"I got it."

He raises his arm to order more wine. And blurts, "I'm *so* glad we're doing this! It's just dynamite seeing you again!"

"Dynamite? You *have* been out of circulation for a while."

He smiles his cock-eyed smile, and it's so familiar, so unbearably dear, I'm afraid I'll pass out.

"Why in God's name did we wait so long?" he asks, leaning in over the table, taking my hand in his. "Even way back when I was with Sam, and we all used to hang out together, I mean, I thought I was in love with her, but if you were anywhere around, I mean *anywhere*, I always knew exactly where you were. What the hell was wrong with me? How could I have been so stupid?"

"I know. I felt exactly the same way."

More wine.

"About you being stupid, I mean."

Wine.

"And about . . . always knowing where you were too."

Deep breathing. Eyes locking for too long.

"I love you, Liam."

"I love you too, Maggie. I've loved you since the first day I saw you."

And just like that, nothing to it, my lonely days are over. Maggie Prentice has snagged herself an upper-deck, dee-luxe stateroom on the ring-a-ding *Bachelor*. All ashore that's going ashore, because, damn it, we set sail at sunset!

Creaky and obsolescent as we are, we leap into this crazy thing like a couple of kids, holding hands, jumping, screaming as we drop from the high barren cliff into the sparkling blue lake. We have our sleepover nights at my place so as not to disturb Gail, who lives upstairs from Liam, with our old-fogey sexual racket. We moan and heave like Tristan and Isolde all over the apartment, orbiting each other the way Gerard and I once did in our womb sea of blood. If our eyes so much as meet as we pass in the kitchen, we'll be back in the bedroom like a shot even if we've just left it. I drop twenty pounds the first month from swooning alone. Well, from that, and my severely curtailed alcohol consumption.

Because, just like in the days of Desi, *pffft!* My craving for the solitary bottle has completely vanished. If I drink at all, it's in Liam's company, and never to the point of babbling excess. It just isn't something a happy person needs to do!

Because happy is what I am. This is *Love* I'm in, and guess what, who knew, I can do it too! Liam, love of my youth, love of my life, is all the Home and Hearth I'm ever going to need from now till my final closing day rolls around.

From an unswept rear storage closet in my mind, I can still hear Gerard's muffled voice, frigid with refusal, insisting, "This is the way you're supposed to feel about the *Father*, not some asinine fool from your pathetic adolescence." But the voice has no power. It's traffic noise. Both Gerard and the Tanteek have been bound, gagged, and banished, the leaden yoke sliding from my shoulders like water. The Untouchables are a distant gang of goofs, two inches tall, and when I think of Desi now, I smile; surely he and Catou must have found rest and peace in Moncton. Everything doesn't have to turn into a horror story just because Gerard says it will.

Though Gerard would be amazed at what else has happened: suddenly, unaccountably, the erratic tide of faith has come in, and *stayed* in. Something deep inside me has loosened its grip and I'm bursting at the seams with trust, joy, and open-hearted gratitude. The all-too-fleeting moments of hope and belief I knew with the Untouchables are suddenly with me all the time. Is this what love can do? Is it because I'm no longer humping through life in my brother's shadow? Or is it one last gift from Desi, unopened till now, the memory of his simple trust and unquestioning child's faith that has somehow become mine, now that I have someone to love again?

Whatever it is that's caused this change, the last thing I want to do is touch it, poke at it, startle it. Make it mad.

By Christmas I've already sublet my apartment, have only a month of tower life left. And I've even told Mum about the momentous change in my life, informing her with a dead-give-away catch in my voice that I have a new friend named Liam Cushnahan. The Irish lilt of his name brings a wan, fuddled smile to her face that instantly makes me want to forgive her every single thing she's ever done to me.

Not believing the words are actually issuing from my lips, I suggest to Liam we drop in on her on Christmas Eve afternoon.

"But be warned. She's as bonkers as they come. We should probably work out a signal so that if you reach a breaking point, we can cut it short."

"I take it there's no Dad in the picture?"

"Nope. He made an early escape, bless his little heart." I clearly remember Liam not hearing me tell him this in his flamed-out bedroom, back when it had been fresh news. And I still don't want to talk about it, still think somehow that it was all my fault, a shameful thing Liam doesn't need to know.

Never mind Liam; Dad would probably despise me if he saw me now with my lacklustre social skills and enormous ass. He'd gotten as far away from us as he could without leaving the solar system. I'd heard from him off and on during my early twenties, slapdash postcards mostly, from whatever exotic locale he happened to be management-consulting in: Ghana, Sri Lanka, Thailand. The cards came to the old family homestead, but were only addressed to me, never Mum or Gerard, with no address where I could write him back. Every scribbled message, every *Greetings and salutations from fabulous Bangkok! How ya been, old girl?* had dwindled him till he'd become as archaic and phantasmal in my mind as Irving Fazola, shrunk to an occasional threatening presence in dreams or a sudden unbidden fury whenever I heard swing tunes on the radio.

I guess he liked me and then he didn't. So I loved him and now I don't. The end.

"I don't even know if he's still alive," I say to Liam now. To which he says nothing at all.

In the car, on the way to Mum's place, my phone rings. I know who it is before I even look; the very ring sounds shaky, querulous, toothlessly belligerent.

"Hello? Hello? Mum?"

All manner of mayhem is afoot on the other end: muffled shouting, the slam of a door, ragged breathing up close to the receiver.

"What the hell? Mum? I know you're there, I can hear you hyperventilating."

"Is something wrong?" Liam asks.

"I don't know, she's, Mum, are you crying? Talk to me!"

"What's the matter?" Liam asks again.

"I don't know. She won't...Mum! I can't understand you! Slow down! Start from the begin...Mum! Slow *down*! Get a grip! *What* happened to Winky?"

"Winky?" mouths Liam, eyebrows arching skyward.

"Her dog," I mouth back. "Okay, that's better. So, Winky's okay? Then wha...what? What did he say?"

The phone continues to boil over in my hand, Mum's voice afroth with sobs, the jagged melody to Winky's crazed, yipping rhythm section.

"Mum, *please*, just relax. We'll be there in ten minutes. You can tell me when...oh. She hung up."

"What's wrong?"

"My brother's there, damn it. I'm not sure I got it right, but I think he told her her dog was going to hell." I've only given Liam the sketchiest outline of my Untouchables career, breezing lightly over Kevvie's death, and Desi, and describing Gerard as "a little moody."

"Jesus! What kind of a jerk is he?"

Mum meets us at the door, her nose red and running, her eyes inflamed. She shuffles wordlessly back to the couch to slump submissively against the armrest, the better to enjoy this extra-special treat, this rare, holiday descent from on high by the son she has adored since the day their eyes first met.

Gerard is sprawled in the big Fionnuala chair, threadbare at the seams, as is the chair, its chintz flowers faded to tired tans and sour pinks. He's haloed in smoke, a full ashtray propped on his praying mantis knees. He resumes speaking as soon as she sits, paying us no mind at all.

"What possible reason could the Father have for wanting to have a special relationship with you?" His voice is bland, unruffled as glass. Liam and I stand paralyzed in the doorway, he with a bottle of wine, me holding a small cake in a box by the string.

"You're like every man who's ever lived; you're here simply

to die." He sucks in a throat-searing drag. "No one but the Bride is going to heaven."

"Stop calling me a man!" Mum snaps irritably, not looking at him. "Or your name is going to be Mud." This anarchic upsurge certainly widens *my* eyes.

I look at Liam, who looks at me, the shock on his face giving way almost immediately to lip-curling contempt. I slip my hand into his free one, praying Gerard won't notice and swing his big howitzer in our direction.

I try to see my twin as someone laying eyes on him for the first time would: his frayed rope of a torso wrapped in several layers of mouldy sweaters, his skeleton shanks forming a draw-bridge to one of Mum's end tables, where he's set his long feet in their Civil War–era grey socks. He looks as if he subsists on damp leaves and ditch water.

Meanwhile, poor, clumsy reprobate, Winky hops stiffly on his bald legs at his mistress's feet, mewling piteously. Gerard follows the dog with his eyes, simpering, "Dear Jesus, please protect my little doggie!" before dropping his voice to a smoke-cured growl. "I've told you a thousand times: life is a testing ground. The damned dog is immaterial. He's just part of the test."

"Good fucking Christ!" whistles from under Liam's breath.

"It's not fair for God to punish Winky! And I've always tried, always, *always* tried . . . to be good." Mum hiccups into her lap.

"Your goodness is filth to him! His ways are not our ways!"

Sobbing raggedly, Mum reaches down to tug at Winky's ears as if trying to prevent him from taking in the dire news.

As for Liam, he puts up his dukes and wades right in, shouting, "Are you fucking nuts?" with such gusto that I have to practically roar, "Merry Christmas, Father Gerry! It sure isn't a party until you get here!" to drown him out.

Gerard shoots me the snake-eye, but he's ready to wrap it up anyway. Mum continues to mutter, directing all her words at Winky's head.

"If Winky can't be with me in heaven, I won't go. And the Father does so like me. I asked him to take my stomach aches away, and he did, so there."

Liam flaps an angry hand in front of his face, trying to clear a corridor of breathable air. Watching him, I have to concede that it isn't as if Gerard doesn't practise what he preaches: his insides are surely a sci-fi wasteland of trash fires and ash by now, the obscene lust for life reduced to a soggy, blackened crust in his mouth.

He gets up, pulling on the familiar black overcoat that he's flung over the back of his chair, one of the sleeves attached by a mere inch of remaining seam. The coat smells like it's been pulled smouldering from an incinerator. On the coffee table in front of him stands Mum's sad little Christmas tree, a miserable pink sparkly thing from Zellers wedged into a saucepan. Two lonely ornaments hang by rusty hooks.

"There's no better prototype of the fallen world than the Christmas tree," Gerard points out, not uncheerfully. "All decked out with cheap, shiny crap." Stubbing out his last smoke in the saucepan, he pronounces with gravitas, "The hard bare cross!" And again, louder: "The hard bare cross! That's all there is! That's all there ever will be." He punches his arm through the good sleeve. "I have to go."

His fell gaze swoops over me as I stand idiotically fingering the prickly tree. It lands on Liam's appalled face. Gerard pulls a black toque out of his pocket and jams it over his head down to his eyebrows, all the while taking Liam's sorry measure.

Mum pipes up boldly to issue a stern warning from her corner. "If I close my eyes, I might just die right now!" She lifts her little chin with firm purpose and squeezes her eyes shut. She doesn't see the front door close. From the window, I watch Gerard shear his ungainly way across the street, a fresh smoke lit. As he brushes the snow with his elbow from the windshield of his car, a black cat springs electrified from underneath it, cannonballing down the street in yowling terror.

I begin removing his traces, dumping the ashtray into the garbage under the sink, cracking open the balcony doors. I order Liam to "Sit down, darlin'," while Mum huddles in her corner, still trying to scrunch herself out of the world.

"What were you fighting about?" I ask her at last, sitting down stiffly beside her. Liam drops uneasily onto the edge of the Gerard-infected big chair.

"Winky." Mum opens her eyes, the beloved name lighting a tiny smile that warms the dry gullies of her face. She gazes fondly down as her poodle scrabbles furiously at the linoleum.

"Isn't he a beaut?" I ask Liam. "Like someone sewed him together out of old slippers and carpet ends." Liam smiles uncertainly before remarking kindly, "He looks like a good old fellow." Winky scrabbles some more, then turns around three times and lies down, his head sinking into a grey pudding of chins.

"When I turn to my son for comfort, what does he give me?" Mum asks him sadly. Winky whimpers in profound sympathy.

"So are you going to tell me what happened?" I ask in the crispest of tones, anxious to thwart any more doggie drippiness.

She sighs abruptly, shallowly, like a child with her hand on the door of the principal's office. And speaks to Winky, not me.

"Those poor little children last year. Gerard told me about them, and I saw the tippy car on TV in the snow. It was just this time and I was thinking about them. So close to Christmas." She hiccups again. "All their little presents wrapped and under the tree." Tears dribble down her cheeks, dripping from her chin onto the damp front of her bathrobe. I'm about to remind her it happened in January, but she barrels over me with a surprising surge of indignation: "Your brother got mad at me for being upset."

"I see. And how does Winky come into it?"

"He told me I wasn't going to see those poor little mites, or Winky either, in heaven, and I asked him why not. And so, and then, he, um, he lost his temper. He, he broke some dishes. They're in the sink." She's fidgeting now, scared of being a tattle-tale. "He said, you're not going to see anyone you know in heaven. He said, he said you're just going to be ass, *assmilinated* like a drop in the ocean. He keeps telling me I'm already dead and I just won't admit it." She turns to me, wide-eyed, her lips quivering. "Mag Mary, does he *want* me to be dead?"

"I don't know. I don't know anything."

"Neither do I," she mumbles sadly. She swerves her eyes and her fighting chin in Liam's direction, rallying somewhat at the sight of his handsome face. "He's the only person I know who makes heaven sound horrible!" One wry corner of her mouth lifts. "I said to him, you just said we wouldn't know anyone there." Her crafty smile broadens. "But I guess we'd have to be there first, so as not to know anyone. Ha!"

"Mum, this is Liam, by the way. Liam, this is my mother, Moira, celebrated in legend and song."

She offers Liam a truly daft smile. He rises beautifully to the occasion, reaching across to pat her arm.

"Maggie told me about the boys and the car accident. It's very sad."

Her face collapses again, and she begins weeping without shame. I rub her back woodenly, as robotic as if I'm washing windows. I have no words for occasions like these.

But Liam leaning over me, murmuring, "Don't let's be sad on Christmas" and "You've been through so much, haven't you?" is beginning to charm the pants off her. When he gets up to go to the kitchen to open the wine, she actually brushes the tears from her cheeks with the back of her hand and winks at me, startling me into a squawk of laughter.

"Maggie told me how pretty you are!" he calls from the kitchen, laying it on thick as he rummages through drawers. "But I'm afraid she undersold you. I can see where she gets her looks all right."

"You stop that now! I'm older than Methuselah's Aunt Mehitabel." Her lower lip still wobbles, but it isn't from tears. She's trying not to giggle.

Liam appears in the doorway. "Which drawer is the cork-screw in?"

Mum fluffs her wispy coiffure as if she's just been approached by a dashing young buck at the CYO mixer. "Next to the sink, dear. On the left. With the cutlery. It's an old thing, I hope it still works!" And when Liam gallantly presents her with "just a tiny sip" of wine in a juice glass, bowing like a snooty mâitre d', she blushes to the roots of her hair.

"Shall we all toast the season?" he asks brightly, sitting back down in the big chair. We raise our glasses limply and proceed to sip quietly.

"Gerard was very bad!" Mum says suddenly, leaning toward Liam in what looks alarmingly like full-disclosure mode. I can't believe this heresy coming from her lips. "He told me the human race is nothing but God's"—she stops for a moment, her dry little hand clamped over her mouth, then seems to undergo a change of heart—"pardon me, but I'm an old lady, and if I say words that are a little chancy, you must forgive me. I'm only repeating what my son the priest tells me. The human race is nothing but God's"—she colours visibly all over again—"God's sperm cells." She upends the rest of her glass for courage, missing her mouth by a few crucial millimetres. "He told me God cares no more for our ridiculous little lives than any man does for..." She skids to a halt, red as a tropical sunset, the slosh of wine dripping from her cheek onto the frayed collar of her bathrobe. She thrusts her empty glass at me.

"Mag Mary, take this away, please. I think I made a boo-boo." I reach for the glass, but she holds on tight; she has more to say, her tone aggrieved, the falsely accused child before the principal, valiantly setting the record straight.

"He said we're an evil smell in the Father's nose. And I told him, I said, I don't believe you! Not those poor children. Maybe me. Maybe *you*!" Her sharp little chin lifts for a moment, the leaping prow of a fast boat cresting the waves; then fear overtakes her, her eyes darting back and forth from my face to Liam's. "The Father only loves the seed that falls on the good ground," she finishes dejectedly.

Liam's eyes are spinning in their sockets. "Moira, with all due respect, er, may I call you Moira?"

"You may," she replies regally.

"With all due respect, Moira, Gerard sounds like a nutcase."

She gazes at him, unblinking, saying nothing for a full minute before blurting defensively, "Well, if such terrible things can happen in the world, then it *proves* there's a heaven where everything will be put right, and where God will swipe away all our tears. That's what I believe, and you're not going to change my mind!"

Liam smiles at her.

"I don't know, Moira. I've always thought the opposite. To me, when bad things happen, and good things happen, and the wrong people die and the good people suffer, it just proves how random everything is. It's nothing personal, and I respect your right to hold a different opinion, but I just don't think there's any proof that a god exists. The dice roll and things happen, good and bad, and that's all there is."

Mum goes very stiff and still. I rear back as far as I can from her line of vision, waving frantic arms at Liam, mouthing, "No!" He smiles crookedly at me and abruptly tacks in the opposite direction. "Maggie, how about you cut us all a slice of that nice cake you brought?"

Passing him on my way to the kitchen, I administer a solid kick to his leg. Meanwhile, Mum sits looking aslant at him, a sly tilt to her head.

"I know you don't mean a single word of what you said," she pronounces at last with remarkable firmness. "Look at you, with a brand-new girl at your age, and I see you, don't think I don't, with the little smoochies in the hallway and the big moony-spoony eyes. You're just pretending because that's the way all you men do. You think you can have a new love in your life and eat your cake and you don't ever ask who baked it for you!"

"Or why there's cake at all!" I call from the safety of the kitchen as I pick shards of china out of the sink and slap slices of cake onto three plates. My words are met with a long and ringing silence.

"Well, I don't see what that's got to…" Liam says at last, but I kick him again, harder, on the way back. He stops, smiling goofily at Mum, who beams back at him.

"Well!" he exclaims after a moment. "Ah! Cake! Isn't this lovely!"

Forks tink against plates. Our chewing is as loud as a chugging generator. Winky's patient, doleful eyes follow every morsel from Mum's plate to her lips. My stomach feels like I've swallowed a stack of T-squares. I need to change the subject. The last thing I want Liam to suspect in me is sloppy religious feeling.

And the *second* last thing I want him to notice is how tightly wound I feel around my mother, how play-acted all this nervous affection is. Like to church, I've come far too late to the mother-daughter business. All the gentle good cheer, the solicitous looks, the fond knee-pattings are things I've picked up from television.

Mum murmurs a tardy grace under her breath: "We give thee thanks, oh Lord, for all thy benefits." Then she creaks forward and sideways to lay her plate down for Winky to finish. He circles it gratefully, doddering like a huge spider missing half its leg complement, licking the plate from every possible angle, his frayed stump of a tail jerking for joy.

"Isn't this nice we're all getting acquainted!" Liam says with forced heartiness. He jumps up and drops to his knees next to Winky, slapping his thighs with gusto. "Come here, boy! Come here! That's a good boy!" Winky flattens his ears, dropping with a thud onto his raw pink stomach and venturing a few, timid, exploratory licks of Liam's hand. I fight down a geyser of irritation. I love Liam to distraction, but there's no call for this sort of thing. Truth be told, the one point on which Gerard and I stand in militant solidarity is that we both vigorously renounce Winky and all of his pomps and all of his works.

Gerard has his own reasons. Mine is flaming jealousy. When Mum was still able to go out by herself, walking the five blocks to Mass every morning, her ancient Maryknoll missal under her arm, or shuffling to the corner store for milk, tea, and a lottery ticket, Winky would keep a berserk vigil behind the front door, barking every four seconds in perfect tempo. The neighbours complained, her landlord threatened, but she would not be moved. "Let him have one more summer, just one more!" she pleaded every year when the vet started making noises about "maybe it's time." No, no, please! He needed one more summer to sniff the carpet, to lie wheezing with his hideous belly exposed. Another summer to throw up everything he ate. With all these "one more summers," Winky has grown to the venerable, possibly record-breaking age of twenty. His rheumy eyes take whole minutes to become unstuck when he wakes up. His pistons chuff and heave the livelong day, emitting foul gases fore and aft, but she won't have him put down. Last summer she forked over twelve hundred dollars of my money for a blood transfusion when the Winkmeister keeled over with acute anemia.

She insists that when the time comes, she'll ease him away gently on her own terms, in her own time, in her own lap. One day he'll wobble up to her with those velvet-painting eyes, swaying on his hairless stilts, and tip over like a cane chair in a windstorm. Then she'll know. Weeping, she'll lay him gently on the oven rack and close the door. Turning the gas on high, she'll sit on the edge of her bed, counting off the minutes. The apartment will be silent, save for the ticking of the kitchen clock and the chortle of Mrs. Penniman's television through the thin walls.

It drives me wild. Why him? Why *him* and not *me*?

She's up now, doing a slow shamble toward the kitchen as if picking her way across a minefield in her pink paddle slippers. She stops to pat Liam's knee as she passes, nearly toppling over into his lap. My ears pick up the faint, autumn-leaf rustle of the diapers under her robe; the whiff of soil in the air isn't all Winky's doing. From the kitchen, I can hear her muttering darkly, "We're not sperms. We're ourselves." And then more loudly: "Teapot, where are you?"

Liam picks an ornament out of the box on the floor near the coffee table. We're supposed to be helping her decorate her tree, after all. He hangs it on a spindly branch and looks over at me sunk amid the springs of the couch.

"You doing okay?"

"Yeah." I get up and pick out a little tin house with a snowy roof to hang. "Sorry about my brother. He likes to go into a tailspin at Christmas. It's a Prentice tradition."

Liam extricates a desiccated brown wreath from the bottom of the box and puts it on his head. He strikes a pious pose, eyes heavenward, and drones, "Oh hear ye, hear ye of little faith."

"Shush!"

Mum shuffles back and forth from the kitchen, bringing in cups and milk and sugar, Winky attached to her ankles like a burr. She lays the cups on the coffee table and puts her hands to her ears, chanting, "I'm not *list*ening!"

"Mum, Gerard's gone."

Returning to the kitchen, she ducks her head inside a cupboard, addressing the plates with authority: "Those little children are watching over us, even though we can't see them. I don't care what you say!"

"Mum, who are you talking to?"

Back in the living room, she draws up short in a sudden patch of fog, muttering, "What did I come in here for?" She looks small enough to crawl through the eye of a needle, with room for her dog and all her dishes besides. From where she stands, I think, death cannot possibly be an evil. Her slow ruin is a gracious, friendly thing, not a wrecking ball but rather a gentle dismantling of her ramshackle, termite-ridden life, the dry grey boards wrenched away one by one, letting in more and more light, till her eyes begin to burn and rainbows spin behind them, and at last the light will grow to such explosive fullness that it will burst her apart as easily as a milkweed pod and carry her up and away into itself.

Liam slides an arm around her shoulders and guides her back to the couch, asking kindly, "May I pour you some tea?" He lifts the pot and frowns, removing the lid to peer inside.

281

"It's empty."

"Oh, for pity's sake! Did I forget to make it?" she cries, struggling to her feet again.

"No, no, you sit. Let me do it," I tell her. "There! You hear? The kettle's whistling. You just forgot the last step."

"I may be a fool, but I'm no fool!" she informs Winky smartly, ignoring me. Sitting there in her ancient yellow bathrobe, its furrows of chenille nearly picked clean, her back ramrod straight, her face set, she's the very reincarnation of Grandma Fionnuala as she grumbles, "Seldom wrong and right again. Well, we'll see about that." Opposite her, Grandma's chair sits empty, unless you count the Angel of Death, quietly knitting, minding its business.

Liam stands at the window, hands clasped behind his back, rocking on his heels.

"I'm just waiting for Daniel O'Donnell to come on," Mum tells him sociably. "Flick the television on for me, would you, dear?" Liam, apparently not hearing, merely smiles at her.

"Mum, let me make you a sandwich," I say as I hand her her tea. I sound like the Caring Adult Daughter in a laxative commercial. I'm thinking of all the fallen boards of her rotten house that it's going to be my exclusive lot to pick up and carry to the dump.

"Daniel and Mary Duff aren't married," Mum twitters on as Liam continues to smile blankly at her.

"You're tipping your cup, Mum. It's going to spill all over Winky."

"She's married to someone else entirely. She has little ones of her own."

"Are you going to come to our wedding?" Liam asks her, amping up his smile into the spangled grin I love so well.

"Daniel married someone else. They're just friends, dear." Her teacup, which she's set down beside her on the couch and forgotten already, topples over as she begins worrying one of Winky's bald spots with her finger. I have to run with a sponge to sop up the puddle before it soaks her robe through. She takes no notice, lifting her dog onto her lap and nuzzling her chin back and forth over his head. The two of them make a grim pair, a surreal, death's-door Madonna and child, both ready at a moment's notice to take their clumsy swan dives into eternity, taking all of their secrets with them.

Liam's benevolent smile evaporates the moment we're back in the car.

"He's got his head up his ass! How can you be twins? He looks like a, like a *coot*! One of those sick old creeps diddling little boys in the back seat of his car before he kneels down to kiss the pope's ring."

"I know. But he's—"

"And your mother. She's a very nice lady, and I know she's missing some marbles, but really, Maggie. I want to feel bad for her, but I can't help thinking she's just asking for it with him. She's as deluded as he is."

"I know. But it's not—"

"I'm sorry, babe. I'm not mad at you. It's all that supernatural garbage. You know, kiss the invisible god's invisible ass or he'll beat the living crap out of you. He *wants* to send you to heaven, of course, but not without the prerequisite amount of ass-kissing and, of course, *you* beating the crap out of everyone else who isn't kissing ass according to your rules. And why? Because some damned book about tribal gods scratched on papyrus by a bunch of illiterate goat-herders says so, and…oh, sorry, Mags. I'm ranting, aren't I? Sorry, babe. I get worked up sometimes, but really, all you can do is laugh. Or puke. Gail and I get such a kick out of the religious programs on Sunday mornings. Have you ever seen—"

"I know it doesn't seem like it, but Gerard's a little more advanced than…"

Where the hell is *this* coming from? *Defending* Gerard? Am I really just a programmed robot after all?

"Why was he getting on her case like that?"

"Because she's stubborn, or, I don't know. He's kind of got a hair trigger."

"Please! He's an *asshole*! If this god of his hates everybody and everything then why doesn't he just leave people the fuck alone? Who needs him? And what about that gang of druggies of his? Why is he going to all that trouble if human beings are nothing but bags of crap by definition?"

"He's a professional contrarian."

"Christ! I couldn't believe him telling her she was here just to die! This asshole elitist, mass-murderer god of his. He's a fucking Nazi!"

"Well, he means, die like a seed dies—"

"Oh, sorry. Die like a seed dies. Whatever the fuck that means."

"It means, a seed has to die before it becomes—"

"And of course what he doesn't say is that if you haven't got your fucking ticket to Jesus-heaven, you can be fucking Gandhi, but you're *still* going to hell. Christ, I *hate* these religious morons!"

"I take it your mother isn't religious."

"Good God, no. She uses common sense!"

I wait as his breathing slows and steadies.

"Really, babe, I'm sorry. I'm not mad at you. I just get, I mean, when these delusionary ghouls start preying on ignorant people..." He smiles. "If I ruled the world, it would be against the law to believe in the invisible magic sky man. Human beings have enough problems. Why make the world safe for extremists and head-cases?"

"We were extremists once," I offer faintly. The machinery in my head has begun to race, cogs slipping out of gear, wheels spinning wildly, as I realize with a thudding heart that this *Bachelor* stateroom of mine doesn't come cheap! If I want to be invited to swanky dinners at the captain's table, if I want a lifetime of swoony nights on the starry deck, if I want to hold on to this man and this life, I'm going to have to swallow myself whole. I'm going to have to deny my past, deny my unsteady heart and the tiny, newborn buds of faith within me, and become Liam's version of Maggie Prentice. Because the real me, the Tanteek's handmaiden, will never for one second be able to cut the mustard on the *Bachelor* shuffleboard court.

"Please," Liam is saying. "We genuinely cared about creating a better world. The emphasis being on *world*."

I can't look at him, blushing for shame for the gaga Untouchables, for trusting little Desi, suddenly feeling so close to them

285

all, unable to remember what I'd found so annoying, tedious, and empty about that old life. This new one seems all at once uncanny, fake, as if, emerging from the Untouchables war zone with the belief that I really could go home again, I've returned to a make-believe happy village scene painted on a frieze, welcomed back by two-dimensional people with gaping, distorted smiles. And behind the frieze lies the real village, in ruins, razed by napalm, fetishes dangling uselessly in blackened doorways...

To which thought I immediately shout back within the privacy of my own head: No! Stop it. Honestly, just stop! Gerard is not a well man. He has nothing to teach you. Keep walking. Don't look back. He says we need to leave everything, that following his version of Christ is worth any loss, but come on! Did it ever *really* work? For longer than a minute? Were there ever any *tangible* changes in your life? And this so-called new faith of yours, what is it really? A rush of pleasant feelings here and there, a good mood, that's all. The whole religion thing is so grey, so nebulous! Your doubts will come back, they always do. And if you're uncertain, you should *be* uncertain, commit to nothing, hold no convictions. Come out like everybody else does with that slippery "Oh, well. Who really knows?" every time the subject veers into perilous view...

Liam isn't finished. "You talk about my mother. Just the other day she was telling some old cluck down the street that she was planning on leaving her body to science. There's a body farm down in the States where they leave corpses out to decompose so they can study the effects for forensic information. When Gail heard about that, she said, Bingo, that's the place for me! Be of some *use* when the whole shebang is finally over. Well, she made the mistake of telling this religious biddy and, whoa! she was all, you can't do that, your body doesn't belong to you, it's a sacred thing, blabbity-blah. Gail told her to stick it in a cold, dark place."

He looks over to enjoy the laugh chiselled on my face as my stomach plummets in a mercifully silent mudslide. He doesn't give one good goddamn whether he's a vessel of wrath or a vessel of mercy, and why should he? He knows himself to be a good man: he hurts no one, works hard, pays his own way, looks after his elderly mother. Gives blood. Leaves a nice Christmas tip for the paperboy. Votes NDP, listens to the CBC…Yes, and he knows no more of truth than the dumb beasts of the field. He's an abomination unto the Father, his proud mind full of idols and creeping things. And should Gerard ever pronounce this final sentence upon him, Liam will laugh till he splits, except, except, if Gerard is right, Liam the mocker will laugh himself straight into a screaming free fall into hell, his heart light years beyond the Gospel's reach. The wisdom called folly in the eyes of the worldly wise is folly indeed to my Liam.

I sit clutching the door handle for dear life, my legs braced rigid against invisible brakes. I know without turning my head that the Tanteek is in the back seat, suddenly having found the voice it lost so long ago, in fine taunting fettle as it stage-whispers, *"If Gerard is right, if Gerard is right, oh dear God, what if Gerard is right…"*

Fuck Gerard, I think. Gerard is insane!

"But you don't trust life without him in it. He knows things you can't bear to hear and can't bear not to hear," whistles past my ear.

God, will I never be normal? Will I never be free of this babbling fear, this ridiculous aberration? Damn it, nobody else worries about this garbage! The enlightened world has marched on! Only the feeble and the crazed lag behind, quaking, shaking our crabbed fists, croaking, "You'll be sorry!" as our eyes bulge and spittle runs down our chins.

Liam, who is looking hard at me, reaches for my hand.

"Maggie, you look stricken! Please tell me you don't believe all this crap! I'm getting worried about you!"

And I think, This is your soulmate, woman! You have to out yourself! You have to tell him how you stood up in public and gave your heart to Jesus! Sure, you did it in your usual half-assed, squinty-eyed, fingers-crossed-behind-your-back way. But you did it. And once in a while, yes, yes, admit it, once in a very great while, it *has* seemed to help, has lined the world up, made moths flutter in your throat. Yes. Yes, it has, and it still does. It's what's kept you going through the darkest of hours whether or not you could ever get a bead on the Father or the Son as they streaked by like lateral lightning, vapour trails hallooing your name…

…yes, and tell him that, in spite of everything, you understand your brother, that there's a force field around him, a kind of bat radar that you pick up through the hairs on your neck. That his low opinion of this brutish and broken world and its tinfoil distractions resonates with you. Confess that your faith is untried, that it's as private as vice. That it all boils down to the twin notional nubs that God couldn't possibly exist, and he couldn't possibly not…

…and tell him frankly that, hard as it is for you to get your head around belief, atheists still seem to you as wilfully dense as Holocaust deniers: muddy-headed, confounded by asses and elbows, braying by the dim nightlight of reason that they're way too big to be afraid of the dark...

For once in your life, you have to tell the truth! Even if it costs you everything. Because if you can't overcome the hurdle of his ridicule, then you're not even close to being serious.

"Babe," Liam says, craning his face forward to peer into mine. "What's wrong?"

Now! Tell him who you are! Speak plainly, fearlessly!

But I want to stay on the *Bachelor*!

No! Go! Speak!

I begin, haltingly, in a thin, aluminum voice not my own. "I don't know. It seems to me that, when it comes to faith and religion, that, well, what I said before about seeds, how a seed dies, well, if life is a sort of seedbed, anyway, if you only look at the seed, its, you'd burst out laughing if someone said there's an oak tree inside that little thing, wouldn't you?"

There. Was that so hard?

"What are you talking about?" Liam asks, frowning.

"I just mean that—"

"Look, Christians just make up all this crap about a god because they're afraid to die. That's the beginning, the middle, and the end of it."

Oh.

Now what?

Gerard would tell me to get out of the car this minute and walk away forever. For what has light to do with darkness, etc., etc. I must return to my old post, my tower lookout, return to monitoring the horizon for the first jagged rips in the seam where the sky is stitched to the befouled earth, waiting for it to curl upward like the flimsy wallpaper it's always been, revealing the massed armies of the Lord, swords high, the avenging Lamb in blinding white astride a horse the size of Asia…

No! *Bachelor! Bachelor!* This has to work! I can't go back, I'll go mad, I'll drink myself into delirium tremens…

Liam pulls up in front of my building.

"I wish I could come up and be with you tonight, but I promised Christmas to Gail. We always fix ourselves chocolatey treats and mugs of peppermint cocoa and spend Christmas Day watching all the old *Blackadder*s together. She's crazy about them."

He suddenly sounds so precious and twee that for one precarious moment my soulmate makes me want to spit bile.

It's not too late to decide for the *Pequod*!

"She sounds fantastic. I can't wait to meet her."

"She's going to adore you! Good night, babe. Merry Christmas!"

"Back atcha, darlin'."

And by the time Christmas dawns next morning, I've washed it all down with a generous, four-Jack chaser, writing the whole incident off as merely atmospheric, the result of being sucked back into Gerard's arctic weather system after sunny vacation time away. My giddiness blows back in, stomach butterflies resume their happy work, and everything in my garden is daffodils and buttercups once more.

By New Year's, I've definitely banished all grief and trouble from my life. Due to move out on the first of February, I haul my antique armoire and swanky sofa to Liam's place, an actual house in a gentrified city neighbourhood, with a huge front yard, a backyard on the edge of a ravine, and great, arching trees, bare now but soon to explode into a rustling canopy through which friendly sunlight will slap and ripple like water. Windows up and down the street will open, kids will tear by on bikes, flocks of birds will take off from the eaves like fighter jets. I'm going be living life on the *ground*, shoulder to shoulder with the rest of the normal human race!

The front yard, Liam promises me, will be the pièce de résistance: a mind-blowing, punch-drunk circus riot of a garden, Mother Gail's exclusive domain, the most spectacular flower show in town.

I dump his ripped bachelor couch and IKEA chairs out onto the curb. Part of me hates to do it; everything he owns or has ever touched is like a relic of the True Cross to me. But my furniture's better. Last to arrive from the fortress is my Montauk chair, deserted now, devoid of alien presence. I hang vintage lace curtains in the kitchen and buy satin pyjamas in raspberry, jade green, and black, perfect for a life of lubricious slip-sliding from one brand-new room to another.

By the end of February I'm officially ensconced as the Missus, washing Liam's socks and underwear in a delirium of love, a real woman doing a real woman's chores! What an exquisite pleasure and honour to look after him, ironing his shirts and hanging them in the closet with the top button done up, like Mum used to do for Gerard, understanding for the first time how satisfying that must have been for her. And I crack a cookbook too, for the first time in my life; night after night, Liam and

I bent double with giggles over blackened omelettes that have to be scraped out of the pan in chunks and soufflés as flat and tasty as particle board.

And I'm amazed at how *long* this new life seems! At night, I lie in my big brass bed, *our* bed now, our soft, joint berth on the *Bachelor*, stroking Liam's polished head as he drifts off to sleep. I'll lie motionless for a long time afterwards, the Eternal Mother, awake long after the children are in bed, full of sweet plans for all our delightful tomorrows. Liam's barren head feels just like a baby's, the only one I'm ever going to have. I find myself feeling abstractedly for the fontanel, the soft spot, remembering some Moriarty aunt or other, decades ago, handing me a squirming baby cousin to hold, Gerard snickering while the cousin's wicked older brother urged me to "feel that spot right there."

"That's where he still has a big hole in his head," he'd crowed as I yanked my hand away in hot horror; my God, weren't people put together any better than this? You could've poked a fork into the kid without half trying!

I know what Gerard would think if he could see me now. Love and babies just make him mad. He'd be sure to come out with some chilled maxim, like, "It's nothing but boring old flesh."

He has the "old" part right. The Liam snoring beside me is the severely compromised version, the copy of a copy of a copy. Secretly I still think I look better over all than he does, round and relatively smooth, whereas naked, he looks weathered, a substantial paunch around his middle but bony in the chest and legs, like a horse too well broken in.

He swears to me he's the happiest man alive. We never stop

congratulating each other for the magnificence, the purity, the indestructibility of this big, fat peony of love that has burst, in the fullness of time, into such gaudy bloom. Our lives are as compressed as gunpowder, ready to blow from the slightest shake as we thump away night after night, yelling, Oh God, oh baby, oh God, oh baby, into pillows and over each other's shoulders.

To the world we're two faceless old farts, Mr. and Mrs. Magoo pawing at each other in a ditzy fog. But I can still see the boy he used to be in every twist and turn of him.

I was in such a hurry to pack when I moved that I dumped entire drawers sight unseen into cardboard boxes. Unpacking at my leisure while Liam's at work, I find astounding things, like a dog-eared Hilroy copybook full of notes on Melville, scrawled in a cramped, jittery hand.

> *Melville . . . depressive type, bitter, esp. after Moby D., no success, all that EFFORT! knew he was genius, nobody appreciates, isolate, moody (!) fear of the big D (!!), DESPAIR!! BIG PRIDE & self-destruction impulse, fear of annhalation, didn't listen to anybody. Wished he dead but afraid to die, oh Herman I get it, I get it, TREMENDOUS SUFERING BECAUSE OF THIS FEAR, but no friends, WHAAAA? No help from relig., also attacked Christianity in Omoo (read?). On life and death this old man walked.*

And right underneath the copybook, my old diary with its rinky-dink gold lock, the gilt-edged pages crammed with the baroque, experimental handwriting I'd employed back then.

I give it to Liam, who flips through the pages packed tight with vicious insults and dire threats directed at Mum. He reads a little here, a little there, till suddenly he shouts, "Here I am! I'm in it!" The two of us sprawl on our backs in bed, kicking and screaming as he reads aloud:

> *A flash of excitement in the middle of this desert of drudgery: that FAR OUT hunk in Romantic (!) American Lit SMILED at me today! I don't think it was a mistake. He was looking at ME! Choirs sang, doves flapped around the room, and stars fell on Alabama! Let me assure you, he's as adorable as the Baby Jesus in party clothes. He has hair the colour of buttered toast, all in ringlets like his mommy rolled it up in rags before beddy-bye. I thought I'd die on the spot!*

"Oh, babe!"

> *We pass INCENDIARY notes all the time, and he always sees the funny, trippy side of everything. Yesterday in class, he made this head out of paper and then stuck his fingers through it like legs and walked it across his desk. I snorted so loud the whole auditorium turned around. I was besnotted with mirth!!*

"I haven't thought about that in forty years!" Liam cries, giddy as a schoolgirl himself.

"I've never gone a week without remembering it," I tell him. "Keep reading. Plenty more where that came from!"

You should get an eyeful of this little honey from behind, his tight little bum hitching up and down. He walks like a matador. He walks like James Brown. He walks like the mighty Mississippi in flood till you go weak in the knees watching him.

This reddens him perceptibly about the ears. "I had no idea you felt that way."

"Of course you didn't. You were too enraptured with your tedious little Movement Chick. You were always telling me, 'Sam's a *Movement* chick. She's just not the groovy, body-painting kind.'"

Love makes me batty with goodwill, faith and hope fairly gushing from my swollen heart. This is a *blessing*, my very own, my first since Desi, and who else would be more interested in hearing about blessings than Gerard, who lives a thousand miles away, his sting removed, fangs filed to blunt edges, a crumpled Happy Humphrey clipping stuffed into his back pocket. Merrily stamping out the memory of Christmas at Mum's, I actually — did I mention I was batty? — *call* him, chattering like a lunatic into the silence of the grave on the other end.

"Please don't laugh, but I think I finally know what grace is. When I look into Liam's eyes I feel like I'm living on the edge of the greatest Mystery of all, and it's so beautiful I can hardly stand it! When I look at him, I can somehow...are you there?" I'm lying in our violently unmade bed, my toenails freshly painted green, calling as if from some sacred grove reeking of musk and cavorting goats. "I really believe I can feel the closeness of God at last."

Hoo-hah! I hear the familiar click of his lighter, followed by a long, weary exhalation. He can barely make the effort to drawl.

"This is the oldest story going. The universe was created solely to revolve around you and the heap of empty illusions you call your life. You're no different from the rest of fallen humanity, so desperate to cling to everything you call *yours*, to make your life seem important. As long as you're doing that, you are lost from the Father's standpoint. All flesh is chaos in his eyes."

"Why am I getting the feeling you don't approve?"

"What do you care?" Teetering on the edge of a coughing jag, he expectorates a wad of phlegm so copious I feel it splash my cheek. "Do whatever you want. But I'd hurry up if I were you. Get these stupid illusions out of your system. If you want to fall for this lie even though you know better, be my guest. This illusion will fail you, don't worry."

I wait for his words to die away completely before soldiering on, amazed at my courage.

"It doesn't feel that way, Gerard. It feels like, I mean, Liam feels to me like, like I'm wearing a tiny picture of God in a locket around my neck. It feels—"

"It feels, it feels! I'm not going to debate with you! Think whatever you want. The sooner you try everything there is to try, the sooner your stupid dreams will come true, blow up in your face and die, and the sooner you'll fall through the bottom of your ridiculous life."

"Well, bring on *that* happy day! Hold on a second while I

slit my wrists in anticipation." I pray the choke of gathering tears is undetectable over the phone. "Sorry I can't get excited about picking up my staff and trudging on to the New fucking Jerusalem till my feet bleed. Who cares that I've been so fucking *lonely* for so long, working, working, putting in my time, and not so much as a hand on my arm"—I stop just short of blurting, "And your fucking Untouchables don't count!"—"nothing, nothing for years and years, so lonely that if the cashier at Loblaws smiled at me when she took the change out of my hand, I'd go home and cry myself to sleep. And now I've had a reprieve, right out of the blue, a *reprieve*, Gerard, and I'm supposed to feel *guilty* about it? I'm supposed to spit this gift in the eye and walk away?"

Supremely unrattled, he exhales another rusty sigh. "How many times do I have to tell you that the true follower of Christ is doomed by definition? He has no name and no home. He is dead, possessing no life but in the risen Christ. Knowing this, he takes no heed for himself. Every day he is ready and willing to die. And you're not. I know you. You're clinging, you're grabbing, trying to outrun your death. Why? You can't, and besides, who cares if the flesh dies? Spirit is all."

"Well, my spirit *likes* my flesh, Gerard," I spit out, my hysteria clearly audible now.

"You must be utterly sold out to the Lord of life and death," he pronounces with infinite calm, just before I hang up on him, hang up before he gets out the word *death*, but I hear it anyway. I always do.

For one sickening moment, the shining present falls away and I see life as my brother has taught me to: a brick hanging by a thread, utterly dependent upon the mercy of the scowling Father. I need a drink in the worst way. But I don't move, sucking back the urge until it passes over and leaves me.

I sit for an hour at the bedroom window, watching the sun sparkle on the backyard snow, the sky so blue, the branches clawing through it so black. I know the Tanteek is sitting scrunched and sulking behind the trunk of the big maple, muttering to itself of void and emptiness and loss, while squirrels dart right under its nose and shimmy up the trees, and Gail's slumbering crocuses wiggle their pointy snouts deep beneath the snow, dying to see what's up, up there.

I have no idea what to expect of Liam's mother, except that she's sure to be a livelier wire than my own. I picture a feisty little fireplug in the upstairs apartment, someone I'll be delighted to call "Mum" if she asks me to. But though I've occasionally heard odd banging sounds that might or might not be music leaking down from her place through the ceiling, by February I still haven't laid eyes on her. Liam tells me that winter's when she has time to socialize, to be "out and about," with no garden duties to keep her home. And when I finally do take up residence, she's just taken off on a lengthy jaunt to Alaska with a gang of superannuated gal pals. Just the fact that she's stumping about amid glaciers and ice floes instead of playing canasta in Florida or, worse, parked in front of the TV crocheting doggie vests is enough to recommend her highly to my imagination.

It's halfway through March before our paths cross, the day I climb into Liam's car on our larky way to take in the St. Patrick's

Day parade. Suddenly, here she is, out of the blue, home from Nome and tucked into a corner of the backseat, wearing a knitted coat the colour of lime Kool-Aid, a Leafs cap tugged down to her eyebrows, and a grin stretching from here to the Arctic Circle.

"I haven't sat in the backseat since I was four!" she shouts in reply to my shy hello. And then hollers, "Roight-o! Orf we ga-o!" as we back down the driveway, capping it with a "Wooh hooh!" that tautens my sphincter to a pinhole.

"I never miss the dumb parade, and I'm not even Irish, for corn's sake, married one of 'em and lived to tell the tale, though that party is no longer among the living, no loss to anyone I might add hee hee, but that's where the handle Cushnahan came from that I should've changed back to my own name, Rasmussen, but never got around to it, just too darned busy having fun!" All of this is yelled into my ear from a centimetre away.

From behind the wheel, Liam grins in my direction, though it's unclear whether the grin is to be read as "Isn't she great?" or "Grating, isn't she?"

I squirm around in my heavy coat to talk to her face to face, preparing to toss in an amusing St. Patrick–themed remark in my Fionnuala voice. I turn just in time to catch the fading of her zesty grin, her suddenly silent face settling into a complex mud flat of wrinkles. She has Liam's slate blue eyes, I notice, though on her they're close set and startlingly wolfish.

The day is shale grey and bitterly cold. We stand on a windy corner watching floats crawl by, unstable copses of cardboard shamrocks in the bed of a pickup truck, followed by a flatbed full of blond girls with aprons over their parkas lurching behind a banner proclaiming: The Polish salute the Irish! Three red-kneed, sombre old gents in kilts and sporrans and tall socks wheeze by on the pipes, bringing sentimental Celtic tears to my eyes, tears that freeze the instant they reach my cheeks. All the while a steady geyser of talk shoots up into my right ear from Gail's direction a good foot below me. With the engine noise and the garbled music and the wind, I only catch the odd word or phrase as it flies by like a blown-off hat: "beta-carotene so cancer can't even *think* of getting started!" and "if you ask me, ginseng is just so much snake oil" and, more alarmingly, "but they're using monkey glands for that now!" Then she lets loose with a delicious, full-octave musical laugh, possibly the loveliest I've ever heard.

Another truck with radio station call letters emblazoned on the side rumbles by. A couple of the station's "personalities," wearing green-spangled top hats, sit slumped and shivering on a bench, waving fitfully at the crowd. In front of them wobbles the comely Queen in her green sash, ice pellets like diamonds in her hair. At the sight of them, Gail whips off her Leafs cap and waves it like a madwoman, standing on tippy-toe to screech, "Happy St. Paddy's Day! It's Gaily-Gaily Cushnahan! Gaily-Gaily Cushnahan!"

She elbows me so hard in the ribs I double over.

"Best part of the parade's when I get to see my buds! They tell me all the time they wouldn't have half as good a show if it weren't for me calling in and keeping things hopping!" She waves and waves as the float rolls away with no sign of recognition from anyone on board. Still the paragraphs keep coming, an endless rumble like potatoes in a washing machine, something about a new citizens committee, getting together a petition, a rehab centre going up somewhere it shouldn't, funds, backbenchers, clout at City Hall, my God, she knows everything, on and on and on and on as the wind spins fierce little cyclones around the miserable school marching bands shuffling past, whipping the girls' hair skyward and gusting Gail's chatter toward me and away. I feel huge and lumbering next to her, my tongue a plug of lead in my mouth, too sluggish to bend around a single rigid consonant.

On the brisk march back to the car, her head swivels continuously this way and that, taking in everything; I swear I can hear the electronic beeping of her third eye. Liam and I trail behind her, our arms around each other, my frozen hand hooked through his belt loops under his leather jacket, his swaying dancer hips bumping against mine. I whisper in his icy ear, "This feels just like the old days, walking home from the Swiss Hut with you at midnight! Remember how you used to lift me?" Up ahead, Gail rounds a corner, and I have a sudden vision of her disappearing—poof!—to leap invisibly over our heads and suddenly reappear, hovering in the air behind us, listening in, grinning away.

Back home, Liam makes hot chocolate while Gail clatters down the stairs with a mammoth photo album full of publicity stills from the TV variety show he'd been on as a regular dancer in the 1970s, spending two years on the freewheeling West Coast after old Sam had been dispatched, doing jigs and polkas and reels in a make-believe English pub.

"Put your feet up, Mum," Liam orders her, though she's already deep into my Montauk chair and hardly has to be asked.

I perch myself on the chair arm beside her, gazing worshipfully at the book in her lap, gasping and shrieking at every turn of the page, for here he is, my darling young one, swinging partner after bouffant-haired partner in his skin-tight pants and blazing satin shirts with long, pointy collars. His hair is intact, chestnut brown and wavy, ringlets trailing down his neck. He puts all the other men in the shade. I imagine every last one of those needle-waisted girl dancers falling for him, throwing open their sweaty dancer thighs and begging for it, scratching each other's eyes out over him. I bet he had them all too, even the boys. Why not? He's irresistible! I'm so proud of him! And what a good-hearted little show it was, so foolish and vulnerable and innocent!

I look over at Liam as he wipes chocolate foam from his upper lip and think, There is nothing sweeter than a dancing man, a man open-armed and undefended. Oh, I am sick, I am just *sick* with love.

Gail is still chirping away.

"He sure had the dancing bug all right, even when he was little he didn't care what the other boys thought, he just had to go to dancing school though it seemed a little fruity to me, but he was a natural just like Gene Kelly, and we did without a lot of things so he could take his ballroom classes once a week."

I pretend I haven't heard all this decades ago, crying out, "Oh my goodness! Did the other boys try to beat you up?" I wince in genuine pain at the thought of it, but no, he treats me to that same cocky toss of the head I recognize from the days when it was covered in curls, drawling, "Naw. The girls wouldn't stand for it."

I figure he must have gotten his moves from his father. Gail has the energy of a typhoon but all the natural grace of a stag beetle.

When she finally kathumps back upstairs with her scrapbook, I follow her; it just seems like the friendly thing to do.

Unlike our place, with three-day-old cups of coffee next to the bathroom sink and balled-up underwear smooched around the sofa pillows, Gail's apartment is a showroom, painted a uniform, high-gloss white like the subway. Windows, tabletops, the TV, spoons, are all polished to a shimmer, the furniture lined up at perfect right angles, edges touching just...so. She leads me on a snappy tour from room to room, bending over every time she spies a piece of lint on the carpet, bouncing up and down like a buoy in rough waters. Then she makes instant coffee, as if we haven't just had hot chocolate, springing up to wash the cups the second they're drained, shrieking, "There's a method to my madness!" And I have another quick vision of her, freshly dead and tidily cremated, flicking a whiskbroom after her own ashes.

The patent-leather-shiny baby grand piano in her living room takes me completely by surprise. I can't imagine her stubby fingers being good at anything calling for precision and delicacy.

"Do you play?" I ask politely.

"Do I *play*? Since I was three, for corn's sake, though Liam has a tin ear, but Charlotte, that's my daughter who lives in Mississauga now, she plays beautifully."

"Charlotte. Of course! Isn't she a nurse? Or a doc—"

"Charlotte edits *Whole Foods Wellness* magazine and runs a holistic health clinic, and believe you me there's absolutely nothing she doesn't know on the subject of nutrition and organic wellness." Gail's nimble mouth slams shut, the subject exhausted.

On the bureau in her bedroom stands a flock of dust-free photographs, picture after picture of little Liam, shooting a cap pistol from his tricycle, grinning sopping wet in baggy swim trunks, pirouetting in a ruffled, watermelon-sleeved Babalou shirt. The photographs are lined up in perfectly staggered rows, smaller ones at the front, bigger at the back. For every five of Liam, there's one of dour Charlotte, engaged in no activity, barrettes pulling her hair back like drapes at a funeral parlour. She has the same even features Liam has, but on her, they're winched in the middle, as if her face is being sucked up her nose.

But one photo of Liam catches my eye, calling me back for a second, a third look. He appears to be about eleven, pudgier than in the preceding or following years. He's in a coat and tie, his hair Brylcreemed flat, his arms, in impeccable ballroom style, holding a flouncy-dressed girl a good six inches taller. The look on his face, the goofy, happy pride as he stands up so tall, so young, so sure of his funny little self, brings smarting tears to my eyes.

"My rogues' gallery," Gail is saying, but she stops short at the sight of my face. I blush like a hot pepper, stammering. "I can't help it. He's just so sweet."

She stands stiff and close-mouthed while I wipe my eyes, and when I pick up one of the smaller photos for a closer look, she steps smartly out into the hall, indicating that the bedroom visit is at an end, thank you very much. I replace the photo and she shuts the door behind my exiting back with a quick snap of the wrist.

Her phone rings and she highsteps it to the kitchen to answer. I stand alone in the living room while she laughs and laughs with whomever, making that lovely, funny sound, like a happy cartoon car revving to life on a cold winter morning. Out of curiosity, I try quietly plinking out the main notes on the piano.

Just as I suspected: D, F#, A, D, a perfect ascending octave.

Winter melts into sunny springtime. Liam and I are sticky with eros, juices bubbling like hot sap, him off whistling to work every morning to program computers, juggling macros and hyperlinks and Booleans the livelong day. I stand at the window to watch him drive up in the late afternoon, to see his eyes seeing me seeing him, torrid grins devouring our helpless faces like flesh-eating bacteria.

I don't see a whole lot of Gail, though from our living room I can hear her oven timer go off, ga-DING, every morning at six, her hard little feet scuttling overhead from the bedroom to the living room to begin the fanatical, twenty-minute piano practice — that was the music I'd been hearing — which she does before she's even sat down for a morning pee. Her hands slam onto the keys like a crash of dinner plates, like she wants to wring the music's little neck. I giggle into my coffee as she thumps out one of Brahms's ballades, the notes bleak and aimless, sloshing around like water in a swinging pail, electrons and protons chasing one another around the vortex at the dead centre of Doom.

The only sour notes in my life come, unsurprisingly, from

Gerard, who finagled my new number from Mum and has taken to calling at irregular intervals and uncouth hours. Once, in the middle of the night, Liam answered, and unable to read the call display without his glasses, roared, "Who the fuck?" into the receiver. Gerard, if indeed it was he, hung up immediately. Thereafter, he's restricted himself to daytime calls, all of which I let go to voice mail and instantly eradicate at the sound of his first wheezy syllable. I check the voice mail religiously the instant I come home from a recording gig or the grocery store, terrified that a call might slip by and be intercepted by Liam as he routinely deletes our daily influx of messages from home security salesmen and young men with dark accents asking to speak to Beyroush.

You'd think I'd never read the Christian rulebook, jumping into the sack with Liam like the fiends of hell were after me, grabbing for happiness like a greedy child scarfing down cookies with two hands till I choked. But if that's the bone sticking in Gerard's craw, does it really matter? We *are* going to be married, and soon! The rest is none of his damned business. He doesn't have to know about me hanging from Liam's neck like a lovesick teenager grinding in the hormone-steamy gym to the Righteous Brothers, ready to die for him in a heartbeat if he asks me to. He doesn't have to see me nauseous with love, watching his hips move like ball bearings inside his pleated Dad jeans. Life on the *Bachelor* is glorious, and no rancid old coot in a long black coat is going to prevent me from tossing like a wood chip on the pounding tides of hope, betting everything on my inflamed carbuncle of a heart.

Yet, there's always a part of me that stands coolly outside

of our thrashing affair, gazing down upon Liam from a great height, loftily deriding his untroubled spirit. I felt it in the rowboat forty years ago, and I feel it now. When he takes his shirt off, I'm overcome with a rush of equal parts unbearable tenderness and withering scorn for his sagging stomach and his white, white skin, with just the hint of last year's farmer tan on his neck and forearms. His unperturbed corporeality: does he have any idea how *late* it is, only a scant cup of days left till the end, the two of us barely held together with peeling bits of dry tape and rotting string?

But the hell with that. I know where I want to be. I know who I am, and I'm no Untouchable. I'm a human being, a woman in love, a person of flesh and heart and heat, and I'm not going any damn where not included on the list of the *Bachelor*'s ports of call.

Still, if that's true, then why am I marrying Liam in the ugliest outfit I could find, a putty-coloured suit a size too small, hideous lace flowers stretched over a lining the colour of cat food, reduced for clearance at the Bay? I know I could have bought something nice, could have spent all the money I wanted. Instead, I choose to appear looking as if I've been packed into a tensor bandage. All this so that Gerard, who won't even know, can't accuse me of taking any thought for my life in this cursed world.

As for Liam, he doesn't even notice that he's marrying the coal miner's burly daughter. Bedazzled, he thinks I look sensational in everything.

Our May wedding is pathetic in its modesty. We don't care.

We're so love-addled, we never bothered to argue about whether it would take place in a church or not; Liam assumed it wouldn't and I said nothing to counter his assumption. Still, City Hall is too bleak and linoleum-intensive a venue to handle a raging passion like ours. So we've settled on a tiny chapel stuck like a wart to the side of a Unitarian church, smack in the fork of the super-highway leading to God slash Void.

It's going to be just the two of us, with only Gail and Liam's friend Mitch as witnesses. Mitch is a long-time bachelor, a fellow computer programmer in the firm where they work. Seeing him hulking in the back of the chapel in his chintzy suit coat, I think there can be nothing more repulsive than an aging man you don't love. And afterwards when we all go to dinner, he annoys me even more, refusing all animal products and alcohol, picking at his fey tomato salad, sipping mineral water through a straw, and mumbling about random mutations in the human genome.

"Too bad Charlotte couldn't make it," I whisper into Liam's ear. "She and Mitch were made for each other."

The reception, held in the pocket-sized library adjoining the chapel, is barely longer than the wedding, the bare-bones vows of which take one and a half minutes, tops. We've hardly begun popping champagne corks and aimlessly milling in small circles when I get the shock of my life.

Gerard strolls in.

Of course he has to wait till the first glasses are being clinked, cooling his heels out in the hall till the mushy stuff is over. He looks a shambles, his hair slicked back with a palmful of spit, his overcoat splotched with fresh stains of unspeakable origin. He's the only person there from my side, a dubious bonus, since I've expected no one. Mum, of course, has begged off, complaining that she feels terrible all the time and never leaves the house any more for anything, reminding me reproachfully over the phone, "You know I'm a part-time invalid."

"I think you mean 'novice' invalid, Mother. In the sense of just starting out, getting your feet wet in the shut-in game." Having her at my mercy at last just never seems to get old.

"I'm a part-time invalid. I don't even get dressed any more. But you tell that nice Liam I'm very happy for him. What church are you getting married in?"

"Sacred Heart," I lied, figuring that had to be a safe bet; there's always one of those around. I held my breath, waiting for more Catholic questions to fend off. But she'd already moved on, talking about the new jacket and booties she was knitting for Winky, whom I imagined lying at her feet like some sad, retired circus performer, decked out in a powder blue sweater tied at the neck with pompoms. I could hear both of them breathing in ragged tandem in her overheated apartment, those last, hard-drawn breaths all they had left to pay the Piper with when he rang at the door, like the paperboys of old, to collect.

But here's Gerard, to whom I sent a terse written invitation, just to let him know we would now be legal rather than living in sin, hoping this might put an end to the calls. I never expected him to show up in a gazillion years. He stands among the other rigid attendees and the minister, holding a napkin with a thin slice of the Loblaws cake I brought in one hand and an unlit smoke in the other. He's wearing his Roman collar, of all things; I thought he'd retired it for good. Meanwhile, Gail, in a yellow blouse with a huge clown bow at the neck and an ancient blue pantsuit with batwing lapels, has been uncharacteristically silent, at least till the moment he walks in. But when he shrugs off his overcoat and she gets a load of that collar, she proceeds to back him against a wall, peppering him with sly questions about abstruse church dogma and pedophile priests.

Gerard stands silently, apparently listening, but his patience gives out after three or four minutes. He cuts her off mid-word, informing her brusquely that he has a funeral to get to, and walks out the door, leaving her standing alone, her bright smile twisting in the wind.

Liam and I are veering perilously close to mutual spontaneous combustion. We're in such an exalted state, we don't give a moment's thought to our tepid guests, only dying for the thing to be over so we can be alone again. We can never get through *anything* fast enough, can't pick up groceries without stopping for a lingering kiss in front of the dairy case, can't go to a restaurant without shoving the plates away to clutch each other's wrists for dear life across the table, frantic to settle the bill and rush back home to bed, our bedroom windows so steamed up we have to throw them wide open, making all the birds, and probably half the people on the block, blush and giggle.

"This is heaven," Liam whispers to me. "I am absolutely in heaven!" We knock back three glasses of champagne apiece and stand, arms round each other, gazing at everyone in the room with a hilarious, hiccuppy love.

"I can tell you everything, can't I?" I breathe hotly into his ear, and he nods, red-faced, like an emphatic puppet. When he excuses himself to go to the bathroom and I'm left for those few moments alone, I can feel his face as it was just before he left, superimposed upon my own, as if I've miraculously *become* him. "I have his face on me!" I cry to myself, slaphappy with girly mirth. And it stays there; it won't shake off! The lights in the room seem schizoid-bright, and I know this is the thing I've been waiting so long for, the very thing people mean when they use the word *life*.

And who knew Liam had turned into a solitary like me? It makes our finding each other again that much sweeter. Other people are so much *work*, we moan to each other: all those dinner parties, dreary jokes, squealing laughter, all that pretending to be interested, all that *acting*! All that having to go out and buy brandy snifters and all the other necessary upgrades that have to be made once you reach your prosperous fifties. It makes you tired just thinking about it.

I pretend that I know exactly what he's talking about.

One by one, his Montreal friendships have all expired, and he's made no new ones in Toronto, save Mitch. It's a relief, he says, to let everyone go. I agree, inventing scads of girlfriends who have drifted away, privately remembering my sad efforts to keep up my end of the conversation with my fellow voice actors, never comfortable, always talking too fast, losing my place, saying anything, telling any lie, just as long as it sounded like it might pass muster and make me sound normal.

After the wedding, Gail grants us a grace period of two days before she resumes dropping in regularly in the evenings, Liam never failing to ask, "Is everything okay?" the minute she pokes her head in. His tone makes me think of someone putting a careful foot onto thin ice, the unspoken "still" before the "okay" fairly screaming.

"Sure! Sure! Everything okay with you?" she crows back, her spirits never less than sky-high, as I imagine her jogging frantically in place, trying to outrun lightning forking against a black sky.

Down she flops then, bright and beaming, into the Tanteek's chair to watch her shows, the TV turned up to old-person decibel level. She's a great fan of live plastic surgery. Liam, who whimpers and covers his eyes at the mere sight of a needle approaching someone's arm, wails, "Tell me when it's over!" as she chortles up a storm, shouting, "Look, look, Liam! They're starting to peel her face off!"

"No!" he shouts, jumping up blind, flapping his hands in terror. "No! Don't do it!"

Gail leans toward the TV, her face ravenous, while I watch, bemused, from my old corner seat on the couch, personally unperturbed by the sight of spurting blood and globs of fat being suctioned into jars. Really, I can look at pretty much anything.

She's in her element, the centre of beloved attention, and, while the commercials are on, she has many, many things to tell us. All I can do is sit there, helpless, as the floodgates burst and the undammable cataract of talk gushes out of her so thick and fast you'd think she were afraid the sun might burn to a cinder before she's finished clarifying her every passing thought. If I try to interject anything, I immediately sense the impatient traffic backing up inside her head, trucks honking, cars overtaking on the shoulder, drivers jabbing their middle fingers at the rear-view mirror. Keeping up with her is like trying to follow a map with print so small I can't even be sure it's right side up. It requires superhuman concentration just to keep my eyes open, never mind navigating the Byzantine twists and turns of conversational qualifications, sub-headings, irrelevant commentary, incidental thoughts, branchings, side roads, rural routes, underpasses, and long cuts.

Then she'll say it all twice more. If Liam moves to another room, she'll trot after him, yipping all the while, even outside the bathroom door. They're a matched set, these two: cup and saucer, salt and pepper, ketchup and mustard. Death and the grave.

Since the wedding, something has darkened in her attitude to me. I know by now that unexpected additions to the conversation can throw her off her game, but when I try to dip a timid toe into her flood-rush of talk, she no longer just waits me out before continuing from where she left off. Instead, she rears up short, snapping, "Oh, really? Because *I* would have thought..." and then proceeds to contradict whatever it is I've said, even if it's a subject about which I clearly possess superior knowledge, like the voice-over business.

She has no such problems with Liam, who agrees automatically with every single thing she says.

To my ears, their conversations sound rehearsed, set pieces they both know so well that they speak to each other in simultaneous monologues, stepping all over each other's lines. It's like two separate talk-radio stations playing at the same time.

At first, I find it endearing that Liam's so kind and patient with her, never letting on that she might be a tad long-winded, that he might be tired or longing for a little peace and quiet. I figure that's what it's like having a mother who clearly adores you and whom you adore in return. What do I know about any of that? Who am I to judge?

Molten with love, I sit as attentive as a border collie, watching Liam's mouth move along with hers, listening to endless chitchat about the day's talk-radio issues: notwithstanding clauses, undermining faith in public institutions, and impacting bottom lines, all interwoven with gardening facts 'n' fancies and hilarious recollections of past highlights of their long lives together, consisting mostly of boyhood gaffes committed by Liam. Once they really get going, there's no way to break in unless I care to enter a third monologue in the race. But I have none to enter, so I simply sit and rub my palms along the creamy surface of *my* beautiful leather couch, thank you very much.

When she finally heads upstairs for the night, I crawl gratefully into bed beside Liam and bark those three little words: "Shove oveh, you." In the morning, I watch him sit on the side of the bed and pull on his socks; it has to be the most touching sight in the world: a bald, middle-aged man in underpants, pulling on socks. Is there anything more pathetic, more endearing, more hopefully rational? I already feel much better than I did the night before, an equal once again, in love to my eyeballs, so happy I could spit.

"Promise you'll never leave me." I cry, sitting up, breathless.

"I wouldn't last a minute without you, babe. Sometimes I think I knew you before we were even born. The day, the minute, the second you arrived on earth," he says, falling across the bed to plow his head into my cushiony stomach. "I must have known it. My heart must have jumped. It's her! She's here!"

Yes, that's how *we* talk, I'm afraid: day and night, nothing but sweet blessings on our lips. We look at each other and see our own best faces smiling back; we look out the bedroom window at the world and laugh with the sheer joy of looking, of being along, unaccountably, for the wild ride of Life. We laugh at the self-important birds strutting around the lawn on reconnaissance missions, laugh at the cool stares of dogs passing us in the street. We laugh at the way The Mystery keeps jumping out from behind bushes, crying Boo!

Well, I do anyway.

The changing panorama out the windows never ceases to thrill me, accustomed as I am to life in a box suspended in white sky. I watch roving gangs of cardinals line up on the budding backyard branches as if for a curtain call, their box-cutter heads tilted coyly sideways. I watch each tree break into leaf, watch lilacs explode into swoony blossom, watch tulips rise and fall. All the while I can feel hope on the back of my neck, ticklish, like excited little bug feet.

I'm flush with a throbbing sense of long-stifled creativity. I decide I ought to write something; isn't that what people with no jobs do? A screenplay, a TV series, anything. I'm pretty smart, and I've known some far-out characters. How hard can it be?

I certainly have the time. My voice gigs are down to one a week if I'm lucky, and the only other times I leave the house are to do a whirlwind check on Mum or get groceries, borrowing Gail's car to drive to my brand-new Loblaws, where, weaned at last from my spinster diet of takeout pizza and lasagna, I lollygag in housewifely mode up and down the aisles, learning where they keep all the stuff a fine cook like me can't do without.

Still, I can't wait to pay up, load the car, zip through the LCBO for wine (the only thing I drink any more), and race back to the cozy safety of home, where I can kick back with...just one...glass of chilled Chablis and watch Gail in the driveway swabbing out her car with disinfectant.

Really? It was only groceries! What does she think, that *I* smell? What's her problem anyways?

In the morning, after seeing Liam off to work, I take my coffee to the brand-new, twenty-first-century computer he's bought and set up for me on a table at the front window. My screenplay chugs ahead as far as: "*Exterior: Outside of a run-down farmhouse in...*" before I take a breather by reading my daily email from Charlotte, who tacked my name onto her six-inch address list the day I joined the family. Barely a day goes by that I don't receive some fervent missive geared to the sisterhood of aging women: jokey messages raking dumb, feckless men over the coals, long lists of strongly biased comparisons of the way the sexes do things, and endless hoo-hawing about fat and hot flashes and how we don't give a good god damn what anyone thinks of us any more. All of them end with some variant on the command: Send this to all the smart women you know! And I think, who? Catou? Barb? Mum? The Tasmanian devil whirligigging beneath my window?

Because that's where Gail is to be found now from earliest morning till well into late afternoon. Her show-stopping garden takes up the entire front yard, and watching it arch its back, yawn, and blush into warmer colour every day makes me a little envious. Her work is so honest and straightforward as she grubs away under the sun, all her plots laid out in the scrubby earth like an ambitious suburban subdivision, seeds dying right, left, and centre into new, glorious life.

Her plots are doing way better than mine. After a week, my opening line has evolved into: *"Interior: a drab farmhouse kitchen in…"* For the next few weeks I pick at a few barren ideas like dried scabs, trying to flesh out Flake and Big Fanny on the page, but by ten, I'm usually picking up the Saturday *Globe* still scattered all over the house, watching old episodes of *Pete and Gladys* and *December Bride* on YouTube, and experimenting with teeth whiteners. Soap operas don't turn out to be half as bad as I'd imagined. When *General Hospital* is over, I slap on some music and dance around the house lip-syncing to Aretha Franklin or Maria Callas, depending on my mood.

Out the window, I can see Gail yanking with unbridled ferocity the first belligerent dandelions that blow in from the jungle next door, where the flora-indifferent Chungs live. She squashes each spidery plant into an old fertilizer bag, as if to say, Ha! That's what *you* get! When the bag is full, she pitches the contents briskly over the fence into the Chungs' yard before lugging an unwieldy industrial vacuum from the garage and proceeding to suck up every last stray twig and leaf and seed from her own, picking up the rogue petals it misses with her hands. Ladybugs and bees busy nosing into new blossoms freeze, holding their breath until she passes. Snails grind to a halt and duck indoors. Lightning flashes, turning the Chungs' great maple an eerie chartreuse; thunder rocks the house, but the fast clouds, taking note of Gail's scowl, abruptly change their minds and head elsewhere. The sun returns, the flowers stretch and preen, and the cicadas pick up their saws and resume their work.

She hails the mailman and every passing neighbour, grinning like the Jolly Roger, her hand shooting into the air in manic good cheer as she cries, "See my handy-dandy new aphid sprayer?" Then she launches into monologue mode, her grubby hands on her hips, her head in constant motion like a bobble-head doll, detaining her victim, who keeps trying to imperceptibly back away, for fifteen agonizing minutes before she finally shouts, "It was ever thus!" at their swiftly retreating backs, bobbing and rearing all the while with intemperate, unnatural laughter.

I watch our neighbour to the right, Mr. Glickman, hurry out to his car, his head lowered, trying not to catch her eye. He learned about Gail the hard way, trying to wrap up a conversation once with a shrug and the time-honoured closer, "Well, what are ya gonna do?" She spent the next forty minutes telling him.

Her energy level astounds me; she doesn't just put my mother to shame, she makes *me* feel like elderly wreckage. Before she sets foot in her garden, she vacuums her entire apartment every morning, hrooming and scraping back and forth on the far side of our ceiling, lifting furniture, banging it down. From the open window I hear the flap of her blinds as she dusts them, the thwap of rugs being shaken within an inch of their lives over her balcony, and finally the vigorous clink of dishes taken from her dishwasher and stacked with gusto in the cupboards. Once a week she marches to the curb to put one tiny, perfectly knotted grocery bag of garbage into a bin so clean you can lay a baby down to sleep in it. I can't imagine what the woman eats, besides royal jelly and jumbo jars of beta-carotene capsules, though when she's downstairs with us, she puts away the chocolate pudding cups Liam always has on hand for her like a stevedore.

Crocuses and daffodils and tulips sprang up in April and May, but they were only the warmup to the garden's blazing opening act: the forsythia that runs along the Chung-Cushnahan frontier. It bursts into bloom one morning completely without warning, illuminating the yard like klieg lights. With every passing day, the baby shoots that poke their heads through the hard dirt, swept clean as a kitchen floor in April, begin, in May, to outgrow their clothes like gangly teenagers, becoming loud and hilarious. By June, they're waving to their pals, milling, jostling, and shoving, shouting lewd suggestions from one strait-laced plot to another. Cardinals and blue jays and finches, the primary coloured birds, bounce about as if on springs, their business never so urgent that they can't stop to obediently wash their grimy little feet in Gail's stainless steel birdbath.

The garden burgeons much the way Gail talks, with themes, variations, repetitions, codas, and recapitulations. Next to it, the Chungs' raggedy-ass stab at a rock garden looks like the foothills of the Urals after Genghis and his hordes have laid them waste. Comparing the two sides of the fence, I can only grab a free-floating Bible verse out of the air: "Unto everyone that hath shall be given; and from him that hath not, even that he hath shall be taken away from him."

It's so startlingly beautiful, this carnival of tufts and stalks and starbursts, and it puts me in mind of nothing so much as Mum's old basket of wool ends, left over from her multitudinous projects: bits, scraps, sequins, rhinestones, buttons in every conceivable shape and colour, the only truly beautiful thing I can remember from our tense, grey household.

And out there with her as she labours, providing a tinny

ostinato to her huffs and grunts, is a portable radio, tuned to never-ending call-in talk shows. Up with the sun just like her, the hosts throw open the phone lines after having scoured the news for the subject of the day, which they and their listeners then spend the morning chawing to mash. Periodically, Gail leaves her work to charge upstairs and call in and, true to her word, gets through at least once a week: Gaily-Gaily, the nutty little lady who does her talking in volume. Often, she and Liam have been chewing the rag on the very same topic the night before, hammering home their points, caulking the cracks, bolstering the fences, agreeing on everything, as if the steady piston thrusts of their jaws is the chugging machinery that keeps the universe humming. Whether the topic of the day is the provincial budget, the federal trade deficit, the insanity defence, or peanut allergies, there's usually room to squeeze Gail in, right before the Paradise Pizza All-Day Traffic Centre report. Wild talk drifts down from her open window of programs put in place, private members bills, and level playing fields, and from the radio in the yard I can hear her yipping at her own heels, seven seconds behind.

"We've got just a minute left. Gaily-Gaily, you have the last word."

"Well, I think you and I are on the same page on this one, although at the end of the day the longest word in the English language is and always will be *if*," declares Gail stoutly, itching to pack an entire thesis into sixty seconds.

If she can't get on one show, she tries the next, as the hosts spell one another, passing the baton every couple of hours, launching fresh topics. She even takes a shot at the sports show, berating the Jays on their latest stupid trade, weighing in on who is or isn't on the juice. There's nothing she doesn't know.

Around two, she heads indoors for another brief piano mauling but is always back in the garden by three, bending with a trowel to respace seedlings planted only that morning or hoovering up errant dandelion seeds blown in from the hostile territory to the left of us.

Karen Chung is the one person in the world who never has to worry about being waylaid by Gail. Karen won't monitor her dandelions and ignores her creeping couchgrass; for this alone, Gail has sworn eternal enmity. When everybody's coats come off in mid-April and Liam spies Karen out front one evening, he remarks on how trim she's looking, that she seems to have lost weight over the winter.

"Let's hope its cancer! I choose to think positively!" Gail chirps, letting loose a pixie-dust scatterfall of laughter.

Karen is a tiny Korean woman, in her early thirties, given to long floral skirts and straw hats, the kind of dainty, delicate person who always makes me feel like the barnacle-encrusted prow of a battleship. Her little boy, an adorable squirt named Sun or San, or Sin, I'm still not sure, pedals furiously after her on his tricycle as she sets out every day to do the shopping, her earth-friendly mesh bags over her arm. Sometimes his rear tire rolls over a bit of Gail's flowery ground cover. To add insult to injury, the Chungs have an unleashed puppy that runs after the tricycle, and who once stopped in the sunny shelter of the forsythia to attempt a quick squat. No sooner did he ease onto his haunches than Gail gave him a swift, hard kick from behind, shooting him squealing straight into the path of an oncoming car that missed him by inches. Karen was too far up the street to see.

Now the dog slinks past our yard, eyes rolling in his head like a horse in a stable fire. Gail's always ready for him, revving the motor of her electric half-moon edger with its precision blade, which makes him take off like the hound of hell, galloping after Sin or Sun, yelping in white-eyed terror.

I'm at the computer as usual, engrossed in funny cat videos, when Gail bangs open our front door one morning in a towering rage. She marches to the front window, leaning right over me, smelling of roots and loam, like she's just been dug up herself. Dropping bits of earth onto my desk, she presses her face as close as she can get it to the glass, snarling, "That bitch's sprinkler is overshooting again!"

Sure enough, water is arcing lazily over the hedge from the Chungs' side and back again, as if it can't make up its mind who it likes better. Gail watches, unblinking, her chest heaving, as the water falls in a fairyland spray straight onto her artful hosta clump, which is not under *any* circumstances to receive water during daylight hours.

"She's trying to kill my hostas. Well, I'll fix her!" Her voice is low and dangerous. "You see if I don't."

She stamps out, slamming the door and clomping up the stairs. Outside, the peaceful sprinkler continues to wave back and forth. Gail pounds from room to room overhead, then sits to play fifteen minutes of Chopin so fast and hard it sounds like a player piano being dropped down an elevator shaft.

In a little while, a squad car pulls up to the curb. Two policemen amble up the Chungs' front walk. I hear muffled voices, a peal of laughter. The cops stroll back to their car and drive off.

Directly overhead, Gail's venetian blinds clatter against the window. After a few moments, Karen comes out and moves the sprinkler back, waving cheerfully in Gail's direction. Gail must have jerked back suddenly to avoid being seen, for I hear one of her vases of artificial flowers smash to the floor, followed by frantic bustling with the broom, the dustpan, and the vacuum.

Minutes later, she hurtles down the stairs and outside. Karen is sitting on her front porch, face tilted into the warm sun, eyes closed. I have to get up and scrunch myself flat against the window in order to see all this.

"Hi, Kaaaaren," Gail calls, her voice all honey and dumplings.

Karen waves back. "Hi, Gail," she says with a wide grin. "How you doing?"

"Just ter*rif*ic!" spits Gail, lock-jawed with the joy of victory. Karen laughs again.

"You seem a little stressed!" she calls, but her tone is friendly, devoid of mockery or sarcasm. Her little boy rolls down the driveway on his tricycle, turning to stare as Gail marches, haughty head high, into the backyard.

I can't help but laugh, thinking, I ought to go over there and make friends. But if I do, what kind of fresh hell will break loose over here?

The golden first summer of my married life deepens. My screenplay bites the dust. By noon I'm already counting down the remaining hours till Liam comes home. Noon is also when

I begin thinking longingly about ice clinking in glasses and Jack's cheery grin and nippy teeth, so much more satisfying than tepid, musty wine. What harm will it do to step out for a bottle? I can hide it in one of the high cupboards, behind the never-used juicer. Who'll know?

But I resist. I try reading instead but am too jittery to concentrate, usually settling for a movie on television. At five, I toss some Shake'n Baked item that even I can't wreck into the oven, watching out of the corner of my eye as Dr. Phil steps up to the plate on the little TV on the kitchen counter, scolding, "YOU NEED"—kaboom, go the drums—"to get REAL!! I want YOU"—Zing! Zoom!—"to draw a LINE, in the SAND"—mass gasps from the studio audience—"right NOW!!!"

Liam pulls into the driveway at long last, a huge bag of pudding cups on the seat beside him. "And a bagatelle to have with supper," he adds, bonking me playfully on the head with a stick of bread.

This bends me in half.

"It's *baguette*, you illiterate cretin!" And Gail, materializing out of nowhere behind him, pokes him in the ribs, shouting, "Woi, Croikey! Oi b'lieve yew just mide a foonay, yew did!"

"What did I say?" he asks, all mystified, as both he and Gail wobble and bob in hyper-merriment and swift bolts of blue lightning only I can see crackle over their heads.

Mum has now taken to calling every evening, once, twice, six times. I let most of the calls go to voice mail too but pick up the odd one out of guilt, especially if I've skipped dropping in on her that week. Invariably she opens with, "I won't be around much longer, Mag Mary." It goes downhill from there.

"I know. You keep saying." Dark silence echoes on the other end, punctuated by vituperative yelps from Winky.

"Hello? Mag Mary? Are you still there?"

"Where else would I be?" More silence.

"You know I won't be around much longer." Her warped voice crawls down the line on shaky hands and knees. Sometimes she'll be incoherent with the weeps after a full day of radio reminiscences of the Auld Sod, where she's never set foot in her life, wailing, "Oh, Mag Mary, please, *please* go for me when I'm gone. Climb St. Patrick's holy mountain and say a prayer for my soul, Mag Mary, please, please, *pleeeease.*" Sitting with the phone wedged between my neck and shoulder, I throw desperate looks Liamward, but he refuses to look my way, and in the set of his shoulders, I can clearly read, "Thank God *my* mother never pulls this kind of stuff."

I shudder to realize how close I came to following her step for step down the lonely, rocky path of her life. This man who sits turned away from me, chuckling with his own mother at some tweedy, overbite-heavy British comedy on TV, is all that stands between my fate and hers. What if the Father should take it into his unfathomable head to rip Liam right out of my arms? What if he should decide that my new husband's cell in hell is now ready for occupancy? Because when *he's* in the picture, giving and taking away as he does according to print far too fine for our feeble eyes, staking my life on one earthly companion is begging for trouble with a megaphone.

"You should get everything squared away with the funeral home now," is the breezy advice Gail tosses over her shoulder when a commercial comes on. My stomach plunges into the abyss until I realize she's talking about Mum, not Liam. "Best thing to do is tie up all the loose ends ahead of time. Oi've got all me doocks in a ra-ow, doock-ay! I'm not going to be a bother to anyone. When you're dead, you're dead. That's all she wrote." Then she lets rip with her merry, musical laugh.

I know that Liam keeps his copy of her sensible living will, fittingly, in his sock drawer. It orders the withholding of all life-sustaining treatment in the event of a terminal condition or permanently unconscious state involving a total loss of cerebral cortical functioning. It also stipulates where her body is to go upon reaching its expiration date.

It doesn't get much duckier than that.

"I'm after quality, not quantity," she insists snappily. "I know what I'm about. Always have."

"Good for you!" Liam says in hearty approval. And next to the brimming well of love in my heart, another, freshly dug, receives the first leaden plops of corrosive resentment.

All of which explains why Liam and I find ourselves in the wallpapered and wainscoted vestibule of a downtown funeral parlour on a beautiful June Saturday, preparing to trudge down the basement steps after a puffy young man in shirtsleeves, whom we've caught, I surmise, in mid-embalm. He leads us down, down, down to where the coffins are kept. Outside, bronzed folk in tank tops with decades to live jog by in the company of robust, springing dogs, and the birds are all in a whomping good mood.

The boy undertaker has a buttery voice and discreetly saddened eyes.

"Anything you need to know, don't hesitate to ask," he oozes in his creamy, golden way. "I'll explain everything."

"Wonderful," I tell him. "So, is the afterlife a disembodied state, a submersion in the great and eternal All, or is it more like the Christian heaven and hell, plus or minus Purgatory and in some cases Limbus Patrum and/or Puerorum?"

Liam pinches me hard. The boy, who either hasn't heard or chose not to, eases open the door to a brightly lit room at the bottom of the stairs and turns to us as smoothly as if he were mounted on casters. He rubs his hands together like a housefly, and I think, with a gentle jolt of summer-morning horror, that his hands probably have someone's dead goo all over them.

"Are you looking for a permanent or a rental?" he asks. Liam and I exchange looks, controlling the corners of our mouths with difficulty.

"A rental is just used for the wake," the boy explains. He probably sets up this little scene every time; I swear he's suppressing his own macabre smile.

We stroll through the coffin display, trying to feel morose. All the lids are open and inviting, like those signs in store windows in summer: It's Cooool Inside! They're as plush as babies' bassinets. One has a cheerful golf scene painted on what's going to be a very low ceiling for some poor old duffer. Another manly black casket has "DAD" inscribed in gold letters on the inside of the lid, right at Dad's eventual eye level. Stripped by death of his name, at least he'll have his title to remember himself by.

On the other side of the room are coffins for Mother, pink and ruffly, plump as pincushions. Angels and crosses are everywhere, and I try to ascertain by peripheral vision if Liam is smirking at them. He knows my mother has real angels as friends; I've seen him and Gail exchange eyebrow-intensive looks over it.

The bloody boxes, it turns out, cost the earth.

I can choose one of the swanky ones, and come off as loving and generous. I can choose the cheapest, appear cold-hearted and mean, and save a bundle. Both impulses run neck and neck. The boy stands behind us lightly wringing his fly paws. He thinks we're a couple of walking antiques ourselves. He's probably eyeing the bone structures behind our sagging faces, pre-planning makeup strategies for *our* imminent coffin debuts.

Upstairs again, we sit around a vast mahogany table as shiny as a concert piano. The boy asks understanding questions in a careful, beige tone. Will there be an obituary? No. No one to read it. No, no one to advise what to do in lieu of sending flowers. The only way it will be a standing-room-only funeral will be if we hold it in Mum's kitchen. Every one of her brothers and sisters are gone, except Baby, who's locked away with a dementia even worse than Mum's. Dad, assuming he can be found, won't care a rap that she's passed on. I doubt her mourners will fill half a pew.

The boy reminds us gently that we have to dress her in something presentable, since she's insisted on an open coffin.

"I want to be able to see who turns up," is her rationale. But the real reason, I know, is that she wants Gerard to see her dead.

"A favourite dress?" urges the boy helpfully. Sure. I'll check through her party clothes and ball gowns. I don't see what's wrong with the famous yellow bathrobe. She's had it since before Gerard and I started school, when it was plush and fluffy. Surely it deserves a showing of its own. I don't know if she even has other clothes any more.

"I take it the shroud is no longer in vogue?" I ask brightly. The boy smiles in neutral, waits a beat, and moves on to the matter of the headstone.

We walk back to the car in silence. It's stuffy as a sweat lodge inside. Liam turns the key, igniting the CBC along with the engine: finger-poppin' jazz, the perfect accompaniment to the hoppin' and boppin', shorts-wearing citizenry all around us, out for brunch and shoe shopping, with nary a care.

Liam's car is a staid grey Subaru, as pristine as the day it came off the showroom floor. I think wistfully of my old, homey Trans Am, littered with butts and coffee cups, parking stubs and lottery tickets. Fred came to repossess it a mere three days after I'd left the gang, the last Untouchable I'd seen. He's now the group's designated driver, and still helping himself to my money, I notice, though there's no one to blame for that but myself: I haven't yet worked up the nerve to cut them off. I keep this, prudently, from Liam.

"We should stop by her place and round up her coffin clothes," I say, watching a shiny gay couple strut past with a pair of handsome hounds.

Liam waits in the car while I trudge up the stairs to Mum's apartment after buzzing the outside door for a full five minutes. She opens her door a crack after I pound and shout for several minutes more. A sliver of face appears, the section comprising her suspicious left eye and a belligerent bit of lip. Winky is running semi-circles around her, yapping death threats at my ankles.

"I'm just looking in, Mum. I can't stay."

"You didn't call me," she complains, hunched in the crack of light behind her door. "Why didn't you call me?"

"You have to undo the chain, Mum. There, right in front of you, the chain. Yes, that one. That's a good girl."

She slouches back to the couch, bones jerking about under her skin, the crazy, grinning skeleton rattling its cage, wanting out. As soon as her eyes turn back to the TV, I duck into her bedroom to riffle through her closet. There's more here than I thought, the rack crammed with antiquated ensembles, blouses in blazing prints, poppy-red and dandelion-yellow pantsuits from four decades ago, when, with Dad so auspiciously removed from her life, she suddenly began experimenting with clothing in colours other than slag brown and cement-block grey. She's contributed many of her barely worn sweaters to the St. Bern's annual rummage sales, but there are still heaps piled on the high shelf, their dazzling fruitiness muted inside zipped plastic bags.

Still, I think, decorum must prevail. Much as I'd enjoy seeing her buried in shocking pink mohair with a jaunty purple tam, she probably won't appreciate it, and Gerard definitely won't. Though these seem like two excellent reasons to proceed, I resist. Poking through the very back of the closet, I finally pull out a sober, dead-leaf brown sheath, roll it up, and tuck it under my arm.

"How are you doing?" I ask as I pass through the living room. "What are you watching there?"

"My show."

"Does it have a name?"

"I don't want to tell you."

"Have you eaten anything today?"

"I'm not stupid."

"What did you eat then?"

"What there was."

"Liam's waiting for me in the car. Are you sure I can't fix you anything?"

"You can't fix anything."

When I get home and unroll the dress, a rush of perfume darts up my nose faster than a garter snake: pine boughs, overcooked meat loaf, gin and lemon, and Gerard's hot, puke-smelling breath in my face. It's her old unfestive Christmas dress, once tight around her middle, now a voluminous thing that will need to be pinned around her shrunken self like swaddling clothes.

The next morning, Sunday, Liam's up before me; I watch him through one squinched eye as he makes his way to the kitchen to start the coffee, taking note of the morning stoop in his posture and the six strands of hair on his head pointing every which way like errant corn stalks in a hastily executed crop circle. Any minute now Gail will burst in, the hinges of her jaw oiled and supple. They'll sit at the table scarfing sticky buns, their chatter picking up speed, sentences overlapping, Gail leading, Liam following, every exchange a bump-free ride of perfect agreement, while I jam the pillow over my head, recalling how I used to do the same thing to drown out Mum and Gerard. Just like them, Liam and Gail have a secret code, a closed universe of their own from which I know I'll be forever barred.

My stomach clenches as a ten-minute drum solo from Gail

evokes overheated honks of laughter from Liam. His strained concentration is as pungent to my nose as animal fear. Because if he steps even slightly to the right or left of the established guidelines, raising a point she hasn't foreseen, everything will come to a tire-squealing halt while she registers the unexpected information, minesweeping it for errors, the merry grin wiped clean off her face and replaced with that tense, furrowed frown I've come to dread.

I feign sleep until they move to the living room for their favourite Sunday morning sport of televangelist-watching, Liam flipping the channels till they find something suitably gag-worthy, causing Gail to spring up in her chair like Nosferatu in his coffin.

"The hair, the hair!" she howls, and I know she's kicking the shit out of my beautiful Montauk chair. "Praise da Lawd!"

"Oh, you're just going to love heaven, you precious people!" I hear Liam say. "Won't it be joy to spend every waking moment kissing God's feet and wailing about how great he is? Won't it be just precious to spend eternity with all those fine upstanding killers of abortion doctors? Oh wait, wait…let's see if we can find that guy who speaks in tongues!"

"Oh abbashinny wagga wagga boom boom!" Gail screams, her knotty little rump thumping up and down. If the Tanteek were in its chair, she'd be squashing it flat, not that it wouldn't be any less ready to spring to life the second she's gone, like Daffy Duck recovering from a steamrolling.

"Won't it be great spending eternity with right-thinking Republicans exactly like you? You don't want to miss that, so don't take the chance! Start sucking up to Our Precious Invisible Lawd now! Every kiss on his ass counts in your favour! Oh no, oh no! We're going to be blessed with music! Sorry, Gail, this is too much even for me." Next thing I know, he's found Mum's favourite, the Mass channel. "And here's your Host!" I hear him holler gleefully while Gail moos with laughter.

Already I've begun preparing myself for these Sunday mornings. Still resisting the hard stuff, I've begun sliding a fortifying bottle of wine and a juice glass down among the dust bunnies under the bed. By the time the hilarity draws to a close and Gail sets out for the garden, I've downed two and a half glasses, my mouth sour, my morning stomach gravely insulted.

I bump my way into the living room. Liam has gone back to sleep on the couch, his face turned away Dagwood-style, and a good thing too, with the reek coming off of me. I shove in behind him and whisper woozily into his neck, "Liam, why can't it be just us?"

He rolls clumsily onto his back, mumbling, "Hunhh?" I stand quickly, dizzily, to get out of range of his nose.

"I have so much trouble keeping up with you guys," I continue lamely, sounding whiny as hell in my own ears. "I want to be first in your life, Liam. I want us to be everything to each other. It doesn't seem like we are any more. I'm sorry. Do you know what I mean?"

He sits up, scratching his stubbly cheeks.

"No."

I'm teetering on the boozy edge of confessing how jealous I am of his closeness with Gail, how I've never had a mother, how without a mother your life-coat keeps sliding off every busted nail you try to hang it on and hitting the floor, how, how, etc., etc.

Three glasses would have pushed me over. Two and a half warn me just in time to clam up. What I'll do is, yeah, that'll be better, I'll call Fred and see if I can't get a hold of Flake and score some more coke. Then I'll be able to tell Liam *everything*. I can talk like gangbusters on coke. I can tell him how lonely and left out I feel seeing him and Gail so tight, and surely it isn't my imagination or just some bitter gripe on my part but something we can fix, like maybe barring Gail permanently from, no, that'll never work, but still, yes, I can tell him everything if I'm high, so that's what I'll do.

"It's okay," I chirp out of a big, toothy smile. "It's nothing."

"You sure?"

"Yeah, yeah. Go back to sleep, darlin'. Fuhgeddaboutit."

I wish to hell I could sleep the way he can. Night after night I lie sweating like a racehorse, soaking my pillow and the sheets down to the mattress. I know this is normal, know my reproductive system, still miffed about its poorly attended opening, is shutting down, rolling up the awnings, and slamming down the grate for good. It gives me plenty of time to toss this way and that, the echo of Gail's voice still throbbing between my ears like a migraine. Is she on her knees, peering down at me through her floorboards? In the wee hours I often hear footsteps over my head, or a sound like her sliding closet door being stealthily opened. Her bed, directly over ours, sometimes thumps heavily. I wonder if she's up there copulating with Satan.

But I know better. She has an animal trap tucked up against the wall of the backyard garden shed, a two-chambered, rectangular box fitted with a trick door in the middle. Raggedy strips of bacon dangle from hooks inside the inner chamber. It's intended mainly for the ravine raccoons that shuffle up nightly to horn in on her *lebensraum* and dig unsightly tufts out of the lawn. Every night some poor creature, all stripes, quivering ears, and soft belly, goes for the bait only to find itself forced to turn tight, frantic circles in her death-box, looking up at last in whimpering terror to see a black, Gail-shaped hole in the stars.

She monitors the trap every couple of hours, every time the frantic rattling of the box signals that she's caught another one. And on this moon-bright night, as I stand sleepless at the window, copping a furtive smoke, I can see her hunkered over the horrible thing, staring the helpless animal down, gazing inscrutable hexes into its uncomprehending eyes, smiling all the while. There's a pail of water at her side. The raccoon stares back, even as its life force is being siphoned into her black soul; it keeps staring up and begging, like life everywhere: Please don't hurt me!

Gail dumps the pail of water over its head. The racoon hisses and claws at the walls of its prison as she trots into the open shed, where, illuminated by her giant flashlight beam, I can plainly see her load and, crack! snap! cock a pellet gun.

Back at the trap, she puts the barrel to the raccoon's neck, still smiling, even with one eye beaded to the gun. And she fires. The gun makes a fun, popping sound, like bubble wrap. She fires again, three, four, five times; the old eyes probably aren't what they used to be. Then she fades into the black, without giving any indication of which direction she's gone.

I look to the tops of the trees, where she might already be crouching, still as the owl that only pretends to sleep, her head noiselessly swivelling. Maybe she's off to a witches' Sabbath in some distant ravine, flapping her batwings, swooping low over phosphorescent swimming pools and garden hedges. And if there is a coven waiting somewhere, how do the other gals stand her? Does she boss them around, blow hot air till the brew in the cauldron boils clean away? All I need for proof is to pounce on her from behind while she's down on her knees trimming the lawn edges with tweezers. I'll lift her grimy sweatshirt, flip her like a pancake, and, lo and behold, on her crepey stomach there it'll be: the witch mark, widow-black, the celebrated third nipple that doesn't bleed when pricked. And along the perfectly sunlit ground, further proof: everyone knows witches cast no shadow in full sun!

Or maybe she's out there alone, chanting necromancy, witching her garden into shameless luxuriance. She is, in truth, a thousand years old, her insides nothing but bubbling sulphur, her long lupine eyes yellow in the blackness as she mutters spells in the languages of moths and bats. Or casts some maleficium to pull her boy back to her and set the Tanteek howling after my shrinking soul.

Behind me, Liam snores like a truck in first gear cresting a hill. I climb back into bed, squeezing my eyes shut, trying to force sleep. Instead, the Tanteek drops from the ceiling like a tiny spider on a thread, lighting on my cheek, slipping in through an ear and beginning to spin, cocooning me in grey webbing from the inside out. "*His blood is on your hands,*" vibrates along the silver threads as they wrap and tighten. "*There shall come in the last days scoffers, walking after their own lusts, who separate themselves, having not the Spirit. Look at you, panting with lust, without shame, wiping your painted mouth and insisting you have done no wrong.*" The Tanteek, taking full possession of its old stomping grounds, pounds through every room in my head, smashing everything that looks like it might be valuable, while oblivious Liam continues to ride the waves of Morpheus beside me, creaking and rattling like the timbers of an old ship.

"*Liam in hell, screaming for mercy, and no way out, no way out ever, ever, ever…*"

I lie rigid as a plank, erasing him from his side of the bed, from his chair in the kitchen, from my side everywhere, trying to get a pre-taste of his absence. I erase him for as long as I can stand before springing him back into life. I know full well that agony is moseying my way, whistling, stopping to smell the roses, maybe already out in the hall, its gnarled rat hand on the doorknob as it whispers through the keyhole, "Ha! This is what *you* get!"

The next day, I get as far as actually dialling Fred's number. Hearing the first ring, I imagine the phone tossed onto the top of a pile of laundry, imagine Big Fanny lumbering over to pick up or Fred carefully marking his place in his Bible before answering. I imagine Gerard's house visible out the kitchen window, and Gerard in it. I hang up in the very nick of time.

My voice gigs have all but dried up. I go for an unprecedented three weeks with no work, and when I do find myself back in the studio, trying to read the warm, maternal copy for a diaper commercial, I'm unsteady, out of control. Once again, it requires countless takes just to work the frog out of my throat. I know they wish they'd never hired me. Crossing the control room to sign my contract, I almost lose my balance. I feel like an imposter, an inept impersonation of the old me. I wonder if maybe I shouldn't waive my fee, having let everyone down so badly.

The sound engineer, whom I've known for twenty years, turns to me just as I'm leaving.

"Whatever happened to that cute little guy you were baby-sitting?"

"Oh, he moved," I get out, stumbling over those three simple words, perilously close to tears. I wave a breezy goodbye and flee for my life.

In the taxi on the way home, profoundly shaken, I give the cabbie my old address, only snapping to life when he pulls up outside my late, great tower of broken dreams. Sheepishly, I pay him and get out. And stand for ten minutes gazing up, up, up at my old window, feeling myself silently seal over with an impenetrable membrane through which I can see out but no one can see in. Finally I hail another cab, which I keep waiting while I deke in and out of the LCBO, barely breathing until I'm back safe in my new bedroom.

Liam has no idea I now wait for him behind the door every evening, my heart in my mouth, my nose pressed against the window, just a yip shy of Winkydom. When his car finally pulls into the driveway and I hear the muffled but sprightly CBC sound of a white girl scat-singing "Fascinatin' Rhythm" from his car radio, I'm so happy I could weep, hustling straightaway into the kitchen so that when he comes in he'll discover me at the stove, absentmindedly stirring, easy in mind and light of heart, leaning in for my evening kiss.

Then it's "Can you hold supper for a few minutes? I promised I'd help Gail move her trap over by the fence."

Up goes my goodwill in a blast of smoke.

"I hate that fucking thing, Liam! You should make her get rid of it."

"Why? It's a humane trap. It's perfectly legal."

"She has a gun, Liam!"

"It's humane," he repeats irritably. "It's not like they're chewing their legs off out there. And as for the gun, she used to let them just die naturally of dehydration until busybody Karen called the Humane Society on her. They came out in a big truck marked Animal Cruelty and read her the riot act."

"I'm so sorry I missed that."

He looks up at me sharply, but I can't stop.

"Last night she caught a cat," I lie, though it certainly isn't inconceivable that she could, and would.

"She did not."

"Did too. It yowled like a cat."

"Come on. She doesn't trap cats!"

"It's a trap! Anything can walk into it. And she hates cats."

"Well, she's just not sentimental about animals."

"But to *shoot* them point-blank? Some little kid's cat?" My throat closes, imagining a poor, frantic child calling plaintively for his kitty, putting up hopeful signs with smudgy black-and-white photographs: Have you seen Mittens/Socks/Felicity? We miss her so much!

"What does she do with the bodies? Grind them up for fertilizer?"

"How the hell should I know?"

"She dumps them in the ravine, doesn't she? Probably goes out there regularly with a bucket of lime, like the Mafia."

"Look, why don't you just butt the hell out! Mind your own goddamn business!"

I watch the two of them in the backyard as they lug the heavy box toward the back fence. Liam says something to her that causes her to burst into silvery laughter, the sound coiling in through the window, raising the hairs on my neck. Trembling, I pour myself four inches from the first bottle of Jack I've bought since I've lived in Liam's house and down it in two swallows.

The mere proximity of Gail has begun to unnerve me completely. Her daytime self sets my teeth on edge; I *know* she's steadily and skilfully crowding me out, talking and laughing more than ever, jamming the air with words, draining it of my rightful share of oxygen, while big lug Liam lumps along beside her, dense as a block of wood, impervious to my suffering. Gradually, imperceptibly, she's sucking him up into her perfectly rounded, dipsy-doodle being, the two of them no more at the mercy of human contingency than the characters in a sitcom.

Furtively, from behind the living room drapes, I watch her outside at work and try to imagine being in the driver's seat behind those wolf eyes of hers. Maybe they see the garden in an utterly alien way, like a cat might, in gradient shades of smudge.

Or are her plants more like the pupils she used to have at her mercy, lined up in symmetrical rows, hands folded, heads bowed in terrified obedience? There's always something that needs immediate levelling or squaring or disciplining, a to-do list that grows like a tapeworm. The poor garden is always being judged and found wanting. She forgives it nothing.

I've never once seen her relax out there, pull up a chair, tip her face to the sun, doze to the drone of the bees. Only once did she have a couple of old dames from down the block over for a swiftly executed tea party on her perfect patch of lawn, a big-jawed moose of a woman in a Tilley hat and a little falcon-beaked creature in long plaid shorts and a plastic sun visor, my old, acid-vision-of-hell cellmates brought to vivid, terrifying life. Gail wore a blouse for the occasion, bustling in and out of the house with niggardly edibles on trays like an unpopular kid bossing her doll and her teddy bear. The three of them huddled over their tea, snorting and cackling at Karen, who sat reading in the sun next door.

But her nighttime self is the true horror, loping through the backyard and through my dreams, her ochre eyes filling with blood, tufts of night pelt sprouting from her ears under the low moon. I picture swooping night birds landing on branches all around her, stepping out of their bird-suits and swarming her legs in their hundreds, malignant wizards whose heads brush her knees. They tell her where the unlocked doors, the loose children are, that she might leap in to snatch them, her claws clumped with the rank mud of her earth diggings, and tear into them with yellow fangs, wiping her bloodied jaws with an old mulch bag. Her lascivious plants sprawl obscenely around her, every flower a leering peasant face, the whole garden rippling with underground laughter at my helplessness and stupidity, as I lurch and stump through the rooms of a house no longer mine, as clumsy as old Ahab on one whalebone leg.

Mum continues to call and call, dribbling sadness into my ear, notifying me over and over that Winky is under the weather and that her stomach hurts all the time.

"It's because you don't eat. Are you taking your meds?" From the other end, a dismissive flutter of sound. "Mum. If you're having trouble remembering when to take your pills, ask Mrs. Penniman to help you. Is that really too much to manage?"

Heartbeats. Yips. Whimpering.

"What will I do if Winky leaves me?" Her panic makes me want to slap her silly; instead of Winky's name, I hear Gerard's, and behind that, the stale ache of my own panic at the loss of Desi.

"Mum! Focus, please! For just one second. I need to know if you're taking your medicine."

"What do you care?"

"Damn it, are you or aren't you?"

"Gerard doesn't care. He never comes to see me any more." A gulp. "I'm afraid, Mag Mary."

"Of what?"

"What if Gerard tells God I don't deserve to be in heaven? What if Winky's waiting for me and I never get there?"

I'm sitting on the front porch, the phone stuck to my shoulder, when Gail passes me, spade in hand, fresh from another

Sunday morning televangelist date with Liam. She raises her eyebrows in interrogation as she circles her right ear with her right index finger, the timeless childhood gesture meaning "Talking to the head case?" I squinch around so that my back is to her.

"Ohhh! Little Miss Sourball!" she throws over her shoulder on a sharply rising note before dragging her lawn vacuum out to hoover the driveway, which is looking a tad dusty.

Mum's voice keeps scratching like a pin in my ear. "Is heaven going to be a nice place?"

"Beats the hell out of me."

"What?"

"I don't know. I don't know. I don't *know*! Why do you ask me these things?"

"You don't like me. I know you don't, so don't try to tell me different."

Silence.

"I'm not that crazy about you either, Mag Mary."

"Fine. I have to go now."

"You think I'm crazy."

"No I don't. I'm just busy."

"I'm not going to be around much longer."

"No, not if you don't take your medicine."

Next door, the Chungs are leaving for church, Karen sliding into the passenger seat of their car in a blue cotton skirt and dainty white blouse, her plain purse over her shoulder, Bible tucked under her arm. Her husband is trim too, funky even, with a spiky haircut and nicely fitting jeans. Sun's face is scrubbed pink, and he clutches a colouring book and a satchel full of crayons. Everything about the three of them is gracious and utterly without guile, but Karen especially: her walk, her gentle voice, the unbothered way she bends to pick up toys left on the lawn. Watching her makes me feel rude as bark.

I imagine them in the pews of one of those swaying-arm churches that always knocked the wind out of me. If I weren't holding my cards so close to my chest in this house, I could lean over the fence one afternoon and sing out, "Hey! You'll never believe this, but I got saved once too! Will you be my friend? You look so peaceful over there! How do you do it? Are you one of those people who believes without question that you are loved by a good God? One who follows your every movement like a proud dad with a new camera, who keeps scrapbooks on you in heaven, who *approves* of you? Are you a complete stranger to guilt, to doubt? Is your faith hard-won but sure?"

She doesn't seem beaten down or repressed; on the contrary, there's a light around her at once subversive and gorgeous, the aura of a person who has no interest in power. Aunt Baby had it, and Desi too, their faces unpinched by cunning and self-protection. I don't even have to see her close up to know it. When Gail stalks among her hydrangeas, silent as an Apache, her grizzled head just one more giant, nodding bloom as she keeps obsessive tabs on Karen's every move, I've seen Karen look up, smile in her general direction, say nothing, and continue sweetly about her business.

Maybe she sees a different Gail from the one I see. Maybe she sees a stumbling, terrified old fool, an object of infinite mercy and concern. Maybe she prays for her, sends waves of healing love over the garden fence, that rare, pure love that stymies evil simply by lying down.

Maybe she's the only person on the planet Gail can't stuff through the woodchipper of her will.

I long to talk to her, long to confess that I know perfectly well I'm supposed to contemplate the old bat in Christ, to see her as a flawed creature like myself, lonely and embittered, fighting tooth and nail to keep afloat the thousands of lies she has to tell herself in order to safeguard her imagined pre-eminence. I know that's why she never stops talking, never stops rearranging and repeating the things she knows, never for a moment stops compulsively patrolling the straight corridors of her mind with a rake, a hoe, and a vacuum. She's scared witless in there. I *know* she's faking every move she makes, every word she speaks.

If anyone can tell when someone is just going through the motions, I am surely that person.

"I've even tried it, Karen," I'd tell her. "I've tried borrowing the eyes of Christ, for seconds at a time! It's like putting on someone else's glasses; everything goes blurry and I'm afraid I'll puke."

Why don't I reach out to her, tell *her* who I really am? Why don't I take this opportunity to salvage a few thin shreds of integrity?

Because she'll say to me, "If you'll only look, Maggie, you'll see there's something to love in everybody."

"Uh-huh. That's what I was afraid of."

Besides, I probably have her all wrong. Maybe she's just dim, or one more raving fundy who's going to lecture me earnestly about the inerrancy of the Bible and the mark of the Beast.

Invite me to go see Benny Hinn with her. Sternly scold me for not even having tried to win Liam for Jesus. I'll be pitched out of the frying pan straight into the lake of fire.

Anyway, I'll never know. I'm never going to speak to her. If she's as good as she looks, she shames me utterly. And if she's just a nut, I'll be crushed beyond redemption.

A week later, just as we're finishing supper, Charlotte shimmies into our kitchen in a billowing orange African bird goddess caftan with vast sleeves streaked in blue. Her thin grey hair trails wispily down her back like tattered shreds of cloud burnt to a frizzle by the roaring sun of her dress. She's huge, having gone all Mama Cass flamboyant in her old age, like the last forgotten hippie just now crawling out of the jungle of Haight-Ashbury.

"I brought you this month's *Wellness*," she says, plopping the magazine down on the table. Her voice, the tipoff to the real Charlotte under all that bedazzlement, is as flat and splintery as an unvarnished two-by-four. "I was just upstairs dropping off some vitamin E and hand emollients for Mum."

"Glass of wine?" Liam asks her. "Oh, come on. A wee dram. We need an excuse to open another bottle." I'm already several drams ahead of him; I began tippling while Dr. Phil was still holding forth.

"Just a drop," she answers, grimacing; you'd think we were foisting castor oil on her. Liam busies himself with the bottle while I leaf through the voodoo bazaar of esoteric homeopathy and eco-conscious regalia in *Wellness*: liver detoxifiers, ionized water, Peruvian ginseng, pillows filled with buckwheat.

Gail drifts in on Charlotte's caftan tails, refusing wine and standing stiff as a hydrant against the sink, her arms folded, her lips tight. Liam and Charlotte in the same room throw her off balance. And yet, there's something about Liam's sister that intrigues me, the way she maintains her flat-line calm around Gail, as if her mother's jagged presence barely registers with her. It almost seems as if *she's* the mother and Gail the persnickety, high-strung child.

"What does synchrodestiny mean?" I ask Gail, looking up from the magazine. She waves her hand impatiently.

"It's just fancy talk for keeping busy." She turns around fast and pours herself a glass of water. Under cover of the faucet noise, I mutter tipsily, "Isn't it about time for you to goose-step over to the Chungs' and borrow a cup of acid?" The only sign she might have heard is a barely detectable clench of her shoulders inside her perky pink tee-shirt.

Charlotte, after a few slow sips of wine, suddenly bursts into life.

"Liam! I almost forgot!" She runs lumpily to the front door, where she left her huge hempy bag. "I was going through stuff in the basement last weekend and you'll never guess what I found!" She comes back, hands held behind her, and cries, "Ta-da!" as she whips out an old record album, dancing it on its edges against the wide, raked stage of her chest.

Liam's quizzical face blooms from a disbelieving smile into a shout of laughter. "Oh my God! Char, you didn't!"

"What is it?" I ask, craning my neck. Liam holds up the battered record sleeve: *Arthur Murray's Ballroom Classics.* "My old practice album! This is hilarious! Whoo hoo! The rumba, the waltz, the mambo, the foxtrot. Look! The foldout sheet with the step diagrams! The tango! The samba! Oh, I have to hear it now! Mum, your record player's working, isn't it?"

"Yes," Gail says, frowning, before she can remember to say no.

Liam is beside himself. "Tequila!" "I've Got My Love to Keep Me Warm!" "Deep Purple!" Oh no! "Sway!" The mambo, with the vocals! "Other dancers may pee on the floor," he croons with tuneless gusto, "but my eyes will see only poo! Me and Danny Purcell used to laugh till stuff came out our noses! Come on! Let's play it upstairs!"

He has the bottle of wine in his hand, and as he passes Charlotte and me, he sloshes more into both our glasses, over Charlotte's feeble protests. We get up and follow him, Gail bringing up the rear, her face screaming that all this is over her dead body. Three extra people in her place at one time are going to wreak holy havoc, shifting chairs out of alignment, denting sofa cushions. "No wine in the living room!" she snaps at our heels, but Liam is oblivious, and he is our leader.

He opens the old cabinet hi-fi in the corner and slaps the record on. Loud.

"I can't believe this! It's been fifty years! It's too funny!" He glugs more wine, turning to smear a kiss on my lips.

"Oh, for God's sake," Gail barks. "Get a room!"

Charlotte, standing next to her, is already flushed with drink. "Oh, come on, Mum," she says with a demented lightness that's quite becoming. "Without sex, where would we be? How else would new souls be able to join us here?" Gail's head swivels up to gape at her, her face a dagger unsheathed.

"What the hell are you talking about?"

Indeed! Two glasses of wine and glum old Charlotte is melting into a metaphysical puddle before our eyes.

"You need a haircut," Gail tells her sharply. Charlotte continues to smile ditzily over the lip of her glass, another big girl just like me, but one who's kept her feet firmly on the ground, and it occurs to me with a sudden stab that *she* wouldn't have let Desi get away from her.

The Arthur Murray arrangements are superbly cheesy. Liam grabs his sister and Gail's face loosens visibly; I know she loves seeing Liam dance as long as it isn't with me, though it's easy to detect her thinly veiled contempt for the shuddering pitch and roll of Charlotte's flesh that makes me look svelte by comparison.

"You're next!" Liam shouts to Gail. "Brace yourself for the cha-cha!"

Gail retreats to the doorway, her body language spelling "I'd rather eat a bowl of turds" in bold caps. She grasps the doorframe, white-knuckled, as Charlotte flails and stumbles, knocking against tables, jiggling lamps.

As for me, I haven't been up here since March, and I know what I want to see.

I slip out the far door into the hall, hightailing it for Gail's bedroom. Yes! There he is on the dresser, grinning, tall in the saddle, his be-ruffled arms around that lucky little gal. My proud dancing fool, all eleven years of him. A wave of maternal love nearly fells me at the knees, as I think, teary-eyed, that there's nothing more beautiful than the light of shy joy and hope in young eyes, at that age especially, when they're poised on the very edge of taking their first flying leap into life.

I lean in to kiss the glass over his bright, sweet face. Courage, dear heart, I whisper with boozy mawkishness. You're going to do just fine! And we're going to be all right. I know we are!

"Are you looking for something?"

Gail has crept up behind me like a cat. I emit a strangled scream.

"Oh! You scared me! I was just looking at your pic—"

"You might have asked first. I don't believe this is your home."

Oh really, I think. You certainly have the run of our place, you wizened old buzzard. But aloud, I only say, "I'm sorry," as I dizzily try to pass her in the doorway, smashing clumsily into her instead, causing her to teeter on her little sneakered feet.

"Get a hold of yourself!" she snaps, pushing me roughly away before reflexively brushing my contamination off her sleeves.

Back in the living room, Liam is dancing alone, winded and red in the face now, swaying his hips and shaking invisible maracas. "I love this!" he shouts over the music. "It's painful! The memories! Thanks, Char! This is so great!"

Charlotte smiles crookedly. Abruptly the music stops, as Gail lifts the arm from the record and slides it briskly back into the sleeve.

"Okay, that's enough. I need to vacuum in here. Out!" Already she's bent over, resmoothing the pile in the rug.

We take our bottle out onto the front steps. The evening is warm and golden. Liam and I sit on the top step and Charlotte stands, leaning over the porch railing, allowing herself a few more itty-bitty sips, a zany smile on her face.

I'm just tipsy enough to feel fabulous. Damn it, I've been running berserk alongside the train of my life for so long, and now finally, *finally*, I've gotten a handhold, a foothold, have flopped myself aboard. There's time to catch my breath, thrill to the stars rushing by, because the train's doing all the work now, and it's almost too much luxury to bear. How can all this amount to nothing? How can there be nothing at the end of it? How can there be *extinction*? The very idea leads to madness, *is* madness! The scudding nighttime clouds, the long-winded leaves, the raccoons mating in the back garden at night once we're done, snapping and yowling and tearing off each other's masks: is it all for *nothing*? Impossible! And Liam knows it too. He knows better than to question this thing. Just because our life feels like grand opera, with the smiting of breasts and shrieks rising to the rafters, doesn't mean what's happening isn't as true as truth can be. Hell, that just makes it *more* true!

Moments later, my gaily hammered heart crashes through the guardrail and over the cliff as Mitch, who only lives a few streets away, wheels uninvited into our driveway on his sturdy mountain bike, his ropey, hairless legs in long khaki shorts, his horrible, bony feet in huge rubberized sandals with bulldozer treads. In no time at all, the conversation is going to turn to programming talk: error trapping, randomizing, if-then statements. And from there to the inscrutability of the mindless universe.

"Oh, excellent," I mutter to Liam. "It's the walking seed-pod."

"What's wrong with Mitch?" Liam asks, honestly perplexed, as Mitch disembarks from his bike and leans it against the side of Charlotte's car.

"Mitch is a twit."

"I think he's brilliant. We talk a lot over lunch whenever we get the chance. I've probably absorbed a lot of his ideas by osmosis," Liam says in a quick, low tone, his staunch loyalty irritating the piss out of me.

"I still hate him."

"You hate everybody." I can tell I've hurt him. But there's no undoing it now, for Mitch is upon us.

"Hello, folks," he says glumly, nodding to Charlotte, whom he can't place.

"Mitch! Come join us, buddy!" Liam cries with far more enthusiasm than the situation warrants. Mitch nods mutely and takes up a seat on the bottom step, stretching out his legs to their full, scabrous length.

"May I offer you a glass of wine, my friend?" Liam shouts, giving Mitch a spirited thump on the back. "Maggers, go get us another glass."

"No thanks. I'm good," Mitch mumbles.

"This is Charlotte, Liam's sister," I tell him, looking up at her and back to him again. "You guys met?"

Mitch looks stumped. I take note of his hands fiddling with one of the twenty-seven cargo pockets on his shorts and think with a lurching stomach of what they must get up to in private, fiddling with the loathsome, atrophying parts dangling inside.

"Charlotte's wearing vegan eyeliner," I inform him smartly. "You can't beat that with a stick." I turn around to Charlotte and explain, "Mitch is a vegetarian."

"Good on you!" burbles Charlotte, trying to focus her eyes. Mitch wipes his hands on his Jazz FM tee-shirt.

"Fingers are sticky," he apologizes morosely. "Just had an ice cream cone."

No one knows how to parlay this remark into further banter.

Gradually, out of the silence, Liam and Mitch ease into work talk. I crane my neck back at Charlotte, who's humming softly as she gazes wistfully into the garden.

"Tales from the crypt," I say, nodding toward the two gabbing men. She smiles, pretending she's heard me. Liam and Mitch are off at a trot with their pivot tables and autofilters, their breakpoints and dropdowns. If I hadn't already gone over the cliff, now would be the time to set myself on fire.

I content myself with watching the cars and bikes go by, and the evening strollers who never fail to stop and gawp at Gail's garden in the rosy light of the setting sun. Beside me, Liam has begun complaining about how inconsequential the young people at work make him feel.

"We should nuke everybody under thirty. Or lash 'em to a post and have at 'em old-school style with a big, old, honking cat-o'-nine-irons," he jokes, trying to do Gabby Hayes and succeeding more than I'd like to admit.

"Liam! My darling! Cat-o'-nine-*irons*?"

It takes a moment for the penny to drop. His eyes grow wide, then crinkle into laughter. Mitch remains totem-faced.

"Yikes! Another brain misfire. Must be all the drugs I did in the sixties," Liam says, grinning mock-ruefully.

"Believe me, I know what drug damage looks like, and you're nowhere close," I say before, breeeeeeep, goes the buzzer in my head.

Error! Error!

"Mitch, you remember the guy at our wedding in the priest collar?" Liam says right on cue.

"Wasn't he your brother?" Mitch asks me with zero interest.

353

"*Twin* brother, poor kid," says Liam, offering me a consoling cheek kiss. "He runs some kind of fly-by-night halfway house for addicts and street people, but it's really a cult. Guy's a wing-nut, and dangerous as hell. He's got these poor shmucks with no self-image and way too scared to think for themselves all following his orders and swallowing this lunatic-fringe religious swill he dishes out."

Mitch glances at me to see if this will be contested. The coast clear, he begins nodding and ruminating before finally adjusting his motor setting to "drone."

"Interesting you mention self-image." He turns briefly, politely, to include Charlotte in his address. "I'm into neuro-science," he tells her, and she smiles again dreamily. He turns back to us.

"I've just been reading up on the latest findings into the nature of consciousness. I think I may have mentioned it already."

"Only endlessly, in passing," I grumble. "You treated us to a lengthy address on DNA at our wedding dinner." Liam pinches me.

"The thinking now," Mitch whirrs on, "is that there's no such animal as the ego, or the self." He winches around again to include Charlotte, but her eyes are closed. "What's actually observable are neurological processes that create the illusion of an ego, what we call a personality. It's all brain metabolism, computers in our heads. They create the illusion of everything we call life, the illusion we all have of being individual selves."

"The brain is matter that thinks," Liam cuts in smartly. "That's one of the few things I remember from Marx."

"When did you ever read Marx, you big phony?" I razz him.

354

"And that isn't even Marx. It's Engels. 'It's impossible to separate thought from matter that thinks.'" Up to this moment, I have no idea I've retained this revolutionary crumb.

"Well, it's still good. The brain is matter, so the mind isn't some airy-fairy thing. I believe in what I can see and touch and smell and..." He trails off, noticing Mitch's impatience to break in.

"Other way around," Mitch corrects with unusual snappiness. "It's what you *think* you see. Take out the two 'you's' from what I just said and you're closer to the truth. It's what think see. The brain thinks, the brain sees. What you conceive of as 'me' doesn't think; instead, your brain metabolism creates, for lack of a better word, the thing, the non-existent essence, the *illusion* you call 'me.'"

"Amazing," breathes Liam reverently.

"Really. And, ironically, since you brought up religious indoctrination, there's a faint echo of Christian morality in all this, as we come to realize through scientific investigation that we're not the masters of the universe we always thought we were. This article I was reading quoted Pascal, who was actually pretty close to the money. I wish I had it with me, I could give you the quote—"

"He said you should never leave your room if you want to stay out of trouble," I blurt, my stomach plummeting at the mere mention of the name.

"Anyhow," Mitch continues, oblivious, "he spoke of how our minds contain the entire universe, which he interpreted as proof of man being created in the image of God and so on, whereas science today will agree that everything really *is* inside the brain,

355

the entire universe, from beginning to end and everything in between. It's also similar to certain Eastern religious concepts, like, we are one with the universe, there's nothing outside of us, we're all the universe, and the universe is us. Not too far off the mark. The point is, there's no person inside your body. There's no me, no you. We are, in essence, just a sequentially connected series of brain events."

"Thank you, Mr. Wizard." I drawl down at him. "Now repeat that speech using no pronouns." I have no idea whether this sounds addled or not.

Liam and Mitch look at me blankly.

"I see, said the blind man as he picked up his hammer and saw," I jabber witlessly. "Liam, pass me that bottle. Oops, almost empty. Should I go get some more?" But Mitch's brain computer has rebooted, and on he rolls.

"Our brains organize sensory input into something that feels to us like a—"

"Feels to *us*? What us?"

"Maggie, shush," scolds Liam.

"—into what feels to us like a narrative. But it's all random, streamed and organized by evolutionarily contingent programming. We're all just complex clumps of evolutionarily programmed genetic material."

"Yee-haw!" I try to whistle, but my inebriated lips refuse to muscle up.

"We ought to get your brother over here, Maggie," Liam enthuses. "Organize a debate. This is a guy who calls people 'God's sperm cells,'" he informs Mitch in triumphant high dudgeon.

"Well, in a sense, he's right. He's using archaico-biological language, but as a descriptive phrase, it captures the randomness and arbitrariness of life pretty well."

Liam nods again. "Except he means it literally."

"Well, life is, literally, an accident. Same way sperm cells serve to perpetuate the race, thrown into operation by random, self-replicating gene pools —"

"Gene pools? Thrown into operation?" I shriek at him, clanging the wine bottle against the railing for emphasis till they can hear it in Sault Ste. Marie. "Have you never been in love then, young Mitchell?" Behind me, a titter from Charlotte.

"What's that got to do with anything?" Mitch asks, turning to face me squarely so that I'm looking straight into his liver-hued eyes. I'm instantly intimidated.

"So life just blindly cracks the cat-o'-nine-irons on its own behalf? Is that all love is, in the end?" I inquire sulkily of the pavement.

"In essence, though you want to avoid anthropomorphic expressions if you don't want to muddy the waters."

"Don't tell me what I want. I want more wine. My brain narrative insists."

"Maggers, you are sloshed," says Liam fondly. Mitch stares straight ahead, stoic as a dead beetle on its back.

"So what part of your brain cell random evolutionary narration contingency made you become a vegetarian?" I demand to know with the belligerence traditionally expected of the sloshed.

"It's purely a health matter."

"Oh ho! That's cold! So it's not the usual song and dance about not wanting to kill animals?"

"No."

"But good health is better than bad health in the random contingency narrative?"

"Maggie, I'm going to have to muzzle you," says Liam, trying to clap a hand over my mouth. I push his hand away and he wrestles me onto my back, laughing, pressing his hand hard over my mouth, instantly replacing it with the other one when I tear it off.

"I can't take this woman anywhere," he tells Mitch. "Hey! No kicking! Do I have to sit on you?"

I struggle up onto my elbows, shouting, "So, what *does* happen when we fall in love, since 'we' and 'love' and 'fall in' are all in our heads, and our heads are also in our heads, huh? Huh?"

"Love is transcendence of the mechanics of the sexual impulse." This flows sweetly, incredibly, from the lipsticked mouth of Charlotte.

"Charlotte! Fess up; you've met someone, haven't you?"

Charlotte frowns, confused. Liam and Mitch study their feet. I'm just sober enough to know I'm being obnoxious.

"I think we're about ready to call it a night," says Liam, tugging at my arm.

"I'm not finished! I want to know, when people go around saying, I only believe in what I can see, like this one here"—I elbow Liam in the ribs—"are they completely delusional, yes or no?"

"Ow! That hurt, Maggie!"

"No, your brain just thinks it did."

Mitch, ever the clarifier, draws breath. "Usually when people say that they only believe what they can see, they're generally asserting a denial of any belief in supernatural agencies, in gods and spirits and angels and so forth."

Charlotte tiptoes down the steps with difficulty, her huge feet finding only the spaces between our legs to make landing. On the bottom step, she treads squarely on Mitch's hand, which he yanks up and shakes vigorously without making a sound.

"Oh! Sorry! Sorry, Mike!" She's whispering, for some reason. "I'll be off," she breathes at Liam and sashays down the walk toward her car.

"Oh! Okay. Bye, Char! Thanks a million for the album!"

"Don't mention it!"

"Girlfriend's got it goin' on!" I yell after her. She slides in behind the wheel with much fussing and adjusting of her saffron tent, checking her lipstick in the mirror before backing out. Mitch's bike, which has been leaning against the passenger side door, crashes to the ground, one wheel spinning deliriously. Mitch leaps to its rescue, picking it up lovingly and laying it back down on its side like a sleeping child.

I politely wait till he's seated before jabbing him *hard* in his Jazz FM ribs.

"If nothing is true, then why am I listening to you?" Apart from a faint wince, he ignores me.

"Hey! I'm talkin' to you!"

"I should probably be heading out too," Mitch tells Liam calmly. But I'm scrambling to my feet, waving the wine bottle, blocking his way.

"Nothing's true, nothing's right, there's no such thing as love. There's no gold in Fort Knox! And if there's no gold in Fort Knox, then all our little love dollars and quarters and dimes aren't worth dick, right? Know what? Siddown, I'm talkin' to you! You *do* sound like my brother! It wouldn't be a debate. It'd be a meeting of the corrupted, evil minds, no, excuse me, a meeting of the neurologically evolved apparati—"

"Maggie, stop being a pain in the ass!"

I sit down hard, snuffling back furious tears, inwardly cursing the bloody Tanteek, that towering anti-Presence, that annihilating Sneer that walks hard on the heels of every single tiny ba-zing of Hope I've ever had. It has me in a headlock, deadlocked and teetering on the edge of the loss of everything my heart clings to.

Just as Gerard said it would.

Next door, Karen is bouncing a big red ball across her driveway for Sun to catch. He misses every time, scrambling after the ball to heave it upward with both hands from between his short legs like a tiny oil derrick. It rolls across the weedy grass and Karen darts after it, her laugh a sweet tinkle in a high Asian register. She returns the ball in the opposite way, raising both hands so far over her head she almost topples backward. The ball sails over Sun and the puppy nipping excitedly at his heels and lands in the middle of the street. He runs after it, screeching to a halt at the curb, looking long and hard from right to left to right again before darting after the ball, his neural circuit board having fired: Warning! Warning! in order to ensure the preservation of his illusory little clutch of genetic material masquerading as a self.

In my head, "Deep Purple" is still playing, and Liam, jiggy on his feet, is laughing up a storm. But it's all wrecked now.

Karen and Sun are wrecked, the nodding, happy daisies in the garden are wrecked, the friendly, deep purple twilight sky is wrecked. There's nothing left but to chin myself on the grim bar of meaninglessness, up and down, up and down, till the day my brain cells mercifully throw in the towel and put this particular unproductive gene machine out of its misery.

What a shame Gerard can't be here to gloat over the life I've tried to save coming apart in my greedy hands.

Sun's red ball sails over the low hedge into Gail's hydrangeas. Liam springs to his feet, diving into the garden to rescue it. He tosses it back with a smile.

"Thank you!" Karen trills from her yard. Liam waves and sits back down again.

Mitch is casting covert looks in their direction. He says something I can't hear to Liam, who shakes his head.

"Nope. Married." Mitch mumbles something else.

"Yeah, I know you like the Asian gals," teases Liam. "She's a nice lady." My breath catches at the sound of this unexpectedly friendly opinion, but it's only a momentary veer off the Gail-sanctioned track. "Unfortunately, she's a bit of a Bible thumper. Last year, she invited us to her church, but when I told her no thanks, I'll give her credit, that was the end of it. She hasn't bothered us since."

"Another seed kerplops onto stony ground," I observe bitterly. Liam laughs, then his eyes grow wide.

"Are you crying? What's the matter?"

"Nothing."

"Yes, something is. Come on, tell me."

"Leave me alone! Nothing!"

"Okay, okay." He turns back to Mitch. "How are you coming, by the way, with that file on the—"

"I just think she's brave, that's all!"

"What? Who's brave?"

"Karen."

"What, about asking us to go to her church? She was damn lucky I never told Gail about it. She would have chewed her in half. All that Bible crap drives her wild."

"Why am I not surprised?"

"What, you're sticking up for the Bible now?"

"So?"

"Excuse me, but, the *Bible*? You're not telling me you believe the Bi…"

It's too late to back out now. My face is redder than Sun's ball.

"Not like Gerard, if that's what you're thinking. But, um, yes, I, uh, guess I, sort of believe, um, some of it."

"Believe what? In God?"

"Yes." This escapes me in a voice so timorous it might have come from one of the ants on the pavement.

And yet, it's like jumping off the high board for the first time! I'm flying! I haven't crashed! I'm still alive!

I'm *witnessing*!

Liam stares at me, agape with something very close to horror.

"And in the Virgin Mary and Yowzah with the son who does magic tricks with wine and fish and bounces out of his grave and floats to heaven? For Christ's sake, Maggie!" For a split second I think he's going to hit me. Instead, he exchanges looks with Mitch, who keeps his wise counsel.

"Well. This is embarrassing," Liam says at last, with a mirthless laugh. "I married myself a *Christian*."

"No you didn't, not really. I'm no good at it." Oh, this is great. Powerful stuff. I *hate* myself!

"So where's your evidence that all that garbage is true? Don't you know all those gospel stories were written by people who lived centuries later, pretending to be eyewitnesses? Jesus probably never even existed, let alone the rest of the fairy tale."

It's my turn to keep my counsel.

"The Church is a corporation, for God's sake. It exists to control people through fear and bleed them dry. It's—"

"That's not the point!" I blurt.

"I see. So the point is…?"

"The point is turning over control of your life and having your sins forgiven." Yes, I say this laughable thing out loud. "The point is facing your guilt and…" I trail off, trying to recall the witnessing power points drummed ceaselessly into my head over the past five years. How to lead the lost to Christ, save them from the power of Satan and the clutches of hell, steps one through twelve. But it's all I can do to stumble over the finish line with my lame closer.

"I have hope now. I didn't before." And fall splat.

"For what? *Heaven*?"

"Is that so terrible?"

The screen door bangs open behind us and Gail stomps onto the porch. We all turn, some of our smiles more brittle than others.

"Don't mind me!" she titters. "I'm not even here!" She gives Mitch an awkward shoulder nudge as she squeezes by us on the steps and quick-marches around the side of the house, where I *know* she's going to crouch and listen.

"What is it I'm supposed to feel so guilty about? What did *I* do?" Liam asks the moment she's gone. He's really angry now. "Christians and their guilt! It's fucking ludicrous."

"But we all sin. We all have things, I mean, we all fall short of the mark." Ah! That's the phrase! "Look at the state the world is in. All of us have had a hand in it, somehow. We—"

"Speak for yourself!"

"I am. I'm just saying that if we admit our sinfulness and" —I'm on a roll now!— "and accept that Christ came to save us from what we deserve, and if we say yes to mercy, then..." I stop. Say yes to mercy? What does that even mean? Who's going to fall for this? Even I don't believe me. Sweat is running down my back; my palms leave damp prints on my jeans. "It's the most important decision we ever have to make, to say yes to mercy or, or to snub it. It's not so hard. And it changes the way everything looks, afterwards." I'm going faster and faster. "You feel safe and cared for and there's a purpose to everything. You feel God is, well, closer. And he, I mean, his presence is..." I stop myself just before the word "nigh" escapes my lips. Okay, I think. Duty's done. Shut the fuck up.

"So what does this mean? You hear voices? God talks to you audibly?" Liam's face is all bent and twisted in outraged incredulity. Mitch, for his part, maintains no expression whatsoever. He looks as if he's observing an experiment in a lab.

I have no answer, so I give none.

"Gee! Guess I'm heading for hell then," Liam smirks. "You too, buddy."

"Oh, Liam!" Fresh tears report for work. "Don't you want us to be together forever?"

He's livid, a hundred times worse than the day he met Gerard.

"I can't believe what you're saying! Why is all this crap coming out now?"

"I don't know." I aim a shaky smile in Mitch's direction. "Our first fight," I tell him dolefully.

"I can't believe this, and I don't think you believe it either. Why are you crying? What are you so upset about?"

"I need things to *mean* something, Liam. Without this, as crazy as it is, without it, everything just, just, crumbles. Even you and me. Please. Don't you understand what I mean?"

"I don't have a clue what you mean. Everything's fine with us."

"Okay, people," interjects Mitch, unfolding at last and rising to his feet. "I'll be pushing off."

"Thanks for dropping by, neighbour!" I shoot at his retreating back. "You've made this a special day just by being you!"

"Cut it out, Maggie! Go inside if you can't control yourself."

"Don't push me! Get your hands off me!"

Liam jumps to his feet, trotting after Mitch as he wheels his bike to the street. I can tell he's apologizing for me.

"Don't apologize! I'm not sorry!" Neither of them looks back. A cackle reaches my ears from the side of the house, but I refuse to look.

Liam comes back up the walk, brushing past me. I grab his ankle like a desperate inmate of Bedlam; he tries to shake me off, but I have him in a vise grip, clawing inside his pant leg, inside his sock, digging my nails into his flesh.

"What the fuck is the matter with you?" His face is purple.

"Liam, please let me explain. Please!"

"Let go of me!"

"Look, I know—"

"Let *go* of me!"

"I will, but please, please, just listen for a minute! I *know* the idea of God seems made up. I *know* it's unbelievable, I know the whole story is slashed full of holes. I understand why you hate it because I hate so much of it too. I mean, the part about the saved and the damned, the blessed 'us' and the outcast 'them,' that part especially, I can't *stand* any of that, Liam. But I can't let it go! It's the only thing keeping me from total, unbearable despair! It's all I've got, Liam! Please understand! Please!"

Helpful phrases float to the surface, begging to be fleshed out with profound apologetics: Our Helpless Estate. A Wretch Like Me. Power, Power, Wonder-Working Power. But all they do is bring back the nicotine-choked Bible studies and Sundays with the fundies as I tried to squash myself into belief like cramming my big splayed feet into a child's pair of shoes.

And yet I know, even with everything I have to lose, that I'm trying to put the most deeply buried essence of myself into words. It can't be true that I have no integrity, because I can feel it fighting like a tiger to get out. Except I'm no better at it now than I was four decades ago in the rowboat. How does one turn the heart's unspeakable reasons into reasonable speech, when cold, unfeeling Reason is looking down at you with the hard eyes of a profoundly offended, betrayed, and possibly soon-to-be ex-husband?

"I'm sorry I yelled at Mitch," I offer humbly, insincerely. "I'm a terrible person, I know. I'll apologize next time he's over."

Liam's face is set in stone.

"Liam," I say to the space between my knees as tears plop onto the cement, "I never thought in a million years I would ever see you again. I didn't know where you were or what had become of you. I didn't even know if you were still alive. Or whether you were married or, or happy. I thought so many times over the years of trying to find you, but I was so sure you hated me. But, oh, I missed you so much, *so* much, Liam. You were the only friend I ever, I mean, all I wanted was to see you again, but after so many years I knew it was impossible. And then, and then you called me."

I wait in vain for his consoling arm around my shoulder.

"I'm just trying to make a point about things that seem impossible, but—"

"My calling you is supposed to prove that God exists?"

"No. Sort of. Please, Liam. I can't prove anything to you. There *is* no proof. If there were, no one would need faith. I just meant, I just meant that everything that's happened to us, our finding each other again, it was like a, like a resurrection. It made the idea of the Resurrection real to me for the first time."

"Are you telling me you *believe* the Resurrection happened?"

"I don't know."

"Maggie, the dead don't come back to life! I can't believe I have to tell you this!"

I don't dare look at him. Now it's Mum's face I can feel on me: wretched, defensive, her jaw clamped tight, hanging on to herself for dear life as Gerard drags her through his thornbushes of words.

"Maggie, I know where this is coming from. You have got

to shake off this power your brother has over you." He's taking charge now, the level-headed man to my weepy, gullible woman. "Are you going to drink the Kool-Aid when he tells you to? This is not healthy, Maggie! This is really, really dangerous. I know he's the one behind all this. You think I don't know about the phone messages he leaves, all that bullshit about me, what the hell was that one I heard, about me being a child of the devil and dragging you to hell with me? Yeah, I know, you thought I didn't know anything about it. You thought you were keeping it a secret. I played the damned message for Gail, and she was appalled…yeah, well, I'm sorry you don't like it, but she deserves to know what's going on, and so do I. And you wonder why she has no respect for you. From now on, I want you to cut him off completely. I'm not putting up with—"

"It's none of her damned business!"

"I don't care whose damned business it is. I don't know why the fuck you don't stand up to that creep. I should have known by the look on your face when we saw him at your mother's. You were cringing like a whipped dog. I don't know what the fuck else he says to you, but—"

"I'll tell you what he says to me! He says, 'He who has ears to hear, let him hear,' and I can't help it, Liam, I can hear! And it scares me!"

"For Christ's sake, Maggie! Let this garbage go! For your own sake, if for no other reason."

"But what if you're turning your back on the only chance you might get to hear the truth?"

"Maggie, *stop it*! This is irrational and it's sick! You spent *way* too much time up there with that lunatic fringe. Pull yourself together!"

I offer him a painfully stretched smile. "You're right," I murmur, trying to sound chastened. "It's all Gerard's fault. Will you beat him up for me?" He doesn't laugh.

"Don't be mad, Liam."

"I'm not mad."

"Don't you like me any more?"

"Don't be ridiculous."

"Can we just forget all this? Can we pretend it never happened?"

"Of course," he mutters, clearly not meaning it.

Gail heaves suddenly into view around the side of the house, just visible in the fallen dark as she fiddles needlessly with the garden hose. Liam sees her too.

"What'cha up to, Gail?" he calls with shaky lightheartedness. "You doin' okay?"

"I'm peachy!" she chirrups back. "Just finishing up a few chores."

"About ready to come in? It's too dark to work out here now."

"Roit-o! I'll be in as soon as I give my annuals one last sprinkly-pie." She hauls the hose behind her down the driveway, vanishing into the black forest of flora, the warden on graveyard shift. Darkness has fallen, the flowers all tucked in and asleep, shivering and sighing in their dreams, trusting Gail to see them through this night and all the nights until the frost ends their brief, shining careers.

"Liam. You're still mad. I can tell."

"I'll be all right. I just need some time."

Time? What does he need time for, I think, panicking. "What do you need time for?"

"This has come as a shock. Can you not understand that?" he answers coldly.

"You mean, like, I say God, you say Void, let's call the whole thing off?"

But he's banged into the house already.

Next morning, I wake with throbbing head and uneasy gut to the metallic tink-tink chirp of cardinals in the backyard. It sounds like they're doing light carpentry out there, making persistent, birdy taps on squeaky tin nails. When I look, there're three of them bouncing on the ground, flashy and overdressed, hopping among the drab sparrows and wrens like clueless angels going undercover.

Gail pokes her merry morning head in as Liam and I are standing nervously in the kitchen, avoiding each other's eyes as we resurrect ourselves with coffee.

"Don't forget your brekky!" she shrieks, her face a gargoyle of mirth. "Most important meal of the day!"

"We won't!" we chorus obediently, our smiles maniacal in turn. The door slams importantly behind her.

After supper she's back, pitched forward in the big chair, taking in an autopsy on TV. This is no actor holding his breath, but a real live corpse, sprawled naked on a metal table like a six-foot ginger root. Knives swish, saws chug and whine. Gail is in full wolfish thrall, watching as if she herself were immortal, a being to whom none of this is of any concern beyond the keen curiosity about just what it is under the skin that makes these wacky humans tick.

Liam covers his eyes with his hands. "Tell me when it's over!" he begs me, his voice breaking as the circular saw screes through the skull.

"You can take your hands away, you big pussy. The commercial's on."

And it's one Liam likes, involving a puppy and flapping laundry. I chuckle ostentatiously, checking his reaction through peripheral vision. He's smiling, but weakly, unconvincingly. I poke him in the side, then try tickling under his arm; after an initial resistance, I feel him soften. Encouraged, I lunge at him and we begin tussling on the sofa like kids. Gail springs to her feet as if she's been shot with a million volts and marches into the kitchen. Liam leaps up to follow her, inquiring solicitously, "Anything I can get you?" From behind, in his jeans with the sagging butt and his shiny, old man's head, he isn't my Liam at all. He's just the elderly stranger whose organ donor card I signed last week.

"Hello?"

"Mag Mary, where did I leave my teef?"

"Look on the coffee table." Out the window, summer is browning at the edges like eggs in a frying pan. Many minutes crawl by.

"Check the floor, Mum." The silence continues, allowing me time to muse that one of the benefits of being obsessed with the fear of loss and death is that, contrary to the popular adage, it always turns out to be *earlier* than you think.

"Mother, where aaare you? Speak! Maybe Winky made off with your teef. Why don't you check the...hello? Hello-*oooo?*"

Now I'm treated to five uninterrupted minutes of the *Lawrence Welk Show*. "When the Red, Red Robin" segues into "I'm Forever Blowing Bubbles," which then hitches up its skirts to kick the bejezus out of "Don't Sit Under the Apple Tree." This is my serenade as I nurse the memory of my pathetic attempt the night before to tell Liam at last how nudged-out, extraneous, and tongue-tied I feel around him and Gail, especially knowing as I now do that Gail thinks I'm a pea-brained Neanderthal, and that he hasn't exactly been standing up staunchly in my defence.

He'd cut me off, brusquely, irritably.

"Just *talk*, babe. Jump right in! No one's trying to exclude you. *You're* the one who sits there like a cipher all night long."

"Mag Mary, why don't you talk?"

"I've been waiting for some sign of life from you, Mother." Eons pass as she mulls this over. Meanwhile I try to imagine myself dipping my oar into heated discussions about by-law reform, just how much bran a person needs to stay regular, and the howlingly stupid drugstore cashier Gail reduced to tears that afternoon, when the only things I care about any more are the hot-button Tanteek issues of death and eternity and God. I imagine dropping one of *those* golden nuggets into the mix, Gail's head whipping in my direction, her face creased into cruel, grey furrows so deep they look fur-lined, as she orders me in righteous indignation to *explain myself*!

"Mag Mary? Who'sh going to...?" Mum drops the phone. It's hopeless, and so are we, Liam and I, growing more elderly by the second, and not nearly as much pillow chewing and sheet thrashing going on as there was a few months ago. I'm losing him, frantically treading water as I watch the rollicking *Bachelor* sail away, a chuckling TV on behind every single porthole.

"Mum, are you still there?" I hear scuffling. Barking. Liam isn't going to lose anything if he loses me. He's complete. But I'll remain adrift forever in the empty ocean of time, alone, unneeded, and forgotten.

"What did I want to ashk you?" Mum's voice is so faint, I know she's talking into the wrong end of the receiver.

"What the hell do you *want* from me, woman?"

Silence. Click. Pause. *Briiinng.*

"Yes! What?"

"Mag Mary, don't you bite my head off!"

"You just hung up on me!"

"Mag Mary? Will Winky have enough blanketsh when I'm gone?"

"Mother, I *really* hope you have something else to worry about in the meantime."

"I'm not going to be around mush longer." Click. Silence. *Briiinng.*

"Hellooooo, Mother." Bleak tract of barren aural tundra.

"Mag Mary? My shtomach hurtsh."

"Why don't you lie down then? Hang up the phone and lie…" Click. "…down."

The summer peaks and topples sideways. August bleeds through September into October. Gail plants bulbs by the crate and sucks up the first leaves the instant they fall with her autumn vacuum, a roaring cylinder attached to a Santa Claus sack that she wears slung over her T-bone shoulder. The racket it makes can be heard in the third circle of hell.

On a Saturday morning, the phone rings, chilling my blood as always. I race to read the call display; it's Gerard, all right. I stand frozen, waiting for him to finish leaving his soul-mangling *message du jour* so I can delete it. But there's no message; instead he calls a second time, and thoroughly panicked now as Liam comes into the room, I pick up.

My brother is blunt as a brick. "Mum has intestinal cancer. She's been in the hospital since Thursday."

"The day before yesterday? And you're only telling me now?"

"Yes. I'm telling you now."

"What happened?"

"She called me on Thursday, completely incoherent. I drove down and had to get the landlord to let me in. She was on the bathroom floor, shit all over her, on her hands, on her robe. She'd tracked it all over the house." He stops, mercifully.

"Was she conscious?" I can see her plain as day, lying splotched on the floor like windfall fruit, rotten through and leaking.

"In and out." I hear the click of his lighter, the deep inhale. "You should probably get over there and clean up. There's a waiting list for the apartment."

"Are you saying she's not coming out of the hospital?"

No answer.

"But what, what do we do? Does she have long?"

"Her struggle is hers alone."

"What the hell does *that* mean? Where is she?"

"Grace."

"Jesus, Gerard! Is there a room number? Do I have to drag *everything* out of you?"

"She's on a gurney in the hall, in Emergency. They're moving her today. Call them and find out." He's about to hang up, then remembers. "I shut the dog in the bedroom. There wasn't anybody home at the neighbour's. So..." He leaves that hanging too.

Well. It isn't as if she didn't warn me.

It's a magnificent deep blue autumn day. Gail is outside with no coat on, putting the last of her garden to bed, shrouding her bushes and trees in burlap, shlerping up stray twigs. I badly want to ask that beaming sky that's so kind to the she-wolf out there if, by any chance, it also knows the humble, tetchy, utterly loopy Moira Moriarty. When she finally leaps out of her flesh and makes a run for it, will it catch her at the horizon like a low fastball, just before she goes over the edge?

And the Father? Where in that empty blue sky is he? Because when death becomes no longer theoretical, when it Tanteek-walks right up in your face, the notion of there being a Father becomes next to impossible to believe. It's like going to a Dylan concert and being convinced Bob magically knows that you, his truest fan, are in the audience, row L, seat 34. Like believing he's looking straight at you from the stage, smiling archly to let you know he knows that you know that he knows.

In other words, it's insane.

Liam offers to drive me to the hospital. Backing the car out of the garage, he leans out the window to give Gail a heads-up. I won't look at her, refusing to bear witness to her pitiful attempt to paste on a sombre face. As we pull away, she raises her right arm in what looks like a Nazi salute.

Mum isn't hard to find. She's still in the hall outside the crowded emergency cubicles, seemingly mislaid amid the din of curtains rattling open and shut, people coughing, nurses bustling, monitors beeping, and gurneys rumbling by.

Her ER doctor, who doesn't know her from Eve, is twelve years old. Apparently, he says, she'd been too embarrassed by her bowel problems to tell anyone. There's a huge, suppurating mass on the right side of her abdomen. Long past the point of operability, it has already spread to her liver and colon. Malignant cells are swarming through her abdominal cavity like schools of lunatic fish.

"She never told us," I mumble lamely, thinking, with an ice-pick stab of guilt, that perhaps her own doctor might have discovered the problem, if only I'd made more of an effort to drag her kicking and screaming into his office.

"The pain was probably manageable until a month or so ago," this doctor replies, not looking up from his chart.

She's lying perfectly still on her gurney, her blue eyes vacant, the pupils shrunk to tiny dots by morphine, twin Pips in the boundless ocean. I'm not fooled. Death is doing the rumba inside of her, thumbing its nose at us, kicking up its heels. If she opens her mouth, the pounding beat will escape, like the noise of a party in the basement when someone opens the door at the top of the stairs.

...

Back in the happy house of brisk Reason, I'm now a source of contagion. The Thanatos virus that has so far been contained within me is now swarming over doorknobs, clinging to the rims of glasses, breeding in the sheets and pillowcases. Liam and Gail have to throw up psychic plastic sheeting to protect themselves from contamination.

Gail flicks on the TV the instant she arrives, throwing herself into her chair, delightedly wiggling her horrible feet in their asinine socks with a different-coloured pouch for each withered toe. They both loudly and pointedly ignore anything on TV involving real-life disaster: collisions, fires, gunshots, in short, any item at all that sounds like someone else's bad news. Gail pounces on the remote at the first hint of trouble, instantly changing the channel to some lackwit reality show that soon has Liam braying like a slaphappy morning-show weather anchor, or a drama with fake murder at the heart, the Mystery acted out for us by clowns paid handsomely to float face down in turquoise pools or sprawl behind steering wheels caked with vermillion gore.

Gail has won. She's planted her skull-and-crossbones flag and is now the official Missus of the house. Our living room feels like some rocky, wild island I can't approach because of contrary winds and perilous tidal currents. I hide out in the bedroom during their long social evenings, pretending to read *The Collected Works of William Blake*, an ancient, never-cracked textbook I found in a cobwebbed corner of the bookcase that will at least make me appear smart if anyone should care to look in on me.

Liam has taken to wearing earphones for hours during his free weekend time, plugged in to teaching CDs on loan from Mitch. When I ask what he's listening to, he replies airily, "Fascinating, really fascinating stuff. Particle physics theory. Energy in empty space and density of matter. How it's entirely possible and plausible that the universe really did come from nothing."

"Eureka! Tell us more, Professor Einstein."

He takes a breath, displays forbearance.

"Basically, it's about how all the old notions of cosmetology are being roundly debunked these days."

"Gosh. All those blackboards covered in equations by dorky scientists in Coke-bottle glasses, just to come up with radiant, pore-refining coverage." But he isn't listening.

"Nobody's ever really *seen* all those electrons and protons and force fields and stuff, have they?" I persist. "Isn't it all just numbers? How do they know those things really exist?"

"Because they explain all the repulsion and attraction in the universe." He readjusts his earphones and settles back into his chair.

"Like, 'by their fruits ye shall know them?'"

"What?" He pulls the earphones out again, visibly irritated.

"I didn't say nuttin'."

He leans back again, shutting his eyes. I plant myself on the chair arm and ruffle his fringe, then lean in to smooch my lips wetly against his outer ear. Over the earphone input, I drawl in my best honey-husky voice, "Tawk tuh me, shugah! It's fuckin' Sataday aftuhnoon! What am I supposed to do while youse is locked up in yuh science lab? I don't see you all week lawng! Izza tought of spendin' time wit' me too harrible to contemplate?"

His sigh is so deep you'd think I'd asked him to help me repave the driveway.

"Okay, fuhgeddaboutit," I snap, getting up. "If it's as much torture as that."

"Am I not allowed a little time to myself on the weekends? It so happens I'm interested in this and I want to know more about it. I can't spend every waking minute with you."

"You could talk to me about it."

"I just did. You're not interested."

"I asked a question, didn't I?"

"You know what I mean. You hate anything scientific."

"Then make it interesting for me."

"Look, will you just find something to do and give me an hour to myself?"

"But I'm lonely. I miss you. We don't spend no moh time tuhgethuh like we useda."

"You don't think *I'm* lonely?" he erupts, making me jump. "You don't think I'd like to be able to share the things I'm interested in with a reasonable person who doesn't go into hysterics at anything that isn't sanctioned by some mouldy priest somewhere?" He's out of his chair now, furiously wrapping up the earphone wires.

"I thought we were over this. Liam, don't go. Can't we talk about it?"

"About what? The Bible? The Resurrection?"

"Liam, please. I'm really wobbly these days, with Mum and everything. Please don't walk away."

Grudgingly, he relents, sitting down on the sofa and patting the place next to him. "Okay. I'm sorry. Come here."

I sit beside him, tipping my head stiffly onto his shoulder. He slips a furtive, teenaged arm around me. Both of us stare straight ahead.

"You want to talk. So talk to me, Maggers."

So tawk to him already. I open my mouth and claw down deep. It takes five minutes before anything coherent floats to the choppy surface.

"My mother's dying and I don't know if I even care," I get out at last, in an embarrassing pipsqueak voice. "She's never been any kind of a mother to me and, oh, I don't know. Just a lot of boring childhood stuff. Old crap. Baggage."

I wait for him to ask, What boring childhood stuff, what baggage? But he leapfrogs over the transitional material and shoots a curare dart straight at my heart.

"Well, it's death, isn't it? You're having to grapple with it now, and I know how uncomfortable you are with the idea."

"*Uncomfortable?*"

"Well, yes. Aren't you?"

"Liam, everyone's uncomfortable. For God's sake, it's—"

"Okay, you're terrified."

"And you aren't?"

He shrugs. "It's a waste of energy. I'm here now. When I'm not, I won't be. There's nothing I can do about it. And it's not like I'll know I'm dead. I won't know anything. It's completely painless."

"But aren't you terrified of *me* dying?"

He frowns, considering. "I'm not in a constant panic about it, if that's what you mean. Of course I wouldn't like it."

"You wouldn't like it."

"Of course not." He thinks a moment before prudently revising. "I'd be devastated, you know that."

"It would kill me if I lost you. It would *kill* me, Liam."

"I think what you're really dreading is your own death."

"So I'm the only person in the world who—"

"You think about it too much. You're morbid. That's what's feeding these irrational beliefs of yours."

"Which irrational beliefs are we talking about?"

He treads carefully. "Look, you're upset about your mother. You're upset because she's coming to the end of her life and is about to become extinct. See? I said it, and look at that wince! I've hit it on the head. Because of your fear, you're all caught up in this idea of an afterlife because you can't face the idea of extinction. And all the God and Bible stuff you picked up from your brother is just tacked on to that as a support for your irrational hopes. And you know you're on shaky ground, because otherwise you wouldn't be so defensive about it."

"You're so completely wrong."

"There, see? Defensive! I know you, Maggie. I know when you're not being a hundred percent up front."

"You're wrong, you're wrong, you're wrong!"

"So you truly believe without question in life after death."

"I have to."

"I see." He smiles into the middle distance, cool as a long drink of water. "Didn't we have this same death conversation once in the middle of a lake?"

"I have to because I can't live if I don't. I'll lose my mind. I mean it, Liam. I'll literally lose my mind. And anyway, you're the one who's nuts, talking about a, a profound mystery like you have everything figured out. Things the human race has been struggling with since the beginning of time!"

"Where do you see mystery? We're animals with limited life spans. Our bodies expire, they run out their warranties, and we have to be cleared away to make room for the next batch. Period. Life marches on for its own sake. Period. I don't care how many flimsy rope ladders you keep throwing up into the sky, hoping to walk off the earth into la-la-land."

"No. No! It *has* to be more than that."

"There's no *evidence* it's more than that! Show me some evidence and we'll talk." He removes his arm and sits back. He has me on the ropes now.

"It's not evidence you can whip a handkerchief off of and say, *Voilà*! It's not math on a blackboard! It's murky and all broken up and, and inconclusive. But it's there!"

"Where? Show me!"

"It's in your heart, you idiot. It's —"

"Yep. I knew that was coming. In my *heart*!" he minces. "What the hell does that even mean?"

Fat driblets of sweat begin rolling in tandem down my sides.

"It means it's not something I *believe* so much. I mean, like believing in, well, in ghosts or reincarnation, or, or, so much as something I, I trust. Like the way I trusted, we both trust-ed" — and now I'm a barrel rolling downhill — "when we found each other again, that love was going to heal us and make us happy, and that it *mattered* and would see us through whatever horror show is waiting for us down the road. Don't tell me you didn't trust just as much as I did! We both trusted instinctively in whoever or whatever it was, in the *source* of the joy we found together. And so, what if it turns out that joy is God, that he's real, against all the odds, just like we both found one another against all the—"

"Maggie." He's still calm. "This is wishful thinking. It's a magic charm against an indifferent universe. Read your Freud. Jesus!" He pokes me in the side far harder than necessary. "Besides. Why does joy have to have some ooga-booga supernatural source? Why can't it just be what it is?"

"Because it can't! Joy can't come out of meaninglessness, not *real* joy. And please," I rasp angrily, gathering steam, "who takes Freud seriously any more? Oh, hold on. Wasn't he the one who came up with the Oedipus complex? Because *there's* something you might want to ponder for a minute or two."

"What the hell is that supposed to mean?"

"Nothing. Okay, it means you cling to charms of your own. There. I said it. You want to sneer at everything that holds me together, but no one can touch the magic amulets you cling to!"

"What am I clinging to, pray tell?"

"Nothing. Forget it. You're a paragon of sanity." We're still staring straight ahead, though his accelerated breathing warns me that his cool is leaking away fast. I decide to go for broke.

"Liam, how can you not be concerned about death and eternity? How can it not *matter* to you? You say those things are meaningless, but at the same time, it's absolutely one hundred percent imperative that you win this argument. *This* matters because you *have* to be right, you have to come out on top! You don't care if you walk all over my heart, just so long as—"

"I don't have to be right. I am right."

"—just so long as you win, but when it comes to the Big Argument of Life, you're going to lose everything! You're facing annihilation and you don't care! All you care about is squashing me like a bug, about pulling off a stupid, pointless victory to vindicate your stupid, pointless life. It'll be quite the feather in your cap, won't it? Are you even human? Don't you even *wish* the afterlife were true? How can you just sit here, completely at peace with a life and death that's meaningless? What's there to be so happy about? You and Mitch insist that life is just an accident, but if it is, then doesn't that turn our whole beautiful story into nothing but random chemicals and synapses sparking and bumping heads? Is that all we amount to, a cigarette thrown out the car window?" I'm deep into uncharted waters now, unable to stop even as I think desperately, Turn back, turn back! You're *way* out of your league. The last thing you want is to founder on the shoals of Mitch!

"Maggie, for God's sake!"

"No, no! Listen! When we first got together, you must have said a hundred times that we were born for each other. Doesn't that seem like, like some kind of *purpose* to everything? Why did you say that if you didn't mean it?"

"Are you so dim you can't tell when someone's using a figure of speech?"

"But, Liam, it has to all *mean* something!"

"Who *cares* what it means!" he shouts angrily. "Why can't you just lighten up and enjoy it?"

"I can't enjoy an illusion! I can't live in a world with no meaning, Liam! I can't!"

"Then find one! But find one that makes sense! You don't need *religion*, for Christ's sake!" He's up now, pacing like a caged tiger. "Religion is nothing but wheels turning in people's brains. It's all manufactured bullshit. The afterlife! Please! When the brain dies, everything dies! Use your fucking head, for God's sake!"

"Would you really care if I died? I don't think you would." I'm shaking like fury now, grasping at every passing straw. "If nothing matters, then why do I matter? I don't, do I?"

"Lower your voice! You sound like a shrew. This is the stupidest argument of all time! I've had it, Maggie. No, don't follow me! Leave me alone! We're finished here!" He heads for the hall closet, yanking out a jacket, rattling all the hangers. Two more coats drop to the floor.

"No, *you* listen, damn it! If I died, would you just think, oh well, she's been cleared out to make space for someone else? Or would your precious void seem like a different place, once I was in it?"

"The void isn't a place," he intones wearily, pulling on his jacket, then pulling it off again. "That's what void *means*. No. Place. Jesus."

"But if you love me, and suddenly I was gone, wouldn't you want desperately for me to still be some place waiting for you, or maybe even looking out for you? Is that such a stupid thing to want? Wouldn't it help you to get through the days, believing that you might see me again, somewhere, some time?" I'm as hysterical as Winky, and just as sincere.

"Maggie. Maggie. You're embarrassing yourself. Looking *out* for me? I'm sorry, but you need serious help." He has a hand on the doorknob, is on the way out; I have to screech at his retreating back like we're soap actors.

"Just *answer me*! Would you be *sad*? And if you wouldn't be sad for me, would you be sad for Gail, your *real* love?"

"Yes! Yes! Is that what you want to hear? Yes! I would be sad!" He bursts into sour laughter. "How childish is this going to get, Maggie?"

"Really? You want to talk about childish? Because you two, you and your mother, please! Talk about childish! You cook up this ridiculous, half-assed version of religion that you've gotten from Sunday morning TV, and the stupider the stuff you watch, the more you love it! It suits your purposes because then you can have yourselves a ball, being so superior, kicking your stupid version of something deep and mysterious and incomprehensible around like bullies beating up on a kid half your size. You don't know the first fucking thing about struggling to find your way in the dark! Why would you even bother to think about it if there's something good on TV? You're totally ignor—"

"Tell me," he snarls, whipping around, pitching his jacket across the room and poking his blotched face up into mine. "If you really and truly believe all this crap, then why are *you* so afraid to die? Huh? What's your problem, if there's really an afterlife and you're on God's good side? I'll tell you what your problem is. First of all, you *don't* really believe it, and second of all, your total incapacity to explain to me what you *do* believe convinces me you don't know what the fuck you're talking about! You need to sit down and do some serious thinking! And until that day comes, shut the fuck up!"

He bangs into the kitchen. The freezer door opens and closes, followed by the door to the liquor cabinet. In a rush of panic, I think, *Not my Jack!* But yes, my Jack; for the next five minutes I listen in gut-clenched envy as jostling ice cubes rush to his lips and tumble back again. At long last he reappears, deep golden drink in hand and shirt collar loosened, looking, as we used to say, suave and blaze.

"Well, if it isn't James Bond with his fucking licence to kill."

He tosses back a neat gulp and replies with frosty hauteur, "It's no use talking to you. You're out of your mind."

"Well, the Bible does call faith foolishness."

Bull's-eye! Spinning on his heel, he storms back to the kitchen, roaring, "The Bible is *crap*!" Bottles clink. Ice rattles afresh. Footfalls skitter across the ceiling.

I stand in the kitchen doorway, hoping to ratchet it down a notch, trying to appear contrite. "If you'd just listen, I already *told* you I have trouble with a lot of it! Liam, you can't drink like that on an empty stomach."

Apparently he can. Polishing off his second drink in one swig, he slams the glass down on the counter. Alcohol seems to focus him, honing his rage to an icicle point. His words march out like orderly ranks of storm troopers, upright and lethal with purpose.

"Listen, if God does exist, why doesn't he get off his fat ass and do something about the suffering in the world? But he never does, never has, and never will." He pours a third drink. I reach for the bottle, but he whips it away.

"Okay, fine! Drink your face off. Too bad you have to get courage from a bottle. Not me. I'm not afraid of looking stupid. I'm used to it." I bite my tongue, clearly not quickly enough.

"Speaking of stupid, why don't you believe in the Greek myths while you're at it? Why don't you believe Zeus is out there throwing thunderbolts at people and coming down to mate with human women? But oh no, you'll say, *that's* stupid! Nobody believes *that* any more. Hah!"

He's sipping more conservatively now, looking noble and handsomely hurt, a wronged husband on *The Bold and the Beautiful*. I ease the bottle out of his hand and pour myself a very tall iceless drink. It goes down like warm Drano, recharging my courage considerably. I will myself to speak softly, allowing my voice to crack pleasantly, sexily, at every pause.

"Here's a way of looking at it. Think of Gail and her garden." Even as I evoke her name, I sense bated breath over our heads.

It also puts a halt to Liam's gallop. His eyes narrow as they refocus on me.

"You know how people pass by and stop and stare," I say gently, generously. "And if they talk to you, they always ask, who's the gardener? It's so gorgeous people right away have to know, who did it? Who made it? It wouldn't occur to anyone to think it just popped up that way by chance."

Liam hawks a wad of phlegm down the drain. "Of course. The old gardener analogy. Had to know that was coming." He turns slowly, fixing me with a reptilian smile. "But you can't stand the gardener."

"That's not true! From her garden, I can tell she has an eye for—"

"Then why are you always huffing and rolling your eyes when she's around?"

"I can tell she has an eye for, for beauty, and arrangement, and that she's meticulous and…"

He folds his arms, eyeing me with frigid interest. Talk about an analogy breaking down.

"I don't huff and roll my eyes. You're imagining things." I try to take his hand, but he shakes me off.

"I can't stand any more of this, Maggie." *Now* he's slurring: thish, Maggie.

"You hate me now, is that it?"

"I have no respect for your ideas."

"I see. You hate everything I care about, but I shouldn't take it personally, is that the idea?"

"I'm going to lie down."

"You're just pissed because I can't stand your mother."

He looks at me long and dangerously. I don't stop.

"But you can sneer at *my* mother. That's all hunky-dory. You claim everything's meaningless, but you still find time to sneer at me, so it must mean something to you that I'm deluded and stupid and that you're superior. Hasn't it ever occurred to you that if everything's meaningless, then even *saying* it's meaningless is meaningless? You can't be right or superior in a meaningless world. It makes no—"

"Listen, I am so damned fu…sick of sheeing you mope around and, moping the fuck around here, no, no, get your hands OFF! ME! Leave me the fuck ALONE!"

I hear a snort from the hall and turn to see Gail tiptoeing exaggeratedly into the kitchen, stage-whispering, "Don't mind me! Just came to borrow some Ajax." Reaching into the cupboard under the sink, she turns innocently to address the ceiling. "People who have invisible friends might want to start thinking about booking a bed at the funny farm." She tee-hees like a happy skylark and ducks out again, but no footsteps mount the stairs. After a moment she reappears, making a great show of retrieving pieces of lint from the hall rug, trying to catch Liam's eye as she bends and rises with impeccable spinal alignment.

Liam puts down his glass and walks fast to the bathroom. There's no time to close the door before flinging himself over the bowl, retching pitifully.

Hah! I think. That's what *you* get!

I retrieve my smoke stash from my underwear drawer and light up. Liam emerges from the bathroom, green of face and noxious of breath. He kicks the bedroom door shut behind him.

"Would you mind putting that out?"

"Yes, I'd mind. Why should I?"

"Because Gail doesn't like your smoke, that's why!" he barks, steadying himself against the dresser. "It's common courtesy!"

"Then she can haul her shrivelled ass back upstairs where she belongs." I belch an aggressive gust into his drawn face, adding loftily, "You think I can't see the void in you? The sadness? The terror?"

He tries to pass me, but I clutch at his sleeve. He rips his arm away. "Put that goddamn thing *out*!"

"You're right! I can't stand the sight of that flap-jawed, brain-eating witch!" From the kitchen, a loud, forced chortle. I raise my voice. "Stupid bitch with her anal garden and her idiotic lawn vacuum and her cat guillotine and her—"

"Who is she hurting?" yells Liam so loudly that he makes himself stumble. He sinks onto the bed, wheezing and bilious.

"The two of you are supposed to be so close, you're so damned smug about it, but anyone can see you're not close at all. You never tell her *any* of the sticky stuff!"

"What sticky stuff?" He rolls his eyes; I can tell it hurts.

"You know what I mean. *Real* stuff. You only talk about inanities, sucking up to her all the time. God forbid you should have to face anything an inch below surface level."

"Are you going to lighten up any time...soon?" He's desperate to destroy me but can't pull in the necessary air. I keep at him, low and even and mean.

"You care about her. You don't care about me. Every asinine, fatuous remark, all that pointless animal murder, every nasty thing she says about me, it's all just fine with you. You never judge her. You treat her like a real friend. She gets all your unconditional love. Why her and not me? You used to be *my* friend! Where are you going?"

He nearly rips the bedroom door off its hinges in his haste. I follow him to the bathroom, watching him grunt and heave for a moment before grabbing the back of his shirt. He can't shake me off and puke at the same time. Even when all the drink is out of him, he doesn't move, remaining splayed over the stinking, splattered bowl, my arms around his panting stomach, my face against his neck, like some gargantuan parasite.

After a very long time, he gets up and I slide off. He stares bleakly at his sunken face in the mirror before proceeding to brush his teeth. I'm standing right behind him, but he won't meet my eyes.

He hangs up his toothbrush. "We're not going to make it," he says hoarsely.

The blasphemy shocks me white.

"Don't say that! You don't mean it!"

"I mean it."

"No! Please! You swore to me this was forever!"

"Who created the problems between us? It wasn't me, baby! Besides, if you're such a good Christian, why don't you try loving someone other than yourself for a change? Why don't you try loving my mother? For *my* sake." He goes into the bedroom and slams the door between us. The lock clicks.

I know Gail is watching from the kitchen, grinning like a death's-head. I don't dare turn around. Ten, fifteen minutes creep by. When at last I look, she's gone, having slipped away as quietly as hope.

But sitting beside Mum in her private room, it doesn't feel so shamefully feeble-minded to be obsessed with the passing away of things. On the contrary, in a place like this, anyone who *isn't* seems puerile and shallow. Flat on her back, she's ceased to be a threat or even a mild annoyance. Her approaching death excites me. I sit in a chair pulled up close to her bedside, and though she seldom stirs, I feel all the while as if I'm watching her pack for a long, exotic journey.

Every time I visit there's less of her, as if her body is regressing, dwindling back into childhood. A nurse has given her a small teddy bear that she keeps wedged in the crook of her arm; it gives her the air of a very brave little girl on her first visit to the hospital. If she's awake, she sometimes tries to speak, her voice a wavering signal buffeted by strong winds. I don't catch a single word.

But mostly she just lies quietly, eyes closed. I have all the time in the world to study the visible parts of her. Those hands that never once touched me in love lie on the blanket, twisted at odd angles. I remember her washing my hair with those hands every Saturday, me standing on a stool, bent double over the laundry sink in the basement as she abraded my scalp with a scrub brush and strong, yellow soap, pinning me roughly by the neck to hose me down with the rubber sprayer. And snapping impatiently at me: "Hold still!" and "Stop bawling! It's not hot!" She always wore her cat's-eye reading glasses for this event, probably because of all the splashing. Her eyes were always fogged in, remote, no help to me in time of trouble.

I could never stop exasperating her back then. But who *is* she, and what does she have to do with me now? I'm afraid at every moment someone will come in and demand to know what I'm doing here, force me to give an account of myself or, worse, of her.

Now I'm the one administering the water, after the nurse has hoisted her dead weight into a sitting position. I'm the one smoothing back the mess of white hair mobbing her shoulders, holding the water glass to her lips so she can take a few sips, watching the water run back down her chin. I watch my own hands too as I swab her off with tissue, hands that have come to look so much like hers, the dark spots dispersed in near-identical patterns, the veins prominent, the skin dry and ridged. Something strange and oddly satisfying rises in my throat as I think, Me too.

Me too, what? I don't know. Me too, old? Me too, a survivor? Are these *Moriarty* hands, the genuine articles, badges of belonging to a family, a history, a past in long-lost Ireland?

Or is it me too who's forfeited a husband, me too who's lost the precious companionship of an adored little boy? Me too, left alone and trembling with no one to pin my hopes on but a phantom God who never calls, never writes, who's stuck in Folsom Prison with problems of his own?

Her head flops forward in sleep as I sit wondering, Is she all packed? Is the celestial taxi on its way? It's impossible to imagine what's keeping her here; she's as brittle and creased as a peanut shell. She could achieve liftoff with the lightest breath of wind, could rise and depart as quietly as a sunbeam sliding across the wall, evaporating into a passing cloud. Traveling light, ha!

At every visit, I telepathically try out some of my stumbling faith talk on her.

"Faith, Mum, is like some dumb, galumphy little puppy who's always at my heels, no matter how many stones I throw at him, who breaks into a clumsy gallop when I try to run away, who I can't shake no matter how fast I run. Is that how it is for you? Do you get it, Mum? Do you know what I mean?"

She gets it. Winky's mother knows what I'm talking about. I can pull out all the maudlin stops with her.

"Or try this on for size, Mum: Faith is like the dorky boy who wants to carry your books home from school, who wants to be your friend so badly, who only wants you to grant him the honour of walking beside you in his hopeless short-sleeved shirt and bow tie, his nerdy stamp albums under his arm, all the things he longs to share with you if you'd just let him come over for a few minutes. And after you've rolled your eyes in his face and called him a dumb-ass gaylord and slammed the door on him, the thought of those stamp albums makes you want to bawl your eyes out.

"You'd give anything to be able to like him."

Liam, meanwhile, bends over backward so as not to rattle me, as if I'll go off like nitroglycerine at the merest jostle. Instead of talking, we banter, laughing shrilly and mightily at the sorriest jokes; I might as well be Gail. We never touch each other, though once I come up behind him at the kitchen table and wrap my arms around his neck, hoping a dorsal approach might still be tolerated. He takes both my hands in his and holds them against his cheek. But we keep the pose too long, and it all dies there.

"I want a Celtic cross for Mum's headstone," I inform him coldly, pulling my arms away and sitting down again.

He stiffens perceptibly, regarding me with the pity reserved for Tourette's cases on the street. But all my bridges are burnt now.

"You think it's silly. I'll never be able to make you understand the whole Catholic thing, so I'm not even going to try." And I ask myself in no little confusion, *What* Catholic thing? Do my words know something my mind hasn't yet caught wind of?

Liam starts to speak, but I cut him off.

"No, don't start. I want that cross. It would make her happy."

"You don't even like her," he reminds me archly.

"Maybe that's why I want it," I snap before the outriders of approaching tears can begin to thicken my voice. Because I'm thinking, really, What says "Moira and Mag Mary" better than a fat crossbeam jammed through an upright, all splintered and cracked? And that circle around it like the big, fat Irish hug she never once gave me.

"I want it. Don't argue with me."

She's still hanging on as November draws to a close. By then I'm spending every afternoon with her, my worst fear playing itself out before my eyes. But I'm not frightened. I'm elated. What better death is there for a doubter like me to behold? This is my chance to crack the codes! To banish fear for good and all! She's played by the rules all her life; surely she has a tremendous reward stored up by now. I want her death to be so meaningful, so eloquent, that it makes me positively look forward to my own.

She continues to lie still, hugging her bear, obediently awaiting orders from the front. Nothing changes from one visit to the next except the spreading bruises on the backs of her hands from the IV drip, the silent infusion of life that keeps her tethered by the flimsiest of threads to the planet. Now my hands, next to hers, look like a child's again.

I envy her her peace, her seeming lack of fear. Keeping vigil beside her, I feel safe, far safer than at home. For once in my life I'm where I'm supposed to be, doing the indisputably right thing. The twilit dimness around her draws me in, blocking out the hospital fluorescence. I fully expect every visit to be my last, badly wanting it to happen while I'm there so that I can peek through the veil as it tears. Just enough to glimpse, perhaps, those six little boys she once prayed so hard for, Kevvie right out front, still himself, front teeth still missing, his dark nimbus of hair as scrappy and linty as ever. All of them waiting to meet her on the far shore—the old River Styx allusion is as good as any—as her wobbly boat drifts in out of the fog, bumping against rocks in the dark. They'll reach out for her like solemn scouts, holding the boat steady. Kevvie will take her elbow like a little gentleman as she clambers onto land, assuring her with a smile: It won't be long. You'll soon be able to put your feet up, Madam. She'll follow them politely, taking small steps, her cracked, brown purse, which she's dragged stubbornly through the veil with her, clutched to her chest. The boys will run on ahead, rounding a bend as she plods after them, and then the very air will slam shut, a black door in a blacker mountain.

Later on at her welcoming banquet, everyone will bang spoons against glasses, crying, "Speech! Speech!" She'll wait till the din dies down, before quipping softly, "Ladies and gents, you heard it here first: No more hunger, no more thirst!"

My reverie is interrupted by the hospital's Catholic chaplain sidling into the room wearing a rust-coloured cardigan over his black priest shirt. Knife-edge creases in his natty tan pants don't testify to a lot of kneeling. He carries the priest's black Bag of Doom but doesn't open it. He nods to me as I move back a respectful distance. I'm positive that he knows me through and through, every evil thought, word, and deed, knows me like the dead know the living.

Mum makes no protest, never asking, Where is my son, where is Father Gerry? The priest sits gently on the side of the bed, the two of them murmuring in low tones, kindred hearts beating as one. I feel I ought to go stand in the hall, scuffing my shoes like a naughty child.

"He is the undefeated heart of weakness," I hear him say, and then, "lower than...something something...ever go." He makes the sign of the cross over her and she follows, dragging leaden fingers to her forehead and across her chest. I keep my head down so they won't see me choke up, as I always do at the sight of genuine Catholic devotion, someone else opening a gift that was supposed to be mine.

He opens his bag then, preparing to give her Communion. I'm sure she'll never get it down, but she does. There's more whispering, hands swishing up and sideways in blessing. The oils aren't coming out today, nor the candles. This is still just a rehearsal.

But it's *her* rehearsal, hers alone. She's bought and paid for every second of this close, professional attention through a life of unflagging devotion. She lies stiff and silent in that narrow bed, and all at once the dawn comes up like thunder as I realize that this woman before me is *real*. Not an uncredited actress playing the part of My Enemy, but a person, separate and whole, as real as I am, her loves and losses as deep and organic and bitter as my own. How can I not have known this before now? Gerard left her in the lurch. Her husband kicked her around like trash in the gutter. I held her at arm's length, held my nose, held my resentful ground. Yet this wisp of a woman somehow has more authenticity than all of us put together.

Does she even know what it is to be untrue to herself?

"If she wants to believe a fairy tale, let her," is what Liam Cushnahan would have to say about this plain and mighty life of faithfulness and survival. Nor would he say it unkindly, his arms folded across his chest, as upright and dry-eyed as a column of figures.

Mum hasn't told the priest who I am. He leaves without looking back at me. She sinks back into her pillows, restless to be on her way.

I drag my chair back to her bedside, peering closely, monitoring the rise and fall of her chest. Yes, I want to be here when it happens, but Gerard has told me he's coming for a visit, and I need to be gone before he shows up. We two have not once met here beside our dying mother. If I see him suddenly looming in the doorway, scissor-limbed and chill in his repellent black coat, the tombstone teeth bared in his smoke-cured face, my heart will seize up on the spot and shoot me straight to the far shore before Mum's boat has even pushed off from the beach.

But it's Gerard who witnesses the passing through the veil, not me.

The phone rings on Saturday morning two days later. Once again Liam drives me to the hospital, but in the parking lot, I freeze. I imagine her lying in there hugging that damned bear, looking so wasted, so piteous, so precious, and I'm enraged beyond endurance.

"I can't go in there. I'll lose it. I'll yell at her: Fuck right off and die! It's no less than you deserve," I tell Liam before detonating into noisy, snot-ridden sobs. We sit in the parking lot for forty-five squalling minutes when at last he heaves a great, exasperated sigh and drives me home.

All my gentle feelings for her have been rubbed out. I can't even remember what they felt like. It's been a month-long cocaine high, and now I'm back on flat, sober earth. I hate her. I want her gone. And I hate Gerard for oozing in the door at just the right moment after half a lifetime of neglect, taking all the honours, twin number one, beloved son. And I hate Liam because he loves *his* mother without condition, and she him, and he loves me with so many conditions and strings and reservations he may as well not bother at all.

Gerard calls late in the evening, asking what happened to me. "Is it over?"

"It was over by two this afternoon."

Over. The last grain of sand through the hourglass.

"Was it easy? Did she suffer? Was she afraid?"

"I need you to take care of cleaning out her place. The landlord wants to come in and fumigate."

"Fuck the landlord! I want to know what happened!"

"Stop pissing me off!" he shouts in a most unsaintly way. And hangs up.

Neither Gail nor Liam has any use for funerals.

"When the Big Day comes, just toss me in the ground and go have a drink!" is Gail's favourite refrain, her teeth thick as thieves as she chortles, it hasn't got *us* yet, ha ha!

Gerard gave the hospital the name of the funeral home, his final contribution before melting into the ether, no doubt sucked up once more into some remote tier of heaven. At any rate, he's not answering his phone. Only Liam and I turn up two days later to oversee the viewing.

It can't be the right body. I have to look twice, three times, have to lean in close over the deserted top half of her in the casket to ascertain if this mole was in that spot a week ago. Surely they've made a mistake, the macabre, mirror image of babies being sent home from the maternity ward with the wrong mothers. And if this *is* my mother, what have they done to her? The light has gone out of her hair; once so white, it's now slate-grey and coarse as frayed rope. They've puffed up her sunken

400

cheeks and given her an overbite, a caking of sallow powder and an inscrutable smile. She looks like the love child of the Mona Lisa and Charlie Chan.

Her brown Christmas dress bunches loosely around her neck. Her hands clasp a pleasingly co-ordinated coral rosary. She's tucked in nicely, and it's refreshing not to see that stale yellow robe, or the rumpled hospital sheets, already looping and flaring like kites in the giant-load hospital dryers, getting ready for whoever's up next.

I have to remind myself repeatedly that there's nobody here, that I'm looking at the crumpled box the gift came in on Christmas morning. Little Moira took the steep steps underground days ago. She's eons away by now.

"Does anyone ever believe this when they see it?" I ask Liam. He purses his lips; I take this to mean yes.

The viewing is scheduled to last three hours. I'm hot with shame, thinking no one will come, even though I finally did put an obituary in the *Globe*. It's going to be just me and Liam, and maybe Gerard, if he re-enters the atmosphere in time.

But I'm surprised. Several elderly but spry nuns from St. Bern's tiptoe in, addressing me softly as "Dear" and patting my outstretched hands. And Mrs. Penniman sits in the last row, sedate and dumb as a post.

Everyone shambles forward in their turn in solemn befuddlement, staring the most bizarre and banal of mysteries in the face. Everyone hoping her presence is noted Somewhere, hoping this papier-mâché charade counts for Something. The sisters kneel and mumble. Mrs. Penniman goes to a great deal of trouble to examine each of the paltry vases of pink carnations I sprang for as if she's waiting for Moira to address her at any moment but not daring to look at the casket in case she does. Liam focuses on his knees if he's sitting and on the far wall when he stands. Everyone whispers, as if Mum's having a nap in there.

Yes, I think: she's tired, she's gone to lie down. Better rest now because in the morning she'll be moved to St. Bernadette's for the Requiem Mass. She'll surely want to be looking her best for the grand finale.

When it's all over, and I've seen everyone off at the funeral home's front door like a good hostess, I remember I left my purse in the viewing room. In the doorway, I'm caught up short; the funeral home jokers are moving in already, shutting the coffin, busy turning screws, tightening bolts. One of them says something disparaging about the Leafs, and the others laugh.

It starts to offend me, and then it doesn't. I can sense her here and not here, caring and not caring. The invisible world must have all kinds of secret paths and hidden corners. She could be anywhere! Or not. The only place she definitely isn't is in that box.

"This funeral is going to be as half-assed as our wedding," I remark the next morning as Liam and I pull into the church parking lot to wrap up the job.

"You're the one who arranged it."

"Don't I know it? Everything done in true Prentice style: scraggly flowers, no music. We botch all our big events. Weddings, funerals, Christmases, all the rituals." I light up one last, antagonistic smoke. "Really. Mum would have been so proud."

In truth, one of the nuns, Sister Gwen, has done most of the arranging, and she's even older than Mum, so I'm not surprised at the spartan simplicity. I don't know the priest, billed in our program notes as Father Leo Tozzi, Principal Celebrant and Homilist. If Mum can hear his muffled voice from wherever she is, she'll know it isn't the principal celebrant she'd set her sights on. Gerard is a definite no-show; it's just the usual suspects: me and Liam, Sister Gwen and her walker, and four or five assorted nuns and elderly ladies who perhaps attend all local funerals. Mrs. Penniman, though, has blown us off.

Father Tozzi has a pleasant, crusty baritone that puts me in mind of a knife rasping through hard bread.

"Come to her assistance, all ye saints of God, meet her all ye angels of God, receiving her soul and offering it in the sight of the Most High. May Christ receive thee, who hath called thee, and may angels conduct thee to Abraham's bosom. Eternal rest grant unto her, O Lord, and let perpetual light shine upon her."

Liam's stern shoulder presses insistently against mine. He's faking it exactly as my father once did, getting up with everyone else, sinking gratefully into the pew when sitting time rolls around again. Father Tozzi walks slowly around the casket, swinging the censer, mumbling Absolution. Unless of course it's too late and Mum is already in hell; as an unsaved Catholic, she certainly stands condemned by Gerard's particular brand of Christian legality. Nor was there a day of my childhood when I wouldn't have wished exactly that for her. But this guy can't possibly know where, or even *if*, she is.

Gerard knows. Maybe that's why he's not here.

The Mass sputters to an end. One of the funeral home boys

approaches Liam as we file out of the church and whispers in his ear. Liam nods, looking strained.

"They want me to be a pallbearer," he tells me, all grim about the gills. He follows the young man back into the church while I stand on the steps in the weak November sun, the hearse nosing against the curb, its back doors falling open.

The cemetery is only minutes away; we've barely settled into the aromatic black leather seats before it's time to get out again. It's nothing like the frigid cemetery we left Kevvie in. On this shiny late autumn day, the grass is far greener than it ought to be, and the rolling swells and little copses of trees remind me of an electric train town. Unbothered people stroll or ride bikes through the winding pathways. It's so peaceful, Death might even be taking the day off, putting his feet up, snoozing under a tree. Sleeping in all day is certainly the thing to do in these parts. De rigueur mortis, I think, wondering if I should risk sharing this bon mot with Liam.

Father Tozzi, smartly turned out in a pigeon-grey Italian topcoat, blesses the grave, sprinkling holy water over the coffin. I hear: *"May Thy mercy unite her to the choirs of angels"* as my jumpy mind harks back to Kevvie's sad burial, never mind how many times I've watched this same, tired scene on TV or in the movies, sombre folks in fashionable black bunched around open graves with nothing in them. I wait for the drama to lift me up, to move me, but there is none. The box sits there, idiotically silent, waiting to be lowered on pulleys only after we mourners have trooped discreetly away, back to put in more time in the City of Life until called here again, for one reason or the other.

I snap back to attention just in time for *"May her soul and all the souls of the faithful departed rest in peace. Amen.*" The sun retreats. Our little band sways and shivers. Looking down at the short line of cars on the road, I see that Gerard is here after all. He's sitting in Father Tozzi's car, smoking. Lieutenant Fred is by his side.

I'm about to walk over when one of the posse of nuns trots back from their car with a black shoebox under her arm. Standing at the head of the grave after a hurried confab with the priest, she whips off the lid and lifts out a pumping, shuddering white dove by its twiggy red feet. She says something I don't catch on the theme of spirits returning home. Then she lets go of the dove. It's off like a shot over the bare treetops.

"Where'd that bird go?" croaks one of the old ladies, jerking her head right and left in utter bafflement.

"Back to town," replies the sister briskly. Liam stifles a snort in his hands. I look up; the priest's car is pulling away, Gerard and Fred never having made landfall.

Mother, behold thy son. Hah!

I stand waiting, listening moronically for some kind of maternal reaction to float out of the whistling void. When none comes, I ask her silently, companionably, "So, Mum. Is it anything like what you expected? Did it turn out to be true that people are valuable after all? Anytime you want to answer is fine with me."

Liam is standing next to the hearse, looking back at me, practically pawing the ground in his haste to escape.

"I'm sorry we have to go off and leave you, Mum. To tell you the truth, I could use a sandwich. But I guess you're used to being left by now.

"Except you're the one who left us. It feels like we all set out together, and you just got sick and tired of the pack of us and dropped back to a walk, and then, poof, you were out of sight, behind the trees and gone."

That's what *we* get. Hah!

When we pull into the driveway, Gail is still out working, the picture of pink-cheeked health, sweeping the bare garden plots with a kitchen broom. Liam rolls down the window. "Still slaving away?" he asks cheerfully.

"Snow's coming!" she shouts back, wagging an accusatory finger at the clear blue sky.

"Come on in and take a load off!" he tells her as I bite my lips off in fury.

"Be there in two shakes!"

We've barely hung up our coats before she bursts in, immediately snapping on the TV.

"Great," I snipe at Liam. "My mother isn't even cold yet and we're back to business as usual." He kisses my cheek and musses my hair. "Come on," he cajoles me. "Be nice."

Before long the two of them are shaking in antic laughter over a *Seinfeld* rerun. They might as well be wearing party hats, tearing around in circles, kids on a sugar high, growing ever crazier the closer it comes to the time Dad's coming to pick them up to go home.

I'm slumped sullenly in my corner, immersed in a vicious interior monologue, when Gail suddenly twists around in her chair to ask brightly, "What are you going to do with the dog?"

With her head cocked to one side, she looks like an especially clever little pooch herself.

Winky. My heart drops forty storeys. I've clean forgotten him.

"Looks like someone forgot to put on her thinking cap," observes Gail with relish, and I know she hasn't forgotten Winky for a second since this whole drama began.

This can only end in tears.

Liam turns on me. "Didn't you get anyone in to look after the dog? Jesus, Maggie!"

I have no tears for my mother, but the thought of poor, abandoned Winky undoes me. I see him orphaned by his empty bowl, just like the pup he was twenty years ago, curled up in the unwholesome pet store sawdust with two mangy kittens and several turds, his life coming full circle as he huddled now, forgotten, in a corner of Mum's dark bedroom, too weak to bark — though could Mrs. Penniman have him? — but then, why didn't she say so at the funeral home?

I turn my face to the window so they won't see my face crumple into full ugly-cry mode.

I vividly remember giving him that irritated kick in his just-voided belly, hoping the balcony rail would give way as he plowed into it, wanting to be rid of him and his ramshackle stink for good and all. My resemblance to Gail in this is not lost on me.

I'm so sorry, Winky, I blubber now, clutching at the sofa pillows. What did you ever do except rush in a frenzy of joy to greet my lonely mother after every parting, a tired old fellow in the winter of your life. I'm so sorry! Can you ever forgive me?

"Give me the key. I'll go see about the dog," Liam grouses,

pulling his jacket back on. "All right, come on, stop it now. Don't cry." He hugs me for a long time, giving me a clear view over his shoulder of tears dribbling down his back, leaving unsightly tracks on the brown leather. He pulls away at last.

"Chalk up another one for your asshole brother," he says as the door closes behind him.

Gail makes a flamboyant production of inching discreetly out the door, then fairly pounding up the stairs. Before she closes her own door, I hear a strangled cackle, followed by little feet running across the living room above me, where she knocks on the window, waving to Liam, as bright as a house fire.

The next day I'm in Mum's apartment myself. Liam and the landlord have disposed of Winky's crumpled remains; his ashes are lying ingloriously at the bottom of the building's incinerator. Now Mum is the one playing Winky's part, waiting, biting her nails, scanning the horizon for the first sign of his miraculously restored little self running to join her, leaping from cloud to cloud. How long can it...yes! Yes! Here comes her baby now!

I'm waiting for Fred to show up with a U-Haul. At Gerard's decree, Mum's bed and dresser, her unsteady kitchen table, and Grandma Fionnuala's chair will soon be glamorous additions to the Untouchables decor. There's also a windfall of loud sweaters in store for the gang. I'm supposed to clean out the odds and ends, taking any mementos I might want for myself before he arrives.

The place reeks of excrement, human and canine; I'm nauseous even with the windows and the balcony door open. The dresser drawers are crammed with junk I have neither the energy nor the heart to sift through. Opening one, I find a messy

pile of notes reminding herself to go to the bank, to call Sister
Angela, to pick up what she'd noted down as "some Muster
Clane." There are stacks of ancient holy cards, frayed and split
at the edges, bound with dried-out rubber bands. And a photo-
booth picture of Gerard at seventeen, with "My Son Gerard"
written on the back in red ballpoint. His acne, in the smudgy,
underexposed shot, makes him look as if he has a full beard.

Stuffed behind the drawer, I find several pairs of old-lady
underpants, the crotches stiff and cracked and stained yellow-
brown. I'd done the very same thing as a child, hiding accidental
stains and streaks in the back of my closet, hot with shame.
Cold water gets out blood, I think bitterly, but look what she
got away with! I slam the drawer shut, despising her all over
again, her coldness, her weakness, her sad, shuffling secrets.
You can't leave, I want to scream at her. You haven't paid! I'm
not done with you, not done scraping up against you, knocking
you around, rattling you silly, anything to try to squeeze a few
hard pellets of backed-up love out of you.

Her whole place screams back at me: Keep out, you! This
is Moira Moriarty's business and hers alone! You're much too
little, and far, far too late.

I leave the door open for Fred; he can buzz himself in, or
not. I don't want to see him and there's nothing here I can stand
to touch, let alone take away.

Outside, everything seems to have tipped sideways, the
world breathed out of the nostrils of My Son Gerard. Life is
nothing but a smear, a scribble, a malignant crucible of testing,
cloudy with poisonous gases. People stream toward me, washing
by like water, antennaed creatures flush with alien purpose.

Trees anchored into the earth look as stupid and arbitrary as upended brooms. I'm leaving her place for the last time, the first in a series of lasts crowding like pigeons around a dry husk of bread. My knees keep pumping, the Tanteek entangling my legs like the leash of a dog gone berserk, turning me in the wrong direction, always, *always* the wrong direction. I'm bawling audibly, and people are going out of their way not to look at me.

Now I know that the Tanteek has been turning me in circles all along. I'm right back where I was at nineteen, turning circles in a rowboat, panting with terror, but now I'm *old*, with no future, my paltry reserves long spent. Everything is as good as gone and there's no holding on to save my life.

I arrive home with three clinking bottles of Jack, and sit on the bed, my face streaked and salt-crusted, drinking to the accompaniment of a bee that's been in the house since September, butting its exhausted head against the window, buzzing like an electric razor with a low battery charge.

A winter-brown bird bonks into the window, making me jump. It plummets, landing unconscious in the empty flower box.

"Mum?" I ask timidly, recalling her winter-brown burial dress. "Is that you?" But who in the history of ever has been able to distinguish a no from a no reply?

I sit dizzily waiting for Liam to come home from work, slipping in the door like a cat with the bottom half of a bird in its teeth. Unless of course hell has chosen today to suck him up, shlerk!, like a stone in Gail's lawn vacuum.

From upstairs drifts the concussive thrash and gargle of Mozart being throttled to death. A fresh Christmas lurks just around the corner, *Blackadders* stacked on the coffee table and raring to go.

Jack-enlivened, I replay Liam's and my last bitter feud over and over in my mind, casting myself as the silent, stoic victim of a cruel tongue-lashing who, when my oppressor has finally spewed his last drop of haughty vitriol, turns nobly and quietly to annihilate him with a telling quote from Blake: *What is grand is necessarily obscure to weak men. That which can be made explicit to the idiot is not worth my care.*

Or how about an original haiku?

Head resists heart, but
Hope leans softly against me
Like a hungry cat.

Suck on *that*, atheist boy!

Or wrap your dim brain around this: Faith is like an untranslatable language, a mountain dialect from some remote back country, spoken by moon-eyed peasants in kerchiefs. Nobody in the big heartless city knows what we're talking about as we stumble around, just off the boat, with our cardboard suitcases, mouldy cheeses under our arms, our shoes made out of old tire treads. Everywhere we go, we're laughed to scorn as we try wretchedly to communicate, signing with our fingers, bleating like sheep in a language that has no spelling, whose metaphors only translate into other metaphors.

Or:

Faith, Liam, is like a voice speaking in a dream that recedes as you awaken: Hear me, my child, and fear not . . . hear me . . . hear m . . . mmm . . . eee . . . POP.

The bubble bursts.

Gone again.

I wake up that night in the middle of a scream, just like in a TV nightmare. Liam sits me up on the side of the bed, an arm around my shoulder, but there's no help possible from all the arms in the world. I clutch the neck of his tee-shirt, my last slippery fingerhold over the crevasse. There's no true thing but death, and it's coming is coming is coming...

"Wipe your nose. Jesus, Maggie." His fine, symmetrical features, as they take in my raw, naked terror, are contorted into Picasso's rendering of "Fine Upstanding Husband, Unjustly Tormented Beyond All Human Endurance, Descending Into Hell."

I continue to cry for a full day and half of the next, with ten-minute breaks scattered here and there. It's mindless, self-propelled weeping; I long to stop out of sheer boredom, but there's no plugging the leak, the bottom plumb rusted out of my reservoir of hope. Liam walks out of every room I enter, his face airtight with baffled resentment. At long last, he lifts me by the armpits, manhandles me into the car, and drives me to Emergency, where we wait and wait, slumped in moulded plastic chairs in identical positions, left hands in our laps, right elbows propped on the chair arm, heads tilted at the same angle against our hands. Our faces, reflected in the darkening window, are straight out of Easter Island, mine still coursed with a steady traffic of tears, the volume mercifully on "mute."

He comes into the office with me as if I'm six. The doctor on call is elderly, harassed, and cranky. Liam is the poster boy for weary rationality as he explains, "She's having some kind of religious crisis. She thinks I'm going to hell."

The doctor taps his pen on his desk blotter, as Liam adds, "I'm an atheist." The doctor nods sagely.

"So am I, so am I." They give each other the secret atheist wink before the doc turns his stink-eye on me, barking, "Sensible people have gotten away from that junk, you know."

"Is she menopausal?" he asks Liam then, as if I couldn't possibly know. The two of them exchange low, knowing words about deranged women and the Change.

"She just lost her mother," Liam adds, turning solicitously to me to ask, "A little over, what? A week ago?"

The hell I'm going to honour his amateur acting with an answer.

Hysterical, pronounces the doctor. Seldom wrong and right again: time of year, time of life, he has my number all right, giving me the old-bat fish-eye, though he's eighty if he's a minute. I can hear him thinking, this is *Emergency*, you damned fool woman; I've got no time to diddle with your change-of-life ding-battery, so take these pills, sir, and give her a stern talking-to.

"What are they?" I pipe timidly in a voice like cracked linoleum.

"Tranquilizers. They go under the tongue. The pharmacist will explain it." He stops just short of adding, "Dearie."

Back home, we're barely in the door when Gail appears, standing outside her door at the top of the stairs shouting, "Hey ho! What's the good word? Where'd ya go, what did ya do, who'd ya see, what did ya buy?" And me with nowhere to hide as Liam lamely tells her we've been at Home Depot picking up a few things, her eyes tightening to crafty slits as she takes in the fact that we carry no bags and my face is so swollen it looks as if wasps have been at it.

I guzzle my under-the-tongue pills in no time. To Liam they're like sandbags; he keeps eyeing me narrowly, clearly wondering, Will they hold? I eye him back, wondering, When did he start tucking his shirt into his dweeby underpants? I refill the prescription once, but they won't let me have any more unless I see the doctor again.

I tell Liam to relax, that they've given me a lifetime supply.

Yuletide looms, the living room ringing to the sound of Christmas comedy specials. A mammoth snowfall obliterates Gail's garden, sending her out bundled in her Canadian Tire parka and Leafs cap to shovel the driveway in the shrieking, mid-storm wind, asserting her dominance even as the snow whips itself into cyclones over the rooftops. She heaves enormous shovel-loads over her scrawny shoulders, slicing the banks as perfectly as wedding cake. The street in the early dusk is like a midway on the dark side of the moon, with Christmas decorations flashing epileptically and inflatable Santas tethered to the ground, reeling like drunks.

Mornings, I stay in bed, not even opening a sleep-feigning eye to bid Liam goodbye. I lie for hours listening to the radio, the volume barely on, my ear pressed up against the tiny speaker as I tune in to the tinny insect voices of a city at holiday time, bug choruses piping merry carols, followed by up-to-the-minute news read to the CHOONG chugga CHOONG chugga of a drum machine. I slide the Jack bottle out from under the bed and drink straight from it as I ease the radio dial experimentally leftward. I'm greeted with a cheerful tizzy on the West Indian station, "de highways an' de byways be blocked wit snow, mon, better stay home wit Lady Ganja, ha ha ha." On the jazz station, a hepcat with a goatee and milk-white eyes is honking spiky, inscrutable, anti-Nativity sounds, improvising on the changes of "So What." A millimetre farther left, and the pterodactyl, chalk-on-blackboard screech of hard-rock call letters introduces two harsh dudes sitting around sharing fart stories, haw haw haw, and giving away tickets to see Succubus and Incest 4U on New Year's Eve. I feel like someone's befuddled grandmother in a stained nightgown who's gotten lost on her way to the bathroom and wandered into the teenagers' party.

Around one in the afternoon I throw off the covers and begin staggering around the house. The morning's drink leaves me nauseous and not even close to satisfying numbness. I note out the front window that everything is shipshape, the driveway one hundred percent ice-free, snowbanks boasting perfect hospital corners. The neighbours are already out slogging along the sidewalk in salt-stained boots, off on merry Christmas errands, though they can't *all* be merry, I think, my stomach pitching ominously; some of them must have crossed over to the dark sides of their lives, must have someone missing, someone who was still around last year, or someone who soon *would* be missing, or someone who had had bad news from the doctor, last night or last week or six nightmare months ago. They're out there tramping through the drifts to or from places forever changed, hollow and chilly, where clocks tick and no one but an unsympathetic cat shares the indifferent furniture.

And me? Would I ever again get to stand in our springtime bedroom watching the sun sink behind the garden shed like a little girl's wobbly curtsy as she sing-songs, "Thank you very much for coming! We hope you liked our show!" Would I ever again feel as I did in those first miracle days in this house, like the call from the governor had come just as the gates of hell were squealing shut behind me?

Liam and I silently eat the lacklustre meals I prepare, greasy platefuls of macaroni with butter or fried eggs under a clogged layer of melted plastic cheese. Gail pops her acorn head in before the slipshod dishwashing is done, and Liam offers her a pudding cup, holding it just out of reach. She mimes a begging puppy, her hands joined and hooked adorably forward, her tongue lolling. Woof woof, she says, and Liam laughs and laughs. The two of them retire to the living room while I chain-smoke six or seven cigarettes, my stash dwindling fast. I know I'll have to leave the house soon to get more, a dreadful prospect at best. I've lost count of the weeks since my last voice job. Up till now, I've been able to handle solo outings to the grocery store and the LCBO, and the hospital to see Mum. But since coming back from Emergency, I've lost whatever shredded tag ends of social skills I'd had left. Going through the front door, having to walk by Gail's sleeping garden frightens me badly enough; having to ask the counterman at the convenience store for smokes is going to feel like asking for detailed directions to Beijing in Mandarin.

But maybe everything will right itself before I run out of smokes and booze. You never know! I mean, really. How long can this go on?

As it turns out, not long at all.

I'm rooting through the kitchen cupboards looking for something to drink, stealthily opening and closing doors while the TV and Gail jabber over each other in the living room. The Jack is gone, and there's no wine in sight. There is, however, every household's untouched bottle of crème de menthe shoved into the back of a low cupboard, but even I won't stoop that low. All right, yes I will. I pour the whole bottle of dental sludge into a tall glass. In the living room, voices have been lowered, which means I'm being discussed. Gail's voice rises out of the indistinct rumble, bristling with righteous indignation: "Please tell me *you're* not going to be out of pocket for some damned religious tombstone. Let her pay for it; the silly, bleating cow was *her* mother!"

I bite straight through the lip of the glass, spitting Christmas-themed, green-streaked, bloody shards into the sink.

Directly behind me, Gail clears her throat. She's standing in the doorway, spoon in hand, on her way to the fridge for more pudding, which she proceeds to scarf innocently before striking a pose against the fridge door, her knobby index finger flush against her cheek Jack Benny–style, her smile bright as a new penny.

"A thought! Maybe it's time we notified the men in the little white coats? Just an idea! I'm just tossing it out there!" She

417

releases a gleeful aren't-I-bad howl, her bared teeth black from the pudding, before trotting off to rejoin Liam.

In one lightning leap, I'm on her, spinning her around, knocking the cup and spoon out of her hand, ramming her back against the fridge, and plowing my fist into her gut.

She's seventy-nine years old and fit as a mutant cockroach; I'm fifty-eight and built like a freight car. It's Mothra versus Godzilla: fifty-fifty odds! My punch seems to hit a wall of rubber bands or the coils of a mattress; for a moment she's folded in two but is still able to grab twin hanks of my hair, pulling me down on top of her as she slides down the fridge, landing hard on her rump. Her facial muscles appear utterly flummoxed, so out of practice are they at registering bewilderment.

My mood has improved monumentally; I haven't felt this good since the last time I knocked the stuffing out of Gerard. I'm euphoric, steam coming out of my ears, the iron tang of blood from my cut lip ambrosia sweet. I'm fully prepared to magnanimously pull away, let bygones be, etc., but she keeps bicycling her hatchet-sharp knees into my stomach, right, left, right. She lets go of my hair to claw straight down both my cheeks with surprisingly sharp nails. It hurts, and I'm thinking, Bring it, bitch, if that's what you want, but at the same time I can't help laughing; the idea of the two of us in a yowling catfight is too funny to stand.

Then, even funnier, from far, far away I hear Liam shouting, "Hey! Hey! Hey!"

Somehow I get hold of Gail's coat hanger shoulders and pry her bucking knees open with one of mine. I sit on her stomach, pinning her flailing arms on either side of her head, all the while wondering how I can possibly have enough time to do all this. Why isn't Liam stepping in, unless, seeing me laughing, he thinks there's no danger.

But there is. I'm *this* close to banging her head on the floor till it splits like a melon and splatters the walls. *This* close to leaning my big knee into her hen-scrawny windpipe until she turns blue, indigo, violet. *This* close to pitching her against the wall like a ragdoll, every bone in her coming unhooked and flopping, her life flashing before her eyes like lightning hitting a hydro pole.

Out of the corner of my eye, suddenly, there's Liam. He's clutching the edge of the sink, knees buckling, sinking to the floor, but oh, so gracefully! He drops like a great heron coming in for a landing, his dancer's arms flung glamorously outward, his head with its silver Einstein corona of hair slumped sideways, a sunflower too heavy for it's stalk. It sags like Christ's head on the cross, if Christ had been mostly bald; his glasses dangle goofily from one ear, as if Christ were being played by Harold Lloyd.

I forget to hold Gail down.

Out she shoots quick as a silverfish to begin sproinging all over the kitchen, shoving me out of the way with her hard little palms, poking the buttons on the phone, taking charge. She jumps on top of Liam and begins rhythmically massaging his chest because she knows everything, which of course includes CPR. I sit inert on the floor and watch as his eyes go from open and glassy to shut, to open, to shut. His life is careening to its end in triple fast-forward time, his remaining years speeding by at the rate of six months to a second. Before my eyes, he's eighty,

eighty-eight, ninety-five, then all cobwebbed over, grizzled with frost and forgetting me forever, washing his hands of Time, passing through the Gate, abandoning all hope.

I want to hold him back by the hem of his shirt, begging him, Don't leave yet, stay, stay here with me on this dazed earth, please, *please* stay with sweet time and beloved place, it's all we know! Don't fly off with the space-cold angels, the flying macros, the winged Booleans. Don't go, Liam! You don't know what's out there!

Time, that mischievous bugger, begins to sploom outward like an elastic band in a cartoon, stretching, stretching, getting ready to shoot the cartoon mouse over the rooftops, over the moon, as I hear in my head the comical *aiiiieeeeeeeeeeeeeeeeeee*, the one I've done a thousand times in the recording studio, aiiiieeeeee, my Liam, my Liam, my own, my own Liam, no, no, no...

Time stops.

And sits there, a cat at a mouse hole, only its tail flicking.

I feel my bottom lip swelling, the scratches on my face fattening with blood like two leeches.

Liam, turned off. Just like that! No longer working. Unfixable.

But black life, life in general, life remaining, *that* will keep on going, dragging me with it like toilet paper stuck to its shoe.

Then gears begin to grind and everything speeds up again. There are paramedics banging on the door; how did they get here so fast, although Gail, naturally enough, foreseeing all possible circumstances, has arranged to live in a house two blocks from the ambulance station. In they rush, knocking into one another in the tiny kitchen like Keystone Kops. I hear "cardiopulmonary resuscitation," "oxygen," "sublingual nitroglycerine," see breathing tubes and paddles intended to jolt a current through him, but even I can see Liam's breathing just fine, though his eyes, I know, are shut, for good, for good.

The bigger of the medics, a burly black woman with the shoulders of a Channel swimmer, shoves Gail out of the way and begins to gently compress his chest, bearing down with all her weight on the heel of her left hand. It's too intimate to stand; who told her she could climb on him like that? Part of me sees him lying there, breathing on his own, eyes fluttering, and thinks, You big faker, who do you think you're fooling? The rest of me says, Dream on, lady, that's never going to work; the unthinkable has arrived, it's here, that unthinkable thing that happens to everybody is happening here, to him, right now. Her shoulders pump while I sit, waiting in preternatural calm for the approaching flat line, the beeping sonar growing ever weaker, Liam's ship slipping toward the black horizon, his stateroom door shut tight, not a soul waving from the deck, leaving, leaving nothing behind but a soundless un-signal as the paramedics ease themselves back onto their haunches, no longer in a hurry as they lay their paddles and tubes quietly on the floor.

Oh, Liam, you're so brave to go first, so gallant, but it wasn't what I wanted, I wanted us to leave together, the police breaking down the doors of our house that had been dark for days to find us lying cold on the floor, the radio playing softly, and us hand in hand and long gone...

But of course it doesn't happen. It so often doesn't.

Liam is resurrected! He crashes back into his startled body, eyes springing open in astonishment at the semi-circle of gawkers high above him, welcoming him home, geez, all this fuss when he'd only gone to the corner store for a carton of milk. His own rusty gears begin immediately to shunt him into forward momentum, the Liam-ness trickling back into his grey face as he tries to push himself up onto his elbows. He falls back again, looking sheepish, and croaks up at the crowd, "What's going on?" and then, "I think I fainted." Then he adds hoarsely, "It wasn't a heart attack, guys, if that's what you're thinking. I got woozy and, whoa, hold on. I passed out."

I'm not taken in for a second. I *know* he's rushing to gather himself, to plunge back into the ways of the world before he can take sober note of just how far down for the count he's been.

Gail, of course, with nothing to show for her sound clocking than mussed hair and an askew shirt front, is hovering in five places at once, blocking all access, barking orders at me over her shoulder: "Pack him a bag, stupid, there are three freshly ironed shirts in the front of his closet, get him warm socks, don't just stand there, you fat pinhead!"

He's going to the hospital, but the worst is over, the big paramedic saying something about a bit more stress than he'd been prepared for, maybe an adrenalin surge, a mild spasm of the coronary artery, ventricular fibrillation, whatever that means. He's almost sixty, it's time, the heart gets flabby, but he's lucky, she tells me cheerfully, probably no harm done, we'll get you into the hospital, sir, run some tests, all hearts are different. Some are more willing to keep chugging along than others.

Gail stands at officious attention, taking mental note, ready to overreact on a dime, but the medic assures us he'll be home and up and around in no time, this is just a warning. He could stand to lose some weight, start battling the bulge, she smiles, patting her own spreading stomach with love.

They help him onto a stretcher, Liam protesting all the while that he's fine, he can walk, there's nothing to get excited about. Gail insists on riding with him in the ambulance, jabbing me hard with her elbow in the doorway where I stand slack-jawed. Standing on the porch, she turns to bore straight through me with her varmint eyes, her bared fangs yellow in the porch light. Then she scampers away, jumping into the back of the ambulance like an Olympic pole-vaulter, leaving me stranded. For a moment I'm frozen; then, suddenly, rabid as Scarface, I bite into the flesh of my right arm so hard I leave a perfect necklace of tooth prints brindled with tiny specks of blood.

"I'll follow you in the car," I call out weakly as the ambulance pulls away, taking its sweet time: no siren, no flashing light; they're probably all having a laugh in the back. Heart attacks, heart attacks, ha ha, not just for the old any more!

I stand for a long time on the porch, coatless in the wind, thinking, Nothing has to end yet, there's still Time. The whole street blinks red and blue and green, the holiday lights blurred by falling snow like tropical fish in a murky pond. I look at each of the lit windows in turn, wondering vacantly, who's looking out at our barren house, bereft of Nativity folderol, while I'm looking at theirs? Who's watching my life come crashing to an end as they sing softly to themselves of roasting chestnuts and Jack Frost nipping noses? How many fires are crackling in piney-fresh living rooms behind all those doors hung with wreaths and ribbons, behind all those warmly glowing windows?

Who's smiling with satisfaction at the festive packages full of sleek espresso makers and silk teddies piled under tasteful trees, waiting to be opened by happy, loving couples? I don't know any of them, don't know who celebrates, who doesn't, who has tons of toys for girls and boys, and who just exchanges gift certificates after their third Scotch.

I don't know a damned fool thing about anyone or anything.

I switch off the porch light and lock the door. The toothy bruise on my arm, throbbing now, smiles grimly up at me, as if to say, "You might want to think about not being here when he gets back. Just an idea. I'm just tossing it out there."

FOUR

I burst into tears as my plane begins to drop over Shannon, the dirty mattress of cloud parting below us, and green Eire smearing into view. Somewhere down there, the band must be tuning up, the pipers stepping into formation, the banners strung and flapping. "Look up, look up!" they're crying out to one another. "For even now, Margaret Mary Prentice (Moriarty on her mother Moira's side!) is here, unseen, yes, but real as rock, hanging in the very air above us!"

Who knows? Maybe a fish will bob up out of the sea with a letter of welcome in its mouth! Hearty, pipe-smoking folk with ham-hock faces, sitting around a roaring fire telling wild tales about me, will fall reverently silent when I (*she!*) suddenly stride into the room!

I'm dropping like a brick over the western edge of Ireland, disguised as the most Irish person ever to draw blessed breath. I'm going to dress in green down to my socks and tell everyone I meet my name's Sheleighleigh McClunahan.

It may as well be. I'm wondering if Gail and Liam haven't already forgotten my real name; it's been three days after all. Gail has surely swabbed away all trace of my contaminating cooties; there's nothing left of me in the house now but a stubborn odour she can't quite mask with lemony-fresh bathroom deodorizer.

No doubt she's splurting off this very minute down the sludgy street in her pristine little car, heading straight to whatever secret hideaway Liam's recuperating in because of course he never came home. Never even called. Nor did I dare call the hospital myself; I was terrified at getting bad news, but even more terrified of hearing from Liam's own lips just exactly what he thought of me *now*. No, no, I told myself, he's fine, most likely propped up on Charlotte's couch, sipping hemp smoothies while she pores poker-faced over her vegan cookbooks, searching out recipes for root broth and spore salad to mend his temperamental heart.

But he was going to stay mad forever and ever and ever and then some.

I needed to make tracks while I still had the chance.

Gail was melting the ice in between the chinks of the driveway bricks with a hair dryer when I barrelled down the steps, pitching my suitcase into the backseat of the cab before she had a chance to straighten up and turn around. "To the airport, driver," I cried, "and *step on it!*" For three days I'd been expecting the cops to come pounding on the door with an arrest warrant for aggravated assault and battery. I can only surmise that she tried her damndest but had so worn out her credibility with the local constabulary, phoning them as she did every time a cat walked on her lawn or a horn tooted after 11 p.m., that they were taking her calls with heaping platefuls of salt.

There's no ice in sight here; instead the Irish Christmas season features cluster-rain that undulates across the road before me like sheets of chiffon. Clamminess permeates everything; I'm shivering inside my dinky rental car as if it were twenty below. Left-side driving turns out to be not as daunting as I'd feared, once I realized that the strange drag and roar of the car's engine were caused by covering my first ten miles with the parking brake on. By the time I've been successfully spit out of the first hair-raising roundabout, my old piss and vinegar begins rising like sap. Look at me! Not just out of the house; I'm out of the *country*! Wrenched myself up and together, scrounged a last-minute cancellation seat, rented a car, spoke to people behind counters without self-immolating, and now I'm on the freeway executing mirror-image driving moves by the seat of my pants, fairly bouncing with euphoria. Hitchhikers loom out of the drench and fog, flagging me down from the *left*, ha ha, young Jimmy Cagneys, their shoulders hunched, their non-hitching hands jammed into wet pockets, collars up around their red ears. I whip through towns and see myself, my mother, and my grandmother striding fast past the shops, chins lifted, mouths tight and determined, reminding me of how old Fionnuala would clamp her lips shut whenever Gerard and I would beg her to say something in Irish. "No, no," she'd say, flinty with possessive pride. "I will not, not on any of your beautiful accounts."

Rain punches and jostles the hedgerows, through which I catch glimpses of the roofless ruins of abandoned houses hiding their pushed-in faces in the folds of hills, just like the wet sheep butting their silly heads against rocks fallen by the road. In a sudden cloud-parting and swell of sun, I spy one damned fine-looking shepherd striding out to chase down the strays and round them up; he's wearing a football jersey and rubber boots, and swings a mighty stick by his side. And I think, Now *there's* a Good Shepherd a girl could get behind! Maybe it was someone like him who came to fetch Mum home; surely she'd earned that much. Besides, Johnny Cash would just get on her nerves.

Perhaps it's only Sheleighleigh-style sentiment, but I can feel every childhood holy card and rosary, every interminable Mass, every inch of Mum's sweet beliefs and Gerard's sour ones settling around my shoulders as comfortably as a rough but warm old fisherman's sweater. It seems that those beliefs are why I'm here: to stake my hope, like they did in their different ways, on something at once haunting and vaporous, and solid as wet stone. And to ram a spine into my mewling, cowering sense of integrity, and decide finally what it is I'm willing to take seriously and stand firmly by for the rest of my life, no matter what anybody has to say about it.

I'm here for a week, and I'm not leaving the West. I left home with this plan in mind, and my first look at the countryside tells me I've made the right decision. It's not just the women who look like me; the whole wind-scoured, rock-strewn place does. It feels like Mum's battered heart, and Gerard's cold, dank one. It's a place made expressly for walking straight into raw winds.

This seems to be something I do particularly well.

On my first morning, I take an early ferry as far west as I can possibly go, to the island of Inisheer. It's beyond freezing on the almost deserted boat; there are no other tourists this time of year except for a dirt-crusted, backpacked, globe-trotting hipster with matted blond dreads and a young Italian couple, clearly newlyweds and calamitously poor choosers of honeymoon destinations. They huddle in the cabin dressed in fluffy Aran sweaters and chic rain gear, nuzzling each other, while I stand stubbornly at the rail in full gale, determined to get the whole experience or die trying.

I walk through the island the whole rain-whishing day, on dirt roads that rise and descend between low walls of piled stones cracked like petrified loaves of bread. It's like walking through the chambers and ventricles of the hardest heart in the world, possibly my own. I've come crashing down from my arrival high; I feel exactly like the sky looks. The rain turns on and off, though the grey never lifts. There isn't a soul about. The few houses I see appear deserted, though there's the odd bit of forgotten laundry hanging limp and beaten on a drooping line, and a tired old pony tethered to a post.

But the wet has already ceased to bother me, since I'm continuously weeping myself, though not out of sadness, I'm shocked to realize. No, it's more a kind of purification-weep, a thorough, abrading scrub-down of the face and the soul.

And there's something else I can hardly believe I feel: Relief.

Relief that something that needed to be over is, at long, long last, over. Relief at letting go of something that was never mine, of stepping away from people who are better off without me, who I'm better off without. Relief to let Liam go, relief at having failed spectacularly at something that was crying out for just such a failure as this.

I feel light as mist as I think, How hard would it be to let everything go right here, right now? To simply lie down and evaporate like cloud among these stones? Slipping behind the gauzy curtain between this world and the next couldn't be any harder here than crossing the road; surely I'd just fall into the arms of the misty-eyed Designer of this wild place, and be carried soundlessly away.

Whoa. Designer? How did *that* come so cleanly out of me without snagging on a thousand jagged little spikes of doubt?

There's a shimmer in the air, a suspicious thickening of the mist, and suddenly the Tanteek bumps up hard against me, like heaven bumping against the stodgy bulk of earth, making it howl.

"*So here you are again,*" I say when I've gotten my breath back. "*You always know where to find me, don't you, goading me night and day, year in and year out with your wisdom and your woe and your madness. But what can you do to me now? Everything's gone, so how can you hurt me? All your nagging can do is keep me trammelled and soft, and vulnerable. Like Mum. Like Desi. Keep me from corroding into Gail or hardening into Gerard. Reminding me over and over that Not Knowing may be a bitter wind in my face, but Absolute Knowing would only make me callous, frigid, and unable to feel any wind at all.*"

"*Oh Mistuh T, I am SO on to you!*"

Back on the mainland, I'm aimless, drawn not to the Christmas-jiggy tourist spots but to sullen small towns whose flat house fronts, rainbow-painted in the time of the Tiger, are now chipping

430

and peeling back to grey in the relentless damp. I visit nothing that isn't anonymous, spending an entire morning under a light snow in a churchyard among moss-eaten gravestones canted like bad teeth. In the spirit of turning over new leaves, I refuse to enter pubs, lunching instead on pre-fab sandwiches and milky tea in dismal cafés, surrounded by irritable last-minute Christmas shoppers and squalling children. Sitting by the window, I watch a bone-drenched dog slink by; a woman across the street in a tweed skirt and curlers shakes a mop out her crooked front door. Her life, the dog's, my mother's, and mine, all seem, in the silvered light, the cloud air, as worthless as a pocked, unreadable tombstone, and just as fearfully and hopefully deep.

Four days in, I pluck up my courage and drive to County Mayo, where Grandma Fionnuala was from, though I can't for the life of me remember the name of the town. But then, it's not towns I'm after. I'm going to climb Croagh Patrick, from where I'll shoot heavenward the prayer for her soul requested by my mother.

In our entire lives, it's the only thing she ever asked me to do for her.

With everything lost and my future drowned at sea, I feel closer to her than I ever have to a living soul. And so sorry, sorry for everything, for things done by me, by Dad, by Gerard, everyone. Sorry for everything, and in need of one last, thorough, penitential scouring before I resume my own solitary life-walk.

Climbing the mountain in the miserable half-snow, half-drizzle of December seems like just the right dose of repentance, though part of me is afraid that somehow Grandma will know; an alarm will sound, and she'll sit bolt upright in her heavenly easy chair, swatting wildly as if a spider were creeping up her leg, shouting, "What's *she* doing there? Off! Get her off!"

I leave at the crack of dawn to drive through bleak Connemara to Westport. I'm in the parking lot at the foot of the mountain by nine-thirty. It's not pilgrimage season, not by a long shot. The mountain hulks gloomily, unencumbered by penitents, free for the tackling. Dubious luck is with me, though, because a faint sun has emerged and the mountain is officially "open," at least for a few hours. I'm not sure if climbing it is legal or not; as usual, I've turned up too late, in the wrong place at the wrong time. But since there doesn't seem to be anyone to stop me, I pull my turtleneck up around my ears and set off on the Pilgrim's Path.

A half hour in, it becomes clear that this is the stupidest thing I've ever done. My hands are frozen raw, and my sweater and flimsy rain jacket are no match for the savage wind. My hair, clumped by the perpetual damp into a thatch of shredded wheat, tears around my face like shrubbery in a hurricane. Half the time I'm walking blind, which would be bad enough, but I've also undertaken this heroic venture wearing flat-soled street shoes, which slip and slide on the muddy path. As the ground grows steeper, gravel and sharp stones bite right through to the soles of my feet. I keep going, pitched forward at a forty-five-degree angle, clutching at rocks and bushes to keep myself upright. I refuse to turn back.

A couple of hours in, I hear voices raised in zestful song coming my way and look up to see a gang of rowdy Germans in sturdy hiking boots, swinging stout walking sticks and shouting boisterous Teutonic hiking lyrics as they descend the steep slope, all of them slanted backward like the grinning idiot in the Keep on Truckin' cartoon. They cast pitying glances in my direction but pass me right by. "Outta my way," I shout at their receding backs. "I'm walkin' heah!" I take ravenous note of their giant knapsacks probably stuffed with bratwurst and schnitzel, thinking, Good! More penance! Twenty minutes later, I'm no longer walking. I'm crawlin' heah. But the *hell* I'm going to quit.

It's at least another two hours before I stagger to the top. I have it all to myself. The view, scudding in and out of vision, is unearthly. I can't believe I've climbed so high. All of Mayo lies on one side, and on the other the blue-grey bay and the Atlantic. There's not a ship in sight: no sullen *Pequod*, no jubilant *Bachelor*, nothing but blank sea, on the other side of which lies home. Yes, home, where the heart is nothing but a four-chambered, blood-pumping valve. Home, where they give you drugs to stop the void from shrieking through those chambers. Home, to where I'm going to have to return only to pack up and leave, to gather up what's left of my savings, find a place to live and some kind of job (*aiieee!*), and to stand on my own once again because my Liam ship, as the saying goes, has clearly sailed.

Maybe it's the thin air up here, or exhaustion, or starvation, but this fully fleshed realization doesn't bring the stinging slap of pain I expect. On the contrary, I feel giddy with exhilaration. Unburdened. Helpless in the best possible way, if that's possible. And it seems that it is indeed.

Eternity encircles me, the sky above, the ocean below, and I belong to it like a bird would, like a fish does. It's the very stuff of my life, passing in and through me, working the bellows of my lungs, in, out, in. Causing me to shout into the wind through a throat that feels as if it's been flayed with a cat-o'-nine-irons.

And…whoo hoo! Listen to that! My voice!!

"Halloooo! Mum! Grandma! Look at me! I climbed the Holy Mountain all by myself! And guess what? Gerard was right! I've lost every single thing I ever turned my heart to!

"But listen! Hear that, you guys? I have my voice back! My own! And it works with the volume turned down too. Shhh! Listen! Hear it now? Quiet and sweet, like I'm chatting with Desi over ice cream cones on a lazy summer afternoon."

The sky overhead, suddenly swept free of clouds, shimmers like a two-way mirror I'm on the wrong side of.

"Who's in charge up there, by the way? Is St. Patrick around? Kevvie, can you hear me? Yo, Winky!"

A plane arcs overhead. The sky pretends it never knew me.

Never mind. I am one among billions, no more but no less.

Deep breath. I clear my throat, and tune my new, clear voice to "Desi-soft." Here goes nothing.

"Mum, all my life I've hated you to the marrow of your bones. No surprise, right? But we don't need to rehash all that now. Because wherever you are, you got there by pulling your-self together, pulling ahead without any of us, and squeezing through that renowned narrow way, the one-size-fits-all death door. And either because you're so well mannered or just out of spite, you left it swinging open for me. You knew I was right on your tail, didn't you?

"It's true, I was. I am. I'm as dead as a seed can be down here.

Exploded. Totally dismantled, turned all the way inside out. And I have to say, it's not that bad!

"I've been worse.

"I guess you know you really blew it with your kids, Mum. You never loved me and you overloved Gerard to death. You ended up wrecking us both, though I concede you had more than generous help from Dad. But then, we kids sure got our own back, didn't we?

"Except, just what is this *own* we got? I don't know about Gerard, but my hands feel pretty empty. And for all you were so, let's charitably say, difficult, it's not like I behaved any differently than you did. I never did an ungrudging thing for you in all the years I knew you. We, Dad, all of us were so miserable, so bitter, so unfair to one another. None of us any damned help to anyone in time of trouble. That *own* we all got back wasn't anything except a long, slow trudge toward...

"...well, toward Gaily-Gaily. That must be what happened to her. Obsessed with getting her own back, whatever that was, from whoever had stolen it from *her*, she went from the clean slate she must have started out as, passed straight through what she might have been, and wasted away into exactly what she turned out to be.

"I guess that's what comes of knowing everything.

"And when I think of how you were struck down, Mum, that crablike thing moving through you the same way she moves through her happy garden, insect arms fiddling everywhere, rump high as a black widow's...and no one to turn to, sticking it out all by your wee gutsy self, toughing it out behind your creased little pouch of a face, with that handful of innocent, laughable things you held dear...I'm blown away. Blown away, Moira!

"But look at you now! Free and clear, and probably up there dishing the dirt about the whole sorry gang of us. Everyone in heaven must be pissing themselves.

"Anyhow. To wrap up, because I have to get myself back on flat ground before dark if I hope to live through the night, here's the prayer I promised you: I forgive you everything, Mum. And through you, everybody else, every last sad, fearful, resentful, malicious one of us, and Liam too, and, uhhh, G...Ga...yeah. Her too.

"And please forgive me for never once having asked you to forgive me."

There. Was that so hard?

"Except—yes, I'm still talking, sorry—except when I lean a little more into it, Mum, it starts to hurt all over again, like pulling a sweater over my head always hurts now that I've reached my arthritic late middle age. It hurts to let you off the hook. Forgiving hurts, and I don't think it's ever going to stop hurting. It's like getting dunked in frigid water, and the shudder, the recoil, the clench in my gut is the only proof that I'm being pulled toward something huge and utterly alien to my nature.

"I don't mind telling you, Mum, I botched everything back home. I really thought I loved Liam. But this thing I'm feeling for you now—*this* is love. This scorch of understanding, when suddenly it's not *me* who's been betrayed and abandoned, not *me* at the centre of the universe, but someone else. My worst enemy. You.

"And yes, Mother, I've taken note of your droll suggestion that maybe I'm only able to love you now because I don't have to see you any more.

"And Liam, for all he's so terrified of facing up to the sticky stuff, he's dead right about one thing. What else can we possibly do but *live* here in the midst of life? Live, and walk, and for God's sake quit jumping and straining and climbing up on rickety piles of chairs to try to see out the high window!

"And bite my tongue off at the root, but Gerard's right too. There's no real home on earth. There's no truly safe place, and no real faith possible without enduring loss piled on top of doubt, with hope and despair hot on each other's heels every step we take.

"I just need to follow what I *think* I know, same as you did. Have the conviction of things not seen, even if I can hardly see, or barely walk. If there are any clues to be had at all, they're surely down here on the ground, but it's just as true that there's no proof of anything. You either decide for faith, knowing it might very well be insanity, or you walk away."

A gust of wind slams into my back.

"Okay, well, that about wraps it up. My spirits are on the ebb again already, and I'm freezing my ass off up here. Plus, the day's not getting any younger. I'm gonna have to let you go, Mum."

The trip back down turns out to be far worse than going up. Banks of fog roll in from the sea, and I'm terrified I'll walk right off the mountain's edge into thin air. My calves cry out for vengeance with every slippery, down-sloping step. After an hour, I'm reduced to inchworming down on my muddy butt, never so grateful to be alone. By the time I reach the bottom, it's blackest night, and the visitor's centre, the restaurant, the craft shop are all locked up and deserted. There'll be no food, no commemorative tee-shirt, nothing to do but limp to the one lonely car in the lot and disappear.

It's my last night. The lady behind the desk at my hotel, perhaps mistaking my cringing, shuffling gait for sunken holiday spirits brought on by loneliness and general decrepitude, informs me cheerily that there's set-dancing tonight at a church hall only four doors down. "Plenty of singles there," she adds with a meaningful wink.

I'm too restless to stay in my room. Tomorrow is Christmas Eve, an auspicious and familiar day to be flying back to the fresh hell awaiting me at home.

Am I detecting a pattern here?

The dancing is in the dingy church basement, the large linoleum floor ringed with card tables and folding chairs. There's a skinny Christmas tree in the corner, and the walls are draped in tinsel bunting and stuck all over with cardboard Santas and stars. The advertised singles are few, all drawn from the over-eighty or the under-eight set. But the live band in their Santa hats is wonderful, with fiddles and pipes till you weaken, as old Fionnuala would say.

I sit at a table nursing a Diet Coke as one by one, friendly folks beckon me to join in the complicated reels and jigs. I shake my head, smiling and rubbing my destroyed calves, but they won't stand for it. They rope me in and assign me a partner, a tiny, grinning little fellow in a spruce blue suit, whom they introduce as "Jimmy Flynn, ninety-one-years young." Jimmy makes a courtly bow, takes my old hand in his ancient one, and leads me onto the floor.

Ninety-one he may be; I can't keep up with him to save my life. He swings me one way, I twist stubbornly in the other. He steers me forward, I stumble back, knees crumpling. I step all over his shiny-shod feet and never stop apologizing. Jimmy never stops smiling. Somehow, no thanks to me, we finish in the right place at the right time. He smiles graciously and bows again as I beg pardon for the eight hundredth time for my oafish ham-footedness. I turn him down for the next reel, feeling guilty, but he's off in a flash with another partner, instantly forgiving and forgetting every egregious sin of my big, stumbling feet.

Back at the table, the small woman with home-dyed red hair sitting across from me introduces herself as Jimmy's daughter. She's wearing an Annie Oakley blouse embroidered with lariats and a square-dancing skirt straight from the badlands of Wyoming. She thanks me for being Jimmy's partner.

"He has the Alzheimer's," she tells me calmly, laying one of her hands over mine in a gesture that both bestows and asks for kindness and understanding. "But he does so love coming here. He so loves to dance. It's the one thing that seems t'keep him goin'."

And all at once I'm awash in one of those inexplicable surges of joy that in a few seconds threaten to blow all the brain's circuits. Because there it is again, that invisible hand scrabbling five unspeakable words into my palm, a spiked message in the inscrutable language of the Father.

The undefeated heart of weakness.

Five helpless little words that split all our pidgin theories and systems like the atom. Five little mystery words at the fissionable heart of a thermonuclear silence, for only silence—of course! —can begin to convey the unspeakable vastness of the What and the Who I'm seeking. The Father...yes, okay. It's as good a name as any to call it, this spirit, this "I Am" that seems to move through me like air through a sieve, this unfathomable Source who informs the weak but undefeated and endlessly merciful hearts of Desi Redpath and Jimmy Flynn, to name just two.

Two in a billion, maybe more but no less.

And what if it should turn out that this ineffable Father is more like Jimmy Flynn than Josef Mengele, or a wolf-eyed monster, or a black void in the stars? After all, Gerard is only guessing, same as everyone else, using information pumped in daily from his own heart. Merciless heart, merciless Father. Hell, merciless *father*, merciless Father! And why should I be surprised at this Father's silence? The only words, the only *clues* from him I'm ever going to fathom are the deeds of love shivered out of me by the seismic shiftings, the colossal shocks and whammies to my own heart.

Maybe what it means to say yes to mercy is to grant it to someone else.

And if he's anything remotely like smiling Jimmy Flynn, maybe surrounding myself with other Flynns might be good for me, might buck me up, put a spring in my step for the miles I have left to walk. There may not be another Liam for me, but damn it, there are Flynns all over the place! There are Desis going begging! And if there are Flynns and Desis and Aunt

Babys in the world, then there's hope in the world, as much as anybody needs to keep on walking.

Hope with a Source. Just as I suspected. Hah!

Nor is my love used up yet. There are a billion good reasons not to fall back into ruin. Why not just keep to my own pace on my own path? Hell, everybody else is! And when this tidal surge of understanding pulls out again, as it inevitably will, when doubt and fear return to litter the empty beach with black seaweed and broken shells...when that happens, I'm officially reminding myself right now, in advance, to just sit tight and wait it out.

I can do it. Hell, *somebody* has to. It takes one helluva big, Tanteek-toughened broad to walk smack down through the middle of the Mystery, and *pay attention, damn it*!

I just need to keep walking.

Well, I walked myself here, didn't I? So I'll walk myself home, weak as I am. Strong as I am. Hope is the thing, hope born of arduous love and harrowing, smarting mercy. Just ride it out, its swells, its ebb and flow, its full, empty, full. Breathe it in and walk, an empty vessel once again and outward bound, till the road spirals up and winds away into wherever it's had in mind all along.

Acknowledgements

I have drawn on the work of many writers before me.

"I love thee, Jesus, my love, above all things…and then do with me what Thou wilt." This is a Roman Catholic prayer traditionally recited at the first station of the cross, when Jesus is condemned to death.

The three astronauts who variously read verses from the book of Genesis during the 1968 Apollo 8 Christmas Eve broadcast were William Anders, Jim Lovell, and Frank Borman. The remarks before the Bible readings are made by William Anders, and the closing message to "all of you on the good earth" was spoken by Frank Borman.

When Liam advises Maggie that she should "ask Alice, because she'd know," he is referring to the song "White Rabbit" by Jefferson Airplane.

Grateful acknowledgement for the quotes (although misquoted by Maggie) from *Moby-Dick*, by Herman Melville, which served as one of the earliest inspirations for this book, so fulsomely do they express the plight of the benighted seeker.

Grateful acknowledgement (and apologies) to Matthew Arnold, from whose poem "Dover Beach" Liam cobbles together his garbled, misquoted recitation in the rowboat.

Thanks and acknowledgement to Luis Demetrio, who wrote the 1963 mambo, ¿Quién Será?, which Norman Gimbel re-wrote into English and called "Sway." The lyrics, "Other dancers may be on the floor, but my eyes will only see you," are, of course, not quoted correctly here.

The actual quote from Friedrich Engels, misquoted by Maggie, is, "Thought and consciousness are products of the human brain... Matter is not a product of mind, but mind itself is merely the highest product of matter." This is from "Anti-Dühring" (1878).

"Come to her assistance...let perpetual light shine upon her" and "May her soul and all the souls of the faithful departed rest in peace" are taken from the Roman Catholic funeral liturgy.

William Blake's "What is grand is necessarily obscure to weak men. That which can be made explicit to the idiot is not worth my care" is taken from the Letter to Revd. Dr. Trusler, written on August 23, 1799.

The line, "[I am] the undefeated heart of weakness," is from the poem "Christmas Venite" by John V. Taylor, from *A Christmas Sequence and Other Poems* (Oxford: Amate Press, 1989).

All Bible quotes (with the exception of three drawn from the New International Version) are taken from the King James Version, with the added caveat that they are as often as not misquoted and inexact, as Bible verses so often are.

I owe many a debt of gratitude, which I list herewith in historical order:

First, to my stout-hearted first readers, who gave up vast tracts of their lives to wade hip-deep through the sprawling monster of a first draft and still had words of succour and encouragement to offer: Arthur Holden, Andrea Trace, Randy Woods, Chloe Gauthier, and Tom Maccarone.

Gracious thanks also to the Humber School for Writers Correspondence Program in Creative Writing and David Adams Richards, whose profound insight proved invaluable in the early, messy stages of the work.

Humble thanks also to my agent, Martha Magor Webb, who read an early draft, detected something worth saving, and steered me in the direction of Goose Lane Editions.

Many, many bows and kissing of hands to Bethany Gibson, my editor at Goose Lane, who, with tremendous patience, brilliance, and unending tact, guided me through the many revisions and rethinkings necessary to find my way to the end.

Special thanks also to Robert Woods, who allowed me unfettered access to his inexhaustible mental archive of big band memorabilia.

Before closing, one more round of deepest thanks to Arthur Holden, who sustained me through many an artistic pout, snit, flight of grandiosity, and descent into blackest despair without ever losing faith in me.

And lastly, to my husband, Tom, who did the same as Arthur but with the added burden of actually having to share living quarters with me.

. . .

Every effort has been made to secure permission from the copyright holders for excerpts of song lyrics, poetry, and prose reproduced (or mangled) in this book. I regret any inadvertent omission.

Excerpt from *Four Quartets (East Coker)*, by T.S. Eliot, © T.S. Eliot 1944, published by Faber and Faber Ltd. All rights reserved, Used by permission.

Excerpt from "Series Of Dreams," words and music by Bob Dylan, © 1991 by Special Rider Music. All rights reserved. Used by permission.

Jane Woods spent a decade working in Canadian regional theatre before settling in Montreal to work as a voice actress. Later, she began translating and adapting French-language films and television series to be dubbed into English. She now lives in Toronto, where she continues to work as a translator.